Summer's Reaping

J.C. Wade

J.C. WADE ORIGINALS

CONTENTS

For Johnny and Shua.
Thanks for beating me up for all those years.
Because of you, I'm as tough as nails.

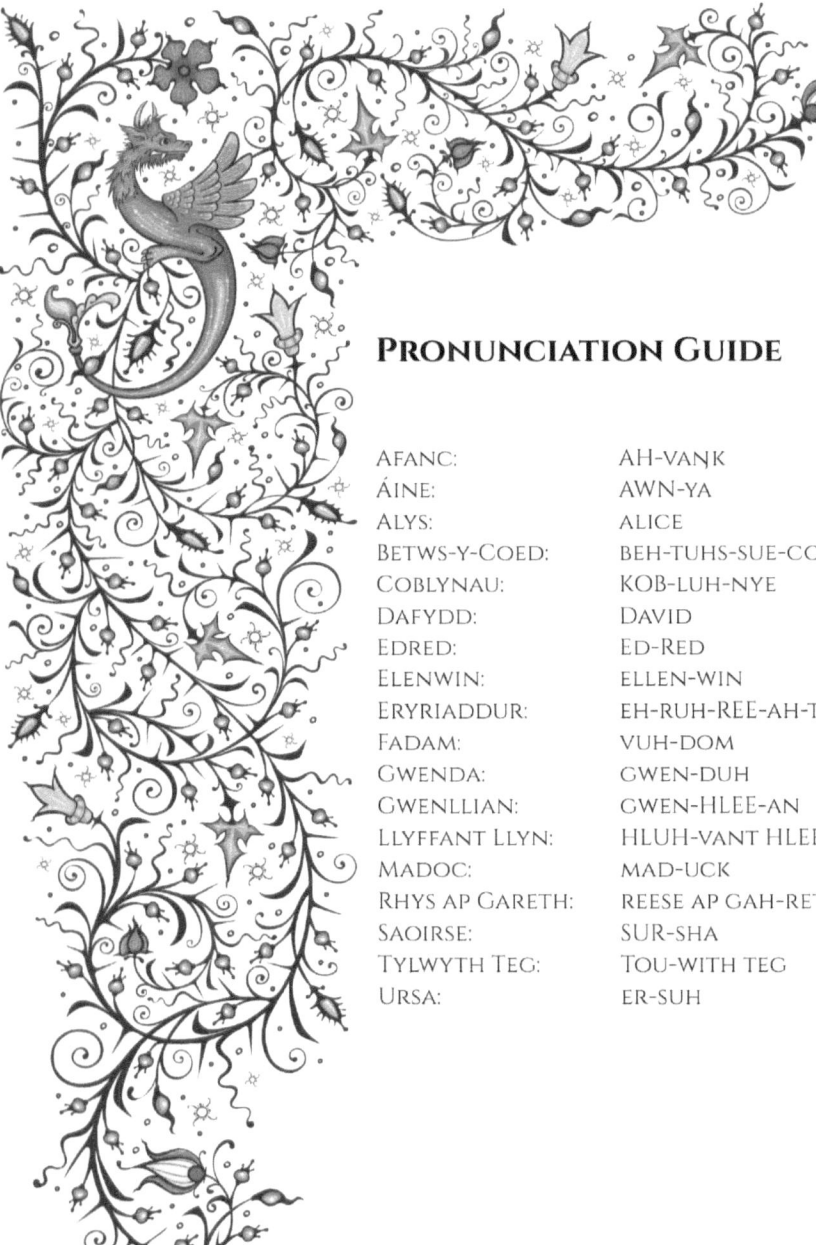

Pronunciation Guide

Afanc:	AH-vank
Áine:	AWN-ya
Alys:	ALICE
Betws-y-Coed:	BEH-tuhs-sue-coid
Coblynau:	KOB-luh-nye
Dafydd:	David
Edred:	ED-Red
Elenwin:	ELLEN-win
Eryriaddur:	EH-ruh-REE-ah-thir
Fadam:	VUH-dom
Gwenda:	GWEN-duh
Gwenllian:	GWEN-HLEE-an
Llyffant Llyn:	HLUH-vant HLEEN
Madoc:	MAD-uck
Rhys ap Gareth:	REESE ap GAH-reth
Saoirse:	SUR-sha
Tylwyth Teg:	TOU-with teg
Ursa:	ER-suh

PROLOGUE

BEYOND

VILLAGE OF BETWS-Y-COED

"I tracked the swarm here," twelve-year-old Saoirse said. The dense forest at her back loomed close and menacing, a boundary drawn by the summer goddess, Áine. Villagers knew better than to venture past her temple, where unholy beasts and fae roamed free.

Until now, Saoirse had obeyed.

She and Edred had walked confidently on the path to the open-air temple, a four-sided stone structure surrounded by towering beech and elms, then pushed past it, wading through the meadow grass to forge their own trail to the Wild Wood.

By some unspoken agreement, their conversation halted once they crossed the field behind the goddess's shrine and stepped into the shadowy confines of the woodland at the foot of the soaring mountain. A lichen-covered stairway jutted from the earth, a silent invitation beckoning them on.

But their people did not venture here. Not where the very air hummed with silent warning.

She'd made it to the pitted stone steps on her own yester-eve but dared not go farther alone. She was brave, not stupid.

"These are proof enough we once frequented the Faerie Hill," she said, glancing at Edred to gauge his reaction.

"Or maybe the Fair Folk set them."

She pressed her lips together as she contemplated their next move. She'd been lucky, spotting the swarm of bees as she placed her family's offering on Áine's altar stone. Not lucky. *Blessed.* The buzz of conversation from the insects amid the long grass had pulled her from her prayer—a plea for a way to help her struggling family.

The goddess had answered her, and she'd followed. At least this far.

"Honey goes for a high price, and there's nothing so fine as beeswax candles," muttered Saoirse, reminding herself why she dared set foot so far beyond the village boundaries.

Saoirse's stepmother, Alys, could no longer wash and mend clothes. She lay sick in her childbed, Saoirse's weak little half-brother, Dafydd, tucked close for warmth against his mother's side.

Mending and washing profited little, but with Papa's milk cows and extra work at the sawmill, they had food enough. Áine's blessing of bees would add much to their meager lives. Papa could stay home more. And perhaps they could afford medicine for Alys.

Edred's gaze lingered on Saoirse's face then on the winding path cut into the side of the mountain. Up, up the stairs traveled, then disappeared from their view, veiled by fir branches, boulders, and shadow.

"I lost them somewhere around here."

She liked Edred for many reasons, but she loved him for his easy acceptance of her word. He nodded in all sincerity as if to say, "Of course you simply lost sight of them and didn't lose your nerve at the edge of forbidden wilderness."

She drew herself up and pulled Da's carving blade from her pocket, snatched from the worktable and held as a talisman. "This one's for you," she said, pushing it into his clammy hand.

He stared at it, his mouth slightly agape. Despite nearly two years seniority, Edred could not hide his fear so well as she could.

"The knife is only to cut down any hive the bees have started to build." If he sensed her lie, he did not mention it. He merely accepted the tool and the heavy hemp sack she offered. "You'll hold this while I scoop them in." She would, that is, if she could even find them—if whatever beasts that might roam the boundary between worlds kept well away.

"Stay close to me, Sers." He stepped first onto the bottommost tread, then paused.

They waited, holding their breath, as if with that one move into the unknown, Edred had sprung some wicked trap intent to devour them. After a stretched silence, where nothing appeared or descended upon them, a smile wobbled to life on Saoirse's face. "Your mother's stories had me all worked up for nothing."

Edred's mouth twitched. "She means to scare us from this place. She wants to keep us alive."

"So do I." She mustered her courage and stepped solidly onto the stairway next to him. "The air does feel different here. Heavy."

They climbed in silence, the only sound that of their labored breathing. Soon, the dim that had hidden the remainder of the path far above swallowed them, too. It seemed to Saoirse that the pressing shadows lived, and the keen sensation of watchful eyes pebbled her skin.

She moved closer to the rocky slope. If she stepped wrong, she'd surely tumble off the mountain, but at least the await-ing tree boughs below would catch her, hopefully. The stairs' switchback turns eventually led them to the ridgeline's gloomy crest. They stood inches apart, her stomach coiled tight.

"There are no birds or insect noises," Edred whispered. He glanced her way. "Sing for me, would you, Sers? It always makes me feel better."

Saoirse shook her head. "I think we ought to follow the in-sects' example." No reason to invite beasts or monsters lurking in the forest to come hunting.

Edred drew himself up, squinting into the shadows that gath-ered in the hollows of branches and slunk around trunks. He stepped off the path, Saoirse close behind.

She ducked under grasping twigs and clinging, mossy beards, barely noticing how the sun's light lessened with each step. The forest floor, littered with detritus, sloped gently into a tree-clut-tered bowl. They crossed it, eyes roving for sign of Áine's blessing or of danger. Saoirse pushed away thoughts that bees would not venture so far and filled her mind, instead, with images of honeycomb and cakes.

They crossed a ravine, thick with brambles and sluffed granite, pushing and pulling each other to the opposite side, where sunlight pierced the dense canopy and chased away the dreary dark.

They eagerly moved toward the sun, and before long, stepped into a beautiful meadow, bathed in light and full of swaying flowers. The white and yellow blooms bobbed in the gentle breeze as if waving them nearer.

Just beyond the meadow, clear water tumbled down rugged stone into a rippling pond, ringed with forest on the far side, much like the one they'd just exited.

"If the bees came anywhere, it would be here." Saoirse scoured the nearest blossoms and, after only a short time, spotted one of her bees. The insect danced upon the flower's cheery center, fuzzy legs dusted heavily with pollen.

"Look," she said, pointing. "Come on, if they've started a hive, it will be in the trees. Let's look over there."

They moved slowly through the knee-high grass to the pond, an errant breeze lifting the hair on Saoirse's neck, making her shiver. They would have to skirt the sprawling pool—neither of them could swim, not that she wanted to get wet—and climb the boulders that rimmed the edge of the green-blue depths to reach the grove.

As they drew nearer the water, a terrible stench—like dead, bloated fish laced with brimstone—filled the air.

"What's that smell?" Edred wrinkled his nose in disgust. They slowed their steps, their wariness increasing as they searched for the source of the odor.

"Maybe there's a dead animal beyond the tree line," Saoirse suggested, without much enthusiasm. What sort of dead animal smelled like *that*?

She didn't want to get any closer to the water. Something about it made her uncomfortable.

"Look! Bees," said Edred excitedly. "By the falls." He indicated an undulating, buzzing smudge that had congregated upon an upper tree limb that overhung the cascade of water.

The world dimmed, and Saoirse glanced up where clouds, gloomy and pregnant with rain, gathered in the sky. One of them had eclipsed the sun.

Edred motioned her onward. "Come on, we'll have to hurry if we want to beat the weather."

Reluctantly, she followed as he skirted the water's edge, her gaze fixed upon the wavy surface as her mind replayed a warning she'd heard since infancy: *Ye daren't set toe upon a faerie glen for fear of beasts and little men.*

But they *had*, Saoirse reasoned. They'd traipsed all over it and nothing—so far as yet—had happened to them.

As if hearing her imprudent thoughts, the breeze grew suddenly violent. Wind whipped her skirts against her calves; the ambient drone of teeming bees withered to nothing, replaced with rasping leaves. Rain pattered on her nose, her shoulders, then quickly turned to a downpour as the seconds ticked on.

Edred slowed. Something in the air, some vibration of warning, sang in her bones. She took his hand without thought. Tiny waves lapped her ankles and soaked the hem of her skirts.

She pushed wet hair from her eyes.

When had they entered the pool?

Edred's gasp came just as she spotted it. There, through the steady flow of the cataract, the snout of some horrible, toothy creature parted the veil of water. Its black, reptilian skin glistened much like a snake. Ivory teeth set along its jaw curled at odd angles. So much she saw before it slunk from some unseen perch behind the falls and entered the lagoon below with nary a splash.

The lake rose by inches as the rain pelted them. How could this be? She hadn't moved from her spot, and yet the pond surged to her knees. Was this some sort of faerie trap?

She stood, unmoving, horrified, as a substantial shadow underneath the surface cut through the water, swiftly as a bird through air. It shot right for them, undisturbed by the sheets of rain.

Edred yanked on her arm. "Run, Sers!"

She jolted from her stupor, battling against her heavy skirts, panting and splashing her way out of the expanding pool. Her heart pounded; her lungs ached. It would catch them at any moment, tear them apart with its hideous jaws.

"Áine preserve us!" she prayed, lunging for dry ground.

Edred stooped as they raced away, scooping up a sizable stone from the earth. He chucked it at the beast. Saoirse didn't bother to watch if his strike landed. Splashes, a menacing hiss, and then they were halfway through the meadow, their gaze intent on the waiting forest.

They plunged in, heedless of grasping branches and ankle-turning rills. They tumbled down the steep hollow with a crackle of dead leaves, and lay in a heap, weeping and shaking. Edred extricated himself from her and pulled the borrowed knife from his belt with quaking fingers, his wide eyes scouring the crest of the ridge they'd just toppled over.

Her shoulder ached something fierce, but she ignored it, clawing her way upright.

"It's gone," wheezed Edred. "Sers, I don't see it."

With a sob, she grabbed onto him, and they clung together. She could not tell where her own trembling stopped and his began.

"We must never come back here," Edred whispered.

No. Never, ever, never.

As they made their way up the other side of the steep ravine, slipping and sliding, grasping tree limbs to steadying themselves on jutting rocks—and looking over their shoulders every other step—Saoirse vowed to heed every warning the elders gave concerning the Wild Wood.

She caught her breath at the top of the gulch, her hands smarting, and eyed a soaked and disheveled Edred. He'd come with her today, despite his own fears, because he simply hadn't wanted her to venture alone.

Her heart swelled with affection for him.

"Come, Saoirse," he said softly, offering his hand. "Let's go home. I think I remember the way to the stairs."

Chapter One

Soul Magic

*E*IGHT YEARS LATER

"There, there, My Sweet," crooned Ursa, lovingly swiping stray hair from her daughter's cold brow. "Do not lose hope just yet." She leaned over the edge of the wagon, whispering into her daughter's useless ear. She could not be too careful. As a magic wielder herself, she understood that even the trees could be listening.

"The grimoire is most specific," Ursa said. She kissed her daughter's unresponsive cheek. Not long ago, it had been soft and warm, yielding to her touch. The sting of tears threatened Ursa's eyes, but she blinked them away, the grief she'd borne for days dissolving into grim resolve.

She lowered her voice further. "Áine's gate is near, where the magic is most potent. Can you feel it, Elenwin?"

The lack of woodland animals further confirmed her suspicions. Not even the slightest breeze caressed the drooping boughs overhead. Instead, the atmosphere weighed her lungs so that each breath obliged exertion.

Even the horse pulling their cart twitched and flinched, flaring its nostrils against the strange magic that oozed between the slender pines. Only her own sorcery kept the animal from bolting.

Ursa's magical talent lay in the persuasive arts. She'd spent the whole of her young life influencing the smallest of creatures to do her bidding. She could induce a spider to dangle from its thread for hours should she wish it, then entice a bird to swoop in and snatch its life away. Mice had proven more difficult, but with continued instruction from the coven and no small amount of determination, Ursa had learned to slip into their simple minds and coerce them to obey. Eventually her abilities sharpened.

If she wanted, she could oblige an army of rats to march to the sea and drown themselves. She didn't, largely because she liked rats. Useful creatures, they.

Such abilities came in handy, especially when searching for evasive potion ingredients or when a living sacrifice must be made. Offerings rarely came to the knife willingly.

Of course, humans presented more of a challenge, but she'd never had greater motivation than restoring her daughter.

This forest, however, this *borderland*, affected every living creature.

Where witchcraft seduced, fae magic repelled. Her long-dead mentor, Agatha, had aptly described sorcery as a wooing craft, for the allure never waned; the urge for greater power only grew with practice.

This magic—fae magic—however, spurned humans.

Still, all the better they went unheeded. They'd travelled for days. She'd prepared for the journey as best she could, Elenwin's body laid out lovingly atop ferns and moss and nosegays to ward off unpleasant odors. She'd placed the appropriate gemstones around her body, each spell cast to slow Elenwin's decay.

The ferns had wilted and the bright stones she'd prepared had nearly depleted.

She retraced the multitude of steps she'd read within the spell book she'd acquired. The underworld was just and fair above all things. "I must not disrupt the balance between our worlds. There must be a soul exchange," she muttered.

Time ran short. The wood grew close and soon, impassable for the wagon, forcing her to unhitch the conveyance and leave it behind. "Gideon will carry you, Dearest." She tugged the blanket covering her daughter more tightly around her feet and tied them together with a line of hemp rope so that they would not flop and sway when she lay across the horse's back.

Next, she hid Elenwin's blackening fingers beneath the folds, the ugly pucker from the serpent's fangs glaring at her like two accusing eyes upon the fleshy part of her hand.

She'd found Elenwin too late, her vacant body sprawled upon the hearthstones. The viper's bite told Ursa all she'd needed to know. She'd warned Elenwin against overconfidence—had urged her to leave the witching pantry well alone—but children often misunderstood the fragility of life.

But hope still lived.

Her eyes stung as she pulled Elenwin into her arms, gasping at the change wrought from only three days since death. Instead of curling and conforming against her breast as a child would, Elenwin's stony body slumped indifferently toward the earth.

A sob caught in her throat. "Do not fear." Ursa did not know to whom she spoke, herself or Elenwin. "We will prevail." This time her voice did not waver. "I needn't tell *you* of my power."

She draped Elenwin as lovingly as she could across the beast's back. It's rolling, wide eyes stilled as her magic further penetrated its brain. It only stamped its hoof once as she secured Elenwin in place. It would not do to have Ele slip from Gideon's strong back and injure herself further.

"Take heart," she said, as she gathered the horse's reins. "I will not rest until I've succeeded."

The forest swallowed their footfalls. Ursa cast out her magic, searching for creatures that might lurk nearby, but when she opened herself to the borderland's magic, she stumbled under its might.

With the recent summer solstice, the goddess Áine's full might and power shone bright as the sun. How lucky for them that when Ursa needed a necromantic spell, it occurred at the zenith of the goddess's power, when her potent magic bled into the human world.

Summer's doorway—Áine's doorway—waited for them, a crack in the world that seeped power from the fae realms. The Book of Undying was hers, passed down from her mentor, Agatha. She had prepared all the ingredients, now nestled in the horse's saddlebags.

All save one.

A sacrifice must be found. *A justifiable exchange*, she told herself.

"You are worthy of life, Elenwin." She hurried her steps, glancing at the bright sky peering between the trees. Elenwin's body would not fare well under the summer sun.

"A soul for a soul, Elenwin. All is just."

Chapter Two

Old Friends

Village of Betws-y-Coed

The well's pulley whined as Saoirse drew up the pail, a tight squeak of irritation that echoed off the stones. Her back ached, but she ignored the twinge as she heaved the burden toward the coping and tipped its contents into her own bucket.

"That old nag in need of water again?" asked a familiar voice from behind. She could hear the smile behind his words and had to fight her own away before turning to meet him. It wouldn't do to grin brainlessly at Edred as other girls did.

She repressed the urge to say something smart, like, *Why no, this water isn't for your mother,* and congratulated herself on her maturity.

Of course, little could be done to avoid the tumble her heart took whenever he drew near, but at least he couldn't see it. Or his mother, who didn't exactly approve of her. Fadam Fortwin liked Saoirse well enough, but her family's lack of fortune made any sort of union impossible.

"I'm scrubbing the tiles today," she explained, allowing him to take the burden from her. Falling into step beside him, she willed the butterflies in her belly away. "You're finished early." She looked him over for some telling reason that he would leave the forge midday.

The Fortwin family owned the blacksmith shop and had grown rich from their venture. The family's industry had helped to expand the population to their village. So too, Edred's shoulders had doubled in size in just a year, and no wonder. At two and twenty, he swung a hammer as swift and as sure as an arrow loosed from the greatest of Welsh bowmen.

He cast her a look that she could not decipher. "Saoirse, have you been to Áine's temple since the solstice?"

Her cheeks heated at the reminder of the celebration, where she'd fumbled all over herself when he'd asked her to dance. She'd ultimately declined his invitation, terrified that if he touched her, her true feelings would slip out of her. That, or she'd make a fool of herself by stomping all over his toes.

"No, I've been harvesting."

He nodded, hazel eyes distant, his brow furrowed. "Of course."

After each summer solstice, when Áine favored the land with her warmth and light, the first reaping took place. The villagers swarmed the fields, cutting and plucking, raking and winnowing. Next came the planting of hardier crops—those that could withstand the season's harsher conditions. With Áine's blessing, come autumn, everyone would have enough to last through the cold months.

Saoirse's yield differed from others. Her father still had cattle, of course, but Saoirse hadn't forgotten about the summer goddess's promise to her—she'd finally found her bees at thirteen, had cut the comb from a fallen, moldering log, merrily fetching the swarm home, stings and all.

"How are your bees?" asked Edred, looking down at her over the knot in his nose. He'd broken it years ago when he'd gotten too close to his father in the forge. Madoc had drawn his hammer back, preparing for another strike, and Edred had caught it with his face. He hadn't needed to learn that lesson twice. The healer had set the break, but the bump along the otherwise straight bridge only added to his charm.

She smiled. "They've done very well over the spring. I wove another skep for them so the new queen doesn't swarm and leave. I'm drumming them into their new home tonight."

Her half-brother, Dafydd, generally helped her cut honeycomb, strain, and pour honey from the older skeps into crocks for storage. But even with his help—often late in the day after the second milking and his deliveries—there didn't seem to be enough hands for the work, especially now that her father had injured himself. More and more of the harvest's responsibilities rested on her and Dafydd. Not that she minded. She'd rather gossip with her bees than with cows.

"That's great." He looked genuinely pleased to hear her bees fared so well.

Her stomach flipped at his interest, and she changed the subject quickly. "Thanks for carting the water. My shoes are sticking to the floor. I'm afraid I'll walk right out of them if I wait any longer to scour the tiles."

He brushed a dark wave of hair from his forehead only to have it flop back. "Are you nearly finished?"

"Finished?" She laughed. "I've only just begun." She started to bump him with her elbow—a goading gesture to make him smile—but caught herself. She gave him a sideways look instead. "There's a place for you in the kitchen, should you wish to give up pounding metal for a day."

As soon as the words left her mouth, she wished them back. A year ago, she wouldn't have thought twice about inviting him to come dip candles or to touch him innocently, but ever since she'd discovered her own feelings for him—and his subsequent courting of Gwenllian, the daughter of the wealthy butcher—every friendly gesture from her whispered a confession.

She wasn't the only maid in the village interested in the kind-hearted and industrious Edred. Áine forbid that her face mimic the soppy, hopeful expressions on other girl's faces.

Still, despite her wishes, her heart ached each time she spied Gwenllian and Edred speaking in the lane. Some days, when Gwenllian's flaxen hair gleamed in the sun and her soulful brown eyes smiled at Edred, Saoirse heartily wished away her own wild, black locks and her common silver-blue eyes.

Perhaps if she adopted Gwenllian's demure countenance and way of speaking, Edred would have courted her instead, despite her lack of fortune.

Even the butcher's daughter's name tasted sweet on the tongue, where Saoirse's bumped and snagged, full of corners.

"Your candles are the best," he conceded, pulling her out of her somber thoughts.

She waved his words away, her cheeks warm. "But you've got enough going on to be dipping candles in my hot kitchen, I'm sure. Have you visited the goddess's temple? Is that why you're back early?"

"I brought the customary portion of goods as tribute, but—it's probably nothing," he hedged, lowering his voice intimately. "Do you recall when we were younger, and we ventured beyond our boundaries?"

Of course she remembered. Even now she could not go to the summer goddess's temple with any sort of ease. Her eyes strayed, as ever, to the distant wild wood and the jutting mountain, teeming with fae.

Saoirse stopped walking. "Why? What's happened?"

He set the water bucket down, uncertainty in his eyes. "The forest near the temple felt *different*, like when we'd found the waterfall at the base of the faerie gorge." He shivered. "Quiet and close."

"Has the water risen?" she asked, hushed. She hadn't paid any attention to the river, being too preoccupied with her bees. It had rained, as it so often did in Cymru, but she'd learned long ago that she couldn't live with any semblance of peace if she fretted about monsters every time the clouds opened.

Of course, eight years ago, any amount of rainfall had worried her. For months she'd prayed for forgiveness, asking Áine to keep her beast well away from the village with the vow to never again set foot upon the goddess's forbidden mountain.

The tight pull of Edred's mouth worried Saoirse. She took a step closer, her heart in her throat. "Has the *Afanc* come at last?"

"Don't use its name," he hissed.

She'd learned the monster's identity through careful questions, placed in the right ears. Legend said that the creature kept the door to Áine's kingdom secure. Some villagers said it did not exist.

Saoirse and Edred knew better.

He shrugged one shoulder, not meeting her eyes. "Mayhap the feeling wasn't quite the same as I remembered." He rubbed his forehead and sighed, casting her an apologetic look. "It's nothing. With all the rain and then the strange feeling of the temple—"

Saoirse opened her mouth to respond, to tell him she would go herself to Áine's shrine, but words failed her. She could not go. Not now, with Papa's lying abed, needing care, not with her endless work. And certainly not alone.

"There you are, Edred," said Fadam Fortwin. She ambled down the lane, her narrowed eyes twitching between Saoirse and her son. They stood far too close than social propriety expected, never mind that they'd been as thick as thieves since they could walk.

Edred bristled and turned to greet his mother. "Good afternoon, Mam."

"What are you doing, dawdling in the street, Edred?"

Edred frowned. "I was inquiring about Saoirse's bees."

Fadam Fortwin's sharp gaze raked over Saoirse, her smile tight. "And how are your bees fairing with you out here in the road, Saoirse? And your father?"

Edred's cheeks pinkened at his mother's less-than-subtle hint. "Mam!"

Saoirse might have laughed if she weren't so annoyed. "We do need water, just like the rest of the village," she said cooly.

It hadn't always been like this between them. The woman's genial acceptance of her had slowly diminished, just as Saoirse's memories of Alys had done. The sharp edge of her memory had worn away so gradually that only the blurred shapes of experiences remained—a feeling of warm affection that both comforted and saddened her.

Saoirse couldn't recall her own mother at all. Both women dead from birthing children. Both buried under the willow, side by side.

But this death, between her and Edred's mother, who had once tended and loved her, cut deeper because the blame rested fully upon Saoirse's shoulders. Upon their return from Faerie Hill, Edred's nightmares betrayed their secret.

Gwenda Fortwin had marched up to her door and berated Papa for mishandling the raising of his daughter. She shouted loud enough for the whole village to hear, "If you don't check her, Rhys, she'll run wild as the fae and drag the rest of us into ruin with her! Her foolishness and your indulgence will be the death of her—and Edred."

The woman had belatedly registered Saoirse in the room, but the flicker of shocked regret in her eyes had quickly given way to resolve. "How dare you, Saoirse," she'd scolded. "Haven't you learned anything from my stories?"

Papa had closed the door on the woman and forbade Saoirse from ever stepping outside of the village boundaries again. He'd swatted her, too, for good measure, not that he'd needed to. She had no desire to ever return to that horrid place.

Ever since, she'd been unworthy of Edred, but they'd stayed close friends. They played under his mother's unyielding stare or in secret, in the hills and valleys of the western hills, away from anything fae.

Saoirse gestured to Edred. "He was kind enough to carry my burden."

The woman's steely eye softened as she looked upon her son. "Yes, he's quite the gentleman." She wrapped her shawl more tightly around herself and shot her son a significant look. "Gwenllian and her family are coming for supper. Best hurry this along and get home in time to make yourself presentable."

Saoirse found great interest in the stones littering the path.

"Of course. I'll be there soon."

After a stretched silence, his ears scarlet, he picked up the bucket, signaling his intent to remain, as ever, the respectful son.

Edred did not speak further as they strolled to her meager home, and her mind spun with what she might say to break the awkward tension between them.

After entering her kitchen, he poured the bucket of water into the overlarge kettle she used for washing, then swung it over the smoldering fire. He paused at her worktable where her finished hive waited, braided tightly into a cone for her bees.

"You've done well there, Sers. I remember your first attempt." His crooked smile banished all lingering discomfort his mother's words had caused. "A rather warped affair, if I remember."

Saoirse arched a brow. "Lucky for you, I'm the kinder of our pair. It would be impolite of me to remind you of your abysmal attempt at droving cattle with Father that summer you turned sixteen."

The flirtatious twist of his mouth made her heart skip. "I suppose I lack the talent of working with dumb beasts."

She smiled brightly at him. "I've had practice enough. How long have we been friends again?"

He laughed, hazel eyes twinkling, and reached a broad hand toward the thick rope of her plaited hair. Standing so close, she was forced to cant her head back to look him in eye.

She held her breath. Sometimes, when Edred touched her in a familiar way, the thread stitching her heart together unraveled itself. Worse, she could not name the cause of the strain between them. Had he adopted his mother's view of her? One day he'd distanced himself, and, bewildered, she'd responded in kind.

Saoirse told herself the alteration came from age. He'd grown up, so had she. Only, Saoirse could not seem to find her feet in their altered relationship.

I miss you, her heart urged her to say. Instead, she pressed her lips tightly together.

He tugged gently on her hair, the smile slipping from his face. "I have to go, Sers."

She busied herself by tying her apron. She couldn't bring herself to add her well wishes to Gwenllian and her family.

"Sers," Edred said, turning at the door.

Her heart flipped as she met his eyes.

"If you go to the temple, don't go alone."

She wouldn't.

Chapter Three

By the Power of Three

HOURS LATER, WITH THE sun nearly set, Ursa had no choice but to stop. The delicate bones of her feet ached so terribly that she limped with each step, but she had no choice with Elenwin riding the horse. Walking slowed their progression, but Ursa sensed Áine's gate nearby.

"We must rest here, Elenwin."

She labored as she removed the ties holding her daughter to the horse, her movements sluggish. Trekking through the oppressive wood only accounted for a small portion of her exhaustion. Keeping the horse from bolting hour after hour required an exorbitant amount of energy.

Still, she could not give sway to her desire for rest. Not yet. She pulled her daughter's body from the back of the horse, grunting as the added weight aggravated her aching body.

Ursa settled her against a fallen log mantled with poisonous, red-capped mushrooms. Buried in blankets, her face hidden from easy view, Elenwin resembled any other body, prepared for internment. Horror clawed up Ursa's throat, making it difficult to breathe.

Falling to her knees, she frantically pulled the covering from her daughter's face, gritting her teeth against a sob at the unhappy sight. Fluid dribbled from Elenwin's nose, most likely from how she'd dangled from her mount hour upon hour. A greenish tinge consumed Elenwin's neck and jaw, radiating up from under the high collar of her dress.

Ursa fumbled for her handkerchief and dabbed the liquid away. "Oh, Dearest, I'm so sorry. There, there, Sweeting. Mummy's here. I'll make it right. Don't you fret." Soon, her daughter's cheeks would pinken and her eyes would clear. They'd shine with light, as they once had.

Looking at the state of her daughter, Ursa suddenly doubted herself. *Could* she do it? As skilled a witch as she believed herself to be, winning back her daughter's soul would require magic she'd never even dreamed of performing.

Tears sprang to Ursa's eyes before she could stop them. She'd ceased wishing on stars ages ago, but now that her entire world had tilted on its axis, she found herself tossing her desperate wants into the ether once more. "Don't leave me, Ele. I'll do anything. Just don't go to Annwn—I cannot go on without—"

The knot in her throat tightened and she lost her words. She sobbed into her fist, her body quaking with the force of her anguish. With so much of her mind now focused on her loss, the knotted coil of magic rooting her rational brain to the horse began to unravel. Frantic stomping and blowing pulled her from her own mind.

She fumbled for the mental connection and latched onto the dwindling tether joining herself to the beast. She barely held it, gulping air.

Don't be stupid, Ursa. She'd lost her composure in a fit of self-pity. Such a display could not be repeated. She must remain level-headed in all things, or she would have no chance at all.

Ursa stood on shaky legs and limped to the horse, its skin twitching as if flies lighted upon its coat.

Careful not to get too close just yet, Ursa inhaled through her nose and closed her eyes, pushing her mind outward. She sensed the horse's nervousness and allowed the animal's panic to flood her. Her nostrils flared, taking in the sharp bite of otherworldly magic that so terrified the steed, an odor her human nose could not detect.

She found that slipping into minds came much easier when she matched her emotions to theirs. If the vessel panicked, so did Ursa. If the animal hungered, so did she. The same terror the horse experienced came easily to her now, for fear lived in the very crevices of her heart.

The beast's mind whirred with images: slinking shadows with gleaming teeth, the unexpected swoop of a predator from above, the sharp stench of brimstone.

Be at ease. There is no danger here. She forced stillness, and despite her eyes being closed to the world, she sensed the horse's ears cease their twitching. Its muscles relaxed as their mingled minds quieted.

We are well. We are whole. None will harm us.

She opened her eyes on a slow exhale, flexing her hands. Rest must wait. The horse needed feeding and protective spells needed recasting. Already the darkening wood pressed close, stippling her skin with dread, a warning that the shield she'd created before entering Áine's borderland had worn thin under the prolonged strain of the goddess's magic. The tension pulled at her limbs, begging her to rest, to sleep, but she could not shrink and wither under the weight of her burden. For Elenwin's sake.

Ursa gritted her teeth and stood upon the sharp bones of her feet.

"Yes, yes, I'll rest soon, Sweeting." She removed the saddle and tied the horse's lead to a sturdy branch, then gathered the vestiges of her lessening magic.

For her spellcasting payment, she drew an incubating duck egg, wrapped in cloth, from the saddlebag. Next, she fished a length of red string and an iron nail from her pocket.

To the uninitiated, a duck egg wouldn't seem much of a sacrifice, but eggs made excellent tender in witchcraft. The symbols of the sacrifice—life, fertility, transformation, even protection—qualified her offering. They came cheaply, not that the cost of the egg was important. The real prize lived inside.

She cradled the sacrifice against her breast as she circled their make-shift camp, ensuring to also include the horse and Elenwin.

"By shell and spirit, strong and true, guard us well, all harm undo."

She stopped and carefully wrapped the string around the egg, ensuring that the overlapping threads crossed several times. *A web to catch would-be evil.* "By knot of red, I weave this charm, protections strong, ward off all harm." Once complete, she took another turn around the space.

Hands steady despite her fatigue, Ursa next positioned the fae-hated iron against the shell. "Iron sharp and iron strong, seal this spell, lasting long." She gently but firmly pierced the bird's protective barrier. Blood oozed over her fingers from the hole, which she industriously used to draw an X on her daughter's forehead. Next, she marked the horse and herself.

With effort, she sank to her knees and, using her fingernails, clawed at the earth until she'd made a hole big enough for her sacrifice.

"By the power of three, so mote it be."

The whispered words rang with finality through the narrow clearing. She closed her eyes against the familiar draw of power that came with casting magic and slumped forward. Breathing heavily, Ursa crawled to where her daughter waited.

Elenwin's hooded eyes stared blankly. Ursa laid her palm against Ele's unyielding cheek. "Hush now, Dearest. Sleep. We are so close. Áine's gate beyond the veil of water lies only a day away."

Ursa curled against her daughter's side then fell into a restless sleep.

T HE FOLLOWING MORNING, URSA forced herself to eat a stale oatcake from the saddlebag. Dreams had plagued her. Images of a lively, laughing Elenwin had quickly turned sour, her smile fading as her jaw grew slack and her body shriveled to dust.

"There will be a guardian at the door," she told Elenwin, quickly forcing the images from her mind. "I will know what it is once we get closer," she said, securing Ele to the saddle. "For now, I only sense the gate's energy."

Gripping the horse's lead, her heart quickened. "This magic is far stronger than anything I've felt before. A perfect location for our purposes."

She'd been wrong about one thing, though: the door turned out to be far closer than she'd first surmised. The horse, no matter how intently she persuaded it to remain calm, grew wild and frantic. She'd had no choice but retreat, to retrace her steps until it calmed itself enough to allow her to remove Elenwin from its back.

As soon as she'd retrieved Ele and the saddlebag, she slipped from the steed's mind. It bolted, blowing and bucking, screaming, as it galloped through the woods.

Ursa sighed. "I hate to see Gideon go, Ele. He was a good horse."

Losing the animal meant that she wouldn't expend further energy in controlling it. All her power must now concentrate solely on whatever beast guarded Áine's door.

Old texts in Agatha's library told of a water guardian, but of what sort? A Kelpie, perhaps? A Mari-Morgan? She hoped for the latter. She'd run into a den of Mari-Morgans as a young apprentice and had found them vastly entertaining. She frowned inwardly. Since they only drowned men, the goddess would not likely employ such a choosey guardian.

Her footsteps slowed considerably now that she carried Elenwin. Twice she stopped to rest under the towering trees. Both times she attempted a scrying spell to discern what might await them, but nothing revealing emerged. Well, that wasn't quite true. A clear lagoon set in a sprawling, grassy field filled her mind. "Could be any manner of creature there," she complained to Elenwin.

The sound of rushing water spurred her on; once she found the swift river, she followed its flow, barely feeling the burden in her arms any longer. The steady current abruptly ended amid algae-covered boulders as it leaped from the mountain.

"I think this must be it," she muttered to Elenwin, as if she might hear her over the roar of cascading water. She edged closer;

tiny specks of moisture painted the air in a spectacular spectrum of color.

Her first smile in a week lifted her cheeks. She set her daughter against a sizeable rock. Far below the falls lay a glittering pond, the ripples upon the surface diffusing to nothing halfway across the expansive pool. She'd scried this very image except for one important element.

She dared to peer over the edge, one hand gripping a tree limb that overhung the torrent. There, deep under the surface, lay the shadowy silhouette of a creature surrounded by the gleaming bones of countless animals.

Her smile faltered. *What can it be?*

She shifted her footing, accidentally sending leaves and a few acorns over the edge. When the debris hit the water, one yellow eye blinked open below the surface. Bubbles escaped the long snout; its tail twitched.

Ursa held her breath, her fist tight around a tree branch.

The creature rose to the surface, its long, strange body exposed. A black, leathery muzzle reflected the sun. Bony spikes surrounded its head in an enormous, threatening mane. They tapered away upon its back, giving way to stiff, light brown fur.

Her breathing hitched, her determination giving way to doubt. Slipping into the minds of rodents and men was one thing. A magical creature of this size and ability likely would prove impossible.

All the air left Ursa's lungs as the creature propelled itself from the water's edge. Thunder sounded overhead, breaking her unblinking stare. She glanced at the sky, which had, moments ago, beamed radiant blue. Now, clouds covered the heavens, bruised with impending rain.

She gasped as her memory caught up with her. She'd read of this creature long ago. Hope surged in her breast.

It hissed as it ambled out of the water, angling its head in her direction.

"How lucky we are, Dearest. If I fail to enter its mind, I can simply sing it to sleep."

The afanc opened toothy jaws and roared. The bellow hit her in the gut, even shaking leaves—and seemingly the rain—from the air. The droplets showered down upon them. The roll of the river increased as thunder boomed overhead.

The river's turbulence swelled with the deluge. *It means to sweep us into the pond.*

Ursa's surprise and fear dissipated like smoke on the wind, replaced with urgency. She rushed to Elenwin's body, clutching her against her breast. "We've come too far to be defeated now."

She matched the beast's emotions, pulling her own fury around her like a cloak, and pushed herself through the brush and over jagged, slick rocks. She nearly dropped Elenwin when her foot slipped off a slimy stone, but she righted herself at the last second, bumping into a tree.

When she'd made it to a safer distance from the rising water, she leaned against a pine and closed her eyes.

The afanc's anger—and her own—entangled like lovers. She wheedled into its resolute mind, slid through with a gasp of effort. *Sleep. Rest. There is no danger here.* For good measure, she hummed softly, using the creature's weakness against itself. The melody brushed against its consciousness, distracting it from wrath and defense.

Had the rain slowed? She opened her eyes, wiping her face with her sodden cloak.

She pushed off from the tree and glared at the river, which had risen a good five feet.

The wind slackened; the rain fell in an irregular pattering of droplets.

She stretched her mind out once more, touching the delicate thread of mental energy that connected her mind to that of the beast.

Her smile returned. "See now, Elenwin. Fate is on our side."

Slowly, she made her way down the mountain, Elenwin draped over her shoulder. She hated carrying her in such a way, but at this point, she had little choice.

By the time she set foot upon the meadow, the gate's guardian rested once more beneath the pond, cradled in a bed of old bones. Magic pulsed from the falls.

"The gate waits just beyond the veil of water, Elenwin. All we require now is a suitable sacrifice."

Chapter Four

Something Wicked

S AOIRSE POURED FRESH MILK into the dash churn and handed the pail back to Dafydd. She tried her best to hide her smirk. "You've got cream on your lip, you know." Her reproof affected him as thoroughly as arrows bouncing off a stone wall.

His broad smile showed his missing front tooth. "Buttercup doesn't mind. Besides, shouldn't I test it to make sure she didn't get into your onion patch again?"

Unable to hold her grin any longer, Saoirse reached over to muss his light brown curls. "Tell me you didn't drink straight from the bucket."

He turned to leave, the pail *thunking* against his leg, and spoke over his shoulder. "I thought you wanted me to always tell the truth."

"Use a cup, at least," she called after him, laughing. "You're likely to spill otherwise . . . and keep Buttercup out of my garden!"

Her words chased him around the corner of the lime-washed barn, the offended squawking of chickens telling her he'd moved on to his next chore: gathering eggs.

Tutting in exasperation, she settled in front of the churn and grasped the handle, but before she could even begin, she heard the muffled call of her father from inside the house.

"Coming, Papa!"

She wiped her hands on her apron as she passed into the common area of their cottage, her boots ringing on the planks.

Her father had broken his leg and cracked a few ribs when he'd fallen from the roof while making repairs to the thatch three weeks ago. Unfortunately, his pleasant temperament had fractured right along with his bones. Rhys ap Gareth tolerated convalescence as well as a fish did air, a trait she'd inherited. Father like daughter, apparently.

He sat in their only comfortable chair, his leg propped on a stool, glaring at the needle he held close to his nose. In the other hand, he pinched thread between thumb and forefinger. Sandy locks fell into his eyes, and he shook them away with an annoyed huff that could topple a sheaf of wheat.

"I don't know how you manage to thread these things. Do you mind?" He held the offending items out to her, his blue eyes apologetic.

"I won't be of any help in this light." She stepped to the window and pulled open the shutter.

She made short work of threading the needle and handed it back to him. "I never much cared for sewing myself, so I rather like that you've taken over for me."

He huffed good-naturedly and returned to darning one of her stockings, which had worn thin at the heel. "When the holes in your stockings grow holes, it might be a good sign to repurpose these and knit a new pair."

Saoirse shrugged, moving to the kitchen table to check on the bread she'd started that morning. They didn't have the means for yarn just then, even with her added income from honey and candles. House repairs and Dafydd's constant need for larger shoes consumed any extra funds. He grew so quickly, their coffers could hardly keep up.

"You can dash the cream if you'd rather. I'll fetch your crutch."

Bang! Dafydd tore in through the door, eyes wide. "Papa! Can I help Wilim search for Fadam Morvel's daughter? I'm not finished with raking hay, but—"

"What do you mean? Is Eva missing?" cut in Saoirse, alarm ringing through her. Last spring a child had gone missing, and they'd found her hours later, washed far downstream. Drowned. The memory of it still haunted her. She and Papa had forbidden Dafydd from playing near the bank ever since. The whole village watched for children near the frothy water's edge, now, terrified to lose another child.

Dafydd shifted his weight from foot to foot. "Other villagers are out looking. Fadam Morvel said that, when they woke, Eva wasn't in her bed."

Saoirse shared a look of concern with her father.

"You go, too, Saoirse. I'll finish the butter."

She tugged off her apron, but Dafydd had already disappeared, leaving the door wide open. "That boy," she muttered, sparing a glance for her father. "You promise you won't do too much." She handed over his crutch, leveling him with a stern look.

"Go, Saoirse. I'll be well enough. Be careful," Papa called after her.

Dafydd had already gained a good thirty paces, but he showed consideration by waiting for her at the edge of the front garden, where their property met the road.

They hurried down the lane nestled among rolling foothills, passing their neighbor's empty fields and barnyards, evidence that others had left their work to help. They lived on the northern outskirts of the village, but the walk was not far except when carting water.

A group of people—four or five—congregated near the well where their path converged with the center of the village, Wilim among them. Her brother's spindly friend resembled a broom, straw-colored hair always standing on end. He waved madly when he spotted them, a gesture Dafydd eagerly returned before dashing into the mingling villagers.

Saoirse frowned at the younger boys' exuberance. They treated the search for Eva like some kind of adventure.

Two women—Fadams Gaber and Sutor—waited there, wringing their hands. Gaber and Sutor happened to be the worst kinds of gossips, but she was glad for their presence. If anyone knew the latest news, it would be them. Thomas, Wilim's elder brother, stood apart from the matronly women, his face drawn.

"What hasn't been searched?" asked Saoirse in lieu of greeting. She nodded to Thomas, who doffed his hat respectfully.

Under normal circumstances, she might ask how the bakery fared since taking over for his father, but the serious nature of their gathering precluded any social niceties, not that she minded. Thomas's lingering stares whenever she'd chanced to meet him in the market embarrassed her. Thankfully, his shyness prevented him from actually speaking to her most days.

Fadam Sutor, thin and wispy as a stalk of barley, spoke first, her worried eyes darting around as if Eva would pop out of the ground like a dandelion. "The riverbanks are being searched as we speak, but . . . ."

The woman didn't need to finish her thought. The swiftness of the river could carry a grown man for leagues, much less a girl of ten. The last drowning had carried the unfortunate girl nearly eight miles. *Poor thing.*

"Another group is knocking doors," offered Fadam Gaber, fisting her shawl about her ample bosom. "Surely someone has seen her about. What sort of child leaves their house before the rest of the world has awoken?"

Her words hung heavy in the air. What sort, indeed? Children of Cymru, having a healthy respect for the dangers that lurked on both sides of Áine's doorway, *never* wandered in the dark. What had tempted Eva from the safety of her home before sunrise?

Thomas's timid gaze flitted to and from Saoirse as quickly as a dragonfly lighting from branch to branch. "Mother is tending to Fadam Morvel while her husband and the other men walk the riverbank." He pulled the cap from his head and crushed it in his hands. "Perhaps she's only hurt her ankle and cannot come home."

"That could be," said Saoirse, though worry gnawed at her. Waking up to find a child's bed empty tested the limits of optimism.

"We're on our way to the temple to pray for Eva," said Fadam Sutor, holding up her offering—a creel cluttered with eggs.

Saoirse's gaze cut through the field to her left, a wide expanse of unripened barley that swayed with the breeze. On the far side stood a copse of trees, cradling the beaten path to the goddess's shrine at the footstool of the Wild Wood. Perhaps she should bring an offering as well.

Another villager stalked up the road toward them, his leather apron abandoned, face smudged with soot. Sweat made his off-white sark cling to his upper body. The furrow between his brows told Saoirse the news of the missing child had reached him, as well.

"Edred," said Fadam Gaber, her voice breathy, "did you hear the terrible news?"

His solemn eyes skimmed over the gathered crowd, snagging on Saoirse. At least her hopeful heart told her it did. She immediately scolded herself. *Don't be such a lackwit.*

"Yes, I heard. I shut down the forge so I can aid with the search."

"Kind of you," said both women seriously, nodding to one another, as if no one else had roused to help, as if they, too, grew senseless around Edred. The thought almost made Saoirse smile.

"Let's go." Dafydd tugged on Saoirse's arm. She heartily agreed, but where to search?

Thomas stepped closer, drawing the crowd's eyes, his voice strangely strangled, "There're some gullies up the western hills beyond the orchard, if one's not careful—that is, if the child went to pick berries or to hunt truffles, she might have taken a fall or become hopelessly lost."

"Could be," said Fadam Sutor, her tone doubtful.

Saoirse privately agreed. What girl of eight would brave the winding trails through the hills with only starlight as her guide? She glanced at Edred, the dubious look on his face telling her he found the idea equally unlikely. But what other option did they have?

"It's a good place to start, in any case," offered Saoirse, giving Thomas an encouraging nod. "What do you think, boys? Does that sound like somewhere Eva would likely go?"

Wilim scratched his nose and shrugged.

"She liked hide and seek and blind man's bluff, but we never played in the hills," Dafydd provided.

Fadam Gabor pulled her shawl more tightly around herself. "It would be good to rule the area out, in any case." The two women said their goodbyes in a whirl of skirts and tramped down the lane toward the temple, their heads bent together as if sharing gossip.

Dafydd and Wilim bounced eagerly toward the orchards, Thomas, Saoirse, and Edred following behind.

The town's crooked rooftops fell from view as they climbed the rolling hills, walking the worn wagon path that wound through the tall grass, Edred slowing to linger just behind. The buzz of grasshoppers and the shuffling of their feet filled the air.

Thomas cleared his throat beside her, staring fixedly at the drooping plum boughs, heavy with fruit. He snatched his hat once more from his head. "It would be my honor—would you allow me . . . that is, I would hate for you to turn your ankle." He kneaded his poor cap so thoroughly, Saoirse doubted it could be reformed to its usual shape. "I offer my arm to you, Saoirse, should you find need of it."

"Erm . . ."

"Mistress ferch Rhys," said Edred from behind, emphasizing her formal title, "is surefooted as a nanny goat. It's the extra toes," he whispered conspiratorially. The sun dappled his rich brown hair, highlighting it in tones of red and gold.

What an unflattering comparison, and untrue to boot! She refrained from rolling her eyes and glared at Edred, who merely wrinkled his nose at her, laughter in his eyes.

Thomas stared at her feet as they peeked from under the hemline of her blue skirts with each step. He couldn't possibly believe this nonsense.

"No, no, Edred. You've got it confused. It's not extra toes, but *brains*." She tapped her temple.

A look of relief softened the tight look of concern on Thomas's face. Thankfully, Edred refrained from teasing more, and Thomas didn't proffer any other body parts to ensure her safe keeping.

In stark contrast to the forbidden wilderness beyond the temple, these woods rang with birdsong. They entered, the boys bounding ahead, calling Eva's name.

Despite searching for hours, they found no sign of Eva.

SOMETHING STIRRED SAOIRSE FROM her restless slumber. She'd had difficulty falling asleep, her mind lingering on poor Eva and her family. The men who'd trekked the riverbanks found no sign of the girl, either.

When Saoirse and Dafydd brought their offering to Áine's altar after supper, they'd had to find a spot to place it among the other gifts. The whole village would be uneasy until they found the girl.

A dull thud sounded outside of the cottage. The wind must have picked up and caught hold of the broken shutter on the barn again. She sighed and flung her quilt to the side, knowing what would happen next.

She really ought to have Edred make a new latch. The old one had rusted away to nothing.

Thud, thud, thud.

"Sers?" called a tentative voice.

Dafydd. At eight, he hadn't quite yet overcome his fear of the dark. He'd shared her room for most of his life, but after she turned twenty, her father insisted on her having her own room. He'd built a loft just for Dafydd, accessed by a sturdy ladder that took up residence in the middle of the common area. Only her brother didn't much care for sleeping alone.

"I'm coming." She yawned into the back of her hand.

She didn't bother with lighting a candle, knowing every inch of space in their little house even in the dim of night. She spied the shadowed silhouette of his head hanging from the open loft, his hair fanning out in a halo of curls.

"Come on, Little Prince, you can sleep with me." When he didn't budge, she added, "It's only the broken shutter."

As if the wind eavesdropped, it took that moment to perform. The resounding *bang* outside propelled Dafydd down the ladder and into the common area like some otherworldly creature chased him. He dodged the obscure chair and mending basket that stood in his way with practiced ease and barreled past her, leaping into her bed.

"I see how well you value my life, leaving me out here alone," she said dryly.

Dafydd's confidence in her came out muffled from under the covers: "It can't get *you*. You're grown."

She couldn't help smiling at his failed logic, but didn't have the heart to tell him that becoming an adult didn't alleviate fears. They only changed shape. "Budge up, you're hogging the bed."

Dafydd wiggled over against the wall like an overgrown caterpillar. She slid in next to him and fought for her stake in the quilt.

The wind whistled through the thatch overhead, the shutter clattering in an aggravating parody of a song.

"Bad dream?"

He nodded against her shoulder. "I thought someone was trying to get into the house," he confessed. "I know Papa said that I needn't worry, that he would keep us safe, but . . . ."

She turned on her side and stroked his hair.

"The healer said it will be weeks yet until the break in his leg will mend," Dafydd said. "How can he protect us if he can't walk?"

"He is not ill, Little Prince. Besides, *I'm* here, and I'd never let anyone harm you. Ever."

"What would you do?" He plucked on a frayed edge of their shared covering.

Saoirse pulled in a breath. "Oh, I suppose I could . . . *tickle* them to death!" Her fingers found the spot in his ribs that guaranteed a fit of hysterical contortions. He kicked her shins twice and elbowed her in the face before she gave up.

She kissed his brow. "Listen to me."

He stilled.

"I would protect you with my life, Dafydd. You're safe. Sleep now."

"Only so long as I stay within the boundaries of the village."
She held her breath for a long second. "Yes."

"Do you think Eva left on her own?" he asked, his voice small.

The question hung in the air between them. "I can't say, Dafydd."

A terrible unease grew within Saoirse. They hadn't found Eva's body, nor clues of where she might have gone—or why. She couldn't have simply vanished. Someone—or something—had taken her. But to where? And for what purpose?

Dafydd interrupted her bleak thoughts. "Saoirse, you say that we're safe here in the village, but what's keeping bad things within *their* boundaries?"

She had the same question. Alys had told her once, long ago, a story of how the fairies stole away humans. Edred's mother had also warned them both from a young age about the dangers of provoking the Fair Folk. Could Eva have done something to catch their interest?

She immediately pushed the thought aside. *Of course not.* What could a mere child do to draw the gaze of the fae?

She remembered then, at twelve, following what she believed to be a blessing from the goddess herself straight out of the boundaries. If she hadn't lost her nerve and circled back to bring Edred along, she might have never made it back home.

Her tongue stuck to the roof of her mouth.

"If I ever get lost, I'll leave clues," assured Dafydd, "so that you'll be able to find me."

"Dafydd, promise me you'll not wander past Áine's temple."

"No," he said, hushed. "Why would I?"

Chapter Five

Dashed Hopes

Two days passed with no sign of Eva. People continued the search, her father even going so far as to ride into the next village, a goodly distance away, in the hope that some kind soul had picked his lost daughter up on the road. Why she should be there in the first place, no one asked. They—everyone—grasped at any explanation, however farfetched.

Every possibility save one.

The rhythmic pounding of hammer on steel rang through the streets, a sharp staccato that mimicked the painful, incessant worries running through Saoirse's mind.

The idea that Eva had ventured into the boundary between worlds—to the Wild Wood—lingered, worming its way into her thoughts. She clutched the broken halves of her shutter latch in her hand, the jagged edge cutting into her palm.

A headache built behind her eyes the nearer she came to the clamorous forge. She winced as she stepped under the eave into the open work area where Edred's father, Madoc, shoveled charcoal into the fire while his son labored at the anvil. The oppressive heat pressed against her, as if wishing to hold her back.

Edred noticed her first, stilling his hammer, his muscular forearms slick with sweat. The vibrant orange of the metal he worked leeched away, dulling into gray dinge. He swiped his forearm across his brow, streaking grime. "Sers," he said in greeting, a question in his eyes.

She didn't often come here. For one, life's necessary chores kept her busy, and secondly, she refused to go where she wasn't wanted. She hadn't been *uninvited*, but the sting in her heart since the change between them occurred bade her to keep away. In the past, her feet had taken her mindlessly—naturally—to his door, but new paths had been forged. Paths that led beyond the touch of his gaze.

Purposefully pushing into his space, therefore, stoked the confused ache in her heart. She took a tremulous breath and lifted her chin, schooling away the sting, dampening it into submission. She had good reason to come, after all.

She lifted her hand and unfurled her fist, silently communicating her needs while she gathered herself. Edred's hair, a rich brown, fell in untidy waves over his forehead. The shadow of a beard peppered his jaw. Her gaze traced the exaggerated arch of his lifted eyebrow.

"What did this latch close?"

Sweat gathered under her kirtle and between her breasts. "The shutter near the barn door. Its banging keeps us up at night. How much to fix it?"

He took the pieces from her, his blunt fingers skimming her palm. She surreptitiously wiped her hand on her skirts then waved at his father across the room. Madoc, finished with shoveling fuel, came to greet her.

"What a pleasant surprise."

Edred took after his father, both tall and deep-chested. They also shared the same straight nose and slightly down-turned mouth, though Madoc's peeked out of a full beard, streaked with gray. They differed in their eyes, however, Maddoc's blue but Edred's hazel—expressively large and beautiful.

Next came a continuous stream of questions and comments that warmed her. He asked after her father's health, commented on the calf Papa lost in the spring, his intent to stop by and chat, and inquired about his recent order of cheese. Last, his eyes smiling, he said, "How lovely to see you, dear Saoirse. You've grown into quite the beauty."

She couldn't help her smile. For all of Gwenda Fortwin's disapproval, Madoc's warm affection and welcoming attention lifted her spirits. By the time he wandered back to the anvil and took up where Edred left off, Saoirse had quite forgotten the gale of feelings that had assaulted her upon her arrival.

Edred smiled in an apologetic way as they both watched Madoc return to work. "It's a simple design. I can—"

A shout pulled them both to the street, where Fadam Gaber scurried, her face aflame. "I've found her! Eva! I've—I've found the lassie!"

Merchants in their stalls surrounded her in the road, doors of shops banging shut as owners hastened to hear the news. Eva's mother, Fadam Morvel, ashen faced, stood upon the stoop of their family establishment nearby, her hand clutching her throat. She did not move from her spot, apparently unable or unwilling to draw closer.

Such a din arose—pelted questions mingled with shouts of relief—that Saoirse couldn't make sense of anything the woman said.

She and Edred moved closer, standing at the edge of the crowd.

"The p—poor girl. She's—I'm afraid that she's d—dead."

Alarm clanged through Saoirse, her heart lurching into her throat. Saoirse stood on her toes, trying to get a better view of Fadam Gaber as villagers hurled more questions at her.

Eva's mother fell against the porch post, a wail of such pain tearing from her that Saoirse's throat closed with emotion. Fadam Morvel slid to the ground and several women rushed forward, speaking urgently into the woman's ears.

Murmurs of shock and concern rippled through the crowd.

"Someone must tell her father. He's searching the river again with Hywel and Tuder!"

"I'll go!"

Another shouted for quiet amid the throng—the miller by the sound and force of his voice—shushing the group. "Quiet! Hush now and let her speak!"

Fadam Gaber heaved for air, her bosom surging against her brown homespun. "I found her—found the poor dear at the temple." Her mottled face twisted, distressed. "I went there to pray, you know, as I have been each day, but—but when I got there—" She dissolved into tears, sobbing into her apron. Her rounded shoulders shook as she gasped, visibly trying to compose herself.

The woman's voice dropped an octave, shocked disbelief lacing her tone. "I found her laid atop the altar stone with flowers all around her, like . . ." She shook her head, eyes wide, as if her scrambled thoughts would order themselves. "But it doesn't make any sense! It's like whomever placed her there *cared* for her . . . her hair newly plaited and her dress laid so neatly." Her shocked expression gave way to anger, her eyes sparking. "But she'd been *disfigured*. Three fingers on one hand and the other—the other had been removed altogether . . . replaced with rotting flesh. Someone sewed the stinking things onto her hands with black thread."

Stunned silence fell over the street as shock ebbed away, replaced with revulsion. Then came suspicion. Eyes roved around the mass, varying gazes full of mistrust and accusation.

The notion that Eva's disappearance had come about through a terrible accident fell to pieces. Someone had lured her from her house while her family slept all around. They'd murdered her in cold blood. Worse—somehow stealing a life grew more horrific—whomever had killed her, had monstrously taken parts of her body and—what had Fadam Gaber said?—replaced them with *rotting flesh*. Whose bits? And why?

Murmurs rippled through the mob and then, like wood lice scattering from under an overturned log, they dispersed. Villagers rushed home, ashen faced, some calling for their children along the way. Shop doors closed.

"Where is Rosamund?" asked a sharp voice from just behind them. Saoirse jumped nearly out of her skin.

Madoc stood there, worry written plainly in his eyes. "Have you seen your sister, Edred?"

"She—she's with Mam at home."

Madoc's eyes sparked with purpose as he removed his thick, leather gloves. "Well, I'll just . . . watch the shop, while I go check, would you?"

Saoirse found Edred's worried gaze. All the color had drained from his face making his hazel eyes a startling golden brown, ringed with green. She doubted they'd get any patrons after Fadam Gaber's news. "I should go check on Dafydd," she said, rubbing the sudden chill from her arms.

"Yes, do." He pressed his lips tightly together, his rigid stance telling Saoirse he shared her fright.

She'd nearly gotten to the well before he called out to her. "Sers!"

She slowed and met his eyes over her shoulder.

"I'll bring the latch to you this evening. Lock your shutters tight. Be . . . be careful."

She nodded, unable to speak for the sudden dryness of her mouth.

Chapter Six

Coaxing a Soul

S HE FOUND DAFYDD IN the milking shed, his flopping curls skewered with stray bits of hay as he mucked out stalls. The vise squeezing her heart relaxed at the sight. She sagged onto the milking stool and caught her breath.

He stilled, worry lines bracketing his mouth. "What's wrong? Is Papa unwell?"

She'd run the whole way up to the house, her heart in her throat, and found it difficult to form words.

"No . . . Dafydd—" she didn't know how to tell him or if she even should. She motioned him closer.

Looking into his green eyes, she decided that the truth—or a near version of it—would likely serve him best. Her honesty would frighten him of course, but that just might save his life.

"Eva has been found. Dafydd, she died."

Little boys were strange creatures. An absorbed light entered his eyes. "Did she drown?"

"I'm afraid it's rather more . . . ." She'd wanted to say "serious," but the word didn't fit, did it? Any fatality suited that description. "Worse." Yes, far, far worse.

His eyes narrowed. She saw his mind working behind his eyes.

"It appears that it wasn't an accident but that someone harmed her. On purpose."

His mouth agape, Dafydd's brow furrowed. "What d'you mean?"

She drew in a careful breath. "I mean that someone killed her."

He stood rigid. "Who?"

"I don't know, but until we know more, we shouldn't wander off alone. We should do our chores together, or at least within sight of each other." She gathered him into a hug. With her sitting, Dafydd met her height. He rested his chin on her shoulder.

"Who would kill another person?" he whispered, confusion evident in his tone.

Her mind skittered, unable to form complete thoughts. Her initial worry that Eva's disappearance had something to do with the Wild Wood no longer fit. She'd heard stories of Fair Ones stealing children, but they never *returned* them. Never disfigured their abductees.

"I don't know, Dafydd, but they'll be caught."

The rest of the day, Dafydd lingered near Papa and Saoirse, uncomplaining at the extra time completing chores together tacked onto the day. He could not do his afternoon deliveries of milk and cheese alone, as per his usual, and had to wait for Saoirse to complete all her duties before they could set out. While she hated the nervous fear that had taken hold of him, so too, she found solace. She far preferred him scared but safe—alive—rather than the alternative.

That evening, just as Saoirse and her father finished washing the dishes, a soft knock sounded. Immediately, Dafydd's worried face loomed in the corner of her vision. She shot him a "don't worry" look. She ruffled his hair as she passed him on the way to the door.

A murderer—even a polite one—wouldn't come upon a family all apiece and announce themselves. "It's only Edred," she said, wiping her hands on her apron. "He fixed the shutter latch for me today."

Relief softened the lines of Dafydd's body. "That's good."

Instead of Edred, Madoc stood there, his grave countenance warning Saoirse that something else—some other terrible event—had occurred.

"Rosamund?" she asked, tense.

"Accounted for. Dafydd?"

She sighed, reassured, and stepped aside, opening the door wider. Madoc's gaze passed over Saoirse and fell upon her brother, who stood in the center of the room.

"Good," he said on an exhale. "Good to hear. I've brought you your latch. Edred is unable to come tonight. Emrys's horse threw a shoe and he's got a delivery of wool to make tomorrow."

Traitorously, her heart deflated a little in disappointment.

"Come in, Madoc. Sit," said her father, his crutch thumping on the floor as he moved to his seat by the hearth.

Their guest removed his hat as he entered, the unusual, solemn expression pricking Saoirse's worry. Madoc settled across from her father, his mouth pressed into a severe frown. "I'm afraid I bring some bad news."

She stilled, bracing herself. What now? Another murder?

"The Saer's daughter is missing." He scrunched his brows. "Carys, I think her name is."

Dafydd's hand slipped into her own, his little body pressed tight to her side. .

Madoc lifted a wide-knuckled hand and smoothed his beard, clearing his throat. "After today's unfortunate news, the Saers hurried home, as we all did, to make an accounting. They couldn't find the girl. They've searched all the usual places."

"No one saw her this morning?" her father asked, incredulous.

Madoc sighed. "Oh, aye. Her mother fed her in the early hours of the day, then sent her out, lantern in hand. You know Carys's been tending the bairns of a family just down the lane."

Saoirse's heart squeezed, picturing the girl's swinging light as she bobbed down the road in the gray dawn. When the girl didn't arrive, no doubt an endless list of chores left little time to run a message back to the Saer's, asking after Carys.

"Áine help us," whispered her father.

Saoirse clutched the fabric of her kirtle. *Please, Áine. We need all the help we can get.*

U RSA PEERED INTO THE moldy grimoire, her lamp held
close to the script. The afanc's humid cave beyond the
waterfall acted as the perfect setting, save for how the misty
air curled the pages of the tome. Despite the damp, the cave's
ancient and enduring space acted like a granite womb, cradling
Elenwin until she could be reborn.

How poetic that her daughter's reemergence into the world
would occur here, at the threshold of the summer goddess's
kingdom, where the very foundations of the mountain absorbed
leeching fae magic.

Ursa glanced at the tenebrous rear of the cave, where Áine's
doorway waited, nothing more than a solid rock wall with the
likeness of an arch etched into the surface. She stayed well
enough away, not having any desire to enter. Áine would not
understand Ursa's desire to remake her daughter, nor would
the goddess approve of how she controlled the guardian beast
that rested at the bottom of its pond, gnawing on old bones,
unconcerned with her presence.

"This time the spell will work," she told Elenwin as she mentally cataloged her list of ingredients. "Soon, you'll step from darkness into the light. I've all the required elements."

Elenwin's decaying, patched body reminded her that time ran short. She lit candles around the sacrificial space. Seven candles, black, for death. Seven more, these red, representing life. "Silly of me to think an egg would suffice as a consecrated sacrifice. It should be my blood given, don't you think?"

She ticked off the required elements to Elenwin, ensuring she hadn't forgotten anything: "The corpse, the living soul to be extracted, a clay vessel to hold the soul, a silver dagger, and a lock of hair from the human sacrifice." The book indicated that the spell be cast under a new moon for heightened magical energy, but Áine's doorway served far better. "Let's begin."

This child, a girl of around nine years, sat against the cold stone wall opposite Elenwin, surveying the scene with benign disinterest. She blinked owlishly, staring at nothing. If Ursa slipped from her mind, the girl's reaction to her surroundings would certainly change.

You're tired. Lie down.

Immediately the girl obeyed, yawning wide as she settled on the comfortable bed of ferns and mallow grass Ursa had prepared. She cut a vibrant lock of hair from the child, the tones of ripened wheat shimmering in the candlelight. A beautiful sacrifice, indeed.

Next, she took care to braid the hair into Elenwin's black, lusterless strands, sniffing at the difference. "You'll be back to your old self in no time at all, Sweeting."

Unplugging a clay jar, she set it between their prone forms, lying side by side.

Sleep deeply, child. Rest.

Once the living girl's breaths evened out, her body softening into an utterly relaxed position, Ursa began. She laid a silver dagger atop the child's rising and falling breast and stood between the bodies, the vessel at her feet. Closing her eyes, she inhaled deeply and began the binding of flesh and soul.

> "Through the weave of fate, the line of breath, I bind thee, child of life, to the gates of death. One heart silent, one heart bound, I tie your spirits, twined and wound. By this braid of hair, blood of kin, Your souls are shackled; now let the rite begin."

The candles flickered, burning brighter. Shadows swayed against the gray wall, silent witnesses of the ritual. Ursa plucked the silver dagger from the living child's body with shaking hands and recited the incantation for extracting the living soul:

> "O soul of the living, bound by flesh, I call thee forth to leave your mesh. No longer shall you breathe or sigh, To death's cold grasp, I say, comply. By this blade, your tether I sever, May your heart beat again, never."

Ursa pierced the air just above the child's chest, severing the soul from its body. Symbolic in nature, the girl did not flinch. A faint silvery aura clung to the tip of her dagger, a living tendril running from breast to blade. She drew up the knife, coaxing the child's soul out of its home, turning the weapon in her fingers as if she wound yarn around a spindle.

The last thread of soul resisted as if wishing to linger, holding itself back. At last, as Ursa tugged it free, the child gasped and then lay utterly still and lifeless. Curious indeed how a perfect body became wholly useless without the magic spark of a spirit, the very essence of life.

Fairly simple to remove, yes, but next came the difficult part: insertion and acceptance of the spirit into the dead vessel.

Ursa carefully guided the drooping, wispy mass into the clay pot at her feet, her breathing ragged. The dagger slipped in her clammy hand, and she clutched it more tightly. This was the point where her spell had failed last time. Such a pity. Such a waste.

She brought the blade over Elenwin's vacant body. An impossible wind stirred the cave, bringing a sound of faraway rushing of long-dead leaves. So too, came a subtle whispering of many voices, heard but not understood. The hair along Ursa's arms rose as magic surged into the space, spurring her on. She raised her voice to be heard over the eerie gale.

"By the same hand, let life be reversed, From the dead, the living soul is nursed. To this silent heart, I give new breath, Arise from the tomb, escape

death's depth! By this blade, I bind you anew,
Through flesh reborn, your life will continue."

She barely felt the sting as she drew the blade over her left palm. Her blood, no more than a black line in the dim, pooled in her palm, welling over the shadowed lines of her hand.

Carefully, she laid the blood-smeared blade across Elenwin's chest and picked up the clay jar holding the soul. Breath held, Ursa tipped a portion of her life's blood into the container, amazed at the change from her previous attempt. The distant whispers grew in volume until the whirlwind surrounded Ursa in an unseen draft, wild and intoxicating. She wanted to laugh in triumph.

Elenwin would live! Her hands shook, and she tamped down her exultation. To solidify the exchange and to ensure the new life spark remained bound to Elenwin, allowing her daughter's spirit to reenter her body, one last incantation must be performed.

Ursa fisted her pierced hand over Elenwin's chest, her blood dripping in a soundless beat onto her stained dress.

"Two souls have danced, now one must sleep, The other, through death's gate, shall leap. In flesh exchanged, life finds its way, By blood and blade, this curse shall stay."

A mighty gust battered Ursa, tossing her clothes and hair. Candles sputtered out. Murky light from beyond the falls lit the space just enough that the two children's motionless bodies appeared no more than shadows upon the dingy floor.

Lifting the clay vessel high over her head, Ursa shouted the last portion of the rite:

> "The living now dead, the dead now alive, By my will, this soul shall survive. Return to me, my child of the grave, By my magic, I thee save."

Panting, she tipped the life force from its container onto her daughter, where it curled and fanned out like smoke from a clogged flue. Abruptly, the wind failed; the whispers ceased. Ursa hungrily watched as the soul lingered over Elenwin, then rose, dissipating into the ether as if it had never been.

She waited, her ears straining in the unnatural silence. She couldn't even hear the roar of the falls over the sound of her own heartbeat. Elenwin did not stir. Her face remained drained of color, mottled with decay.

"Rise, dearest. At least o–open your e–eyes."

Elenwin did not obey.

Tears blurred Ursa's vision. She sank to her knees, pulling at her hair. Her keening wail bounced off the walls, a mocking echo. "I felt the magic!" she screeched. "I don't understand. How—where did I go wrong?" Ursa sobbed into her hands, salt from her tears stinging her injury.

Her desperate hope had burned to cinders yet panic still scorched her as time drifted away like so much smoke in a breeze. Too many days had gone by. Elenwin's body could not wait much longer. Had she misinterpreted Agatha's spell? She poured over the text again, clutching the book to her, her eyes roving over her mentor's scribbled handwriting. No, she'd done it all, just as prescribed!

She set the book aside and stood, pacing the uneven ground, uncaring when her foot sent a creel of eggs from the temple toppling. The spell should have worked! It *must* work.

"I cannot give up. *I will not.*" She staggered back to Elenwin's side, stepping over the lifeless sacrifice, and relit the candles surrounding the space. She seized the grimoire once more, her finger skimming the words.

She reread the spell, words jumping out at her as if the divine intervened on her behalf, wishing to point her in the right direction. The spell mentioned a heart three times. *Three.* A holy number.

"Yes, that must be it," she said on an exhale. Relief flooded her. She stroked her daughter's hair, streaking it with blood. "A new heart, dearest, then the spell will work."

Chapter Seven

Scrying Pool

THE WHOLE VILLAGE TURNED out for Carys's burial. The sobs of her mother wrenched Saoirse's heart. Saoirse clutched Dafydd against her side as the girl's family laid stones over the fresh grave.

Her village, like any other, understood loss. Death lived amongst them, a silent member of their community, but *these* deaths brought far more than sorrow.

Funeral-goers shot wary glances at their neighbors. Did she really know the thatcher and the fletcher as well as she supposed? What about the milliner, who held his hat so steadily at his waist? Could the murderer be here, and if so, did they tremble, or did they hold steady in the wake of their destruction? Despite carefully assessing each villager, she couldn't imagine any one of them harming Eva or Carys.

The child's chest had been abominably cut open, her heart replaced with a gruesome lump of decayed flesh that the village healer identified as a human heart. Saoirse clenched her eyes shut and squeezed her father's hand as she imagined what poor little Carys had gone through.

The remains had been well tended to: her body washed, her hair combed and braided, her dress arranged neatly about her shins, and last, a bouquet of chamomile had been placed in her folded hands. Just like Eva.

Whoever had arranged the girls had even taken the time to tuck a merry blossom behind their ears. Why butcher two children only to carefully arrange them for burial?

Thomas coughed into a closed fist, pulling her gaze across the grave. She could be wrong, of course. Her inability to place the blame on her neighbors didn't make them faultless. A baker would not know how to carve organs from a cavity, nor stitch fingers upon a lifeless hand. *Would he?*

What of the butcher or the tailor? Her gaze slid to the people nearest her, assessing their tear-streaked faces and their kerchiefs clenched in white-knuckled fists. Who could perform such abhorrent atrocities?

Once all the stones lay heavy and grim atop the grave, people shuffled away, conciliatory mumbles falling from leaden lips. Saoirse offered her own apology to Carys's despondent parents as they passed, no doubt as comforting as a rocky pillow. Carys's mother, unable to stand, fell against her quaking husband, her howl of pain lifting the fine hairs along Saoirse's neck.

Edred stepped beside Saoirse and Papa, his ashen face drawn as he gazed at Carys's parents. "I'm organizing a town watch. We'll take turns walking the lanes and keeping an eye on things."

Papa patted Edred's arm. "Aye, good idea. I want to be involved."

Edred nodded. "I thought you might." His gaze fell to Saoirse and lingered, his mind working behind his eyes. "You're close to the temple trail, perhaps with vigilance, our sharp eyes will catch something."

Papa touched the brim of his hat in farewell. "I'll watch the road." And with that, Edred moved away, speaking quietly to the grieving parents.

The sun beat down on her shoulders; sweat beaded upon her skin as all three of them plodded home, birds calling merrily from the trees, and insects buzzing unconcernedly. Papa had insisted on coming along to the funeral, of course, but his sluggish pace forced them to linger in the heat.

"It's only been girls so far," her father said softly, breaking their silence.

She clutched Dafydd's hand. Guilt swirled in her gut as her father voiced her own thoughts. Shamefully, she'd never been more grateful to have a little brother instead of a sister. Perhaps his sex alone would keep him safe. "Regardless, we cannot assume Dafydd isn't in danger."

She tugged on her brother's hand, forcing his attention.

"Remember what we decided?" Papa asked. "Don't go alone with anyone, Dafydd, no matter how well you know them. Until we find out who's doing this, we must assume the worst of everyone we know and love."

Dafydd nodded, his face gone white to the lips. A surge of protectiveness coursed through Saoirse. She'd do anything to keep such distress from him–to keep him safe.

"Even Wilim?" Dafydd asked.

"I don't think Wilim is harming children, but until we know more, there'll be no running off to play. Do you understand?" Her father's gaze swept to her next. "At the meeting this morning, did they say if anyone else had been taken?"

"No," she answered. "Thankfully, no one else has gone missing." *Yet.*

"Perhaps it's finished, then," Dafydd suggested, visibly brightening.

Saoirse didn't have the heart to suggest otherwise.

Soon after the discovery of Carys's body on the altar stone, everyone gathered in the town square. Tokens and prayer offerings that had covered the shrine had been taken—presumably by the murderer—lending credence to Saoirse's belief that the killer could not live amongst them, for how could this person carry off flasks of ale, a fold of cloth, loaves of bread, pitchers of cream, and countless other items without anyone noticing?

Saoirse placed a hand on his forearm as Dafydd ambled to the edge of the road and inspected a particularly whippy stick. "I can watch our road, Papa, if you'd rather lie down. You've been on your leg a lot today."

"Kind of you, Saoirse, but I'd rather you stay close to Dafydd tonight. Try and distract him." They set into motion once more, the *clunk-clunk* of his crutch dampened by the packed earth.

"There's something I don't understand," her father whispered, glancing at Dafydd, who walked a short distance ahead, savagely beheading grass tassels with his new-found weapon. "Why return the bodies? Do they place them upon the altar as some sort of . . . some poor excuse of an apology?"

Good questions. And just as puzzling, why replace healthy body parts with rot? And to whom did the decomposing flesh belong?

Her father continued, apparently not expecting a response: "The murderer must be someone the children trusted. How else could they lure them away?"

"The village has grown quite a lot in the last five years," she supplied. "Perhaps we don't know everyone as well as we supposed."

"True," he conceded, his gaze lingering on Dafydd. "I'm glad a watch is in place, in any case. I can see down the lane a good ways, especially on starry nights." He glanced at the sunny sky, unobstructed by clouds.

"I'll set your chair at the end of the garden after dinner." She hesitated as she formulated words. "What did . . . Papa, do you mind me asking what you found most helpful after Mother and Alys's deaths?" She rushed on at his frown. "I want to *do* something. *To help*. Offering an apology is not enough. What use are words after losing a child?"

Sweat glinted off Papa's forehead. Eyes wary, his mouth pressed into a tight line. They rarely spoke of his wives, of her and Dafydd's mothers. She'd peppered him with endless questions when young, of course, all of which he'd given short answers to.

His unwillingness to speak of her mother had injured Saoirse's young heart, but then Alys had come and enveloped her with so much love that the splinter in her heart had healed.

After a stretched silence, he said, "You're quite right. They don't have room for your words, no matter how well-meant."

"But there must be something I can do," she pressed.

The crunch of their feet on gravel as they neared home forced him to speak louder. "When my Tilly died, my grief was different."

Saoirse's heart lurched at the mention of her mother.

"Losing Tilly nearly broke me. I barely had enough sense to care for you, let alone myself. Neighbors helped a lot with that, especially Madoc."

Her brows raised. *Madoc?*

"He'd show up, pick up a pitchfork, and help me feed the cows, deliver milk, whatever I needed. All without a word."

Saoirse had no memory of this, being an infant at the time, but the story endeared her to Edred's father all the more. "Why didn't he say anything to you?"

He pursed his lips, considering. "I suppose . . . well, as you said, words are useless. They come with an expectation of acknowledgment or a response. With Madoc, I didn't have to be solicitous or even polite. He simply arrived and lent his hands. Mayhap you can do that for these families."

Yes, perhaps she could.

Dafydd trotted up to them, his fist outstretched. "Look," he said, breathless, and unfurled his fingers. A crimson leaf hopper sat upon his palm, antenna twitching before it chanced its escape and leaped away in a brilliant array of colors. His face fell, and he surged after it.

"Let it be," said Papa. "How would you like to be snatched from your home?" then immediately cringed at his words in light of recent events.

"I didn't mean any harm," Dafydd lamented.

"Of course you didn't," Papa offered, "but let's leave living things in peace, aye?"

"Come," said Saoirse. "We've got chores anyway.

URSA CLUTCHED A POSY of pungent mugwort in her fist as she settled upon a rock at the edge of the afanc's pool, placing the lit candle by her side. The sun shone high in the sky, dazzling the surface of the water. The languorous ripples borne from the falls kissed the muted reds, gray-blues, and greens of the smooth stones that bordered the bank at her feet.

Deep below the water's surface, the afanc slept under her control. She traced the shadowy line of its sleek body, spiky mane splayed flat against its shoulders.

Their mental connection, a glittering tendril of gossamer, pulsed in time with the creature's heartbeat, slow and languid. The beast would surface soon, as it often did, to take air and feed upon the creatures in the surrounding forest. She sensed its hunger.

As always, time ran short.

She could not stop the decay of Elenwin's body, no matter how diligently she recast preservation spells upon her. Equally alarming, each day that Ursa imposed her will upon the powerful fae beast guarding Áine's door, the greater the draw upon her magic.

Weariness tugged at her eyes and limbs. Her bones seemed to sag within her body so that each movement required that much more effort. She had to ensure her next sacrifice would be her last, for neither she, nor Elenwin, could withstand much more of their taxing circumstances.

Without a coven, she had no sisters to commune with, no one to suggest why the necromantic spell had failed. Twice.

Yes, she'd made changes: her blood instead of a fetal duck's, a new heart to beat true. But how could she be sure those changes would suffice?

She'd taken it as a sign from the gods when she'd stumbled upon the bitter, spicy herb for communing with the dead on her way to deposit the second child in the temple. Mugwort would enable her to speak to Agatha, her long-dead mentor.

Perhaps if she connected with the witch's spirit, she could learn, with absolute assurance, how to successfully complete the necromancy spell. She yearned for Agatha's wisdom, for a compassionate ear. A mother's understanding. Oh, how she'd suffered, alone and desperate!

Ursa gazed at her reflection, distorted by ripples but clear enough for communion with the dead. She lifted the mugwort and deeply inhaled its scent, reminiscent of damp soil. She tore a leaf from a sprig and set it upon her tongue. After years of practicing her arts, she no longer minded the bitter, camphoric flavor that snaked up the back of her throat, knowing the outcome outweighed any distaste.

Ursa lifted the candle and speared the mugwort through the small pyre, holding it there until the plant withered, giving up its magical properties. Returning the candle to its seat upon the rock, Ursa next held the smoking mugwort before her and fanned its astringent fumes toward her nose, inhaling deeply. Already her mind lightened, her skin tingling with anticipation.

"By this flame, I seek connection. Bring forth wisdom with clear intention."

Closing her eyes, she stilled and conjured an image of Agatha in her mind's eye. Her mouth curved upward as her friend and teacher slowly evolved into being: tall and lanky, with hair as black as a raven's wing. She pictured her flinty eyes that constantly assessed, that peered beneath the surface of word and deed to the heart of a man. Ursa imagined the witch standing before her, flowing robes choked with snake and duck eggs and sachets of herbs.

Her smile grew, her eyes stinging with suppressed tears. She missed her friend fiercely.

"Spirits of those who've gone before,

Cross now gently through this door.

Agatha, I call you,

If willing, share your wisdom true."

Ursa opened her eyes and sat upon the wet shore, her skirts thirstily pulling in moisture. She peered into the water. The world fell away; the thunder of the falls was nothing more than a gentle hum.

"Come, share your message, your voice I hear. Speak if you will, I welcome you near."

She sensed Agatha's entrance into the earthly realm by the change in the air. It stilled and grew heavy as if a shawl had been draped across her shoulders. Agatha's voice whispered across her mind even as her mentor's image transposed over her own in the water.

Agatha had heard her plea and come. Quiet elation raced along Ursa's limbs, settling in her middle, warm and comforting. Such communion required no words from the departed. Supernatural communication came through mental images, feelings, and a sense of knowing that pervaded all else.

Sister, Agatha seemed to say, and with the greeting came an outpouring of tenderness that brought fresh longing.

"Dear Sister," Ursa said, hungrily searching Agatha's image in the water. "Many travails have befallen me. Elenwin is dead, and your spell to retrieve her spirit has failed. I glean power from a goddess's doorstep. I use my own life's blood in the ritual. My chosen sacrifices are pure and undefiled. What more need I do?"

Twin reflections in the water rippled and swayed like leaves upon a raging river. Ursa stilled her breathing and closed her eyes lest she lose their connection in her own urgency.

She waited. She must be patient and open her mind to receive Agatha's message, unmottled by her earthly fears.

Peace settled over her heart as protective sigils played across her mind, emblems invoking defense and confinement. What could this prompting mean? An impression brushed across her subconscious mind then: *A circle of salt, enhanced with rosemary or rue.*

But what protection could she possibly need?

Could it be that the circle wasn't meant for her, but for the spirits—Elenwin's and the sacrificial child's? Ursa sat straight, her thoughts tumbling. What if, without a protective circle, the spirits of the village children had fled? Surrounding the spell with salt, rosemary, and rue would ensure the life force could not leave. It would be forced to linger, where she could then persuade it to do her bidding.

Gratitude filled her, lending new life to her weary bones. "Thank you, dear Sister." Ursa blew out the candle. "I honor your presence."

Now she must only search out these ingredients and select a new sacrifice.

"Tonight, Elenwin, you will live again."

CHAPTER EIGHT

THE NIGHT WATCH

THE SUN RETREATED, PEERING around the steep angles of the mountains that encircled their village, casting long shadows upon the unobstructed view of the lane. The sky's brilliant array of pinks and oranges, coupled with the homey, lazy hum of Saoirse's bees, contended with the distress currently gnawing through her.

A small carving knife and a block of wood in hand, Saoirse moved through the front garden, crowded with poppies, foxglove, and lavender, to where her father sat just outside the gate, at the road's edge.

"I'll finish the mending if you carve me a new straining ladle for my candle making."

A pair of Dafydd's breeches clutched in one hand and a threaded needle in the other, Papa looked her over skeptically. "What's happened to you? My daughter, wishing to patch holes?"

Saoirse tried to laugh, but her grin slid from her face. "A knife is better than a needle in this case, wouldn't you agree?" She canted her head downhill toward the village, a silent reminder of his task. "If something were to happen, I'd rather you have a better weapon than yon wee barb."

His eyes hardened, all vestiges of teasing forgotten. "I'm prepared." He dropped the items in his lap and pulled their one, well-stropped blade from his boot. "I merely wanted to take advantage of what's left of the light."

Saoirse planted a kiss atop his head, her arm wrapped around his shoulders. "Be careful, Papa. Call out if you need me."

He gripped her wrist as she moved to pull away. "Don't send Dafydd to the loft, aye? Keep him close the whole night."

"I will," she promised.

Inside, Dafydd sat near the hearth, winding spun wool around a dowel. The last of the daylight shone through the open shutters, limning Dafydd's curls a burnished gold. She stared at his silhouette. His tongue poked out between his teeth as he set to unknotting a bramble in the yarn.

"It's time to lock up," she said into the quiet of the room.

Dafydd carelessly shoved the spindle and pile of yarn off his lap and into the basket at his feet, no doubt further snarling the mass.

Saoirse groaned inwardly. "You know you'll have to untangle that tomorrow."

He frowned at the basket as if the strings were to blame and not his carelessness before stalking over to the nearest window.

He pulled the shutters closed and clasped the latch. "I'll secure the inside if you see to the barn."

"Already done," she said. "The animals are all tucked in." She moved to the hearth and held a rush to the embers, igniting it into a beckoning flame. She'd light more candles than usual tonight. Dafydd wasn't the only one nervous as a rabbit in the open.

Saoirse helped him to wash, tilting the water pitcher over his cupped hands. "Did you mean to lock the door with Papa outside?" Dafydd scrubbed his cheeks and the back of his neck vigorously. "How long will he sit out there?"

She offered him a towel. "Let's stay in my room tonight, hmm?"

He stilled, the rough pass of the cloth along his neck slowing. "Why is Papa sitting in the garden, Saoirse?"

She had no wish to lie, but what good would come from scaring him further? "He's only keeping a keen eye out with goings on of late."

His brow furrowed. "Aren't you worried for him?"

Of course she worried, but only children had gone missing, not adults. Nor would their father watch alone. Other men would walk the lanes, ensuring their safety. Why, then, did a warning pulse through her with each heartbeat?

"Papa is quite capable," she insisted. "Even with a broken leg. Don't worry for him."

She gestured toward the loft. "Time to change for bed."

In the summer months, they usually slept with the shutters thrown wide, allowing the breeze and starlight to bathe

the house. With the windows covered, a sense of entombment threatened, which she chased away by setting to light another half-dozen tapers. The rational part of her brain rebuked such waste, but the jittery, anxious portion firmly scolded the other into submission. *Needful, not wasteful.*

As she set to the task, Dafydd announced his presence by jumping the last few feet off the ladder to the floor with a loud *thunk*. She clutched the candlestick she held tightly, her other hand held to her heart to still its racing.

"I'm ready," he announced, apparently immune to her and Papa's worries. So much for needing to distract him.

She picked up a spare candle and handed it to Dafydd. "Take this to my room, if you please. I'm just going to check the windows and the door again."

Once satisfied everything was latched good and tight, she washed her face and neck and hung her overskirt and bodice on the peg inside her bedroom. She climbed under the covers, leaving a handful of candles burning in the other room for when she needed to let Papa in the house.

"What shall it be tonight?" she asked. She had no intention of sleeping—probably couldn't, even if she tried—and planned to tell Dafydd stories until he slept.

He fluffed his pillow and settled on his side, his eyes bright with reflected candlelight. "Tell me a faerie story about the puka!"

Saoirse frowned. "Dafydd, you've heard those stories a dozen times. Besides, wouldn't you rather hear something more . . . pleasant?"

"It is pleasant! Please?"

In her current state, she had no desire to speak of the shape-shifting faerie known for playing tricks on unwary travelers.

"How about a tale of the Tylwyth Teg and the changeling?"

At his approval, she settled her back against the wall. "Long ago, in a small village—"

"Like this one!"

"—in a small village much like our own, there lived a poor but hardworking farmer named Cadfan."

"Oh, can't you make his name Dafydd?"

She sighed heavily, casting him a wry look. "I'll never finish this tale if you don't stop interrupting me. Now, where was I?"

"Dafydd's farm sat on the edge of a wild and mysterious forest," he said. "A place people rarely ventured, especially after dark!" He practically vibrated with excitement. "He and his wife had a wee babe called . . . Wilim." He giggled and then added, "They'd always heard the tales of the Fair Folk who lived in the hills, but they never spoke of them. Oh, and they kept an iron horseshoe above their door!"

Saoirse couldn't help her smile. "That's right. Let's see . . . one autumn evening, Dafydd's wife put the baby to bed while he tended to the flocks in the fields. She sang a lullaby, not knowing how her words carried through the chilly air nor how the shadows from the forest crept closer to their home."

Dafydd stilled as she continued the story. "As the night deepened, she began to hear strange sounds—almost like footsteps outside—but when she peered out the window, she could only see a mist rolling over the moorland."

"What was in the mist?" Dafydd asked with solemnity, though he knew the story well.

She carried on, ignoring his interruption: "Soon, a chill seeped into the room, and the fire flickered as if a draft had slipped in. The baby began to cry in his cradle, wailing and writhing in his swaddling. The mother rushed to comfort him, but her heart ran cold when she saw how wee Wilim's features had sharpened. When the babe met her gaze, his warm brown eyes glittered silver and his wail cut off with a smile too wide for his tiny face. The laugh that escaped him mocked like a distant echo.

"The mother knew just what to do. She'd heard the whispered warnings of the Tylwyth Teg, how they stole human babies and replaced them with fairies to bring mischief and woe to those who kept them. She rushed to retrieve the iron over their door—as all faeries fear its touch—and raced back into the room. 'If you're my true son,' she said, 'then you will have no need to fear this metal. If you are not Wilim, I will know.'"

Dafydd pulled the quilt up to chin. "How did she get Wilim back?"

"Well, she'd heard from the village elders that a changeling could be forced to reveal its true nature through cunning or fright, so she pressed the horseshoe against the babe's foot. At once, the creature shrieked, its cry like a winter wind tearing through the cottage. Its face twisted with rage and, for a brief moment, its true form flashed before her—a wiry, misshapen creature with long, pointed ears and eyes that burned like hot coals.

"The changeling leaped from the cradle and hissed in a voice like rustling leaves. 'You think you can outwit me? Your son is ours now, and you'll never see him again!'"

Her brother sat up in bed, eyes wide. "But the faerie didn't account for Dafydd, who heard his son's cries upon the moor."

"Quite true," Saoirse answered. "Dafydd recognized the chilled fog as a mark of the Tylwyth Teg, and when he heard wee Wilim cry out from the ether, he pulled his iron blade and chanted in a voice strong and clear,

'By iron and fire, by earth and by sea,

I call upon powers to set my child free!

Be gone, false spirit, return what you stole.

The hills take back your wandering soul!'"

Dafydd rose to his knees and slashed his fist through the air as if he held the iron blade. "And then he clove the mist with his knife as the changeling's scream rocked through the valley." Dafydd struck the air again. "The mist retreated into the mountains, and when he ran home, he found his wife and a restored Wilim. The end."

Saoirse laughed. "Yes, that's right. The faerie was no match for a mother and father's love and courage. Between them, they saved wee Wilim. The Tylwyth Teg knew better than to challenge them again."

"Another," demanded Dafydd. He flopped back down onto his pillow and stifled a yawn. Saoirse couldn't hold back her own.

"All right, but just let me peek outside and check on Papa."

She draped a blanket around her shoulders as she exited the room, unlatching the door to stick her head outside. The moon shone brightly upon Papa's dark head, sparking his hair silver. After the changeling story she'd just told, she couldn't help but shiver. "All right, Papa? Do you need anything?"

He lifted the block of wood in answer. "I've plenty to keep up with. Lock the door behind you, aye?"

When she returned, Dafydd lay asleep, his breathing even, his mouth slightly agape. She blew out the candles near the bed for safety, kissed his head, and moved to the chair by the hearth. Even if she'd wanted to sleep, she wouldn't have been able to. With Papa outside and her nerves on edge, she'd only toss and turn. She might as well get some work done.

She set the knitting basket atop her lap and commenced the tedious task of untangling the heap within.

Saoirse awoke with a jerk. The bundle of yarn she'd so diligently picked apart now lay at her feet, all her effort of neatness destroyed. She winced at the painful crick in her neck and rubbed at her bleary eyes. How long had she been out?

She stood and reached to take the candlestick off the little table near the chair and stopped short.

Her heart lurched. Only a stubby wodge of wax with a tiny flame remained in the pricket. She hadn't merely nodded off. She'd slept for *hours*. A quick assessment of the room told her every candle had burned very low indeed. She snatched what was left in the pricket and moved to the door. Had Papa's knock awoken her?

But when she moved to the door, the bolt had been thrown. A spike of fear lanced through her. She'd locked the door—hadn't she? Had she somehow missed that one crucial step last night? Outside, Papa still sat in the chair at the gate, head bowed, as if his chin rested on his chest. "What sorry protectors we make," she muttered.

She grimaced at the brightening horizon. How long before he'd surrendered to sleep? She'd rouse him just as soon as she

checked on Dafydd. She retreated inside the cottage. The gut-
tering candle afforded little light, but her feet carried her to her
room without issue.

"Good morning, Little Prince," she said, lifting the flame
higher. The weak halo broadened to encompass the lumpy quilts
devoid of Dafydd. "Dafydd!" she cried. She fisted the quilt, re-
moving all possibility that she'd somehow missed his sleeping
form. She raced to the shutters and threw them wide, letting in
the pale dawn.

She screamed for him as she bolted for the front door. "Papa!
Wake up! I can't find Dafydd!"

Her father started with a snort, half-turning in his seat as he
fumbled for his crutch. "What's that?"

She didn't wait for him, but turned back into the house, again
calling for Dafydd. Maybe he'd gone on his own to the loft to
change and . . . and fell asleep or bumped his head so he couldn't
respond. Panic surged through her. She took the rungs of the
ladder too quickly and missed a step, bruising her cheek on the
wood as she crushed herself against it to keep from falling.

In the dark triangle of space, the dim outline of his pallet
remained neatly made. His work clothes sagged from where they
hung along the back wall. Her heart sank. Regardless of the
unlikely possibility he'd left to do his chores without rousing her,
still, she held out hope.

Her brain latched onto the only other explanation. Perhaps
he'd gone to the privy. *Yes, that's it.*

She dashed down the ladder and squeezed past her father, who'd just limped to the door. "I'm checking the privy," she called as she rushed out.

Sharp bits of straw, pebbles, and twigs gored her bare feet as she barreled around the side of the house to the necessary. "Dafydd! Are you in there?" She didn't wait for a response and yanked the door open. *Empty.*

She squeezed her eyes shut against the wave of panic that threatened. *Think, Saoirse!*

Perhaps he wasn't long gone. Yes, maybe someone patrolling the village had seen him, even stopped the murderer from— She shook the suspicion from her mind and ran back to the house. She would find him. There had to be a simple explanation.

Papa still stood in the entryway, his face ashen, staring at the empty space that had once held Dafydd's shoes.

Her hands shook as badly as her voice. "Papa. *Oh, Papa.*" Her knees wobbled and she had to lean against the door to stay upright. "I fell asleep," she wailed. She pressed her fist to her mouth in an attempt to keep her anguish contained.

Swallowing her sobs in great, gasping gulps, she wiped her eyes and forced herself upright. "I—I'm going to get help." She nodded vigorously, her hands flexing. "Perhaps someone else has seen him." She whirled away from the jamb and shoved her feet into her boots, not bothering to dress further, not caring if anyone saw her in her chemise. "You stay here, Papa, in case he comes back."

"I'll check the barn."

Her breath burned her throat as she tore down the lane. As the well came into view, she slowed. A dark shadow smeared the cobblestones—a distinctly *person-shaped* shadow. She pushed her tired legs harder and fell to her knees at Thom's side. Gripping his shoulder, she yanked him onto his back. He blinked at her in a confused fashion.

"Saoirse?" he slurred. "What're you doing? Why am I on the ground?" He scooted to a sitting position and groped around for his hat. "What's happened?"

Her chin quivered. "Thom—" His name fell from her lips with a sob. "Did—did you fall asleep, too?"

He scratched the back of his neck, his mind working behind his eyes. When they refocused on her, he said, "I suppose I did. I'd just left the orchard trail and made it here when I . . . well, I can't rightly say what happened. One minute I was walking and the next . . . here you are."

"He's gone, Thom. Ring the bell. Wake the village. Dafydd is *gone*."

CHAPTER NINE

A FAVOR

A JAGGED PIECE OF glass had invaded her heart, sharp and cutting. It stirred with the smallest memory of Dafydd's disappearance. Each time she glanced at Dafydd's missing shoes near the door or his hat dangling from the peg on the wall, the keen-edged shard shifted, slicing her anew.

Dafydd had disappeared despite their locked doors and shutters. He'd left, regardless of his fear of the dark and his new-found mistrust of people. The door's bolt had been thrown and he'd—apparently—walked out into the night while the rest of the house slept.

Why? How?

He couldn't stand to be alone after sunset, refused to sleep alone. What must he feel now, without her open arms and a shared quilt?

Her hands trembled as she arranged the kindling for a fire. Supper must be made. Dafydd would be hungry when they brought him home.

Papa *thunked* into the house, his face white to the lips. He'd seemed to age ten years in just the space of six hours. She'd seen her father face loss before—quiet, stoic, like a stone wall braced against the wind, taking every blow the storm threw but never crumbling. But now, the deflated set of his shoulders alarmed her.

She stood abruptly from the table; her chair shunted backward with a rude scrape. "What news?"

Papa pulled off his hat, his whiskered throat bobbing. "Nothing as yet." He placed his hat upon the peg by the door and moved painfully to the chair near the hearth. He sat with a beleaguered sigh and rasped his hand over his red-rimmed eyes. "The whole of the town has come back from their searches but, as with the others . . . ."

Saoirse paced in the small space of the common room as her father stared at the wall, unblinking. Her eyes burned and she pressed the heels of her hands to them, forcing emotion away. Sitting idle chafed. She'd cared for all their animals while Papa had helped manage the search in the village.

She'd searched too, of course, but had come home only an hour ago to start supper. But carting water for boiling the barley and scrubbing the neeps hadn't assuaged the desperate panic stirring in her belly.

"He lives still." Her whispered words fell like a stone between them, a brash clatter in the pressing silence. Her father didn't even flinch. "He's alive," she insisted, turning to face him, fisting her hands at her sides.

Papa's eyes told her another story. His hope, it seemed, dangled by a thread.

"*No*, Papa. I refuse to accept that he's dead. I won't give up."

His gaze sharpened on her at last, and a part of her rejoiced at the anger written in his eyes. "You think I want him slain?" he demanded, his voice hoarse. "Dead or alive, I cannot search for him as I wish, not that it would do any good. No other child has been found alive!" He hurled his crutch across the room in a sudden riot of emotion.

Miraculously, it did not break. Her father, on the other hand, fell to pieces. He bent double and sobbed into his knees, his rounded back shuddering. A briar of unintelligible words tangled in his hands.

She found herself crouched by his side, clutching him to her. "I will go, Papa. I will go out again and look."

His anguished gaze lifted, his breathing hitched. "Every possible hiding place has been searched. Nothing has been found—for any of the stolen children. What option is left to us?"

His words smacked of surrender. She stared at him, her jaw slack. She snapped it closed. Perhaps after helplessly watching two wives weaken and pass, her father had no more resistance left in him. She, for herself, brimmed with defiance. Dafydd *would not* die. Not if she could help it.

"Whoever has taken him . . . whatever hole this *monster* has dragged him into, I will find it and pull him out."

In a whirl of skirts, she marched to her room and threw open the chest at the end of her bed. She removed her knapsack and stuffed it with whatever potentially useful item her fingers touched: a length of gauze, flint, an extra pair of clothes. Next, she gathered a lantern and a handful of candles, her fingers unsteady.

She moved to the kitchen and added food—bread, cheese, apples, a bunch of carrots—and a small knife. She'd sharpened it just yesterday. A glint of mid-morning light traced the edge before she tucked it in her belt.

At last, she turned to her father, whose swollen eyes regarded her. In her distraction, she hadn't noticed him rise. He stood awkwardly on his good leg, his white-knuckled grip on the back of the chair steadying him. "Where can you possibly go that hasn't already been scoured?"

Her heart pounded in her breast. "The only place left."

Her father drew in a sharp breath, his face ashen. "You can't mean to . . . Saoirse, it's dangerous!"

"If you had the ability, you'd go in my stead. We both know it."

His acceptance came slowly: in the softening of his eyes, in the slant of his shoulders. "You'll need cold iron. It would be your only hope against the fae."

His words offered her small comfort. He didn't want her to go, but he would not forbid her, either. "Yes, Papa."

His eyes watered. "Oh, Saoirse, I wish I could go in your stead. Here, take this instead of that wee kitchen knife." He bent to retrieve the weapon from his boot, but she hastened to him and stilled his hand.

"You might need it here. I'll . . . I'll stop by the blacksmith shop before I go." She needed to ask a favor of Edred, anyway.

They stared at each other for a long second, teetering on goodbye.

"I'll—I'll be back soon." She kissed his cheek, pressing her nails into the palm of her hand to keep her tears from manifesting. She set her insubstantial weapon on the table. She'd get something more fitting for her journey from the forge. Her boots thundered across the planks in the silence and her hand fumbled with the latch.

"Courage, Saoirse," Papa said, his voice warring between pride and grief.

"I love you," she said.

The soft thud of the door as she left rang of finality. Would she ever make it back home? Then again, without Dafydd, home would never be the same.

The sunny walk into the village proper stung. How dare the sun shine when her world had crumbled? Pitying glances from the few neighbors still about incensed her. The look told her they expected Dafydd's body to appear in a few days' time, that there was nothing more they could do.

He lives. I will find him.

The forge's silence hummed in her ears. As the building came into view, the jagged piece of glass in her heart snagged. She stopped in her tracks.

The bright glare of Gwenllian's hair appeared all the more beautiful against the dark wall of the blacksmith shop. She lifted her chin, gazing worshipfully into Edred's face, highlighting the graceful turn of her neck, milky white as a swan. Perfect and alluring.

Saoirse's mind urged her to look away, to leave, but she couldn't. She required cold iron and something else. A favor that only Edred's family could give.

Gwenllian stood on her toes, bringing her pink mouth to the corner of Edred's. His hand lifted to her elbow, cupping its sharp curve to steady her.

The ache in Saoirse's breast intensified as if a fist clenched around her heart, impeding its beat.

As they parted ways, Gwenllian dipped her head, her cheeks blooming pink. Edred's contemplative gaze followed his lover as she crossed the street and disappeared into a nearby shop.

Saoirse pulled breath into her lungs, willing the stab of pain away. How often did they press their mouths together? Frequently, from the looks of it. If Gwenllian was comfortable enough to do so openly, in a public street, they'd probably shared lots of kisses in private.

If only the tenderness she harbored for Edred burned as cold as the iron she required. Saoirse thrust those thoughts away and forced her feet forward, shoving the emotion welling within her away—deep, where the pain would not be seen in her eyes.

Edred did not notice Saoirse until she stepped beside him, his gaze lingering on the shop his sweetheart had disappeared into. Starting slightly, his eyes searched her own, kind and familiar, but then the same pity she'd seen in others shadowed his face. His mouth opened, no doubt wishing to share his condolences, but she stayed him with a hand.

Pity cut worse coming from Edred.

"Two things, if you please. I need a knife—a proper weapon that's right for my hand. And cold iron," she said, proud of the steel laced in her words.

"Iron?" The sympathy etched on his brow morphed to one of censure as realization dawned in his eyes. "*No*, Sers. I know what you're thinking." He dared to step closer to her, to lean into her intimately as if they shared a secret; she closed her eyes against the sensation his nearness elicited.

He lowered his voice, "The fae, nor their creatures, steal children and harvest their body parts. Dafydd isn't on the Faerie Hill."

She glared. How could he know? "I locked the door, Edred. I'm sure of it. When I awoke, the bolt had been thrown. Only magic could have opened it."

"Or Dafydd," he suggested.

Her breath left her in a rush, as if she'd been slapped. "Can you give me what I need or not?"

He ran a hand through his hair, mussing it till it resembled a wind-swept bird. "Your glare isn't as terrible as you think it is, you know." He crossed his arms, leveling her with a knowing look that only irritated her further. "You're thinking of going alone, of course."

She clenched her jaw and needlessly readjusted the bag on her shoulder. He knew her far too well.

When she didn't respond he swore under his breath. "Do you really think your father needs to mourn the loss of both of his children? This is madness. We agreed never to return."

Anger surged through her. She barely refrained from striking him. What had gotten into her? She'd never hit anyone in her life. For some reason she did not wish to examine, Edred's disapproval stung. Even her father didn't dare to stop her. Or were they both just that desperate? Edred had always followed her without censure or complaint, but now—

She shook her head to rid herself of those thoughts. That had been then. *Before.* Their easy camaraderie had morphed and changed into some unnamable creature. Were they even friends any longer?

"*We're* not going anywhere," she quipped, focusing on the bright display in the weaver's shop window next door, blinking her hurt away.

"*Sers,*" he prodded, his voice soft.

Sers.

The tentative grip she held on her emotions slipped away. He'd used the nickname all their lives, of course, but after witnessing the shared kiss between Gwenllian and himself—after his objection to Saoirse's plan—using the nickname smacked of betrayal.

She gritted her teeth, leveling him with a caustic scowl. "Don't call me that!"

Surprise flitted across his face then disappeared as quickly as pulling the shutters. "All right," he said, lifting his hands in surrender. "I can see I won't be able to talk you out of it." With a sigh, he turned and walked into the dim of the forge. She followed, then waited as he sorted through a bucket of oddly shaped metal pieces of varying sizes and lengths.

He pulled a roughly spherical piece of iron ore from the jumble about the length of her thumb but when she reached for it, he fisted his hand around it. "What exactly are you planning?"

Saoirse had no real strategy save for tramping across forbidden paths for the second time in her life and looking for clues. She wouldn't tell him that, though. Saying it out loud would only serve to heighten her own fears and further ignite Edred's skepticism. She barely trusted *herself* to see this through.

"I need . . . I need you to look after my da. In case the worst happens." She pressed her lips together, unable to meet his eyes.

Edred stilled for one long moment, his gaze a weight.

She fumbled for words, snatching them as soon as they surfaced in her brain. "The villagers have searched everywhere, haven't they? You along with them. And myself. It's only a hill, after all, and I'm older now. Stronger. Less prone to . . . to fright." Áine preserve her, she was a terrible liar.

"Saoirse." He reached for her, but he stopped himself, his calloused hand falling away. After some internal battle she could only guess at, he said, "Your father will be cared for."

She slumped in relief and took a faltering breath. "Thank you, Edred. Really."

He pulled a blade from his waist. "It's iron. It should fit you well enough and it's sharp." He drew in a breath, his censure melting into concern. "I came to see you this morning you know.

I stopped by after looking by the river for—" He grimaced, then added, "I'm sorry about Dafydd."

She took the proffered knife with trembling fingers and thanked Áine when she successfully slipped it home in the leather sheath on her belt. The lump in her throat made speaking difficult. "Me too," she managed. The world swam and she pressed her eyes closed, hard.

When she opened them again, Edred unfurled the fingers of his other hand. She plucked the ore from his palm, careful not to touch him.

"Pray for Dafydd. And for me." She didn't wait for his response, and turned her back on the forge, her village, and everything her heart begged for. Perhaps she could not have Edred, but she could have Dafydd. All she had to do was find him.

A hand grasped her shoulder and turned her on the spot. "If you insist on doing this, at least wait for me to pack a bag. I—"

"'Lo, Edred!" said a jovial voice. Geordie, a farmer from the opposite side of the village had entered, doffing his hat. "And you, Miss. Oh, it's you, Saoirse. I'm sorry to hear of your brother. Terrible news."

Normal speech left her. She swallowed hard and lowered her eyes, her hand fisted around the strap of her bag. Words really were useless in such a time.

"Er, begging your pardon," Geordie said apologetically, no doubt sensing the tension in the air, "but your father said you'd have my oxen shoes ready."

Edred pinned Saoirse with a hard look. "Don't move. I'll be right back," he whispered. He walked Geordie into the little office room where business was conducted. As soon as the door swung shut, she wheeled about, eager to leave, her face heated and her eyes pricking.

People simply assumed Dafydd dead. Well, she'd never been one to let other's certainty become her truth. She couldn't wait around for Edred, nor did she wish his sense of duty upon her conscience. Just because he'd followed her once up the long stair as a child didn't mean he was obliged to do it a second time. With only one thing left to do, she pocketed the ore and walked up the lane, to where she'd left the cart laden with her skeps.

She'd give anything to have Dafydd back. Surely Áine would hear her prayer with such an offering: her most favored possession in the world. Their usual gifts to the goddess consisted of cream and honey, neither of which seemed a suitable sacrifice to bring Dafydd home.

"Hello," she said to the woven hives as she crested the small hill. The six skeps she'd created and the flourishing life within seemed to return her greeting. Dozens of droning bees hovered, many of which landed on her. One crawled across her chest, and she set a finger in its path, waiting for it to climb onto her hand.

"Thank you for everything you've done for my family and me." She swallowed the lump in her throat. "I'm taking you to the temple meadow." She brought the insect up to eye level, the lines of its body dissolving as tears gathered in her eyes. "It's a quiet place. Lovely, in fact." *Save for the menacing Faerie Hill.* Not that the bees would mind.

The insect lighted from her finger, signaling to Saoirse that she shouldn't dally any longer. With her pack amongst the skeps, she lifted the handles of the milk cart and pushed the conveyance away from home, away from the village, and up into the foothills of the forbidden wood.

The well-worn track to the temple, free from large stones, eased her going. Saoirse thanked the gods for that blessing. Her bees wouldn't take kindly to too much jostling.

Áine's temple—currently vacant of villagers—sat amid a field of verdant, knee-high grasses. Gifts from desperate villagers to Áine littered the altar stone, leaving Saoirse little room to place her bees. Thankfully, the open-air building—constructed of timber and stone—would allow her bees to come and go freely. She'd just have to set them on the floor.

She slowed to a stop at the base of the temple steps and wiped sweat from her brow, her breathing ragged. She didn't know how Dafydd carted dozens of milk jugs to homes and businesses every day. *He's strong.* The thought lent her hope.

Slowly, carefully, Saoirse lifted each board holding the individual skeps and mounted the steps to the temple. She had to place her feet precisely so as not to topple the heavy, burdensome hives. One by one, she settled her colonies on the floor of the temple surrounding the altar.

She'd leave the trolley here. The next person to come and pray, to offer some beloved trinket, would know to whom it belonged and return it.

"Do you remember the day you blessed me with the idea of bees?" she asked the goddess, knowing in her heart Áine listened. Saoirse closed her eyes, enjoying the comforting thrum of her swarms.

"Dafydd is gone. Someone has taken him, as they did with Eva and Carys." The knot in her throat swelled. She sank to her knees. "I o–offer you my b–bees in payment . . . all I have of worth. Keep Dafydd safe. I'm going up there—into the deep wood. It's the only place I can think to look. Guide me, if you would. Help me save him in time."

She gulped down emotion. "He—he's so very afraid of the dark."

A breeze cooled her cheeks, caressed her neck.

The droning of her bees grew louder as they crept from their homes, likely coming out to see what all the fuss was about. Hundreds of them flew around her in darting masses. She lifted an arm to protect her eyes, carefully rising to her feet. The vibration of bees grew in volume until it played in her chest.

What on earth? Had the trek to the temple upset them so much that they chose to abandon their hives altogether? The swarm's agitation increased, and so she withdrew, stumbling down the steps.

If they left, her offering to Áine would be for naught. She had nothing else to give.

Her stomach fell as she helplessly watched the cloud of bees vacate the temple. They blazed into the sun, tiny specks darting this way and that. She followed the horde with her eyes as they furiously raced into the field, but they soon disappeared.

She'd grown so accustomed to speaking to her bees that she nearly called out, to beg the mass to return, but they were only insects after all, and no matter how well she loved them, they could not love her in return. Was this to be her lot in life?

She stood at the corner of the temple, staring at the empty skeps. Dafydd had vanished with no clues on where he'd gone, and now her bees had abandoned her.

Would Áine do the same?

"Enough," she told herself, slinging her pack over her shoulder. Standing here, worrying, wouldn't do either of them any favors. "I've already lost half the day."

She forced her feet through the drooping, tasseled grasses, scattering grasshoppers. The hated mountain cast a long shadow on the field, and despite the heat, she shivered.

Her steps slowed as she came upon the trailhead, where stone steps waited, flanked by two lichen-spotted conical sarsens, pitted and aged. Much had changed since she'd last dared to step beyond the boundary of the village, or perhaps, the looming shadows amid the weeping cedar and fir boughs couldn't compete with her memory. Creeping vines encroached onto the switchback trail. Up, up, it wound, disappearing behind shapeless gloom.

Suddenly Saoirse was twelve years old again, a shudder passing through her as the detested sensation of potential doom returned. This threshold—a magical, invisible line drawn upon the world—warned her away once more. Saoirse's dread cut deep. Perhaps she would not need to go so far as the afanc's pool. The vast mountain had many trails and hiding places, no doubt. Dafydd could be anywhere.

As her foot touched upon the first stone step, buzzing filtered into her thoughts. Her gaze roved over rock and broom, skimming every eclipsed crevice and inky shadow, until she spotted them. *My bees.*

Perhaps they hadn't abandoned her, after all. Had Áine heard her prayer? Had the goddess used the insects as a guide?

Yes, that must be it.

"Thank you," she whispered.

The bees swarmed ahead, moving in a smudged haze against the forest, as if leading the way.

Saoirse drew up her courage and followed.

Chapter Ten

Breadcrumbs

S AOIRSE PANTED AS SHE climbed. The towering trees
blocked the sun, dimming the world to twilight. Several
times she tripped on the uneven steps, but she didn't dare focus
on her feet when the encroaching wood leered down upon her.
She forced her bunched shoulders to relax as she studied the inky
pools between trunks and reaching ferns.

A branch creaked overhead, complaining as if some unseen
burden lighted upon it. Saoirse could well imagine a dozen terrifying creatures from her childhood nightmares and clenched
her fists to still their trembling.

Her bees had disappeared, but her options narrowed to two
points: keep going or turn back, and she had no intention of
returning without Dafydd.

She warily regarded a precipitous drop as she took another
sharp bend in the trail, trying and failing to recall exactly what

would meet her at the top of the long stair cut into the rocky mountain.

She'd expended all her energy in *forgetting* the wood in the weeks following her last venture beyond the village boundaries. Only a hazy reminiscence of grasping tree limbs and flashes of the scaled, toothy creature emerging from beyond the falls remained. *Dafydd, please don't be there.*

Eventually, legs spent, Saoirse reached the end of the long stair. She gratefully slumped against a large boulder and drank from her water skin, her gaze drawn to the void between trees, expecting to see some kind of feral beast staring back at her.

The steps emptied onto a semi-flat, broad saddle between two craggy peaks ringed with aged, gnarled trees. Their trunks twisted like so many ropes, as if fierce winds had shaped them. Far above, on either side of the wide clove, rocky crags—some with sheer, weeping faces—peered down at her.

The scene could be beautiful were it not for the sensation that slithered across her skin, as if unseen eyes regarded her. She listened hard, hoping for the hum of bees, but only unnatural silence pressed in on her.

She swept her gaze overhead, lingering on a trickle of water seeping through the rockface—staining the surface the color of rust. *Like blood.*

Her younger self and Edred had traipsed straight ahead, into the bed of close pines with spindled, broken branches, but a variety of other options lay before her. To the left, the landscape sloped upward, broken boulders scattered amid the trees like fallen crumbs from a giant's plate. Farther afield, up the rising topography, the trees grew too densely to hint at what awaited there.

The forest to her right sloped gently downward, crowded with vegetation and mingling shadows. At some point the landscape had to rise again, as evidenced by the hovering mountain jutting into the sky, but so little could be seen amid the curling trunks that Saoirse discounted that as her first option.

Each possibility bristled with unnamed menace. Now, standing at the precipice, her courage wavered. Perhaps she'd been too quick to cast off Edred's offer to accompany her. The world loomed vast and unfamiliar—and Saoirse, all at once, felt unbearably small.

Immediately, the image of the shared kiss between him and Gwenllian rose in her mind, and she winced away from the pain. "Do not think of him," she whispered to herself. "Courage, Saoirse."

Frightened but determined, she replaced her water skin and rose. As she considered her next move, her eye caught hold of a dark silhouette amid the rusty pine needles littering the ground straight ahead. She edged forward, her breath hitching as the familiar object took shape.

Dafydd's shoe.

She recognized the bruised leather at the toe, where his ever-growing feet constantly scuffed and scraped against cobbles. *There*, at the heel, a pucker of rawhide had worn a sore upon his foot after Papa had reinforced the sole.

Her hands shook as she lifted it, light and plain and terrifyingly, unmistakably *his*.

He *had* come this way.

Oh, Áine, preserve her; she'd been *right*. But the initial stab of vindication that speared through her quickly gave way to dread. The fae had stolen him away—like the changeling from her story—and now she must fight back with iron and rhyme.

Her stomach churned. What chance did she stand against the Fair Folk, armed with a wee bit of cold iron and fireside warnings? Daunting enough facing a murderer, how could she possibly fight creatures possessing magic and otherworldly cunning?

She clutched Dafydd's shoe to her breast as a memory surfaced: "If I ever get lost, I'll leave clues, so that you'll be able to find me," he'd assured her. And he had. He could be close, in a hollow or a cave. "Dafydd!" she bellowed. She turned in a tight circle, listening hard, but the surrounding forest swallowed her call.

She cried louder, "*Dafydd!*"

Enduring stillness answered.

She couldn't stand here all day. She must choose, but where to search first? The murky wood, hampered by scree? The ghoulish hollow to her right? Or straight on, through the pines, which would lead her to the faerie pool . . . to the monster that lived within?

She narrowed her eyes, scanning the tree line for further signs. Finding no other trace of him among the evergreens that led to the afanc, a quiet relief settled over her. She turned instead to the boulder field—sun-dappled and sparsely treed—where the light chased shadows more easily.

The forest floor, shrouded with crackling leaves, announced her every step. She called out every so often, winding around oak and spindled birch, over a field of rocky rubble, roaming deeper into the woods until the clearing in which she'd found Dafydd's shoe disappeared.

A sound reached her then, difficult to decipher with her clamorous footfalls. She stopped in her tracks, waiting, holding her breath, Dafydd's shoe gripped in her hand.

There. It came again, like a single, sharp note from a bird. Or a little boy.

The detritus held no evidence anyone had gone this way. Outside of her own trail, the ferns remained unbruised; the lower branches of trees unbroken. Worse, she could see nothing more belonging to her brother.

The cry sounded again, splitting the silence. This time, she thought she caught the end of her name. Did he call out to her, but the distance or the terrain garbled his words?

"Dafydd!"

Only the black knots, like so many sightless eyes blotted along the birch trees, stared back.

"Help!"

She whipped her head toward the desperate sound and raced deeper into the thickening wood. "Dafydd! I'm coming!"

Shoving at branches, she scrambled over fallen trees, her breath quick. Her feet tangled in roots, spilling her onto the ground. Her hands smarted, but she rose at once, ignoring the pain. She raced toward the cries of distress as it echoed through the trees.

At last, she stumbled into a sizable clearing and gasped. In the center of the small dell stood an ancient oak; its gnarled roots curled out of a mirrored moat of water. Fog drifted over its surface, misting the air and clouding the rocks and plants that crowded the edge. To Saoirse's nightmare-filled brain, the stones became squatting bodies, the plants, spiked heads, spearing through the haze.

She shook the thoughts away, her gaze roving. "Dafydd?" she said, her voice small.

The tree's wide-spread limbs strained upward, its patches of leaves unnaturally still, as if the mighty oak held its breath.

The air had gone suddenly cold; Saoirse's breath blossomed in the air, mingling with the churning fog. Something within her shouted a warning. Her heartbeat, already drumming wildly, galloped against her ribs. Pounding. Thrashing. *Leave*, her mind insisted.

She'd heard Dafydd call for her. She wouldn't leave. Not yet.

Fog rolled away like a curtain over a marionette's stage. Just then, a ripple appeared in the center of the glassy water as if an unseen finger touched the surface. There, in the reflected branches of the oak, half-obscured by the lobed leaves, perched Dafydd, legs straddling the center fork.

She inched toward the pond's edge, her gaze flying up to the spot in the actual tree—to the space Dafydd should be sitting—then halted.

On this side of the world, the oak remained empty. Only in the reflected pool did Dafydd sit, clutching the broad branch before him. Was he trapped in some distortion of reality?

"Please!" The voice matched Dafydd's. *Almost*. She studied the face in the strange pool, squinting through leaves. "What are you waiting for? Come! Help me down!"

She dared shuffle closer, leaning to peer into the water. The reflection stared back with a face that resembled Dafydd's but . . . *no*. His features were distorted—wrong—with eyes too wide and mouth that stretched unnaturally. The air grew heavy and thick, pressing against her and filling her lungs.

"Come into the pool."

This time she could not mistake the *wrongness* of the words, as if two voices spoke as one, both menacing and alluring. Every cautionary tale she'd been fed as a child rang like a crier's bell in her head. Terror seized her muscles.

Apparently realizing that Saoirse had caught onto the ruse, the thing in the reflected tree slithered free of the branches, drifting to what should be the forest floor. Only, as Not-Dafydd's feet touched the strange, lucent liquid, did a head press against the membrane of water. It emerged; Dafydd's features washed away as water cascaded from its bulbous head, revealing ember-like eyes and a saw-tooth grin that brought Saoirse's heart to her throat.

Its oily voice mocked: "If you will not enter, I will come to you."

She fumbled for her knife at her waist, careening backward. Any lesson on what to say or how to defend herself fled from her mind.

Not-Dafydd continued to rise from the water, and Saoirse, her blood gone cold, whirled around and bolted through the choking brush, crashing through branches, stumbling. She gasped for breath, panic turning the edges of her vision dim.

It followed her—charging from somewhere to her left. Fir boughs snapped—close. So close. Any second, it would pounce. She'd never find Dafydd. Her father would never know what happened to them.

She ran faster, a desperate cry rasping from her.

It shouted after her, rough—demanding—mere feet behind.

She pushed her legs on, forcing her body beyond its capacity. Branches struck her face and then it crashed into her with a chittering cackle. She slammed to the ground. Jaws gnashed near her ear as needle-like claws bit into her shoulder.

"Not fast enough," it hissed, scratching at her clothes.

Saoirse dragged in a breath and tried to push herself up, to scramble away, but the creature held her fast. She strained against its weight, her muscles screaming as jagged nails raked down her back. A screech tore from her, and suddenly, the load lifted.

A snarl followed by a wet crack filled the air. Saoirse clambered to her knees and twisted around. She shoved hair from her face, slashing wildly, but her blade only cut air.

The grotesque creature writhed on the ground, limbs jerking as dark ichor spattered the fallen leaves. It shifted, taking on the partial images of Dafydd, then Edred, before morphing into Saoirse's likeness. She stared in shocked stupefaction at the faerie as it changed.

Edred stood over the monster. *Edred.* He'd come. He'd *saved* her.

He fisted his forge hammer, sullied with black blood. As the monster's altered appearance blinked into a wispy shadow—then evolved back into a sharp-angled, stubby elf—Edred's hammer fell down upon it once more. Saoirse winced away, screwing her eyes shut as the blow's crunch echoed through the wood.

The creature's strange, gnarled fingers opened and closed ineffectually. It heaved a few stilted breaths. Only when it rattled its last, did Edred holster his weapon and come to her. He lifted her, pulling her to her feet.

He followed me.

"Edred." The word snagged in her throat. A desperate sob escaped her; she fell into him, clinging. She couldn't help her gasping, wrenching tears. Though he held her with strong arms, they trembled as much as she did.

"Are you hurt?" He turned her around, swiping her tangled hair out of the way where her plait had unraveled.

She hissed, arching away from his probing fingers.

"Your dress is torn, and your shoulder is bleeding." His voice quavered slightly as he inspected her wound. "I don't think the cut is deep. The strap of your bag saved you worse injury."

He dropped his hands, but when she met his gaze, his concern melted away. The beginnings of a storm churned behind his eyes. "You're lucky I followed you . . . that I got here in time."

"I had to come," she said. "You think I'd leave Dafydd for dead?"

"I want to find Dafydd just as much as you do, but what makes you so sure—" He pointed an accusatory finger at the dead faerie. "That thing could have killed you or—or stolen you away."

"Yes!" she spat, not in any mood to tiptoe around his feelings. "You're right. It might have taken Dafydd!"

Suddenly, she wished Edred hadn't killed it. What if the creature had hidden her brother in some hole or in that moat? Perhaps she could have bargained with the monster to free her brother. Her sudden ire vanished, leaving an empty hollowness in the pit of her stomach. No, not empty. Fear roiled there like a dozen coiling snakes.

"I found his shoe just near the head of the stair. I—I heard him cry out for me," she said, her voice thick. "I *wanted* it to be him." She wiped tears from her cheeks.

The sharp line of Edred's shoulders relaxed. The tempest behind his eyes softened. "I know. Of course you did, but they're tricksters, Saoirse."

He motioned her away from the dead creature, holding a drooping bough for her to duck under.

"Tell me what happened."

"I—I followed Dafydd's cries . . . just—" She swallowed hard, wobbling and in a daze. "Just like in one of your mother's stories," she explained. "I nearly fell for the ruse, but something about the eyes and the pull of its mouth . . . ." She shook her head to rid herself of the image in her mind. "When it started to rise out of the water—" She shuddered. "How did you find me?"

Edred's lifted brow showed his surprise. "You were screaming for help." He rubbed the back of his neck. "I've never heard you scream like that. I tried to find you, but I realized quickly that I was running in circles. No matter which path I took, I ended up at the same glade with a ring of mushrooms in the center." He frowned. "I didn't dare cross them."

She let out a shaky breath. "Good thinking." But *had* she screamed for help? It all happened so fast. Perhaps whatever lured her with Dafydd's voice had also lured Edred with her own; a trap to ensnare them both. She lifted her hem to step over a fallen tree. "How did you find your way out of the loop?"

He slowed and pulled at a leather cord around his neck, freeing a pendant from under his shirt. She stopped walking to examine the smooth, dark rock—like any other river stone—save for the hole in the center and the delicate silver filigree wrapped around it. It radiated warmth where her fingers touched, either naturally or from the close contact with his skin.

She let her hand fall away and resumed the march downhill toward the saddle.

"A hag stone," he explained. "Mam's had it for years . . . says it protects against magic spells and the like. I looked through the wee hole here, in the center, and saw the *real* wood, not the magical illusion set for me." He shrugged and his voice softened. "I, er, borrowed it from her chest before I came."

Did his family know he'd come for her? Did they approve? Apparently not, if he had to sneak a magical artifact. Wouldn't his mother have forced the thing on him otherwise?

As her heart slowed and relief settled, emotion knotted her throat. Edred's sudden emergence—his apparent defiance against his mother for her sake–unraveled her resolve and fresh tears filled her eyes. She couldn't meet his gaze.

"Thank you for coming, Edred," she said thickly. She groped for his hand and caught it in an awkward squeeze. "I'm glad you came."

He shot her a half-hearted glare. "If you would have waited like I asked, we could have defeated that thing head-on, together."

Soon they emerged from the denser forest, and the saddle came into view below. The sun sank toward the western edge of the world, and her heart plummeted at the change. "We've only a couple of hours left until dark. Which path of terrors do you suggest next?"

Edred grimaced. "Where did you find his shoe?"

She led him down the slope, around the broken boulders, and to the spot a stone's throw from the top of the stairs. She'd have to scold Dafydd later. The next time he left a clue, he ought to be more explicit about which direction he'd gone, not that she ever wanted to repeat this terrible venture.

"This place hasn't changed much," Edred observed. "It's still just as–"

"Shh! Do you hear that?" A low drone reached her from somewhere within the hated pines that lead to the monster's pool. Her heart lifted. "My bees." Her smile wobbled only a little. "I left them at the temple."

"For Áine to lead you to Dafydd." His gaze softened. "You sacrificed your bees."

She couldn't speak. Her throat had closed.

He carefully lifted her pack from her and slung it over his shoulder. "Then we'd best follow them."

Saoirse stared after him. She'd always loved him for his easy acceptance of her word, but now, despite her best efforts, she could not school her heart to forget him. He'd come for her—and for Dafydd. She loved him, just as fiercely as she always had. Curse the stars that had ever set her heart in his keeping.

CHAPTER ELEVEN

BEYOND THE VEIL

S AOIRSE'S STOMACH CHURNED AS she and Edred slipped between skeletal pines. Branches creaked overhead, despite the stillness of the air, as if whispering to one another.

She adjusted the knife in her hand, which had grown slick with sweat. Despite her silent prayers that the bees would lead them down another path in this part of the forest, they soon found themselves standing at the precipice of a deep hollow—one she remembered all too well.

The mouth of the fissure abutted an imposing granite escarpment that even the most stout-hearted of goats would likely not dare to cross. From its origin, the break ran in a jagged line down the side of the mountain, disappearing behind weeping firs and felled pines.

Her younger self and Edred had tumbled into the crevasse's yawning maw and escaped by holding onto roots and each other, clinging to tree limbs, and balancing on stone knuckles that jutted from the earth.

Crossing the throaty gorge as an adult would likely be easier, but her increased strength and ability did not change the fact that an afanc lurked beyond the opposite rim. The ravine stood as a threshold, one that, if crossed, would slow them considerably. Especially once they rescued Dafydd.

"There must be another way to the meadow," Saoirse whispered. Something about the space demanded reverence, never mind that a great, hulking beast might hear them. "One that doesn't require a climb."

Edred shrugged. "I expect a faerie can cross it quite easily, even with a human child," he offered, his voice equally low.

She glanced at the long, reaching shadows surrounding them, evidence of the sun's rapid descent. As Edred sloughed off his pack and rummaged in its depths, Saoirse stepped to the edge.

"That's new," she said, pointing to a large, felled tree spanning the gulch a short distance away. The tip of the tree angled down into the gorge and couldn't be seen from their vantage, but the wild tangle of roots across the expanse fisted into the air.

"Uprooted," said Edred, coming to join her. He'd produced a coil of rope from his sack, which now dangled from his shoulder.

"Yes, but—" she squinted through the dim to the opposite side. "—Does it look like a path has been worn in the underbrush? Just there, leading away from the roots."

Edred frowned and scooped up his bag. "Let's get a closer look."

She followed him along the rim, skirting holly and fern. "The grass is trodden down," she noted. "Perhaps an animal trail."

They exchanged a dark look. *Or wee folk.*

Where the end of the tree surged from the rocks, a clear trail blazed, littered with discarded, green pine boughs, as if torn and tossed away. Astringent evergreen filled the air. *Freshly broken.* Saoirse's dismay intensified.

Sure enough, on the upper half of the pine, dozens of severed limbs protruded into the air like so many spiked barnacles. Someone—or something—used this as a bridge. Frequently.

Had the afanc made this? Surely something so large could span the distance in a single leap and didn't require such amenities. Which monster was worse? The fae or their pets?

"I guess we won't be needing this," he said, shrugging off his rope and replacing it in his bag. "Are you ready?" asked Edred, his voice tight.

"Not even a little."

The corner of Edred's mouth twitched, but all too soon, he stepped onto the tree over the steep embankment, his arms thrown out for balance. He walked narrowly but swiftly to the middle, then stopped. He looked over his shoulder at her. "It's sturdy enough. You can follow."

"Great," she muttered. Her mouth ran dry. "Coming." Saoirse's trembling fingers made it difficult to sheath her blade.

She scrambled atop the trunk. Worn bark sluffed under her feet as she set her pace, heel-to-toe. She teetered slightly but kept her balance all along the lengthy pine.

Her bees had gone ahead, but she didn't worry herself over them now. Something told her she'd find them right where she desperately did not want to go.

She heaved a sigh as she found solid ground again, ignoring Edred's outstretched hand. Disregarding her rule and touching him in such circumstances would be easy. However it might comfort her now, later, she would regret the reminder of how well his warm solidity consoled and heated her. She'd worked too hard to pluck each tender stitch of yearning from her heart to thread the needle yet again.

She pulled her knife and walked in stride with Edred to the edge of the meadow, where trees gave way to verdant pasture. The sun did not bathe the open space as it had on their previous visit. Instead, it hid beyond the jagged line of trees on the opposite side of the field as if peering through firred fingers, too afraid to watch their approach.

The wind whipped the long meadowgrass into a frenzy, dipping and swaying drunkenly, as a leaf upon turbulent waters. A sudden gust pulled at Saoirse's skirts and hair; strands lashed against her face.

Edred's uneasy gaze met her own in silent warning. *This doesn't bode well*, it said. She swallowed convulsively, then stood on her toes, craning her neck to look for the afanc. "Do you see—"

A keening wail pierced the air. Saoirse's heart shot into her throat. She tensed even as Edred clapped a hand around her wrist and pulled her into a crouch. Her hand trembled under his, where she fisted her knife.

"What is it?" she hissed. "I don't see anything."

Edred's face paled. When nothing immediately happened, his clenched jaw relaxed slightly. "It could be—yes, I don't think it's a monster. There must be a cave nearby. The wind whistles over cavities . . . makes the chambers breathe and moan."

She didn't care for that description at all, but her heart eased itself down her throat, back where it belonged.

"There," whispered Edred, pointing toward the falls. "Your bees."

In the tumult, the insects had swarmed in an agitated, fevered mass along one of the many limbs of an elm close to the cataract of water. Their tree sprang from the rocks, its thick branches twitching in the sudden storm.

"Of course they're near the water," she groused. Fear gripped her heart as a cold sweat beaded upon her skin. *Where the monster lives.*

Edred squeezed her wrist before letting go. She instantly missed the weight and surety of his touch, and she scowled at her heart's treachery.

"The rain's held off," he murmured. "Perhaps that—that thing isn't here just now."

She shot him a doubtful look, and he shrugged. "Just trying to keep a hopeful mind," he offered. "Don't touch the water." Bent almost double, he rushed for the falls.

Like she needed reminding. She followed him, her gaze darting between the wind-swept branches that housed her bees and the churning faerie pool.

Edred raced to the sharp boulders that lined the falls and ringed a portion of the pond. He peered into the water, his dark, wavy hair whipping about his head like a flock of starlings. She reached his side, her breath short, and stared in horror at what rested below the rippling surface.

He pointed needlessly at the dark silhouette under the water. The monster that lived in her nightmares now lay amid countless bones. Was Dafydd in there? Torn to bits? Her lips parted, a faint croak escaping.

Edred brought his mouth to her ear. "I don't see any clothes," he whispered, apparently following her train of thought.

No, they wouldn't find any, would they? Both the stolen children had been returned. Dead and mutilated, yes, but not torn asunder or gnawed upon.

She looked around them for clues—another shoe, per-haps—and spotted something odd in the dusty trail amid the boulders: oblong indentations. Scuff marks of differing sizes, as from boots. Footprints of the human kind. She tugged on Edred's sleeve, too afraid to speak.

He followed her gaze to the jumble of overlapping traces in the dust. A sudden gust of wind nearly toppled her. She clutched onto Edred but immediately changed tactics. She leaned against a boulder, her hair flying about.

"Do you hear . . . chanting?" he asked, his face ashen.

Saoirse listened hard. Amid the crash of the falls and the turbulent wind, whispered words—as if from many voices—as-sailed her ears. They rose and fell in cadence, there and gone again. Mouth gone dry, she nodded and followed Edred up, up the winding path that led to the silver ribbon of water.

Edred stopped at the would-be end of the trail. Bees dipped and raced around them in a frenzied fashion. Saoirse followed his gaze beyond the slippery rocks to a ledge behind the falls. A dim cave yawned wide, from which a maniacal laugh rang out. Well, she heard *that*.

Edred eased his hammer from the loop at his belt, his knuckles white, his jaw tight. Saoirse fumbled in her pocket for the cold iron Edred had given her.

The chanting came again, but the wind carried the words away before she could make sense of them. Was it a faerie or a human that dwelled within?

Only one way to find out.

A muscle jumped in Edred's jaw, his pupils blown wide. With a curt nod, she followed him off the path and stepped behind the veil of water.

Chapter Twelve

Monster Interrupted

THE LOW-CEILINGED THROAT OF the cave, spotted with algae and moss, descended sharply. Saoirse covered her nose with her elbow to dampen the reek of rotting flesh. Had the afanc stowed away some poor, half-eaten victim? Her mind readily supplied images of moldering body parts attached to freshly dead girls. An icy finger ran along her spine, making her shudder.

Shrill wind wailed through the tunnel, pushing at their backs. Saoirse's heart thundered in her breast as flickering candlelight radiated toward them, illuminating the pitted surface of the widening cavern.

The chanting came again: "By this blade, your tether I sever." The grim words filled the air and lifted goosebumps on Saoirse's flesh. They froze in their tracks, while the wind moaned as if in protest.

Edred's wide eyes met her gaze. One side of his face glowed softly from the ambient light, the other half cut with shadow. Her pulse reached a fever pitch.

"May your heart beat again, never," came the chanting, enthralled female voice.

The words grounded Saoirse and pulled her from her frightened stupor. She nodded to Edred, and together they exited the tunnel opening into a small chamber littered with candles, herbs, and stolen goods from the temple altar, but Saoirse only had eyes for the woman standing betwixt two prone forms—forms that appeared to be children.

Candlelight tossed jagged shadows over the woman's filthy dress and tangled hair. Her hungry expression raked over the bodies, too absorbed to notice she had company.

One child lay covered with a blanket; only a portion of raven hair spilled free from their wrapping. The other child was dressed in what looked to be a night rail. A mass of curly hair the color of amber splayed across the filthy floor.

Saoirse knew that hair—knew that it smelled of sunshine and mischief, and if she touched it, it would be as soft as a fawn's ear.

Dafydd.

Saoirse couldn't breathe. A fist gripped her, squeezing relentlessly. She started forward, but everything slowed to a crawl as the woman swiped the air just above her brother's chest with a silver blade. Had she meant to miss?

Saoirse lifted her own weapon. She'd cut the woman down for this. How dare she hurt children! How dare she touch Dafydd!

As Saoirse left the shadows, a strange wisp of bluish haze clung to the woman's dagger, connected to Dafydd's chest; she coaxed it upward, tugging gently as a spider draws silk for a web.

"Stop!" bellowed Saoirse. "What are you doing to him? Leave him be!"

The woman jerked in surprise; the ethereal substance threading from Dafydd's chest snapped. A portion of the bluish haze snaked back into him and disappeared. He flinched once, then lay perfectly—frighteningly—still.

"No!" screeched the woman, her face twisted in ugly desperation. She clutched the stone vessel to her chest and hurriedly let slip the other portion of whatever she'd taken from Dafydd inside. The woman glared daggers at Saoirse, holding the jar as a dragon guarding a clutch of eggs. "Look what you've done!"

The woman raised her knife to strike Saoirse, but Edred—pushing past her—blocked the attack with his hammer. He gripped the woman's wrist so fiercely that she dropped her weapon with an outraged cry.

"No! Curse you," she shrieked, her dark eyes wild.

Saoirse fell to Dafydd's side and shook him. "Dafydd! Dafydd, wake up."

His eyelids fluttered, but he did not surface from his stupor.

"The faeries take you, blood and bone," hissed the woman. She spat at Edred and tried to rake her nails down his face, but he held her wrist too tightly.

The witch wailed, collapsing. Her full weight yanked her from Edred's grip, and she broke free, stumbling. In her haste to flee, she tripped on the other body and fell, her head striking the cave wall with a dull, wet crack. The container holding whatever she'd pulled from Dafydd slipped free of her hands to settle atop the soiled wrappings of the second child.

"He will not stir," said Saoirse, checking a sob that bubbled up in her throat. "Edred, I cannot rouse him!"

Edred whipped his head between her and the fallen witch, but he inspected the woman first, no doubt ensuring she would not rise and pounce on them. "Still alive," he announced. "Best hold onto this, though. No telling just what she did to him." He handed Saoirse the clay vessel and pocketed the witch's silver blade, pulling back the woman's skirt, which, in her fall, had covered the face of the second child.

He reeled backward with a curse, his hand covering his nose. "She's dead," he cried. "Long dead!"

"Who is it?" Saoirse asked.

"No one from our village that I can tell."

That explained the putrid smell. Bile rose in her throat. Swallowing hastily, lest she be sick all over Dafydd, she peered into the bowl containing the strange haze that had come from her brother's chest. She tilted it to catch the light from the dozens of candles littering the cramped space, her breath held tight in her chest. Whatever that woman had done to Dafydd sparked silver and blue, much like the sun atop a black, rippling river. "What sort of magic is this?"

"Dark," answered Edred grimly. He rummaged around the cave, knocking over a basket and a few candles.

As the weight of his words penetrated her brain, her heart sank. How could she possibly combat such wickedness?

Edred returned to her side and offered her a thick tome, well-worn and frayed along the edges. "This was among that circle of candles," he informed her. "Looks like spells." He sneered in disgust.

Setting aside the jar, she took the book carefully. The stained pages, full of scribbled, cramped writing seemed to whisper. She frowned as she read some of the pages' spells. *Withering Hex. Blight Touch. Nightmare Curse.*

Dark magic, indeed.

"Maybe the village healer can make sense of this and use it to help Dafydd," he suggested. Swinging his bag from his shoulder, he fished inside, eventually producing his coiled rope. "We should tie her up."

Saoirse nodded absently, her gaze falling to her brother.

He stared up at her.

Joyous shock and relief surged through her. He lived! Book forgotten, she ran her hands over his limbs, searching for further injury. "Oh, Dafydd! Tell me where it hurts, Little Prince!"

But he made no sound, nor did he return her embrace.

"Dafydd, what's wrong?" she asked, leaning back to peer into his eyes. Devoid of emotion, he stared blankly at nothing, as if he looked through her. Did he not see her, not recognize her? "Dafydd?" she whispered, searching his face for any sign that he heard her. "Dafydd, it's me."

He blinked slowly, his eyes empty of their usual spark.

A guttural roar split the silence.

Startled, they whipped their heads toward the cave entrance. The afanc.

Edred swore colorfully and pulled the knot he'd tied around the witch's wrists tight. "Come," barked Edred, pulling Saoirse and Dafydd up to their feet. "Quickly now."

How could they make it out of the cave, past the pool, through the meadow, and across the pine bridge with a barely conscious Dafydd? The creature would devour them all as soon as they stepped foot outside.

Edred dashed to the exit, swallowed whole by the shadows lingering there.

She swayed on shaking legs and gripped Dafydd's shoulder to aid him, though he stood without support. Emotionless, his face slack, he didn't even seem to notice her at all.

Edred returned seconds later. "It's out of the pool . . . sniffing the air. *Hurry!*" He lunged for Dafydd and pulled him toward the cave entrance, tugging his hammer free in one swift motion.

As they rushed for the exit, the forgotten clay vessel followed, scraping across the uneven stone floor as if tethered to Dafydd. "Look!" she cried, following its path. "It's moving!"

Edred looked over his shoulder, panic written in his eyes.

Saoirse scooped up the jar, her gaze touching on, then discarding, useless artifacts spread around the room. She had to find something to cork it. Whatever the witch had taken from Dafydd, she wouldn't let danger befall it.

Shifting stones grated outside amid the rumble of the falls. Edred swore under his breath, the same word in quick succession. He lifted his hammer, both fists wrapped around the handle. If the afanc had started up the trail to its lair, they could not escape—not without battling it upon the uneven, slippery rocks. Would the afanc remember them?

Edred's shoulders tensed, chest rising and falling in shallow bursts. "We're trapped!"

They would die here, perhaps as they ought to have done at twelve and fourteen. An urgency to tell him she loved him, that she was sorry for pulling him into this mess filled her. The words spilled into her mouth, choking her.

But in seconds, the moment passed. Edred jerked his chin toward the back of the cavern, where the dark pooled thick as honey. "Go, take Dafydd. Find a hiding place."

He pushed Dafydd into her arms and retreated to where the curved wall adjoined with the tunnel entrance, his back to the granite, his lungs working like a bellows.

She couldn't let Edred fight alone. She would settle her brother in the dark and rejoin Edred. Together they might stand a chance. She maneuvered them through the circle of candles and detritus, and—praise be—found the discarded wooden stopper on the ground.

She wedged the plug into the cruse's opening and urged Dafydd into the darkness. Miraculously, the cave extended. A threshold of sorts had been carved out of the rock just beyond the line of shadows. The antechamber, small and narrow, would offer little protection, but what other choice did they have?

When complete darkness veiled them, she sloughed off her bag and, squatting, rooted inside for a cloth to wrap the jar in. She thrust the container into her bag. As she rose, she placed a hand against the granite wall to steady herself, and at her touch, a strange light throbbed into existence. She stared, stupefied. The rockface *glowed*.

"What—" came the feminine voice of the witch. She'd awakened, apparently, moaning and groaning, her words slurred.

Saoirse's fear spiked. Edred could not fight both the witch and the afanc.

"Stay here," Saoirse whispered to Dafydd, pushing his back into the corner, then she retreated the short distance to the shine of candlelight.

Saoirse pulled her blade as the witch struggled to right herself. Blood dribbled from her hairline. She swayed as she endeavored to stand, but her bound hands prevented easy movement. She rose to her knees, grunting as she righted herself, her joined wrists pressed against the floor.

She glared at Edred, whose divided attention roved from the entrance to the woman.

"You!" the witch howled.

Just then, a guttural snarl rolled through the cave. It thrummed in Saoirse's blood. The afanc had arrived, its great, toothy snout sniffing the air as it pushed its way into the cave.

"You fools!" the crazed woman screamed. "Sleep!" she cried, clawlike, bound hands outstretched toward the monster lurking in the cave entrance. "Obey me! Sleep, I say!"

Edred tightened both hands around the handle of his weapon, the cords of his muscled forearms flexing, ready to strike.

"Sleep! Rest!"

Amazingly, the questing, toothy snout bobbed and weaved, dipping to the floor, only to twitch up once more as if resisting her command.

Edred shuffled backward, his breath hitching.

At last, the beast settled with sigh, yellow eyes closing, and its bulky body slumped, blocking the exit.

The witch swayed on her feet, but her gaze went to the dead child she'd accidentally trampled in her fall. The blankets had slipped free, revealing a ghastly sight. Saoirse gagged.

"Oh, Ele. Oh, Sweeting. Mummy's sorry." Her cries quickly turned to rage, however, as her glittering eyes fell upon Edred. "Look what you've done! I'll take your eyes for this! I'll pluck them from your skull myself!" She lunged for him but he caught her easily.

"You'll do nothing of the sort," hissed Edred, his own eyes blazing. "We're taking you to the village to burn."

The woman's angry glare swung to Saoirse who stood, stunned, at the back of the cave, Edred's iron blade clutched in a fist.

"The boy is lost to you now," the witch goaded. "His soul is severed. Only Agatha or the goddess can help you now." She chuckled darkly. "And both are far beyond your reach."

"What have you done to him?" demanded Saoirse.

"You interrupted the spell, you witless creatures!" The woman swayed and screwed her eyes shut against the tears that gathered there. "Lost. Like my Ele. He's but a portion of himself." She drew in a restorative breath and opened her soulless eyes, black and fathomless. "But I envy you. Even half a soul is better than none." Tears streaked down her cheeks even as she laughed, the sharp sound bouncing off walls.

"She's mad," Edred said, disgust lacing his tone.

"Two souls have danced, now one must sleep," the woman sang. "The other, through death's gate, shall leap. In flesh exchanged, life finds its way. By blood and blade, this curse shall stay."

Was that a spell from that horrid book?

Edred took hold of her bound wrists and shook the woman, effectively shushing her. "Enough. Say no more. You've much to answer for, witch." He yanked her toward the mouth of the cave, making the woman stumble, but he stopped short. The afanc–though sleeping–guarded the exit. "Make it move. We're leaving," Edred demanded, but the witch only wept, her eyes clenched tight.

Repulsion rang through Saoirse. The witch had killed and mutilated Eva and Carys— had intended the same for Dafydd. "She's a monster!"

The woman twisted, her crazed eyes leveling on Saoirse over her shoulder, arresting and eerie. "There are two kinds of monsters, my dear. The worst of which lives inside you. What will *you* do to restore the boy?"

Saoirse could not answer. She clenched her fists, itching to strike the horrid woman, to shake her until her teeth rattled. The woman deserved much worse than that for murdering and mutilating two girls—for attempting to do the same to her brother. Saoirse would do much for Dafydd, but she would *never* resort to such darkness.

Gulping deeply to steady her breathing, Saoirse returned to Dafydd, putting distance between herself and that wretched woman. She wanted nothing more than to scoop him up and go home to Papa and the healer, but something told her the witch spoke true: Dafydd would require far more than what herbal medicine and rest could provide.

"Move the creature," Edred demanded of the woman once more.

Saoirse returned her attention to the softly glowing etching along the back of the cave wall. Dafydd stood before it, arms slack, solemn and unmoving. As she stared, the faint carvings in the rock deepened, its blue hue burning brighter. The throbbing color fanned outward, filling the designs, coalescing to form an arch.

More of the witch's magic, or something else?

Saoirse's skin tingled as she drew nearer, a warning tiptoeing up her spine. What had first appeared to be the scrolling, intricate design of pillars wrapped in clinging ivy, fell into sharp relief. Not vines, but *words*.

She squinted at the script, her nose mere inches from the granite wall.

To pass through me, you must give what you hold dear. I ask not for wealth, nor for fear. What am I, that thrives when love is shed and opens only when desire is dead?

"She refuses to force the afanc to leave," Edred said, as he drew up beside her. "We'll have to climb over the damned thing. What—what is that?"

"There's a . . . a door here," explained Saoirse. "It just started glowing. Look, there's words."

"Don't!" cried the witch from the larger chamber behind, her voice shrill. "Don't enter Áine's gate!"

Saoirse's stood rigid. *Only Agatha or the goddess can help you now.*

Saoirse did not know who Agatha might be, but she knew the goddess of summer well enough–her entire village prayed to her. She, herself, had been blessed with Áine's gift of bees at a young age. Would she find favor with the goddess now? Would Áine restore Dafydd?

"Áine's door,' she whispered, awed.

Saoirse lifted a tentative finger to a radiant symbol. A spark of vibrating energy raced along her bones and up her arm at the contact. She withdrew her hand immediately.

What would you do to restore the boy?

She glanced at Dafydd's vacant face, and her heart pinched.

"I will do this," she vowed. She would enter Faerie and bring Dafydd to Áine or die trying.

Chapter Thirteen

Beyond the Gate

THE WARMTH OF EDRED'S body soaked into Saoirse's arm from where he stood beside her, lending her comfort. She repressed the urge to draw nearer. The witch and the afanc frightened her, but the prospect of a changed Dafydd—a half-soulless Dafydd—terrified her.

"What does it mean?" Edred asked, his eyes roving over the glimmering arch. He'd left the witch slumped against the wall near the dead child—presumably her own. The witch sobbed quietly, hunched, gazing at the slack lines of the girl's face as if she only found beauty there instead of rot and reek.

"What am I that thrives when love is shed, and opens only when desire is dead?" Saoirse read aloud. "It's clearly a riddle."

She was rubbish at puzzles.

Edred frowned. "The answer could be sacrifice or . . . or letting go." He ran a hand through his hair and expelled a breath.

"It'll likely be something symbolic. You know how the old stories go."

Yes, all the heroes sacrificed their old lives when entering Faerie. They often lost wives or children.

"So, the door could open if we relinquish something cherished?" she mused aloud. What could she give? She'd already given her bees. Dafydd was lost to her—or so it appeared—despite him standing mere inches from her. Not that she would ever give him up, whole or incomplete.

A desperate panic rose up in her for his abrupt change. She latched onto his little, cold hand, frisking warmth into it.

"Yes, I think that must be it," Edred said, his tone stony. "We cannot enter without a sacrifice. I don't think it has to be physical. We could give up something from our future or . . . or even a memory." He furrowed his brow, considering. "It might be easier—less painful, maybe—to give up something from the future. If we don't know what we're missing, how can we be affected by it?"

Saoirse frowned. "What about all those tales of maidens giving up future, first-born children in exchange for some favor?"

Edred rubbed the back of his neck. "Well, I wouldn't suggest that, of course, but something less valuable. Something you could stand to get by without."

"No, I think giving something up from the past would be better. That way you know exactly what you're leaving behind."

Edred shrugged, glancing back at the witch through the narrow threshold that separated the antechamber from the larger room. "Whatever we decide, we should do so quickly."

Saoirse clenched her fists, her mind reeling. The sooner they entered the gate, the sooner Dafydd could be healed. Whatever she chose, when the time came, the faeries always got what they bargained for, no matter how painful for the humans, so she must choose carefully.

She glanced at Edred, a worried look on his face. Sacrificing a memory might be the best option, but which should she choose? Memories of Alys, of her childhood spent with Edred—of hearth-side stories told by Fadam Fortwin surfaced in her mind. But as each appeared, she clutched them close to her, guarding her memories with a fierce possessiveness, as if letting go of even one would empty her entirely.

How might her life change if she forgot Alys's songs or her tender lessons? What story might she give up from Edred's mother, when each experience might prove lifesaving beyond the gate? Nor could she part with any memory from Papa, whose quiet courage during strife might prove their ultimate salvation.

She repelled any further loss of Dafydd. What if, in the end, all she had of him lived in her mind?

That left Edred, her best friend. They had many memories together.

"What do you want to do?" asked Edred, his focus returned to her and the doorway. "The afanc blocks the exit, but maybe we could climb over it if it continues to sleep."

"I've no intention of leaving," she said, even as her heart stuttered with fear. "The healer cannot restore Dafydd. You heard the witch. Only Áine can help him now. You should go. Bring the woman to the village."

Edred shot her a dubious look, shifting his weight. "Sers—I'm not sure that's wise. She mentioned another name. An Agatha. We could search her out—try that route first."

What assurance did they have that the witch would lead them to this unknown woman, whomever she might be, or that Agatha would be trustworthy? "I trust Áine before I'd ever trust that mad woman."

Edred's mouth pressed into a thin line. He sighed, his eyes softening. "You've always been far braver than me, Saoirse."

She might have laughed were the circumstances different. She'd only ever been brave with Edred at her side. This time, she would have to go alone.

As if reading her thoughts, he leveled her with a stern look. "Forget it. Don't even try to convince me to stay behind."

"Well, someone needs to take that woman down the mountain in case . . . in case Dafydd and I don't make it back."

She could not voice her other concern, that if Edred accompanied them, and he lost his life, she'd be to blame. Stepping through the faerie gate just might mean he forfeited his future life with Gwenllian. How could she live with herself, denying him happiness in search of her own?

He shook his head in denial. "We will tell them together, after Dafydd is restored."

Despite the fears plaguing her, a large part of her sagged with relief. Gratitude for her faithful, loyal friend surged within her breast. Áine help her, but she couldn't stop loving him. "I—I think I'm ready. Are you?"

His nostrils flared, his eyes roving over the door. "I doubt any amount of preparation could make me feel ready for this." His mouth tugged up with a reluctant smile. "But that's never stopped us before."

His words warmed and saddened her at the same time. Yes, they'd been a pair once upon a time. She resisted the urge to squeeze his hand and, instead, squared up to the arch. "Very well. How do you expect we go about it? Do I need . . . blood?"

He huffed a humorless laugh, his brow raised. "Let's try opening the door *without* cutting ourselves open and see what happens. Are you sure you wouldn't rather I try first?"

"Quite gallant of you," she said pointedly, "but no. This is my adventure. I'm the one who dragged you into this." *As usual.* She ignored the stab of guilt her words brought and offered him a smile.

"As ready as I'll ever be."

She searched her brain for what she might give to appease the riddle.

There was, perhaps, one memory she could part with. A painful one for her, but a sacrifice all the same: the memory of when she'd realized she loved Edred in the same way that Papa had loved her mother.

She wouldn't need the memory beyond the gate—preferred to pluck in from her consciousness even on the best of days. Without it, perhaps she could find happiness.

If she lived.

She'd discovered the depth of her feelings at seventeen. Simply and naturally as the rising sun, one day her heart skipped a beat when he'd smiled at her. And when his hand grazed hers in a myriad of innocent ways thereafter, a terrible longing had taken root in her, as if—with each caress—a needle pierced her, stitching a line from his heart to hers. The tug and drag of each needle stroke grew unbearable as time progressed, however.

Her thoughts had lingered on him constantly, and she found herself inventing reasons to steal moments together, despite the duties that tethered them to their respective families. Sometimes, he'd oblige her, slipping away from a chore to walk with her in the orchard. Other times, he could not break free, and he'd turn her away. Yet always, Saoirse yearned to be near him.

She desired to laugh in his arms under the cover of night and to work beside him in the light of day—to build a life woven with his. The realization had both startled and excited her.

But other young women began to vie for Edred's attention, casting him sweet smiles and contriving little, maidenly quandaries to draw him near. Worse, Edred responded to them no differently than he responded to her. Jealousy crept into her heart, and she put up a mask of indifference. She'd quickly lost the courage to confess her feelings; better to remain his friend than to risk losing him altogether over a love that might not be returned.

She cringed at the notion of losing her precious, if futile, feelings for Edred, but she would make that trade for Dafydd. And if Áine accepted her sacrifice, all the better for her heart—even if the reprieve did not last.

Her face grew hot. "I don't—can you step away? I don't wish you to hear."

He lifted a curious brow, but obliged her. Of course he wouldn't assume her offering to be anything embarrassing.

She waited until he retreated into the main chamber. The witch spoke something, but Saoirse did not care to hear. The cool granite soothed her heated palms. She leaned in, her lips so close, she nearly kissed the ancient stone. "Áine, hear me," she whispered. "Thank you for helping me find Dafydd. He's alive, but—" Tears reformed, and she blinked them away.

Saoirse glanced at her brother, who stared without sight beside her, his sway nearly imperceptible.

"I wish to enter Faerie and, for my sacrifice, I willingly offer a memory." She cleared her throat softly, steadying herself. "Only one," she repeated firmly because gods and faeries twisted any hint of ambiguity. "I freely give the realization of my romantic feelings for Edred, in exchange for entrance into the Summer Court."

For one terrible moment, nothing happened, but soon the arch's glow increased, filling the back of the cave with the light of a hundred candles. The air grew heavy and a low, grinding rumble echoed throughout the cave, resonating in her bones. A curious sensation swept across her mind, gentle as gossamer and vague as a half-remembered dream.

Then the smooth, cool rock under her touch fell away. She gasped and yanked away, flexing her fingers. For a moment, it appeared as if her hands had disappeared—that they'd sunk into the shimmering blue surface reminiscent of a cloudless sky.

Had it worked? Had Áine accepted her offering?

A chill wind slipped along her skin. Even Dafydd shivered. The veil of blue in the center of the arch darkened to black; the length of the cave deepened, stretching out like an arm, pointing the way. She lifted a tentative finger and pressed it into the pitch, gasping when she met no resistance.

"What is it?" asked Edred, coming up behind her. "Did it work?"

She gaped at him. "You can't see it? The rock melted away . . . the path extends." She gestured at the extended tunnel.

"No," he said, drawing closer and slapping a hand upon stone. Strange.

She licked her lips and grasped Dafydd's hand. Would he, like Edred, find barricading stone?

She placed Dafydd's palm next to Edred's seemingly-hovering hand.

Edred jerked as a portion of Dafydd disappeared into solid granite.

"The witch severed his soul," she said, as if that explained why Dafydd could walk through but Edred could not. "Perhaps the magic does not see him as a—a person."

"We'll restore him, Saoirse," reassured Edred. "Go."

Saoirse nodded and gathered her courage. She wrapped an arm around Dafydd's wooden shoulders and pulled him close. Fear gripped her. With only one step, she'd leave the human world behind. "You'll follow after?" she asked Edred.

"Of course."

With one lingering glimpse at her friend, she filled her lungs and propelled Dafydd over the invisible barrier, her fingers clutched around his arms. The air shimmered, rippling with the percussion of her penetration into Summer's realm. A wave of magic washed over her as she crossed the threshold, an invisible caress across her skin not unlike walking through a spider's web.

Chapter Fourteen

Summer Court

Á INE, GODDESS OF SUMMER, sat upon her throne of living vines, centered under the domed glass of her hall. Servants tied gauzy curtains to stone pillars, inviting the fiery sunset to spill across the loamy floor.

The last petitioner bowed an exit, leaving her alone. Well, not quite. A servant or two still remained.

Brackenholt, Áine's chief attendant Greenman, stood beside her, the rough bark of his skin painted gold in the fading sunlight. Curled tightly, young fiddleheads sprouted from his arms and wrists.

He offered her the ledger containing desired blessings: a wilting garden here, a struggling flock there. An imbalance of wild beasts in the deep wood of Rowanshade required attention, and a drought endured upon the heathland.

"This came for you while holding court," he said, his voice rumbling like distant thunder. He plucked a black envelope from his leafy head and offered it to her, his twisted, twig-like fingers cradled together, nestlike.

She glanced at the offered correspondence and set the ledger aside. "Has Thistleroot finally taken charge of the cockatrice wreaking havoc at Castle Gwys?"

"I believe she's still occupied with the task, Fair Lady."

They shared a private smile as she plucked the letter from Brackenholt's leafy hands. "Met her match, has she?"

Brackenholt shrugged, creaking slightly. "Your Ladyship knows how the humans work themselves into a dither over land ownership. It would make more sense to surrender the castle to the cockatrice than lose lives to it."

Áine broke the letter's seal—a spider dahlia jauntily placed atop a skull. Why would Death send her correspondence? "Quite so," she answered, her attention divided. "I'm sure the poor beast has had quite enough of those shining knights with swords challenging it at every turn."

"There is another matter that we haven't yet discussed today," Brackenholt said. "The bees that young maid returned to you, they've swarmed into the borderlands."

Áine lent him half an ear. "How singular," she said, lifting the letter. "It seems congratulations are in order. There's to be a child. Do you know, in all my time as goddess of summer, I don't think there's ever been a *birth* in Annwn."

Brackenholt's interrogative grunt sent the little moss sporophytes along his brow fluttering. "Quite. Shall I send the parents a congratulatory gift?"

She waved him off. "No, I'll deal with that. What were you saying, Brackenholt? Something about—"

A unique sensation, much like the prickle of static before a summer storm, brushed against her mind. Something had shifted within the boundaries of her kingdom. She sat up straighter, canting her head.

"My Lady?" asked Brackenholt.

Her magic enabled her to protect her realm, tend the land, bless her subjects, maintain the balance of nature, create beauty, and oversee the festivals and rituals of worshipping humans—just to name a few—all at once. While she delegated some of her tasks to her servants, most fell solely to her. One of which being entry points.

"Call for Carreg, Brackenholt."

"Is something afoot, Fair One?"

She tapped Death's letter on her knee, her lips pursed. "Someone's passed through the Monmouth gate."

"You intend to alert the coblynau?"

Áine stood, her crown of gorse heather casting a sharp shadow upon her flowery throne. "Yes. They will find any intruders swiftly enough, but I would have someone I trust on the task. I would know the purpose of their visit, and should I have need of them, I'd hate for them to be *inconvenienced* by some of the less-than-savory creatures in the mines."

"And if they aren't of need to you, Fair One?"

"Then the matter will take care of itself, I would guess."

"I will make inquiries in the grove, Lady," the Greenman said with a creaky bow and a whisper of leaves. He moved away, his great loping strides eating up the distance from her throne to the stairs that stretched into the meadow.

Áine crossed the expanse of her hall. Who might have come through the gate? How long since that door was last breached? A century? More? She could scarcely recall. Well, whomever had come, they better not have harmed her guardian. She frowned, imagining her pet injured. Yes, she would get to the bottom of this quickly enough.

Thankfully, whoever had entered the mines wouldn't get far without the notice of the long-nosed creatures that constantly sniffed out and knocked upon stone, looking for the richest veins of Starfire Quartz, silver, and gold. Though mostly friendly, the gnomish coblynau's personalities varied as widely as humans.

One such of their kind, Carreg, had only recently brought information to court detailing the miners' new-found vein of magical quartz within their intricate network of tunnels—tunnels into which the southern doorway spilled.

She'd approved the new dig, and he'd gone on his way. Thankfully, the trees in her kingdom could get a message to him before he traveled too far. Their manner of speaking—through the wind or birds—far surpassed the work of any bipedal courier.

She took in the sunset's brilliant, warm hues as she exited the hall into a verdant meadow. Horses grazed in the distance, the coral tones of the fading light stroking their backs and manes.

A flock of swallows took flight, soaring and diving as one. "Let's hope Carreg reaches our visitor before the trowes find them."

Chapter Fifteen

What the Dark Brings

A GREAT WHOOSH SOUNDED, carrying with it the faint tang of metal and damp, but it certainly smelled better than the nauseating reek on the other side of the door. She squinted into the dark. The ambient glow of the arch at her back illuminated close granite walls for several paces, then all else fell into darkness. She gripped Dafydd's hand.

She turned toward the magical door and gasped. The way had already shut, but Edred's form remained visible. A ghost of the granite partition overlayed the portal, blanketing his person and the candle-strewn room beyond in the irregular, pitted lines of the cave wall. The light afforded to her did not come from the arch, but from the witch's numerous candles.

She glanced into the darkness that awaited them and kissed Dafydd's head. "It's all right. I brought my own," she told him, though he did not betray fear. Indeed, he showed no emotion at all. "I appreciate your stoicism," she muttered as if he had any choice. She removed her bag and dug through it. Her fingers trembled, fumbling for tapers. "I've enough worry for the both of us."

She pulled out her cloak, the shoe she'd found, and an extra shirt for Dafydd. "Hold this, would you?" she asked, offering him a candle. He did not move to take it. He didn't even acknowledge that she spoke to him. The knot in her throat obstructed her next words, so she wrapped his limp fingers around the wax and squeezed.

He held on, staring into the void. Would the goddess even be able to help him?

Stop it, Saoirse. Of course she'll restore him, won't she?

Tossing her cloak over her shoulders, she next helped him into the extra shirt and replaced his missing shoe. "There, no more hobbling."

What's taking Edred so long?

As willing as she'd been to trek alone into danger to save her brother, Edred's separation increased her fear. She stared at her friend through the haze of spectral stone. Was he stuck in the cave with those monsters? Saoirse didn't know which beast was worse–the witch or the afanc.

Edred leaned close to the partition as if to share a secret. Whatever he surrendered, the stone kept his words from reaching her.

Finally, the echo of scraping stone pealed in her bones. The lucent granite thinned like a skin of ice melting on a pond.

Edred's eyes, wide with awe, immediately found Saoirse and Dafydd.

"Grab a candle!" she cried before he stepped through and sealed the gate.

He retreated into the larger antechamber and returned seconds later, the flame stretching shadows along his jaw. He didn't even hesitate as he stepped across the threshold. "All right?"

She gripped his forearm. "I was nervous you'd be stuck in there. The witch?"

He glanced back at the reformed barrier. "She's muttering to herself and weeping in turns."

Her gaze lingered on the opaque stone and the room beyond, the curve of the tunnel preventing her from seeing the woman. "I don't like leaving her, Edred. I wish we could tell someone in the village, but I'm glad you insisted on coming along."

He shrugged awkwardly, his gaze falling to Saoirse's hand, resting on his arm. "I don't like leaving her either," he admitted, "but you would have done the same for me had Rosamund been taken."

She brought her unlit candle to Edred's flame, lifting the gloom marginally as the wick caught. He was right, of course. She would gladly slip beyond the boundaries of their worlds for him. "What are friends for, if not dragging them into danger?"

They walked down the narrow corridor without speaking. Their twin halos of light repulsed the darkness. It leaped away from them, only to shrink and skulk along their backs as they passed fissures and crags. The narrow passage dipped and rose, their footfalls mere whispers, ghost-like and hollow.

"Has your mother told you any tales of Áine's kingdom?" she asked, gathering Dafydd against her. The absolute silence pressed in on her, as weighty as the mountain atop them. Maybe she could break its spell by speaking, but the rough, damp walls absorbed her voice.

Edred rolled his shoulder and stretched his neck, no doubt in an effort to relieve tight muscles. She experienced a similar strain along her rigid shoulders.

"Only that the kingdom is rumored to be rich in bloom and color. I've heard nothing that can aid us here," he said.

She pressed her mouth closed lest her fears speak for her. She'd expected to enter a lush realm at the peak of life and abundance. Instead, they walked through the oppressive pitch of endless night.

Suddenly, their candles guttered from a phantom breath. Darkness surged, tossing shadows along the walls. Saoirse's heart stuttered along with her flame. They froze in their tracks. Saoirse let go of Dafydd to shield her light. If it went out . . . . She swallowed hard.

"Wait here," Edred whispered. He dared to lift his fragile flame higher and crept forward, one hand moving to his belt, where his hammer hung.

Had the chill increased? Saoirse sidled closer to Dafydd.

Edred's wavering, lone glimmer in the darkness struggled against the smothering void, but as he pressed onward, the glow along the walls illuminated a widened pathway. Another few shuffles forward, and the nimbus of light touched only air. The walls fell away. Gloom yawned wide and vast.

A chamber or something else?

The stiff column of Edred's spine relaxed slightly. "It's all right. The path diverges here," he explained. "The currents of air converge, making a draft."

Saoirse expelled a tremulous breath and urged Dafydd forward with her arm. Her beeswax sputtered but held true.

She huffed a shaky laugh. "For a second there, I thought—"

A tapping sounded from somewhere behind—above?—them. No, it rang all around, a faint knocking that grew increasingly louder.

Three taps, then silence. Three more.

The hair on the back of Saoirse's neck stiffened. "What was that?"

Edred's face, already pale in the candlelight, lost all color. His gaze roved from the walls to the low ceiling. "I—I don't know."

A creaking groan rolled through the tunnel, reminiscent of a plank of wood under tremendous strain. Tiny fragments of rock and dust fell from the ceiling.

Her breath hitched, and she tightened her grip on the stub of her candle. Warm wax pooled between her fingers.

"They're coming," Dafydd said softly, devoid of alarm. Eyes glazed, he stared overhead at the slick, dribbling ceiling.

"Who's coming?" she whispered, the sound barely more than a gasp.

"The monsters," breathed Dafydd.

She followed his gaze. Horror lanced through her as a phantom handprint appeared on a drier bit of rock overhead. Too-long fingers fanning out from a palm—spider-like—stamped the stone, wet and glistening. Another appeared, drawing nearer.

"Run!" ordered Edred.

She grasped Dafydd's hand and jerked them into motion.

Edred took the path leading left, running headlong into the unknown. Her candle flame weakened, bent with the force of their escape.

Don't go out! Please! she prayed.

Something skittered overhead, raining bits of rock and dirt upon their heads. Hoarse, rasping breaths filled the tunnel, excited and eager, mingled with the slap of feet—or hands—upon rock.

Faster.

She couldn't let go of Dafydd to shield her flame. It faltered and died, plunging them into near blackness. Her heart lurched.

Edred, as if sensing her plight, slowed and turned. His frightened, drawn face loomed at her in the surrounding dark. He reached for her.

She clawed at the air, grabbing for his hand, but he was suddenly snatched backwards, pulled off his feet in a whoosh of startled breath.

"Edred!"

His candle fell to the ground. The flame dimmed to blue, struggling for life. The halo of weak illumination darkened the world to a single eye within a vast, empty gulf.

His grunt rang in her ears. A scuffle. A hiss. And then all fell silent.

Fear froze her limbs. Her heart tripped and galloped.

Saoirse groped for Dafydd lest something try and take *him*, too. She grasped his shoulder and pushed him backwards until he stood against the cold wall of the cave, shielding him.

Eyes wide, desperate for any sense of what might be bearing down upon them at that very moment, she tried to look everywhere at once, but the dark blinded her.

She pulled her knife—a neat *snick* in the quiet. Whatever might hunt them, she would not make it easy for them. She would die fighting.

Holding the weapon eased her fear enough to focus her mind. Seconds passed; the silence thickened. She listened hard, but only the sound of her own ragged breathing filled her ears. The weak flame of Edred's felled candle dimmed further, barely lit.

She must retrieve the candle and right it. Quickly, before it died completely.

Mouth dry, limbs quaking, she crouched. One hand still clutching her unlit candle, the other pressed against Dafydd's chest. She set her blade betwixt her teeth and tentatively reached into the pitchy gulf. By some miracle, nothing pounced upon her. Slowly, she set the candle on its end and watched, desperate—as the flame grew stronger.

She struggled to stand, her legs unstable and her breath thready. She mapped out the edge of Dafydd's arm, his shoulder, and leaned in to whisper into his ear lest anyone—or anything—be lurking nearby and overhear.

"Do you know what took Edred?"

A nod.

Understanding what sort of monster stole her friend away ought to help her form some semblance of a plan, but fear overwhelmed her. And how could Dafydd possibly know? Did his half-soul allow him sight between worlds? She pressed her mouth to his ear again. "Did you see it? Are there more?"

He shook his head, his chapped lips scraping against her cheek. "The girl told me that the dark faeries stole him away," he said levelly.

Girl? Saoirse blinked, confused. "But it's just us here, Little Prince." She swallowed with effort, her skin pricking. "Do you see her now?"

As if in answer, the tapping began again. It sounded farther away, a taunting echo rolling through stone. She tensed.

He pointed to his left, where the drag marks of Edred's heels marred the dusty path in the weak corona of light. The hair along Saoirse's neck pricked to life. "She went that way?" she whispered.

Dafydd only stared.

The ghostly tapping rumbled, reminiscent of stone falling down a distant mountain. Her questions about the unseen girl would have to wait. She retrieved the light and held it to the beeswax taper, brightening their space marginally.

Pushing it into his hands, she said, "We best move along now. We've got to rescue Edred. Mind you don't burn yourself."

CHAPTER SIXTEEN

DEVILS

S AOIRSE CREPT ALONG, LED by the two grooved lines in the dust from where Edred's feet had dragged along the tunnel floor. Dafydd walked sedately beside her, the taper held loosely at his side. Wax dribbled onto his shoes.

The chaotic tracks in the dust showed Edred's attempts to break free, to fight. Other marks appeared, narrow, oblong unshod feet, presumably from his attacker. The black lump of Edred's bag lay in the center of the path. The woven strap had been cut in half.

By a knife or claws?

A clanking crash echoed down the tunnel, making her jump, but she could not tell its origin–in front or behind. She lifted Edred's bag and tied the severed ends together before slinging it over her other shoulder.

She dared to walk faster, her knife slippery in her clammy hands. Then, quite suddenly, the pathway disappeared.

Dafydd stopped beside her; they both stared at the jagged edge of the stone precipice just beyond, a break in the trail where the path had fallen away. The fissure spanned at least four feet, not impossible to cross but daunting all the same. Cool air rose from the cleft.

She lifted her candle higher, trying to discern if Edred's tracks continued on the other side, but the light barely shone past the gaping hole. Saoirse toed a small rock over the edge and strained her ears for the signal that it had found the bottom. Silence.

She grimaced, her fear growing. There was nothing for it. They'd have to jump. She eyed Dafydd and replaced her knife. She'd toss him across first and then follow.

"Wouldna risk it," said a creaky voice from just behind.

She screamed, her heart pitching into her throat. She grabbed Dafydd, trembling. Wax spilled down the back of her hand, hot and stinging, but she ignored the pain.

A snap of fingers and a flame sprang into existence. Two beady black eyes set in a face like a winter apple stared back at them from about knee height. The creature's hooked nose hung over its wide, thin mouth, and a wispy brown beard punctuated its angular, long face.

The creature lifted his—at least, she assumed it male—burning thumb and set the glimmer of light atop his head. No, not his head, but atop a hat—a resin-covered, grimy, green stocking cap, upon which perched a stubby candle. The same dull brown hair on his chin also puffed about his pointy ears.

Though his flame was small, the tunnel filled with light.

She couldn't find her voice.

"I say, I wouldna risk it," he repeated, louder this time as if she were hard of hearing.

"R—risk what?" she asked stupidly.

He clucked his tongue. "It's a long fall. If it doesna' kill ye, ye'd wish it had."

Asking *what are you* seemed rather rude, so she settled on, "Wh—who are you?"

"Kraglin's the name," he said, eying them with a measure of disfavor. "It's been quite some time since we've had human guests. What brings ye intae King Clatterby's mine?"

King Clatterby. Hadn't she heard a story once as a young girl of the coblyn king who helped human miners? Coblynau, while rumored to play innocent pranks, could be described as amiable. Perhaps he would help them find Edred.

"Please, we've lost our friend. We need to find him, and then we'll be gone. We seek an audience with Áine."

"Och, that's what yon stramash was all about? Heard ye carrying on all the way from my stope, I did."

"Stope?"

"Aye," he affirmed. "Where I was working the ore," he added at her dumbfounded expression.

She loosened her grip on Dafydd, and he sidled to her right side. "Look—Kraglin, my friend was abducted by—by something I couldn't see." She glanced at Dafydd, who did not show the slightest interest in the goings-on. "My brother says a monster took him. We need to get him back. Can you help us find him?"

Kraglin's eyes widened slightly; his shoulders rose to his ears. He shushed them, flapping his long-fingered hands. "Do ye wish tae call the diawls down upon our heads?" he hissed. "Dinna speak of 'em!"

He called them *devils*? She glanced over her shoulder, suddenly overcome with the sensation that one such creature reached through the dark for them. "Why? What will they do once they've caught someone?"

Kraglin waved them closer. "Come away from the ledge. They climb walls as well as any spider. If one should be creeping upon us, they'll snatch you quicker than a bat honing in on a wee midge."

She suppressed a shiver and edged closer to Kraglin, Dafydd in tow. "They stole my friend, Kraglin. What will they do to him?"

The grimy lines upon the creature's face deepened at his worried expression. "Big lad? Human like you?"

She nodded.

He made a sound of regret in his throat. "They likely havenae had such a grand meal in an age."

Saoirse's stomach turned over. She tightened her arm around Dafydd's shoulders.

"They . . . *eat* people?"

Kraglin nodded. "Aye. The dark eleves hunt our young, who cannae use magic against them. We dinnae let our little ones leave the shelter of the burrow's safety. If they do, they are forever lost to us. Humans would be a great temptation for them. O'course they might draw out this feast—make a spectacle of 'im."

Saoirse twisted around, still clutching Dafydd, to stare into the black unknown, imagining hidden eyes watching them. Had they already killed Edred? Did they feast upon him even now? Revulsion made bile rise in her throat.

"I cannot leave him," she whispered. She faced the little coblyn. "Where have they taken my friend?"

Kraglin shook his head, the light from his cap dazzling her eyes. "We do not go there."

She straightened her spine, thinking of Papa. He pressed on, always. She called upon courage she didn't possess. "You–you needn't go. I will. Only tell me how to get there."

The coblyn's eyes narrowed. "You can't mean to go and *live*. And what of the lad, there?"

Yes, what of Dafydd? She couldn't very well drag him into a den of devils. Perhaps she could see him safely settled in with the coblynau—in their burrow—and if . . . if she died, maybe they would return him to her father. Unwell and half of himself, yes, but alive. The thought did not lend her any comfort. No, she must see Dafydd restored, but how?

She swallowed her apprehension. "I would ask a small favor of your king, Kraglin. Would you bring us to him?"

He eyed her for one long moment but nodded. "I suppose I could, at that. It's been some time since we've had any visitors from the outside world." He turned to go and then stopped short. "Of course, it's customary for a visiting nation tae bestow gifts upon the king. Are ye prepared for such?"

She stammered. "I have no riches—only what I brought on my back."

Kraglin frowned and rubbed a dirty finger under his long nose. "No sparkling gems or luminous trinkets?"

She shook her head, her heart falling. How much would she lose before restoring Dafydd? "I've only some food and candles."

He scrunched his forehead. "Have ye any tales or songs? Can ye make music?"

She nodded. Yes, she could . . . at least her father and Edred often asked her to sing for them. "I have songs."

Kraglin tapped his long nose. "Let's hope you're good, then!"

They easily followed the coblyn, thanks to his bright light. They walked through narrow tunnels and vast caverns and around mirrored lakes, twisting and climbing until Saoirse could no longer remember their path.

They passed more coblynau, all industriously picking away at the ancient rock, the *knock-knock* of their tools reverberating through the stone. Some pushed wheeled carts laden with sparkling pebbles and winking gems, producing a rumble that sounded in her bones.

"That knocking," she said, ducking under a spiked stalactite. "I heard that right before the dark elf—that *thing* took Edred." She craned her neck, her gaze leaping from shadow to shadow. "Are we in danger here?"

Kraglin grunted. "Nay. The devils dinnae dare tae pass the sentinels. Bad magic between them. Old magic."

She frowned at his back. "Sentinels?"

"Aye, hulking dragons. Ye didna see them just as we came into the largest cavern? Och, I suppose they're easy tae miss if ye dinna know just where tae look. They're asleep now, ever since the great battle in Monmouth Mine, but if they get a whiff of their enemies, I reckon they'll wake as sure as bedrock."

Kraglin happily told the tale of the sentinel dragons as they wandered through the intricate mine.

Long ago—as it always goes in faerie stories—deep underground, the red and white dragons dwelled. Great coveters of riches, they greedily hoarded away the fruits of the mountain until every discovered precious stone had been claimed. When the last gem had been obtained, they began to steal from each other.

This, of course, did nothing for their friendship, and a terrible feud began.

"Their battle threatened to collapse the mountain," explained Kraglin.

"Who caused them to sleep?" asked Saoirse, scrunching her shoulders as the path narrowed.

"Weel, we canna be certain, but we *think* t'was the very devils that took your friend. Áine told us that the devils, having no natural home of their own, hatched a great plan. They pretended friendship to the sentinels, promising fealty to both the red and the white, but in reality, planned the dragons' demise. If they ever awake, the fiends what tricked them will pay with their lives."

Saoirse hunched over; the roof had lowered so greatly. "Good thing they're there for you, then. Even dormant they're keeping you safe."

Kraglin huffed. "Aye, wouldnae wish for the hulking beasts tae be stomping us flat. Ah, here we are," he added, triumphant.

They shimmied out of the tunnel into a small chamber no larger than her bedroom. The door, if Saoirse could call it that, rose out of the ground. Six stalagmites speared the air, much like pickets. Five from the ceiling stretched between the six on the floor, forming a toothy gate. Two coblynau stood guard, tiny obsidian spears in hand. They wore splendid armor made from animal bones. A patchwork of threaded clam shells adorned the slightly taller coblyn on the left. The other's headdress consisted of what looked like a red and white spotted fungi cap.

"'Lo," greeted Kraglin, straightening up with no small amount of importance. "We've visitors from the Brightlands. They've need tae speak with the king."

The guard on the right eyed Saoirse and Dafydd with wonder. "Why, they're giants!"

The guard on the left snorted. "Ti'n Dwl! If ye ever left the Delve, ye'd know humans are nae giants. Havena ye heard the tale o' Branwen ferch Llŷr? Now, *that's* a giant!" He settled his beetle eyes on Saoirse and bowed. "Welcome tae Monmouth Mine."

"But where're yer beards?" said the guard on the right, squinting up at them. "And how do ye sniff out rotting air or sullied water with such inferior, puggish noses?"

Lefty slapped his palm to his face and groaned. He grumbled something in a language Saoirse did not recognize, and then an argument broke out between the two guards.

Kraglin, having quite enough, motioned them through the mawish gateway. She and Dafydd had to turn sideways to squeeze through, the rocks fit so tightly together. If anything much larger than a coblyn tried to rush past the gateway, they'd have a difficult time, indeed.

They left the guards, still bickering, and came into a large, expansive cavern. She stared upward at the spiraling walls, carved with holes like a life-size honeycomb, lit with hundreds of sconces.

Coblyns of all shapes and sizes roamed along ledges. Dozens of ropes hung from pulleys, from which industrious faeries hefted heaping bundles in baskets and buckets. They pulled the ropes below with surprising strength, speedily delivering their charge to waiting fellows above.

The air rang with voices and the squeak of stone wheels, but it gradually faded away as she and Dafydd followed Kraglin, picking through the throng of working wee folk. A hush fell over the commune as, one after another, coblyns paused their labors to stare. They could spot Saoirse and Dafydd easily enough, being three times their size.

Saoirse's awe lay dormant, dampened under layers of urgency and fear. In different circumstances, she would keenly take in each face and ask countless questions. Now, she could only think of Edred, who, at that very moment, no doubt suffered. She refused to believe he might already be lost to them.

Kraglin led them across the cavern, shouting instructions: "This way. Mind your feet. Yes, that's right. Make way; can't you see we've got important business?"

They passed a rather buxom coblyn cradling a swaddled babe, who gripped its mother's beard tightly in a tiny fist. Saoirse's stare caused her to bump her head on a hanging bucket, sloshing her with water. She stepped over a set of metal tracks set in the floor, upon which two carts sat, laden with broken bits of granite, each peppered with glitter.

"He'll be just through here," Kraglin said, pointing to a stout door, apparently leading to an adjacent chamber. "Stay here while I pop in and speak to him."

Dafydd placidly gazed about them while Saoirse's stomach churned. How could she possibly rescue Edred and ensure Dafydd's safety? Could she leave him here?

Countless coblynau pressed closer, filling the cavern floor with colorful, waxy caps and pointed ears. Eyes peered down at them from the hive-like ledges above, increasing her uneasiness. She forced a smile, hoping it didn't look as strained as it felt, and curtseyed in a wobbly fashion.

"H—hello."

Whispers rose amongst the crowd, and soon, a rift in the throng split the ocean of faces as they made way for a single faerie. This coblyn carved a line in the throng. Long gray hair, plaited in two thick ropes, fell over sagging shoulders.

"The Stone Singer," said a coblyn nearby, awe lacing its tone.

Saoirse gripped Dafydd's hand so tightly he squeaked.

"Sorry," she muttered, as the old coblyn—the Stone Singer—stopped before her.

Within this coblyn's silver beard, dark gemstones winked, sparking onyx, like its eyes. The faerie peered at Dafydd, its withered brow crinkled in a question. "Why, whatever have you done to the lad?" it asked in a rusty voice.

Saoirse pulled Dafydd closer, her arm around his shoulders. "I've done nothing."

"He's got a terrible hole in him, just there." It lifted a long, arthritic finger to his chest and poked the space over his heart. "I can see the jagged edges of him. Torn straight away. Weeping and ragged." It tutted and lifted its strange eyes to Dafydd's face. "Does it hurt, boy?"

It grunted disapprovingly when Dafydd didn't respond. "And you," said the Stone Singer, its gaze narrowing onto Saoirse, "you hold the missing piece. Toting it around like a pet toad."

Saoirse didn't care for the coblyn's assumption that she had been the one to cause her brother such terrible injury, nor that they carted his soul around for whimsy. "I'm off to set him to rights," she said firmly. "That's why we're here."

The Stone Singer's withered mouth tugged into a frown. "King Clatterby's magic—our magic—lives in stone and earth, not in blood and bone . . . nor spirit, for that matter. We cannot aid him in this."

Saoirse didn't have the strength to explain everything to the old coblyn. She hadn't expected their king to restore Dafydd, of course, but after so much *wrongness* in such quick succession, having her trouble pointed out to her seemed suddenly, impossibly, heavy.

They'd barely crossed the threshold of the goddess's gate, and obstacles already mounted. Would she ever make it to Áine? Even if they made it to her, would the goddess deign to help Dafydd?

She'd so adamantly insisted that the goddess *would* answer her plea that she hadn't even considered an alternate possibility. She forced down a rising panic. "Don't worry," she whispered into Dafydd's curls, not sure if she reassured her brother or herself.

Kraglin reappeared then. "The king is quite busy, but he's agreed to make a little time for you. This way. Follow me. Step lively."

Glad to leave behind so many prying eyes, she ducked under the stone lintel and followed Kraglin into the next room to meet King Clatterby to dare risk asking a faerie for a favor.

CHAPTER SEVENTEEN

A BARGAIN IS STRUCK

F AERIE LIGHT CAST PRISMS of color along the ceiling
and walls, dazzling Saoirse's eyes. A narrow path wound
through cascading piles of gems, jewels, and precious metals,
leading to the center of the room, where a set of overlarge silver
scales sat. More wheeled carts atop inlaid tracks further cluttered
the areas.

Despite the high ceiling and wide walls, the cramped space
forced Saoirse, Dafydd, and Kraglin to huddle together. No one
noticed them at first. A handful of coblynau, each with a strange
glass affixed to an eye, busily inspected colorful, polished stones
piece by piece, too intent on their work to look up. Another set
of wee folk hefted gold nuggets onto one side of the scales. The
other held what looked like granite cobbles, winking silver-blue.

Kraglin cleared his throat, drawing attention, and bowed
from where they stood at the entrance. Saoirse followed suit,
curtsying politely, though to whom she wasn't sure, for each

coblyn dressed in the same manner, and none so richly as a human king.

"Your Majesty," said Kraglin to a rather rumpled faerie. His apron, dusty from tumbled stone, had a tear along the hem. He separated himself from the group at the scales, wiping his knobby hands on his trousers in a markedly unregal manner. His beard, a rich rust color, curled into a wave at the tip. Bushy hair poked out around his pointed ears, much like dandelion down.

"Might I present the Brightlanders I spoke of?" Kraglin said.

The king openly appraised them as if they were strange gems carefully procured, wondering at their worth. "Mmph, and what is your name?" he asked Saoirse.

She had to clamp her mouth shut on the impulse to answer truthfully. Every child in her village learned early on to never give *real* names to the fae should they be so unlucky to encounter them. Doing so gave them power over you, and being bound to a faerie's whim never ended well. Not for humans, at least.

"You may call me Lady Traveler," she answered. "And this is my brother," she added, gesturing to Dafydd on her right.

The king lifted bushy brows. "Lady Traveler and Brother." He pursed his bottom lip and hooked his thumbs under his apron strings. "Weel, I'm not like to be so blunt, but I'm rather busy—we all are, as you might've noticed. Say your piece then, and be on your way. Why have you obliged yourself to enter my mine?"

Saoirse, taken aback after Kraglin's kindness, stammered at King Clatterby's less-than-warm reception. All the coblyn tales painted them as friendly to humans. Clearly, the stories needed modifications. So far, King Clatterby seemed prickly as nettles.

"Good day to you." Her mind spun, looking for how to proceed. She'd never met a king before–human or otherwise–but had expected something less frank. How could she possibly persuade a disgruntled faerie king to aid her?

Her brain latched onto faerie traits. As good a place to start as any. The fae appreciated honesty, being unable to lie themselves, and Clatterby asked for brevity.

"Well, Your Majesty, I've lost my friend to the—the dark elves." She twisted her fingers together. "I'd appreciate your help–"

"It's customary for emissaries from other kingdoms tae present neighboring sovereigns with *gifts* afore asking for favors." King Clatterby somehow looked down his nose at her, despite his small stature. "Or do humans overlook old customs?"

Saoirse's face heated. "Er . . . " She'd mucked this up badly, hadn't she? Should she sing now or—

"Came in from the borderlands," supplied Kraglin unhelpfully. "Through Áine's gate."

"From where else?" asked Clatterby. "They didn't very well dig their way in from the Brightlands." He barked a laugh at his own joke. "Humans aren't likely to dig their way out of a hole, much less tunnel through a mountain!"

Saoirse forced away the rising panic that gripped her throat and ticked off other important guidance regarding faeries.

One, they never made promises lightly and expected to be paid—in full—no matter how steep the price. Two, their skill in twisting promises and contracts to their advantage outpaced even the cleverest of human minds. She would have to tread very carefully should they ever strike a bargain and start speaking of terms. Three, fae loved honorifics—especially using titles like Lord and Lady.

Well, she hadn't messed up there. *Your Majesty* was perfectly acceptable. Wasn't it? But he'd clearly taken offense at her lack of a gift.

That must be it. She stood straighter. "My Lord, I mean no slight. I'm simply . . . on errand and was waylaid by . . . by our common enemy. And, as Kraglin explained, I came by way of Áine's gate, not knowing what I would find on the other side."

There. Perhaps if she saw her as an ally, he'd be less fractious. She tallied her remarks: she'd used another honorific, she got to the point, and had even avoided upsetting anyone with the mention of the dark elves.

He peered at her sideways as if looking for a blemish in a precious stone.

"My purpose," she continued, "is to reach Áine as soon as possible. I came without the intention of disrupting your day." There, honesty, too, she added to her list. He could find no fault in her, surely.

He grunted, unconvinced. "You mean to say you wished to slink through my halls and enjoy the safety of my kingdom without announcing yourselves? And now, because something has been taken from you—not by our hands—you wish me to aid you?" He made a sound of regret in his throat. "Are all Brightlanders so assuming?"

Someone tittered in the room.

Saoirse wanted to point out that his halls offered little in the way of safety, seeing as how Edred had been savagely abducted, but she held her tongue.

King Clatterby smiled in the same false way as some of the girls in her village, and her confidence faltered. "If yer so intent tae reach Áine, go," he said, falsely sweet. Then his words hardened: "And may the earth keep its wealth far from you. Stingy—" The remainder of his speech fell away to mumbles as he turned, clearly dismissing her. He barked orders in their guttural language. The surrounding coblynau sprang back into industry.

Saoirse's ears burned with embarrassment. She couldn't just leave Edred to a terrible fate. And while Áine could certainly help her friend, she could be days away. He needed rescue *now*.

Kraglin shuffled beside her, looking uncomfortable. "My apologies," he wheezed. "He's in a right state this evening. The Stone Singer found a much-needed vein of Starfire Quartz, but it encroaches into enemy territory."

At her blank look, Kraglin explained furtively. "Starfire Quartz holds immense magical power. It ensures our tunnels remain stable and our defenses impenetrable. Its magic keeps us hidden from the devils below, among other things." He lowered his voice further. "We must mine the Starfire before they do—and all without them knowing, but how? We are not warriors. We stay alive by hiding."

Saoirse eyed the king's back, who presently squinted at a tallied slate a clerk handed him. Apparently, the king had already forgotten them.

If she could find a way to help the faeries get their coveted, magical quartz, perhaps he would agree to help her. But how?

Saoirse bit her lip, her worry increasing. Could nothing ever be simple? She must rescue Edred—very soon—but she daren't bring Dafydd along. Even whole, she would not bring him into further danger. Watching over him so carefully in his current state, she'd likely get them both killed in her distraction.

But Saoirse refused to give up. Ignoring Kraglin's hiss of warning, she moved deeper into the chamber, her feet sliding over scattered bits of treasure. "Your Majesty," she said, loud enough to be heard over the clatter of stone in the scales. "I'm afraid there's been a misunderstanding. I do have a gift to offer you."

The king half-turned, one eye magnified into a shining onyx orb in a glass he'd pinched between brow and cheek. "Eh?"

She chose her words carefully, emphasizing the distant and exotic—well, at least, she hoped they'd be considered such by mine-dwelling coblynau. "I am tasked with keeping the stories of our people," she exaggerated. "I sing them to the sun-touched hills and the endless sky to honor our gods."

She held her breath. He didn't need to know that every child sang the same songs on feast days, nor that she wasn't especially tasked with keeping the old stories alive in the minds of the village children. Every person did so.

Sure enough, Clatterby's irritated visage relaxed. The little eyepiece fell from his face and dangled on a chain clipped to his collar. "A story weaver? Why didn't you say so from the start? Mmph. A song for the sky, you say? I have not seen it for some time now. Is it still blue?"

She curtseyed. "It is, Your Grace. In fair weather, it is as pure as some of those stones there," she said, pointing to a pile of gems. "And on stormy days, it's as dark and foreboding as the granite that lines your halls."

Clatterby pursed his lips. "I suppose we can work and listen at the same time." He folded his arms across his narrow chest, but he could not hide his interest from her. It glittered in his eyes. "Let's hear it then. What song befits a mountain or the sky? I would hear it here, under miles of stone."

Saoirse considered her options. They had no songs expressly for the sky nor the mountains, though she could likely create one were she not so nervous. Most of the songs shared around hearths centered around victories and losses of past kings.

With her heart aching and her limits stretched, one song sprang to the forefront of her mind—a lament befitting the pain in her heart: the fall of Cynddylan. She grasped it as eagerly as a drowning man would a lifeline.

A heroic king of her country, Cynddylan ruled over his lively halls as they rang with joyful noise, only to fall eerily silent and empty. A terrible enemy utterly defeated him, and his ultimate torment came in the form of enduring after all else was lost.

Perhaps Clatterby, who balanced his subjects' lives on a narrow blade and lived in fear for their lives, could appreciate the story of a human ruler's losses. Possibly, the lament would soften his heart, and he would agree to aid her.

A lump had already formed in her throat, thinking of the tragic Cynddylan, for loss had colored his life just as surely as it had her own. Indeed, it threatened her again. She closed her eyes against nerves and the sudden, rising tide of emotion and cleared her throat.

"Silence in the quiet tower, oh lord of battles, who contended," she started, her voice wavering for the first two notes.

"Why, her voice is high and as sweet as a bell," someone remarked.

Saoirse closed her eyes, focusing on the words. "Men who marched to Catraeth, noble their host. Mead filled their cups, their pledge, their boast."

She sang of the king's home, of the green mountain that cradled his people. Of the sea's bright roar—of each man, woman, and child—who fell by the sword and stared, sightless, into the heavens. Of his hall, now bristling with thorns and swept with cold.

"Alone. His hall empty, Cynddylan mourned. Woe to us, woe, two brothers, woe; my sister perished too. I spoke my word beyond measure, and I walked for a long hour. A court without souls, a bed of sorrow. Woe to me, king of naught."

The room rang with stillness as the last note faded. She opened her teary eyes. Clatterby, his face a mask of avid, breathless wonder, stared. In fact, every coblyn in the room had ceased working and gaped, mouths slack—some wiped their water-filled eyes.

"Your voice is very good," Clatterby said gruffly. "You could charm even the most sinister of beasts to slumber."

Someone entered then, pulling all their attention to the door. Another colbyn stood in the entryway, his face tanned and eyes tight with worry.

"Stonewarden! Someone has breached Áine's gate!" His mouth snapped shut as he pushed into the room, and Saoirse and Dafydd came into view.

"Carreg," said the king in greeting. "Aye, we've noticed."

The newcomer straightened his cap and marched up to the king, sizing up Saoirse. "The goddess charges me with relating their purpose here. What is it they want?"

Godesses's charge. Could he mean Áine? Saoirse desperately wanted to ask questions but kept her mouth closed lest she breach another faerie courtesy.

Clatterby waved a hand in her direction. "She's lost someone and needs help finding him, it seems. Is that right?"

Nearly right. Edred's rescue hadn't been her purpose in coming through the gate, but she wasn't about to split hairs. She licked her lips, her heart leaping. "Y—yes. I lost my friend in the tunnels. Something took him."

The collective intake of breath at her words had her rushing on. "I need help finding him."

"We cannot help you," said the newcomer—Carreg.

Saoirse spoke quickly. "Of course, I understand if you can't send anyone to go with me the whole way; I'll go in alone if I must." Her belly turned over even as she made the vow. Pausing, she took in the shocked, fearful faces staring at her. "But I cannot

. . . I won't leave your mountain without trying to retrieve my friend. I require a guide to show me the way I *should* go."

She moved back to Dafydd's side and urged him to stand before the king, her arm draped around his shoulders. "My real purpose in coming through the gate, however, involves my brother. You might have noticed he's not quite . . . usual for a human. He requires healing that only Áine can provide. An ailment in his soul."

Each coblyn listened intently, a dozen glittering eyes boring into her.

"I can't possibly bring him along to rescue our friend," she pressed. "I ask that you allow him to stay here—at least until I return. Once I have Edred, we'll make our way to Áine and leave you in peace."

One of Clatterby's shoulders twitched as if uncomfortable. "And what if you don't return? Better for you, I think, tae run along an' make yer petition tae Áine. You could have Brother set tae rights by supper time!"

She fiddled with her sleeve, her brow furrowed. Her death seemed a likely outcome. What chance did a farmer's daughter stand against the sort of creatures other faeries feared? If she died, what would become of Dafydd and her father?

As if sensing her thoughts, Clatterby continued. "Saving your friend is noble, I'll give ye that, but is it no' also a wee bit foolish—and greedy to boot? Listen tae reason, Brightlander. Your friend is likely already dead—you needn't prove your honor in dying, too." He narrowed his eyes on her. "Would you really leave your kin behind for some man from your village?"

Saoirse frowned. Perhaps the king was right. Afterall, Dafydd was a child—an injured one—and wouldn't the coblyns know best? They suffered endless torments from their enemies.

When stated plainly, as Clatterby had done, plunging into danger for a dead man made no logical sense. The choice should have been an easy one, shouldn't it? Still, Saoirse faltered.

Edred had come for her. He'd followed her up the long stair into the Wild Wood. He had killed that creature—had *saved* her. The knot in her middle tightened. Could she simply abandon him?

She tried to imagine leaving with Dafydd for Áine's court, tried to picture herself content and happy at home with Papa, safe in the warmth of familiar hearth light. But the vision would not hold.

Clatterby's simple solution turned her stomach sour. Even if she could not explain, even if it cost her everything, she simply could not live with herself if she abandoned him—dead or alive.

She exhaled a breath, her choice, though now made, gave her no comfort. One would think that she'd be accustomed to running headlong into dangers unknown by now, but the hollow, empty-bellied terror churning inside her only seemed to grow.

She held Clatterby's gaze. "In that case, I'd ask that you do what I failed to do and bring my brother to the summer goddess yourself, and then, once he is made whole, return him to our village."

He eyed her skeptically. "That is no small request, Lady Traveler. How do you intend to pay for such a bargain? A song will not suffice in this case, I'm afraid."

What more could she give? She strained her memory, trying and failing to recall what she'd offered Áine in order to enter into Faerie. Her first-born child? She doubted she would be so stupid.

"I have no wealth. Only stories and the work of my hands."

Clatterby's shrewd eyes sparked with interest. "We have wealth enough. What can you build with your hands?"

"I keep cows and bees," she answered automatically. She grimaced. She no longer had bees, but perhaps she could again—if she ever made it home.

"Cream and honey," said someone in a tone laced with longing.

The king glared over his shoulder at the guilty party before fiddling with his beard, his mind working behind his beetle eyes.

"Yes, it's been many years since we've tasted anything so sweet."

Clatterby snapped his fingers, and his clerk rushed to his side, stone slate and etching tool held at the ready. "Once you are dead," he said unfeelingly, "I will take Brother to Áine myself and then see he is returned home."

"And in exchange?" she asked.

Scratch, scratch went the etching tool on the slate.

Clatterby considered her. "In exchange, Brother will provide ten jugs of cream and five jars of honey each full moon until his eighteenth year."

Her insides squirmed all the harder. "But Your Majesty, I said *I* keep bees, not my brother. If I'm dead, how could he provide such a large quantity?"

The king considered this briefly, rocking onto his heels. "Mmph, a fair point, but I'm sure he's an industrious lad—or will be, once he's restored." He eyed Dafydd dubiously, then added, "And what better motivation to fulfill a bargain than for a martyred sister?"

She scowled. "Five jugs of cream and two jars of honey." She ignored the fact that she had no bees whatsoever and hoped that Dafydd had gleaned enough knowledge from helping her that he could start a colony on his own. "And only on feast days."

Every eye in the room bounced from Saoirse to Clatterby. The clerk held his marking tool mid-air.

"Feast days!" he laughed. "No, that willna do at all for such a grievous charge. There are many of us to be fed, after all, Lady Traveler." He frowned and tugged at his beard again, but the bargaining seemed to enliven him. "Seven jugs of cream and three jars of honey. A fair deal, wouldn't you agree? Of course, failure to deliver will incur penalties, but surely a promising young human like Brother can honor your word. No?"

Saoirse bit her lip. Papa could help him, but seven jugs of cream was a steep price to pay. And the honey! Impossible without bees.

Remember for what you're bargaining, a little voice reprimanded her. Cream and honey for a *whole* Dafydd's safe return.

"Six jugs of cream and three jars of honey."

The king grunted, his shrewd eyes narrowed, but ultimately relented. "Ah, fine. Six of cream and three of honey, every full moon. I accept."

The clerk's frenzied markings ate up the slate. Coblyns smiled and muttered to one another, no doubt celebrating their boon—albeit prematurely.

The air vibrated with finality. A stone hung low in her belly. What had she done? Hastily, she added, "But I get to choose who will guide me to the dark elves' home and"—she raised her voice to be heard over the noise—"if I don't die, we will owe you nothing."

Clatterby laughed at that, apparently finding the idea of her living absurd. "Yes, yes, of course," he said, chuckling. "Make your mark here, if you please."

The clerk turned the tablet to face her and offered her the thin etching rod. The forked, crooked markings upon the slate meant nothing to her. How could she be certain it contained their true bargain?

She glanced at Kraglin. "Can you read this?" she muttered to him, hoping the king would not hear her and take offense that she questioned its veracity. While the fae could not tell lies, they could certainly bend words to make them fit their agendas.

Kraglin lifted his chin, his eyes roving over the markings. He nodded firmly to her.

She sighed and made her mark at the bottom of the page, the scratch of the utensil making her finger bones itch.

The characters upon the slate glowed bright blue, then faded away, save for her name on the bottom: Lady Traveler.

Chapter Eighteen

Winning Elenwin

U RSA OPENED SWOLLEN EYES and stared for long minutes at Elenwin's slack and mottled face. "I've failed yet again, Dearest. Take heart. I do not give up so—" But her words hung in the air, unheard. She sat up straighter. The sensation of Elenwin's unseen presence that regarded her every move no longer warmed her. *Gone.* "Elenwin," she keened. "Why have you left me?"

Utterly alone for the first time since her daughter's birth, emptiness consumed her. How could this be? How could her sweet daughter move on, knowing her capabilities?

Naughty child. Selfish, faithless child!

"Come back," Ursa demanded, steel in her voice. Unfallen tears trembled on her lashes. "This instant!"

She waited, breath held, for the returned perception—for the *feel* of Elenwin's soul drawing near, but it did not come. Cold walls and spent candles surrounded her and the creature. "You are my sole companion," she whispered, glaring at the afanc's ugly snout.

Another onslaught of weeping threatened, but she willed it away, gulping air. Why would her daughter leave? Had she lost confidence in her mother? Ursa froze, her mind working. *Yes, that must be it.* "Ele doubts me," she said to the roar of the falls, aghast—offended.

She drew in a ragged breath, her resolve solidifying. Well, she'd just have to remind her daughter once more of her power. Nothing could be more persuasive. Elenwin would sense her mother's power, and her faith would be restored. Her spirit would return to her, apologetic and eager. She need only revive her daughter's trust.

She eyed the small space, the tools of her trade littered about. Useless without the silver blade. That brat had taken it from her. Ursa clenched her hands into fists, the nails biting into her palms, reopening her half-congealed wounds. She welcomed the pain. The pain grounded her, a sharp tether to the present.

She stilled as a sudden thought brushed across the landscape of her mind. The blade needn't be so extravagant and costly as a silver knife. Nature offered far more sacred cutting implements. She need only find a hawthorn tree—dually symbolizing life and death.

The knot in her throat loosened, her sorrow and indignation replaced with cold purpose.

She inched her way to the cave's entrance where the mist of the falls dampened the walls and blanketed the sleeping afanc. She cast out her mind to their mental tether, examining the magical thread in her mind's eye. It pulsed in time with her heartbeat, strong and sure.

Sure it would not wake, she lifted her bound hands, pressing the rope against one of the creature's protruding, serrated teeth, and sawed away at her bindings.

"You're in need of a reminder, it seems" she hissed, her voice a promise. "You will see what I'll do for you, Elenwin. You will return to me and then we can begin anew."

The tight press of rope unraveled from her skin. She flexed her wrists as a bitter smile traced her lips. She stood and stroked the afanc's leathery snout, its exhalations warming her skin. "Wake," she whispered.

The afanc's reptilian eyes blinked open, gold with a black, slit pupil in the center. A rumbling growl charged the air and reverberated through her bones. "I am your master. Obey me."

The monster's snarls faded away, its keen intelligence sparking down the magical tendril that connected them. "Hungry, aren't you?" she crooned, her hand sweeping over its massive head. She stroked the mane-like spikes protruding at the base of its skull.

"Feast you shall," she promised. "Descend upon the village and eat your fill. Only," she added, amending her thinking, "leave me the children, if you please. I have need of them."

It pushed itself backward from the tunnel and slipped through the veil of water. Already, thunder rolled.

"You see, Elenwin," she whispered to the empty chamber. "Do not doubt me."

Chapter Nineteen

Hasty Plans

S aoirse settled Dafydd in a small chamber belonging to a coblyn family some way up the great, spiraling cavern ramp. While low-ceilinged and filled with miniature furnishings, the room boasted a clean and stable bed—and a good thing, too. When Dafydd sat on the small mattress, the frame didn't even creak.

The matron, a dark-haired lady coblyn with silver streaks in her hair and a patchy beard, had a no-nonsense aura. She showed no annoyance at sharing her space with a human boy. "All my bairns are grown with lodgings o' their own. Dinna ye fash. He's most welcome!"

"He doesn't need to take your bed," Saoirse said. "I can make a pallet on the floor for him."

"Nonsense! He's a guest! Besides, my husband willane be home tonight, as he's working the late shift."

Dafydd fit the room better than Saoirse. She stooped, nearly bent double as she draped a blanket over Dafydd's knees.

Saoirse bit her lip. How could she leave him here with strangers, even willing ones? But she couldn't possibly bring him along. He would die, just as she likely would. Her throat tightened with fear, and she had to blink away sudden tears. Death had always seemed a distant thing–as far away as the moon. Now, it leered at her, waiting just around the corner.

She crouched before Dafydd, her heart rending. "I hate to leave you," she whispered, her voice thick. "I'll do everything I can to . . . to come back for you. I promise—"

She stopped herself from making an oath she could not live up to and kissed his forehead. "I love you, Dafydd. If I don't see you again, tell Papa that I did my . . . I did my best. Tell him I'm s-sorry." On the last word, she turned her face away. She didn't want Dafydd's last memory of her to be sullied by weeping.

She lifted her chin, forcing down fear and uncertainty. She must be brave for Dafydd. For Edred. She studied Dafydd's face, pale and slack with exhaustion, his eyes dull and distant. His apathetic attitude pinched her heart like an iron vice. The Dafydd she knew—her lively, curious, maddeningly mischievous little brother—barely existed. The spark in his eyes had dimmed to cinders, hardly flickering.

Had the witch's spell broken him so much that he couldn't even remember her? Her chest tightened further at the thought, a raw ache spreading through her ribs. Would he relay her message to Papa?

A stocky figure appeared in the doorway, silhouetted against the light from the great cavern. "The Stone Singer waits for you at the gate," he said, his voice like gravel, rough and low. The handle of his pickaxe poked up above his shoulder, its haft worn smooth from years of use, and an assortment of chisels dangled from his belt.

Yes, time ran short. She glanced at Dafydd one last time. He'd succumbed to his tiredness and closed his eyes, his legs curled to fit upon the bed. Love for him swelled within her breast. "Gods be with you," lingered on her tongue, but she would not speak such final words.

She swallowed hard and leaned to press her lips to his forehead one last time, her falling tears streaking his pale skin. "Rest, Dafydd," she whispered, her voice trembling. "Pray for me if you can."

With steps as heavy as her heart, she followed the servant from the room. She couldn't falter now. For Dafydd's sake, for her family's sake, she had to believe this wasn't the end. Not yet.

The coblyn's work in the cavern ceased as she followed the servant down the winding ramp. Every eye traced her movements. Whispers followed her, awed at her choice to willingly descend into the terrible dark of the devils' den.

"She's mad," one old coblyn said, its voice laced with wonder.

"Pitiful waste of working hands."

"Such courage!"

She didn't *feel* brave. In fact, she had to force each step. A desperate hollowness had taken up residence in her heart.

"Has no one warned her?" someone asked from the crowd, voice pitched above the muttering. "Has no one told her what they do to those they catch?"

Oh, yes, Kraglin had told her plainly enough. She forced a swallow and turned her attention inward. *I have the Singer. I have Áine's blessing. I have Papa's hopes and Edred's life as motivation.* These must be her mainstays.

Her choice to have the Stone Singer show her the way to the devil's den had been no idle selection. Initially, she'd thought of Kraglin, who had been kind from the start, but then his words came back to her as he'd brought them to the coblyn burrow.

The devils dinnae dare tae pass the sentinels. Should the dragons wake, they'd make quick work of 'em, and make no mistake.

Dragons. Stone ones, at that, who'd once ruled the mountain. And, according to Kraglin, they hated the dark elves.

From there, a half-witted, incomplete plan sprouted in her mind: If anyone had the capability to restore the beasts, a faerie with the title of Stone Singer would be it.

Could she convince the Singer to reanimate the ancient creatures? The coblyn might agree if she could lull them to sleep once more. Assuming they completed the improbable task, how could Saoirse then persuade them to rid the mountain of the dark elves before the dragons devoured her whole?

Her stomach dropped. Real dragons, not mere tales of fire-breathing beasts brought low by knights and sung about in village halls, but a living, breathing monstrosity of scales and fangs. And she—small, fragile, and human—must *reason* with it?

She shivered and tried to imagine herself standing before the creature. Her voice steady and commanding, persuading it with wit and courage. What could she possibly say? And then, in a fit of mutiny, her imagination conjured a vision of fiery eyes that bored into her soul and teeth sharp enough to sever her in a single snap. Saoirse's throat parched, dry as ash.

The foundations of her feeble plan threatened to erode, but Edred's face flashed in her mind, white with terror in the glow of the candle flame just before the monster had swept him away. She could not leave Edred in a nest teeming with sharp-toothed, ravenous devils.

How could she do this impossible task? Every part of her rebelled at the thought.

But you've faced a monster once before and lived.

Yes, she had. In fact, she'd faced three fiendish creatures, if she counted that horrid witch. Saoirse's hand drifted to the hilt of her knife, hanging from her belt. At twelve she'd only had her wits. This time, she'd go into the unknown armed with iron.

They reached the bottom of the spiraling ramp and cut through the throng of staring coblynau.

"May the tunnels lead you true," mumbled a colbyn she passed.

"Luck as rich as gold, girl. You'll need it," said another, doffing his hat, his eyes pitying.

Before long, the servant brought her to the burrow's exit. There, standing at the toothy gate, the Stone Singer waited. She leaned on a staff, her dark eyes intent upon Saoirse. Next to her stood Caregg, the messenger sent from Áine. He inspected her curiously as if he mistrusted her. No wonder Clatterby appointed him emissary. The two of them shared similar temperaments.

"I know King Clatterby agreed tae only the one escort through the mines," Carreg said, his small chest puffed up importantly, "but I'm comin' along as well. I'm on an errand, you see, for the goddess. She'll be expecting a full report, and I intend tae give it." He nodded once, as if to say, "Just try and stop me."

Saoirse frowned inwardly. Convincing the Singer to awaken the dragons might prove all the more difficult with another coblyn there to protest. Inducing one would be hard enough. But two?

She could not voice her displeasure at Carreg's coming without arousing suspicion, however, so she nodded tersely, her nerves roiling. "Lead the way," she said, then squeezed behind the two escorts through the jagged gate.

Once alone, and the glow from the cavern lost behind the tunnel's curves, the Stone Singer paused. She lighted her fingers and held them up, torch-like. The blue-hearted flame reflected in her black eyes.

"Why have you come under our mountain, girl?" The Stone Singer asked. "Tell me true. I'll know well enough if you're fibbing."

Unsettled by the Singer's words and piercing black gaze, Saoirse had trouble finding her voice.

Carreg lit his own fingers and touched the flame to the stubby candle atop his green and red striped cap. It blazed brighter than it should have, illuminating the whole space. His eyes narrowed in a marked manner. "Aye. No human has entered Faerie willingly for a century at least, and 'ere you come, bouncing along, demanding tae be shown passage through our tunnels straight tae our enemy."

"I don't *bounce*," Saoirse retorted. "And believe me when I say I'd like nothing better than to stay well away from the dark elves."

The Stone Singer's unflinching gaze unsettled Saoirse. "I do hope this friend of yours is worth all the effort."

What could she say? She'd already teetered on leaving him to whatever wicked fate had beset him, but some part of her—some lingering ache in her heart, had set her feet on this path. She could not abandon it now.

"I've given my reasons for coming," she said coolly, unwilling to wrestle with her fears and doubts again. She leveled a stare between the two. "But perhaps humans aren't so quick as coblyns to abandon their own."

To Carreg's credit, her words hit true. The disapproving line of mouth hardened, at least, while the Singer merely raised a wispy brow. "I do hope you know what you're doing," said the Stone Singer.

The urge to bark a sardonic laugh bubbled up inside of her, and she clamped down hard on the impulse. She'd never doubted herself so fully as in this moment. "Yes, I hope that, too."

The Singer smiled softly, the corners of her weathered face gentling. "Come along, then. Your fate awaits."

Let's hope there's more to my destiny than death. "Lead on," she said, proud her voice did not waver.

CHAPTER TWENTY

AN AWAKENING

S AOIRSE FOLLOWED CARREG AND the Stone Singer
through twisting tunnels, and eventually, into an expansive
cavern, lit with blazing braziers. The flamed sconces washed the
stone in wavering orange and amber hues, illuminating the massive room. Toppled stone pillars littered the floor in mounds of
rubble—as tall as her house in some places.

Far above, a narrow, jagged gap in the ceiling revealed the starry heavens, explaining the scree upon the ground. She stared up
at the whisp of velvety line of sky, longing for home. No mining
equipment lined the walls or hung from the ceiling here—no
pullies or buckets—no cart tracks marred the floor.

"What room is this?"

"This is the crypt. Kraglin would have brought you through
here on your way to our burrow," informed the Singer, her voice
echoing softly.

Even had Saoirse paid closer attention to their route, she wouldn't have been able to remember all the twists and turns he'd taken them on. The shock of Edred's abduction and her urgent need to get Dafydd to safety had narrowed her awareness to the point of her shoes—and putting one foot in front of the other.

"A crypt you say?" She turned in a tight circle as she walked to the center of the room, careful to avoid tripping over a fallen portion of ceiling. No burial niches lined the walls. No bones littered the floor. No ghostly-white winding sheets caught her eye.

"Not a coblyn crypt," the Stone Singer explained, "but of the dragon kind."

Her heart leaped. They'd arrived so soon, and she still hadn't devised a way to persuade the Singer. She licked the dryness from her lips. "But . . . where are they?" she asked, peering into shadowed corners.

Carreg scoffed softly. "Why, you nearly tripped o'er a portion of one just now."

She looked down at her feet but nothing surrounded her boots save for bits of rocky debris. Only a foot away, a column of stone lay upon the ground, as if a stalagmite had grown weary and laid itself down to rest.

"That's a tail you're gawking at . . . and that's the body," Carreg said with a sweep of a hand.

She turned to a lumpy mass of what she'd assumed had once belonged to the roof. The wall of stone rose well above head height and looked no different from any other overlarge, mis-shapen boulder to her untrained eye.

Evidence of dribbling rain and sunlight stretched along the "dragon," the same width of the gap overhead, so that moss and other plants grew in crevices atop the block of stone. "*This* is a dragon?" Saoirse asked incredulously.

"Aye, a part of one," answered Carreg. "From so close, I can see how it might be difficult tae get the full effect," he added fairly. He motioned to the crenulated grooves in the megalith, streaked with green and alizarin algae. "Here's her hind leg . . . see her paw? Just there."

Her? She'd take Carreg's word for it.

She followed the sweep of his finger as he outlined the undulating, angled lines of the supposed foot buried in a puddle of stagnant water. Yes, she could see it now. A proportionately large appendage—at least as long as Edred was tall—and lined with parallel ripples of tendon and sinew that ended in four sharp claws.

An actual dragon. "But it's . . . *huge*," she lamented. She gulped as the full weight of her plan settled upon her shoulders. *And this hulking stone is only its leg!* Áine help her.

"This one is Eryriaddur the Red," the Stone Singer informed. "The white dragon is just there, buried under all that rubble." She indicated a second massive jumble of stone a good fifty paces away. That pile had none of the smooth, clean lines of an animal that the red dragon had.

"What happened to it?"

The Singer shrugged. "Who can say? They've been like this since our kind arrived. My guess: a portion of the wall or ceiling crumbled atop her. We only have gossip and what little Áine has told us."

"Or the devils below did this to her," suggested Carreg.

Saoirse peered closer at the red dragon. What she'd initially taken for irregular striations of algae or mineral deposits streaking over the stone were, in fact, overlapping scales. She walked along its length, taking in every bulge and dip of paralyzed muscle.

"How did the dark elves put them to sleep?" she asked.

"Trowes," corrected the Singer, ignoring Carreg's sharp intake of breath at her using their enemy's name. "If you're going to fight them, you ought to know their name."

Saoirse blinked at the Singer. Finally, a proper name for the dark elves she would confront. Her trepidation grew. She understood the wee folk's fear, for trowes were denizen creatures of dark places—savage and malignant faeries. They had easily overpowered a grown man—and killed coblyns with little effort—how easy for them to strike her down, as well. She swallowed heavily, her nerves frayed as walked to where the dragon's head rested.

An angular, horned head, long snouted, with two slits for nostrils at the end, lay upon two forepaws. How had she not seen it before? Now that her mind had caught hold of the shape and contours of it, she couldn't *unsee* a dragon.

"They're both so large. How could the trowes possibly defeat them?" Saoirse asked. How could she, tiny in comparison to the hulking beast, stand a chance?

"Only those involved know for certain—and I'm no' keen on asking the devils for details." Carreg said. "Come on, the exit is this way." He swept his hand to the right, where the black hole of a doorway stared at them.

Nerves made her limbs jittery. Now or never, Saoirse. *Courage.* "I—I wonder why you have not woken them yourselves," she said, wincing inwardly at her bluntness. She'd never been one to beat around the bush.

The Singer raised a brow while Carreg sputtered, his face tinged red.

She pressed on. "Surely the dragons would not be angry with you should you wake them. They're principled creatures, aren't they? The dragons would no doubt thank you for your service then rid you of the trowes for good."

Of course, Saoirse did not *truly* know if dragons were as principled and honorable as fables claimed, but if all other of Fadam Fortwin's tales rang true, why not those involving dragons?

"They're dragons," Carreg scoffed, his tone laced with biting sarcasm. "Once they rid us o' the devils below, I'm sure they'll be keen for a nice chat o'er tea." He rolled his eyes. "Dinna forget it's us that came and took up residence in their halls after their demise. What if we're just as unwelcome?"

"But . . . ." she said, thinking fast, "but they covet riches, don't they?"

"Yes," said the Singer, the word drawn out in a way as if to say, "So what?"

"Well, why assume they would dishonor your king and people? If it's true that they coveted riches, why not strike a bargain? Surely the dragons would welcome a kingdom's fill of coblynau to dig endlessly for wealth."

The Stone Singer's shrewd gaze glinted in the torchlight. "An interesting perspective."

Saoirse stilled, surprised that the Singer had not instantly discounted her words. *Could this possibly work?*

"We're nay waking dragons," Carreg barked. "Enough! Come, Singer. Let's get on with it."

But the Singer's feet stayed rooted to the floor. Her gaze travelled from the red dragon, to the buried white one.

Saoirse bit her lip, her heart bounding. She barely breathed. "Why *not* wake them?" she pressed, her gaze boring into the Singer. "If the worst should happen, and they aren't interested in striking a bargain, turn them back to stone." This seemed rather heartless to Saoirse, but she kept that bit to herself. *They can work that out later.*

The Singer pursed her lips as if in thought. "Perhaps—"

Carreg's mouth fell open. "You can't honestly be considering such a scheme. Sister, we've taken o'er the dragon's home since their demise. They willna look favorably upon us claiming the mountain's ore and gems!"

"What have we taken over?" the Singer asked. "We live in fear for our lives—we cower in our corner of the mine and hope we don't run out of Starfire lest the trowes gain the upper hand and devour us all. We don't use ill magic, as the trowes do. We weren't the ones that whispered lies to disrupt the dragon's alliance. They have reason to hate the trowes, but not us."

She leveled her enlivened gaze upon Saoirse. "Clatterby has decided to mine the quartz I found beyond our boundaries. It runs straight into trowe tunnels. If we move forward with this, I'm afraid many of us will die. But so, too, we must quarry the stone. If we don't—"

"But—"

"Nay, Carreg, the human is right. Our skills will be of particular interest to dragons. After all," she added lightly, "we aren't the ones that turned them to stone."

"You can't mean to—they're *dragons*!" he sputtered. The *thunk thunk* of the singer's walking staff overtook his words as she moved closer to Saoirse. The Singer peered at the red dragon's face.

"Shouldna we speak tae King Clatterby first?" Carreg squeaked, scurrying after his counterpart. "Or Áine? What if they disapprove?" He gulped. "This could mean our heads!"

"Unlikely," muttered the Stone Singer, bending close to examine one of the curling horns of the immobilized dragoness. "At least for me. What would he do without a Singer? Our resources already run dangerously low, and the veins I've found are all in trowe territory."

"Oh, that's just fine for you, innit?" he mocked.

"Would Áine really take your heads?" asked Saoirse. The idea didn't sit right with her. Áine, the benevolent and doting goddess she admired, wouldn't harm the coblyns for righting a wrong done to majestic creatures.

Carreg's frightened gaze fell upon Saoirse. "She is a goddess," he said, as if that clarified everything.

When Saoirse's expression remained blank, he waved an impatient hand. "You know their temperaments, I'm sure. All seasonal goddesses are willful, ruled by whichever whim pleases them on any given day."

"That can't be true," Saoirse protested, shaking her head, refusing to believe her goddess could be so treacherous, so false. "Áine is generous and caring. She gifted me with bees—"

"Aye, she *can* be," Carreg interrupted, his voice sharp enough to cut through her argument. "But she is also fickle, Lady Traveler. Easily slighted, quick tae anger, and often growing bored with less . . . godly pursuits."

Saoirse opened her mouth to object again, but Carreg pressed on, his tone carrying urgency. "She tends to the land well enough, cares for her kingdom as a whole, but that care doesna always extend tae individuals, does it? We are but pieces on a board to her. Pieces tae be shifted, sacrificed, or swept away if it suits her grand designs. Her generosity comes with limits, her kindness with conditions."

He took a step closer, his steady gaze pinning her in place. "Do you know how many of us have suffered due to our enemy, yet she doesna lift a finger tae help?" He shook her head. "The goddess approved the new dig the Singer found, but what will it cost us? How many will die in the process of mining the Starfire Quartz so close tae their territory?"

Saoirse's stomach churned, a sickening mix of doubt and disbelief twisting inside her. "But she helped me," she said softly, clinging to the fragile image of the goddess she'd grown to love and trust.

Carreg shrugged, unfeeling. "Perhaps you amused her. Maybe she found herself in a benevolent mood that day. Listen, human. I know Áine. I've served in her court for nigh on fifty years."

How can this be true?

For a moment, silence stretched between them, heavy and uncomfortable. Saoirse's heart raced as she struggled to reconcile Carreg's grim portrayal of Áine with the being whom she wanted to mend Dafydd's soul.

A cold weight pressed against her ribs, chilling her. Would the goddess deign to help her again? What if, after all her trouble, Áine refused?

Saoirse sagged. Doubt weighed down her heart. She'd counted on Áine's favor and now Carreg warned her not to rely upon it.

Is that why King Clatterby had so readily agreed to escort Dafydd to the goddess's court should Saoirse die? Because it didn't matter to him whether the goddess repaired Dafydd or not—only that he kept his end of the bargain by simply bringing him to her? Take Dafydd to Áine and *ask* for the favor, then bring him home to Papa, healed or not.

"I'm no' saying she doesna care at all, Brightlander," Carreg said, his tone softening. "I'm saying she cares in her own way—a way that is not human. Don't forget that, or it may cost ye dearly."

"Áine will not take our heads for waking a creature that lived in her kingdom for eons of time," the Stone Singer said dispassionately. "But whether the goddess chooses to aid you further, I cannot say."

The Singer's words lent her no comfort, but Saoirse had come too far to turn back now. How might Papa advise her?

An image of him swam in her mind's eye, desperate and fearful at once. *Courage, Saoirse,* he'd said as they parted. What she wouldn't give for his kiss upon her brow now.

"If Summer will not disapprove of waking the dragons, will she condemn the loss of the trowes?" Saoirse asked hollowly. If Carreg's evaluation of the goddess proved correct, she must tread carefully not to offend her.

Carreg winced at the use of their enemy's name but prattled on. "Who's tae say?" he cried, throwing his hands up in the air. "But if Áine does not mind, Clatterby certainly will."

The Stone Singer swiped a finger over the stone and then promptly stuck the accumulated dust onto her tongue. "Hmm, yes," she said. "That's quite true. Clatterby will mind a great deal." She turned to Carreg, a smile stretched across her wrinkled features. "I'll be sure to tell him you were against the idea."

She resumed her investigation of the stone, tapping an arthritic finger against the rock, her ear pressed to the surface. "I will, that is, if we survive."

Carreg pulled his beard, his face crumpled in agony. A string of unintelligible words fell from his mouth—none of Saoirse could decipher but understood all the same. She knew a prayer when she heard one.

Still, Saoirse couldn't believe her luck. She hadn't counted on the Singer's easy agreement. Were all fae so suggestable? Should this sudden decision worry her? Did the Stone Singer have a hidden agenda, one that would conflict with her own?

"It might not work," the Singer said. "I know this stone, but does it know me?"

Carreg groaned and pulled his hat over his ears, tossing the light from his candle around the room.

"Where should I stand?" asked Saoirse.

The Stone Singer, busy rooting in her robe pockets, did not look at Saoirse. "Oh, far enough away not to be eaten, I suspect. I'm sure they're quite hungry at this point. Let's start with this one, eh? It's not buried under a ton of rock."

Saoirse scurried away, ushering Carreg along. The coblyn yelped softly, no doubt startled, but didn't resist. They moved behind the tail of the white dragon, staring in equal measures of fascination and fear.

"You planned this all along, didn't you?" he growled.

"I'm sorry, Carreg," she whispered. "I couldn't think of any other way." Could he understand? "But—it's *Edred*, you see. I *must* find him. It's my fault he came. I've always—" She frowned as a half-formed thought itched the back of her brain. Some whisper of thought, like an idea or a realization—stirred then died, falling back into shadow.

A sharp and clean note vibrated through the air, and Saoirse forgot her stupor.

The Stone Singer had laid her staff upon the floor and stood before the dragon, wielding two slender metal rods, forked at their tips. They glinted in the flickering light, catching Saoirse's attention as well as any spell might.

With practiced precision, the Stone Singer lifted the device in her left hand and struck it against the dragon's stony flank. The second tone, this one of a lower register but just as pure and sweet, hung in the air. The lovely pitches twined together, pulsing through the air, piercing Saoirse's chest. They seemed to play in her blood, enlivening it so that it coursed as merrily through her body as a babbling spring.

A soft current of air tugged at her as if alive—as if she waded through a stream and the water pulled at her ankles, only she wasn't standing in water, but in a room full of thrumming magic.

The dragon's inert surface, patched with algae and time, shimmered faintly. The crevices between scales glowed softly, as a crusted ember in the hearth. The flare grew until flecks of stone cracked and fell away, revealing glints of a gleaming, crimson hide beneath.

Saoirse gripped Carreg's shoulder so hard, he had to bat at her hand. With a whispered apology, she dared to lean closer, eager to see it all.

The glow spread quickly, veins of molten gold weaving through the stone like fire awakening in the heart of the earth.

The Stone Singer hummed, her voice rising and falling in a perfect crescendo, in perfect tune with the ringing bouncing off the walls.

Saoirse clutched her chest, overwhelmed with strange sensations that shot through her. The music stirred her. It spoke to her without words, moved her so that she wanted to weep and dance together. "What is it?" she asked, gasping. "It's so beautiful."

A faint rumble shook the ground beneath their feet. The dragon's massive body twitched. Saoirse gasped and took an instinctive step back.

The Singer raised her voice an octave; a single, clear note that pierced the air like an arrow.

The dragon groaned mightily, a sound like the grinding of ancient stones deep within the earth, mingled with the low roar of a distant storm. Cracks spread like lightning across its form.

Silence fell. Saoirse couldn't breathe.

A glowing, fierce eye snapped open, brilliantly gold with a narrow, vertical pupil.

CHAPTER TWENTY-ONE

RIGHTEOUS ANGER

W ITH A FINAL, RESOUNDING *crack*, the stone encasing the creature shattered.

Rocky debris rained down upon them. Saoirse covered her head with her arms and squinted through the dusty haze. The large, dim silhouette of what Saoirse could only describe as a living mountain, shifted in place.

"Watch out!" cried Carreg.

Saoirse ducked just in time as the oxblood tail of the dragon swiped past in a great *whoosh* as it spun in a tight circle.

Saoirse staggered backward, her eyes wide. Eryriaddur bowed her back, her forepaws splayed, stretching in a markedly fe-line fashion. Joints popped; claws dug into stone. The dragon yawned wide, exposing lines of wicked-sharp teeth.

It snapped its massive jaws and rotated its head upon its serpentine neck. "Well," it said in a voice like sleepy thunder. The words rolled through Saoirse, vibrating her bones. "I feel as if my joints have calcified—" Next came a rumbling purr of a chuckle that played in Saoirse's blood. "But I suppose that's not too far off the mark."

It seemed to take notice of the Singer finally. Calm as day, she replaced her instruments into her pockets and retrieved her staff.

"And what might you be?" asked the dragon, its tone imperial.

"I am Brynlor, Singer of Stone. I am a race of faerie called coblyn." She leaned upon her staff and dipped in an approximation of a bow. "I have awoken you after many centuries of slumber."

"Have you?" It blinked, as if trying to recall a dream.

"It is believed that our common enemy turned you to stone."

The dragon's grunt rumbled through the cavern. Eryriaddur's eyes narrowed as she sneered, exposing deadly teeth. "Yes, the nasty tricksters. I recall." The dragon dipped its head closer and sniffed. "You smell different than the trowes."

The dragon peered about the room, its long, scarlet neck bending elegantly. "But what do we have here?" It stepped closer, its footfalls surprisingly light. Vibrant yellow eyes peered intently at them from mere feet away.

Saoirse's knees wobbled, and Carreg whimpered.

It sniffed, ruffling Saoirse's hair and skirts.

Carreg, face wan, bowed. "Eryriaddur, Lady of Flame and Keeper of the Mountain!"

Saoirse sensed the dragon's grin, much like she knew when her cat smiled. "Can't be. That's *my* name."

"F—forgive me," rasped Carreg. "I—I'm Carreg, vassal to King Clatterby and oathbound emissary to Herself—er, to Áine, that is."

"Yes, I thought I smelled her favor upon you. But who is the Clatterby you speak of?"

"He—he is our king. King of the coblynau. We, er . . . we live here, in the mountain. We share it with the . . . with the trowes." The word must have tasted bitter on his tongue for the look on his face.

"You live in concert with the trowes?" asked the dragon, acid lacing its tone.

He shook his head, his hat falling askew. "N—no, mighty dragon. We hide in fear for our lives. They've taken for their own the depths of the halls you and your sister built, and we've carved a living from the upper portion."

"My halls are overrun you say? With trowes and coblyns alike?"

Saoirse, sensing the conversation turning against their favor, cleared her throat, drawing the brilliant, terrifying gaze of the dragon. She clenched and unclenched her fists. "Wise Eryriad-dur," she said, curtseying. "I am travelling through your beauti-ful halls with the intent to reach Summer Court." She swallowed heavily. "My company was beset by the trowes—they took my friend. The noble coblyns have endeavored to help me."

The dragon sniffed closer. "A human? But—" Its nostrils flared as it dragged in another lungful of air. "Hmm, how in-teresting. You, a human, yet you have the goddess's favor as well. Are you also an emissary to Summer?"

Saoirse's throat closed. How unnerving to have so many teeth mere feet from her face! "I am not, but I gratefully accept and treasure any boon she bestows."

"Well spoken," said Eryriaddur, lifting her head as she sat upon her haunches. She fluttered her black wings, sending dust flying, and canted her great head as if puzzling them out. "You have united against the trowes and so thought to wake me," it said perceptively. "How long have I been asleep?" As if suddenly remembering her once-friend-turned-nemesis, she said, "And where is my sister, Ishara?"

The Singer moved forward. "She sleeps still," said the Stone Singer, pointing with her staff. "Right in front of you."

The dragon's gaze swept over the pile of rubble, from which the spikes of a tail intermittently protruded. Saoirse had mistaken them for more of the countless stalagmites that littered the cave. "Has the ceiling crushed her?" Eryriaddur asked, her words tinged with worry. For a magical being sworn to fight its peer over riches, she certainly sounded concerned.

"I did not dare to wake her," said the Singer, "and you begin your feud again and crush us."

Eryriaddur eyed the coblyn, her gaze piercing and cold. "Bold of you to assume I cannot control my temper."

The Singer only blinked up at the dragon, unfazed by the remark. "We know well the story of your hatred for one another. Áine told us of your feud, but not of how you succumbed. I don't think she knows herself."

Eryriaddur's barked laugh rebounded through the cavern setting rocks aquiver. "We did not always hate one another.

Sisters, we claimed this mountain and spent decades making it our own. We shared all and loved each other well."

"What happened?" asked Saoirse.

The dragon's gaze flitted to her, then rested upon her buried sister. "When the trowes first arrived, they claimed to only wish to serve us. What a triumphant boon, to have servants as well as riches?" She chuckled darkly and Saoirse squirmed. She had planned the very same for the coblyns. She held onto hope, unwilling to give in to doubt when so much depended on the dragon's cooperation.

The dragon's talons clacked upon the stone floor, as if agitated. "Over time, with flattery and deceit, they slowly set my sister and me at odds. Eventually, their poisonous words drove a wedge between us, and we forgot our love for one another. I believed their claim, that Ishara envied my wealth and contrived ways to steal it from me."

"And so you warred," said Saoirse. A familiar story for human kings and peasants alike. "But how did this happen? How did the trowes overtake you?"

"By the time we realized their treachery, it was far too late." The dragon paused, her great jaw clenched tight.

Saoirse imagined tears gathering in the beast's eyes but the next moment, she blinked, and the perceived emotion vanished.

"We met here and made truce, but the trowes, knowing our changed hearts—and our shared realization of what they had done—fell upon us. Using the magic they stole from Starfire quartz, they wove a dark spell upon us and turned us to stone." She shrugged and resettled her wings as if uncomfortable. She sighed heavily, her sad eyes roving over her fallen sister. "I fear she is past waking."

"Let us try to rouse her," said Saoirse. "Can you shift the stone?"

Eryriaddur hesitated. "I fear knowing the truth of it. If I leave her as she is, I can still hope that she merely sleeps. What if she is truly gone? We are the last of our kind."

Saoirse's heart ached for the dragon. "I know something of loss," said Saoirse.

"Oh?" asked the dragon. "And how did you overcome your losses?"

Saoirse's voice, though small, echoed in the room. "Healing only comes, I think, after pain. You must shoulder it and walk on, no matter how it burns." She swallowed, thinking of her own mother, of Alys, of Dafydd's soul torn from his body, and of Edred. She swallowed away her emotion. "But, your Ishara may still live."

The dragon's gaze lingered on the rubble, longing clear in her eyes. "I wish it to be so," she admitted, her rumbling voice somehow tender. "I have much I would say to her."

The Singer nodded. "And unfinished business in the bowels of the mountain, no doubt."

Saoirse cut her eyes to the Singer, glad she shared Saoirse's vision for what must come next, but *two* dragons awakened might prove more than they could handle.

"Reunited or not, knowing is the kinder choice in the end," the Singer said.

The dragon's saffron eyes bored into Saoirse, then the Singer. "All right," she said softly. "What's one more upset? Stone Singer, if you would do the honor?"

Carreg and Saoirse moved away from Ishara's tail, backing up against the wall so that the Singer and Eryriaddur stood on one side of the white dragon, and they on the other.

The singer cleared her throat and hummed the same two-toned note as before, ringing her forks with magical precision. The stones covering the dragon glowed with blue effervescent light. They throbbed before the tell-tale clattering of shifting rock filled the room. The hummed notes rang in Saoirse's ears as the stones—both large and small—rolled away in a cacophony of rumbles and scrapes.

Saoirse stared in stupefied fashion as the dragon's body came into view. Protected from algae and mineral deposits, the white dragon's stone form glowed as a star in the night sky. Her scales glittered like specks of diamonds in granite.

Her delicate, opalescent wings didn't fare well under the fallen stone. Torn and crumpled, her wings, at least, fared better than her forelegs, which showed breaks in several places. And there, at the base of her skull, the elegant stem of her neck had been crushed to dust.

A droning, mournful cry from Eryriaddur filled the air, followed by a roar that shook the foundations of the earth. Saoirse covered her ears and squeezed her eyes shut. Eryriaddur's lament pierced through her. She knew the dragon's pain—had lived with the same ache in her heart for as long as she could remember.

No way Clatterby could miss that noise.

"Trowes!" the dragon bellowed, then belched fire at the ceiling.

Heat bowled into Saoirse.

"They will pay for this," growled Eryriaddur. "What holes have they crawled into? Tell me! They'll taste my fire!"

CHAPTER TWENTY-TWO

THE TROWE DEN

"I CAN SHOW YOU the holes they climb out of to snatch our children," the Singer supplied, her tone icy.

"Climb on then," growled the dragon. She coiled low to the earth, vast body curving like a sleeping mountain, so they might ascend.

The Singer set her staff down and climbed upon the dragon's forearm, seemingly unafraid. "I've always wanted to ride a dragon," she said, flashing Saoirse a wide grin. When the Singer couldn't reach the edge of Eryriaddur's wing to pull herself up, Saoirse climbed atop the dragon's scaled arm and took hold of the coblyn's feet. She heaved, pushing with all her might—Basalina, Dafydd's minder, had spoken true, they were made of sturdy stock—until the Singer reached a protruding barb and pulled herself the rest of the way.

Saoirse climbed up next, the dragon's scales as smooth as slate, and hooked her left hand around the sturdy edge of a leathery wing. With her right hand, she gripped the Singer's outstretched arm and, together, she found her seat between two bony spikes.

"You next, Carreg," Saoirse said, waving her hand. His face had gone rather green, but only after a brief hesitation, in which the dragon turned its head to peer at him, he sprang forward with a squeak. Saoirse, holding onto an elongated spike with her left hand, leaned far over the side of the dragon and pulled Carreg up with a grunt.

"Which way?" growled the dragon, sniffing the air. "I cannot smell them."

"Straight ahead," supplied the Singer, thrusting out her arm as a charging knight upon a noble steed.

Eryriaddur's spiked back cradled them safely as the beast wound through her old routes, deep in the belly of the mountain. Saoirse grasped the curved barbs, ducking her head as Eryriaddur belched sulfuric fire.

The dragon wove through majestic halls, carved with fire and ice, lighting aged pyres set atop stone columns with a burst of flame, revealing abandoned, pilfered rooms. Bits of jewel-bright fabrics, tattered and shredded, littered the ground.

The entire network of abandoned, ransacked rooms came to light, all of which must, at one time, have shone with wealth and beauty. Now, every hoarded scrap of finery lay scattered and broken amid crushed stone.

Some tunnels had collapsed completely—either purposefully by the trowes or as a product of time. Twice the coblyns and Saoirse nearly lost their seats upon Eryriaddur's back as she spun and hammered her barbed tail against obstacles. She dug through debris with her forepaws, growling and muttering until she cleared a blocked passage enough to squeeze through. Each time, Saoirse feared the scrape of the ceiling as Eryriaddur crept along tight spaces while Carreg gasped and prayed at her back.

Deep in the earth they traveled. Down, down until they came to a lake teeming with eerily glowing fish and ringed with stones. Here Eryriaddur let them off and stopped to drink her fill. Carreg swayed on the spot, his eyes wide with apprehension. The Stone Singer, however, seemed quite at ease. She hummed softly as she bent to examine the pearly swath that lined a clamshell.

Eryriaddur's angry muscle softened as her great frame drooped into lines of sorrow. Even the livid light in her eyes dampened. "What has become of my mountain?" she asked, though Saoirse instinctively knew the dragon did not wish for an answer. "My halls stand empty, and every beautiful thing has rotted away or been stolen from me."

Saoirse, unable to speak, patted the dragon's massive elbow, the sharp stones crumbling underfoot like so much hoarfrost. She lifted her boot and stared in confusion. Hollow stones, lined with gold? Shards littered the floor, winking bright gold in the low light.

"What are these?" she asked, bending to retrieve one of the strange rocks.

"These were once my children," Eryriaddur said hollowly. "My sister's and mine. Or they would have been, had the trowes not murdered them. They certainly played us well. What fools we were, and now . . . now I don't know if any male dragons yet live. I fear I am the last of my kind."

Saoirse cradled the shell in her palm, her heart aching. "I know words are useless," she said softly. "I cannot say I understand what you must feel, but I—I mourn with you. This is a terrible thing."

Eryriaddur stared at her for a long moment, unblinking. "What a strange human you are. I can see why Áine favors you."

The Singer stepped carefully through what Saoirse had assumed were clam shells. "They steal our children and anyone too engrossed in their work to realize they've stumbled into danger. They hunt us for food and wear our skins as mantles."

Saoirse's stomach soured, fear and disgust warring inside of her. Poor Edred. Was he still alive? Her blood turned icy.

The dragon huffed, disgusted.

"They took my friend," Saoirse added hollowly. She held the broken shard in her hand, light and fragile as her hopes. "I've no idea how long ago. There's no sun or stars to judge the passing of time under this mountain. He could already—" She swallowed hard. "I hate to ask it of you while grieving, but can we go now, and retrieve him? Even if he's . . . if he should be lost to me, if there is aught left of him, I would bring him home." Her voice cracked on the last word and she wiped at her eyes.

In answer Eryriaddur lay down upon the stones. "Climb up, then," she said gently. "And hold tight. I can't promise your safety once I reach their den, for I plan to lay waste to it, utterly."

Saoirse set the broken bit of shell carefully amid the other fragments—she didn't think it right to keep it—and scrambled

up Eryriaddur's foreleg. She grasped the curved edge of the dragon's membraned wing, pushing and pulling herself atop her
back. Saoirse reached down and pulled Carreg and the Singer up
as well.

"I don't think you're the last," Saoirse said, suddenly recalling
one of Fadam Fortwin's hearthfire stories. "Go north, to Scotia,
and search out the Beithir. He is told to rule the skies with
thunder and lightning."

"Lightning, you say?" said Eryriaddur thoughtfully. "I just
may. First, let's hunt some trowe. I'm awfully hungry."

T HE FIRST SIGN OF trowes came after a series of dizzying
downward turns. "I can smell the fiends," growled Eryriaddur softly. "I think it best we do not speak after this point. I
wouldn't want any sentinels to alert their fellows."

"Be warned," said Carreg, "the light will be sparse. They
prefer the dim, where intruders find themselves lost before they
even realize the danger."

Saoirse had trouble finding her voice, so she settled for a nod. She desperately wanted to hold her knife, but dared not lose her handhold upon the dragon.

Despite Eryriaddur's bulk, she padded silently through the tunnels, which grew so dark that Saoirse could not even see her vice-like grip around the dragon's spines.

Saoirse spotted her first trowe as they turned a corner to a larger room, lit with small rush-like lights set upon the walls. Three tunnels led off from this room and, squatting just before the middle passageway, sat the trowe—a bent, goblin-like creature with long, pointed ears and gray, pallid skin, picking meat from a freshwater clamshell.

Dozens of empty shells littered the ground at its feet. Its clothes resembled dried mushrooms, held together with spider silk—at least that's what she told herself it looked like. Hopefully not the skin of the coblynau.

It turned its head, revealing two long slits for a nose upon a misshapen face. It sniffed the air, its curled lip exposing sharp teeth made for tearing flesh from bones.

Eryriaddur wasted no time. Before the creature could so much as breathe, she leapt from her place like a great cat upon the trowe, crossing the sizeable distance in a blink. Saoirse hung on for dear life, her body lurching with the movement. With a neat *snap*, Eryriaddur clamped her jaws around the trowe.

The flex of the dragon's throat as she worked to swallow undulated against Saoirse's legs. She gagged, clenching her eyes tight.

Eryriaddur shuddered and spat out a foot. "They taste just as foul as they look," she grumbled.

"We'll take your word for it," said the Singer from behind Saoirse, who didn't sound at all disgusted. In fact, Saoirse thought she was rather enjoying herself.

"Well done," praised Carreg softly. "Where to now?"

The dragon scented the air, her long neck outstretched. She lifted a forepaw and pointed. "One of these," she said. "Or all. We'll have to check each." She lifted a claw to her lips, indicating they must return to silence.

The first tunnel ended in a grotesque larder, where bits of coblyn and other, unidentifiable body parts hung from hooks. The Singer gasped while Carreg moaned. Shovels, pickaxes, and clothes lay in sorted heaps.

"I'm so sorry," whispered Saoirse, but Eryriaddur shushed them all as she backed herself out of the tight space.

The middle tunnel led to a lake, in which Eryriaddur helped herself to six more trowes. She chomped the first they came to right in half while swiping the next from the water's edge with a claw. She crushed it and tossed it aside before she opened her mouth and discharged an inferno of white-hot, liquid fire that splashed and hissed upon the stones. The trowes shriveled to husks in the blink of an eye. It happened so quickly, they hadn't even had a chance to scream. Steam rose from the water from the intense heat. Sweat beaded Saoirse's brow as she lifted a hand to her face. The stench of burning flesh stung her nose and made her eyes water.

Eryriaddur turned with a whoosh of her tail, gouging the earth with her spikes, and slunk silently into the last tunnel.

This path had a gate of sorts, patched together with the shafts of coblyn tools, bones, and roots braided into rope. Eryriaddur pushed past the unguarded gate, breaking it to splinters as if it were nothing more than a sheaf of wheat.

This tunnel descended sharply to the right, the light dimming near-to-nothing. Only the rare, weak rushlight afforded any sight, making Saoirse's fear grow. The air grew impossibly warmer as they came to the end of the tunnel. What could that mean?

She strained her eyes and her ears but heard nothing. The acrid stench of sulfur permeated the air. Eryriaddur huffed. The sudden skuttle of stone on stone erupted in the silence, and the dragon spewed fire. The abrupt brightness burned her eyes; Saoirse cringed away, the silhouette of a handful of melting trowes seared on her retinas. Her stomach turned as they slipped from the dragon's wide back.

Light from their smoldering remains illuminated the space. A dome-like cavern, but too low for Eryriaddur to fit comfortably. Twenty or so paces into the center of the room, the floor fell away, revealing a cliff. Ropes and pullies hung from the ceiling just above. No, not a cliff, but a *hole*, roughly five feet across.

Eryriaddur edged closer, her nose working, her neck outstretched.

"The entrance," whispered the Singer.

The coblynau and Eryriaddur had described the trowes as living in such places, but Saoirse had assumed it a slight upon their character, like calling someone a worm or vermin, creatures drawn to wickedness. Saoirse hadn't realized they meant the term literally. The mines, after all, were nothing *but* a system of hollows to her. This pit, however, could only be described as ominous, a dark maw set in bedrock, fringed with tangled roots and the stench of damp rot and spoiled eggs.

Too small for Eryriaddur's bulk, but large enough for scores of the creatures to crawl out of at once and overwhelm them should they be discovered. How many lived below? Hundreds? Thousands?

Saoirse glanced at her scaled companion. Eryriaddur craned her neck low, examining the hole with a golden eye that flickered like a dying star. Nostrils flaring, she pulled back with a sneer. "I can smell the fiends amid the reek of alkaline. Many of them."

"A warren of shadows down there," whispered Carreg unhelpfully. "I can't see anything."

"There's no way for me go in quietly," said Eryriaddur, hushed. "I could break the rock—melt it, but that could cause you injury. I'd just as soon stick my head down and burn them to char if it wasn't for your man, Lady Traveler."

Calling Edred her "man" made heat bloom on her cheeks, but she said nothing. One doesn't correct a fire-breathing, bone-snapping dragon.

"Can't you simply sing the stones?" Saoirse asked the Singer. "Widen the hole to fit Eryriaddur?"

"There's nothing *simple* about singing stones, Lady. You think I move the mountain at random? There must be a plan in place . . . trusses built. Coblyns to shunt debris. I know nothing of this rock here. Sing the hole bigger," she mocked. "You want the whole floor to collapse, or the ceiling to come down on our heads?"

Carreg, apparently taking pity on Saoirse, placed a calming hand upon the Singer's arm. "There's no telling how vast their den is—how many other tunnels lead into their nest. Even if she could sing a larger opening, the process would alert the devils prematurely. Some might scarper off with the man . . . stuff him in some hole for a tasty meal at a more convenient time—begging your pardon, Lady," he added at Saoirse's grimace.

The singer turned to Saoirse, eyeing her in a most disconcerting way.

"What?" she asked, dreading the answer.

"Dinna you see?" said Carreg. "You'll be needing tae climb down an' get him."

The Singer pressed on, ignoring Saoirse's working mouth, opening and closing like a fish. "We can draw them out once you've got inside. Eryriaddur will make quick work of them, I'd wager, but you must get your friend first."

"We could search for a secondary entrance," offered Eryriaddur kindly.

Saoirse chewed her lip. Finding a new tunnel system could take hours—or days—and Edred had already been in the trowes' clutches for several hours. Knowing the exact amount of time was impossible. "He can't wait any longer," Saoirse said, though her voice wavered.

"So it is decided," Eryriaddur whispered.

The singer cleared her throat. "Very well. If this is the plan, we should leave this hole . . . draw them farther away, where the tunnel is narrower, or where it would be easier to trap them."

Fear gripped Saoirse's heart in an icy fist. They were leaving her for a better position? She placed her hands upon her knees and breathed deeply to little affect. Her heart still hammered in her chest.

"Ye've got yer knife, Lady?" asked Carreg.

Saoirse's fingers fumbled at her belt. She pulled out the blade with a soft hiss of iron on leather. "I—iron. I've heard you don't care for it much."

Both coblynau eyed the blade with little affection.

"It burns us," the Singer informed. "It *will* aid you, but you should take this, as well."

She removed a necklace, lifting it from the folds of her robe. An azure crystal throbbed with soft light at the end of the chain. "Starfire Quartz, infused with a charm. It will hide you for a time—keep the devil's senses dulled to your presence."

"For a time?" she asked, taking the offered talisman.

"Like all magic, it depletes with use. If we wish to remain hidden from our enemies, we must constantly search out and mine the crystals." She lifted the stone resting on Saoirse's breastbone and blew against it. The light within grew brighter. "It is now active. Hide it in your bodice so the light will not be seen."

The Singer took Saoirse's hand in her own and kissed it. "Use your blade well."

Saoirse worked hard to swallow as she shoved the Starfire Quartz under her dress's collar. Warmth spread across her skin where it touched her.

Use her blade well? She only ever used a knife to carve honeycomb, mince beef for pies, or scrape the whiskers from Papa's chin. She'd never struck anything with malice, had never sunk her blade through anything so close to resembling a human.

But she had no choice. Carreg spoke but she could not decipher his words. She nodded absently, as if the action could convince her brain of sudden abilities, perfect for rescuing a man nearly twice her size. It didn't help.

She shuffled to the edge of the hole, black and seemingly endless. What horrors awaited her inside? She understood Dafydd's childish fear of the night—of perceived monsters that lurked in shadow, for she felt them too. An image of the grotesque trowes flashed in her mind and she shivered.

"Tug on the rope three times once you're down," whispered Carreg, who had materialized at her side. His face had gone white to the lips. "We will count to three hundred, then we will announce our presence. With luck, you'll find your friend whole and alive. Find a new way out." His glinting eyes bored into her. "Courage, Lady. You must brave the dark alone. Stay alive."

Courage. Papa had asked the same of her. *Oh, Papa. I'm trying to be brave.* What she wouldn't give to have him here with her. He would lend her strength.

"What of Dafydd?" she asked, her voice trembling. "You'll ensure he's cared for."

"Of course. I will bring him to Áine myself."

Saoirse licked the dryness from her lips. "A—and if I should succeed, how will I find you again?" She balked at the sheer impossibility of her task.

Thankfully Carreg didn't warn her against such an unlikely outcome.

"Climb high. Find a track or—or a cart. Search for any sign of coblynau, and we will find *you*."

She blinked rapidly and wiped her trembling hands on her skirt. "Th—thank you, Carreg."

Saoirse tried very hard not to sniffle. She wiped her eyes on her sleeve and returned her knife to her waist.

Carreg pulled the rope to the edge of the abyss. "For you, mistress."

Chapter Twenty-Three

Into the Pit

T HE PULLEY DIDN'T WHINE as she pulled the rope. Trowes, however deplorable she found them, at least took self-preservation measures seriously. What good would hiding be if their machines gave them away?

The light faded further still as an indistinct shape loomed in front of them. A basket, just large enough to fit one person at a time. And forget it holding Edred—not that they planned coming back this way.

"You'll not start counting until I'm at the bottom," she confirmed, stepping carefully into the woven basket, the rope pulled tight in her grip. She could not see from what it was made, but it did not creak or bend as her weight settled into it.

"No," said Carreg. "We'll await your signal."

Slowly, she lowered the basket, hand under hand; the last of the light disappeared, leaving her in absolute darkness.

Áine, if you can hear me in his pit, I could really use your help.

The heat grew more intense. Small lights flickered below, helping her gauge the length of her descent.

Five feet.

Ten.

Was that the beat of a drum or her own heart?

The tunnel walls ended. She stared at the smooth expanse of the cavity's ceiling and stilled.

Not lanterns below, but fires, illuminating the cavern in a hellish light. They dotted the space, which was certainly as large as her village. She took in the expansive room as quickly as she could.

The sprawling trowe's nest was a chaotic amalgamation of stone huts carved into the rock walls and crude shale structures cobbled together with what appeared to be sinew and bone along a far wall. At least a hundred trowes gathered near the center of these huts. Their wiry forms moved to the rhythmic, primal pounding of a drum. It rattled in her chest. *Boom. Boom. Boom-boom.*

Through the center of the cavern, a black river stretched, like a vein of ore, marked with lines of brilliant shades of orange and angry red. The throbbing colors covered the cracked surface like finger lightning. She followed the river with her eyes, searching for its source, but the cavern held its secrets, ending in a dark so complete she thought perhaps the world ended there.

She dared to descend further into the thick, acrid air, the coarse rope biting into her palms. Sweat beaded her skin. The sound of guttural chants joined the drum. In the center of the trowes, a bier projected into the air. Its blackened wood displayed ominous bone talismans. Empty skull sockets stared up at her.

And set atop the high platform was Edred. Saoirse nearly let loose of the rope in shock and horror, but caught herself at the last second, the basket trembling.

His broad shoulders strained against the ropes, his desperate face red and slick with perspiration. His dark hair clung to his forehead. Relief that he lived shot through her, then dampened. He wouldn't live for long. Clearly, the trowes were up to something. Their behavior reminded her of a celebration of sorts. Or a ritual. One that involved Edred.

She had to move, and fast.

Down, down, paying out rope as quickly as she could, Saoirse did not stop until the basket—made of bones, she realized—juddered against the ground a good distance from the event.

Her hands stung but she ignored the pain and jerked the rope three times in signal, then stepped over the rim of the macabre contrivance. She dashed into the welcome shadow of a craggy stalagmite a few paces away.

She heaved for breath, the heat searing her lungs. How could the trowes live in such a state? Did they have some terrible magic that allowed them to withstand the heat? Or, perhaps, the creatures were simply that unnatural, to enjoy this hellish place.

She dared to peek around the edge of her hiding spot. The surging mass of trowes parted. One trowe, festooned in bone armor and a headdress topped with long gray hair strode through the crowd, holding aloft a sizeable rock. He tossed it into the strange river, which hissed and popped in a riot of fiery splatters.

A few trowes, standing too close, fell victim to the splash and collapsed to the ground, howling in pain. Instead of helping their fellows, those nearest ripped into them, shrieking and fighting each other. Limbs torn asunder, those in possession of the fallen trowe bodies, darted away, growling and snapping, as dogs protecting their food.

Saoirse, swallowing bile, recoiled behind the stone column once more.

Hurry, Eryriaddur. Distract them.

The drum's cadence increased, and the chanting trowes grew louder. She chanced another glance around the rock as the bone basket slowly rose in the murky air.

Thankfully, the trowes' attention belonged solely to the bedecked trowe that had tossed the rock into the molten river. It dipped a long-handled *something* into the fiery depths, which instantly erupted into flames.

Saoirse stared in horror as the trowe brought the torch to the base of the pyre and set it alight. They were going to burn Edred alive! Her friend fought all the harder, squirming and writhing, but his bonds held.

She tensed, her muscles coiling. She had to do something, but what? Flames licked at the legs of the stand. Black smoke snaked upward. The chanting trowes exploded into a frenzy. They squealed and laughed. They danced and cheered as their presumed leader climbed the structure, seemingly unconcerned by the spreading flames.

It pulled from some unseen place a glinting, obsidian blade, decorated with what looked like teeth and hair. The trowes quieted, all eyes eagerly pinned upon Edred and their priest or leader—whatever position it held.

The obsidian-wielding trowe lifted the blade high over his head and spoke in a hissing, guttural tongue. The fire stretched along the beams, reaching higher.

Saoirse pulled back, her mind whirring. She could draw them away—jump out and shout to distract them—but what good would it do either of them? Edred would soon burn and then they would have her, too.

Where was Eryriaddur, anyway?

Just then a sound reached her: the clear, pure tone of the singer's magical tools. Saoirse looked up, just as every other living being in the cavern, to behold that the Stone Singer stood in the basket, held midair. Her voice echoed through the domed structure, clear and beautiful, mingling with the knell of the vibrating metal she held.

The stone hiding Saoirse glowed blue, and then the room erupted into violent chaos. The trowes covered their ears, screeching and hissing as the Singer was lifted higher, higher, then out of sight, back into the hole in the ceiling.

Finally! Relief shot through Saoirse. The trowe on the pyre shouted a command as the last echoes of the Singer's melody faded. The stones' throbbing light withdrew, and the hoard of trowes shot into motion. Impossibly, they climbed the walls like so many spiders, in a swift, undulating wave along the rock to the hole in the ceiling. From Saoirse's vantage, the walls appeared *alive*, moving swift as a mountain stream.

Saoirse could wait no longer. The flames grew violent, crackling and spitting as it ate up the wooden legs of Edred's platform. She did not stop to think that the climbing mass of monsters might notice her movement, nor that some of the trowes lingered behind, one of which still stood atop Edred, staring up at its fellows streaming into the ceiling's hole.

She made her move, her fist clenched tight around her knife. Slipping from the shadows, she ran, her eyes steady upon the pyre. Her bodice clung to her, soaked with sweat, making the fabric pull at her skin as she pumped her arms.

She jumped over a fallen trowe, and when she chanced a look at Edred and his captor once more, her heart seemed to stop altogether. The flames were just under the platform now. Smoke swelled, mostly hiding Edred and the trowe, but she could still see portions of them, peeking through. The trowe lifted his knife above his head, his long-fingered hands fisted around the hilt. Was he going to stab him? More words tumbled from the trowe's mouth.

Saoirse pushed her legs faster, racing, her heart thumping wildly. Thirty feet. Twenty-five.

A roar sounded from above and trowes fell from the hole, some burnt, others bitten in half. Their bodies dropped like stones toward the earth.

Twenty feet.

Fifteen.

Screams erupted, high-pitched and shrill. A trowe sprinted from the right, slamming into her. She hit the ground hard and rolled. Her lungs didn't work. She couldn't pull air. She forced herself upright. The trowe seemed just as dazed. It shook its head and scrambled to its feet. The trowe's blinking eyes narrowed in suspicion in Saoirse's direction.

With a menacing snarl, it crept forward on all four limbs and swiped at the air, just missing her.

Could it not see her? *Of course, the Starfire gem!* She'd forgotten!

It snatched out once more and caught hold of the hem of her skirt. She wrenched it away, but the damage had been done. It had found her. Saoirse rushed to her feet just as the trowe pounced. It dragged her down, climbing over her, chittering nonsense. The creature's hands swept up her body and wrapped spindly, clawed fingers around her throat. She thrust her iron blade into its belly with a grunt.

The attacking trowe fell away, shrieking, holding its wound. She gulped air. More, hot and thick. She forced herself to her knees and found once more, the pyre. The roar of the flames as it consumed the bier filled her ears. Terror gripped her heart. Within seconds, it crumpled, sparks flying. Heat rolled into her.

Her dry throat tore at her outcry. *Edred.*

She stumbled to her feet and lifted a forearm to block the intense heat from searing her eyes. Loping shadows raced past. She swiped at them belatedly, her eyes trained on the inferno that held Edred's body.

Smoke blinded her, but she forced her feet forward, listing to the left to see around the collapsed pillar of spewing fumes. There, beyond the billowing cloud, she saw the obsidian-carrying trowe and two others dragging a listless Edred toward the far wall. All the breath left her with a relieved sigh. They'd pulled him from the podium before it fell. She coughed and staggered toward them. Her lungs burned.

A cacophony of screaming trowes fell from above—the thud of their bodies added to the chaos. Some dropped into the molten river, breaking its crusted surface.

Thud. Another body fell, this one only two feet away, and she jumped, unable to keep her eyes from the grisly, crumpled body. She gagged and stumbled on.

She followed the trowes that dragged Edred into the shadows between a cluster of huts, away from the intense heat. Immediately her exposed skin, tender and stinging from the heat, found relief. Her breath came easier, and her vision cleared as the smoke lessened, just in time for her to see Edred's booted feet disappear behind the rounded hut.

Saoirse pushed forward, her feet barely stirring the ash-strewn ground. Fear made her tense. Her heart thundered in her ears. Huts, offset from one another, cluttered the space. She rounded the curve and could not see where they'd taken him. Had they put Edred in one of the structures?

She slid along the curve of the nearest hut to its entrance, low to the ground and dark. She stooped to peer inside but could see nothing except shadowy outlines of crooked furnishings. She moved to the next dwelling. Trowe voices, low and guttural, told her they still lingered, but where?

She risked a glance around the hut, and her breath caught. The trowes had stopped in a narrow, shaded alley a short distance away, Edred slumped on the ground between them. His ash-matted hair appeared singed. His ruddy, slack face was covered in soot. She stared at his face, his chest. Did he live?

The trowes appeared to be debating what to do with their prize. Despite her inability to understand their speech, their intent rang clear as they pulled knives, gesturing to his limbs. Did they intend to divide him up here to make him easier to carry?

Two of the trowes argued, gesturing toward a dark hollow in the rock. A tunnel? The third trowe—still bedecked in bone armor, barked a command, sharp and clear. He pointed to Edred's middle and one of the trowes drew nearer, knife held at the ready.

Without thought, Saoirse leaped out, her white-knuckled grip on the blade slick in her hands. The trowes barely had time to turn before she fell upon them, a furious cry ripping from her throat. Her weapon flashed in the dim light, plunging into the side of the nearest creature. It hissed in pain, staggering away as dark blood seeped between its spidery fingers. She lost sight of it as it scurried into the dark.

The second trowe reacted faster, drawing a wickedly curved blade from its hip. Its eyes darted from place to place, unable to see her. One of the other trowes fisted a handful of ash and threw it in her direction. The powder coated her face and bodice; it wafted up her nose and stung her eyes.

Saoirse ducked as the black glass of a blade arched toward her. The obsidian whistled past her ear and glanced her shoulder, slicing through fabric and scraping skin.

She gritted her teeth and kicked out. Her foot caught the trowe in the shin and it stumbled backward, throwing off its balance. It fell atop Edred, losing its knife in the process, as the third trowe stalked forward. Its black eyes locked onto the dusty smudge announcing Saoirse's whereabouts; a cruel smile curled upon its warped face.

"Foolish," it rasped in a strange accent. "You die here."

Her heart in her throat, Saoirse gripped the cold iron in her left hand hard enough to hurt. The odds that she survived this had always been low, but if she should die, she would do so defending her friend. She would not let them cut him to pieces.

"You first," she spat.

The fallen trowe stumbled to its feet and, miraculously, Edred groaned, stirring drunkenly.

Hope speared through her heart. *He lives!* The fear that had gripped her loosened its hold marginally. "Edred!"

The third trowe moved fast, as quick as a striking snake. Saoirse wheeled to the side, barely missing its blade. She reset her feet as the second trowe pounced upon Edred, its wide, black teeth clenching around his arm.

Edred came to with a sound halfway between a gasp and a shout, and gripped the gnawing creature around its throat with his forge-strong grip.

The last trowe dove toward her. It caught her around the legs, toppling her. She hit the ground, and all the air from her lungs whooshed out. She had enough presence of mind to slam the cold iron against its head. Again and again, she pummeled the creature, but its bone headdress prevented any real damage. She slashed at its back and side with her knife, crying and muttering half-formed oaths, but her blade merely glanced over its armor.

The creature snarled and climbed her body, its sharp claws digging into her; she fought all the harder. She kicked and thrashed wildly but it held fast.

"I suck marrow from your bones," it promised in its guttural speech, and opened its maw, ready to clamp down on her throat. Apparently, trowes preferred the intimacy of shredding victims apart with their teeth in favor of weapons.

Saoirse couldn't even scream. She pressed the cold iron against the exposed side of its face. Instantly the skin there hissed and smoked. The trowe shrieked and lifted a gnarled hand to the grotesque burn the stone had made in its cheek.

She wasted no time and plunged Edred's iron blade in its neck, swiping hard. Blood poured from the gaping wound, spilling down its front and onto her bodice. She shoved and kicked it away, then scrabbled to her feet.

Gasping and crying, she groped her way to Edred, who now stood on shaky legs. His fist sailed past another trowe—the first she'd knifed, she realized. Blood dripped from its side. It must have circled back, seeing that she and Edred were nearly overcome. The throttled trowe lay on the ground just behind Edred's feet.

Edred favored his left side, hugging his elbow tight against his rib. A rope still clung to his right knee, twining through his legs and around his feet, but the fury burning in his eyes lent her hope like nothing else in the world.

The trowe, apparently realizing he was sandwiched between two determined humans, snarled and scurried away.

CHAPTER TWENTY-FOUR

ESCAPE

"S ERS," HE RASPED, LIMPING toward her, his hand out-stretched.

Her initial relief at seeing him alive fell away into shock and horror. The fore and middle fingers on his right hand were missing, leaving bloodied stumps smeared with ash and muck. *His hammer hand.* He hunched into himself as he stumbled forward, his elbow pressed tight against his side.

Anger mingled with pity as she hurried to him. She caught him as he staggered, his eyes and teeth overbright in his begrimed face. She squeezed him about his shoulders, her eyes burning from smoke and emotion. "Oh, Edred, I came as quickly as I could!" she said, her lips numb. He trembled in her embrace, and her worry for him intensified.

She pulled away, peering at his ribs. "Let me see," she prodded. "What else is wrong?"

He allowed her to see, lifting his elbow and exposing the holes in his shredded, bloody tunic. There, through the slashed fabric, three deep gashes still wept darkly as if claws had raked open his skin. Even in the poor, orange light, the white of his ribs shone through in one terrible gash.

"At least both injuries are on my right," he said in an attempt at bravado. "I can still punch the fiends with my left hand."

Her heart lurched but she forced calm, taking deep breaths. They needed to move and fast. She lifted his left arm and pulled it around her shoulders. "Lean on me. That's it."

"You came," he said, his words thick with emotion, eyeing the fallen trowes around them. "How did you find me?"

"I came from there." She pointed to the distant hole in the high ceiling. Trowes still clung to the walls, but they did not swarm upward into danger. No doubt, between the trap they'd sprung and the demise of their fellows, those left alive scuttled back to the safety of their lair. Screeches filled the gloom, setting her teeth on edge. "Let's go. I don't have time to explain."

Eryriaddur took that moment to roar loudly; it shook her bones, even from so far away. Immediately following, flame burst through the hole above. A handful of trowes fell like tumbling embers from the hearth to crunch into a bloody, blackened heap upon the bedrock.

He gasped, tensing against her side. "What *was* that?"

She craned her neck, searching for an escape. "A dragon," she explained distractedly. The bone basket she'd come in on lay in a shattered bundle upon the floor. Of course she hadn't counted on it as an escape route—no way it would fit two human-sized people—but now that the option had vanished, panic clawed its way up her spine once more. Where were they to go?

"Watch which holes the trowes slink into," she advised. "We need to find an escape."

Standing exposed in the open aisle between the huts certainly wouldn't do them any favors. Already shadows moved at the edges of her vision—more trowes, either drawn by the commotion from some secret place or those escaping the dragon's wrath.

Thankfully, many stopped to feast upon their fallen comrades, dark shapes hunched and scrabbling over still-warm-albeit-broken bodies. Saoirse grimaced, her stomach churning, and tightened her grip on Edred's arm, her voice low and urgent. "Let's get out of the light."

Edred lumbered on, his movements sluggish and clumsy. He leaned heavily on her. Saoirse's muscles ached in protest. "S—Saoirse," he mumbled, his voice hoarse. "Where are we—?"

"Shh." She cast a wary glance behind them. "Later. Just keep moving."

They wove through the narrow gaps between the huts, their path lit by the glow of the pyre and other fires smoldering in the distance until they came to the end of the row. She settled Edred against a hut—sturdier than they looked—and pulled off her underskirt, nearly tripping as it caught on her boot. She tore into the fabric with her teeth, creating a hole, then ripped the skirt into strips, her mind racing all the while, her gaze roving over shadow and rock.

"How did you get here?" she asked. She wrapped a length of torn fabric around his grisly hand, still weeping, with shaking fingers. The material darkened with his blood, and she tied another strip around the missing digits.

Edred winced. "No idea. The first one dragged me through tunnels a long way—or maybe it only felt like a long way since I didn't make it easy on the damned thing. I got away once, and wandered in the tunnels for a time looking for an escape, but, in the dark, they seized me again." She caught sight of his scowl as she tore another strip from her underskirt.

"It took my hammer," he added with no small amount of regret, "had to bite off my fingers to get it away from me. Took the witch's blade, too."

She stilled and leveled him with an apologetic look, guilt swimming through her. Despite Edred's insistence that he come, if she had demanded Edred go back home once he'd found her in the woods, he'd still be whole and hale. What would Edred do now, without the use of his right hand?

"Don't," he said. "Sers, I would do it again. I'd follow you anywhere."

Heat bloomed in her chest and spread to her face. Something stirred within her mind and heart–like a half-remembered song, one she'd sung countless times without thought, but no matter how she strained her mind, the missing lyric stayed just out of reach.

She shook her head, dismissing the sensation. She'd puzzle it out later. "This will likely hurt," she warned and pulled the length of ripped fabric around his wounded side tight. He grunted, the portions of his face angled toward her losing color, but he did not complain further as she knotted the ends.

She peered around the last of the huts, looking for lurking trowes. "What happened next? After your hand?"

"More came, and they carried me—couldn't fight them all." He squinted into the dim, taking in their location. "I can't be sure, but I think they pulled me in through a tunnel over there." He pointed to the black expanse of wall she'd seen from the basket—where darkness pooled, absolute.

"It's hard to know," he said, an apology in his tone. "The way was utterly dark, but I recognize that set of stone pillars there."

In the distance, at the very edge of throbbing firelight, the vague shape of dozens of thin stalagmites jutted into the air, reminding her of the afanc's teeth.

How perfectly ominous.

She followed a handful of scurrying trowes with her gaze, each of them heading in the direction Edred had indicated, and grimaced. Hurling themselves into the dark with trowes terrified her beyond words, but they had little choice.

"Do you think you can wield a weapon left-handed? We need to find you one."

In answer, he looked about them, and seeing a long bone hanging as a talisman from a hut doorway—she didn't want to know to whom it belonged—he shuffled over and yanked it free. He seemed to move a little easier. Perhaps her binding lent him some support, or maybe his smoke-addled brain had finally cleared.

He stepped on one end of the bone and pulled against his booted foot with his good hand, muscles cording along his arm. A sharp breath escaped through his teeth, his jaw tightening as his body tensed against the strain. Sweat broke out upon his brow, but soon, a crack sounded as the bone fragmented. He lifted it and examined the jagged end. Panting, he said, "This will do."

"Come on," she urged, her stomach in her throat. *Now or never.* She dashed out of the relative safety of their hiding place for the shadowed recess closest to the wall. Edred followed in a crouch, his weapon glowing softly in the dim.

A grunting, tearing sound emanated from pitch dark, and her mind readily supplied the image of needle-like teeth tearing flesh from bone. She stopped in her tracks, and Edred nearly bumped into her. He stopped as well, his warmth radiating into her arm.

What she wouldn't do for a candle! But no, candles would likely only aid the trowes in spotting them, yet fumbling, blind, put them at a sore disadvantage. She could barely see her hand in front of her face, and the dark only increased the closer they came to the supposed tunnel exit.

Edred's sharp intake of breath came soft in her ear—a sound of realization—but it alarmed her all the same. She thrust out a hand, fumbling for him. Had something gotten hold of him? Her fingers brushed against his bicep, but he did not struggle or go stiff with pain.

Silent, he communicated his desire for her to hold his weapon by pressing it into her chest. She groped for it, holding it tight, and waited, her heart in her throat.

The rustle of fabric from Edred mingled with the trowes' grunting and gnawing.

His arm grazed hers, and after a brief, yet eternal moment, he pressed something else into her, standing close. His hand—and something warm—bumped against her forearm, then slid down to her hand. She grasped it, learning it with her fingers. Smooth as a river rock, threaded with leather and thin wire, and in the center, a hole. *The hag stone.*

She relinquished Edred's bone weapon and brought the stone to her eye. She peered through and smothered a gasp. Through the hole, the black world changed. The curve of the cavern wall shone blueish white as if sketched in chalk. Obstacles littering the path were bathed in the same strange lines, defining edges and corners.

The trowe, fifteen paces away, sat on its haunches, pulling apart the elbow joint of a fellow, the blood on his chin etched a gruesome white. So, too, the remainder of the distance to the tunnel was painted in gray tones, clear and absolute.

She pulled her knife very carefully so as not to make the slightest sound, but Edred's hand fell upon her shoulder. He squeezed, and she knew he did not mean for her to do the deed. She wanted to protest in favor of his injuries, but his hand already quested for the return of the hag stone, his knuckles skimming her cheek.

She relinquished it to him, growing unnerved as she sensed his leaving. She shivered, eyes wide in the dark.

A scuffle, a snarl, the sound of bone hitting stone, and then the sharp intake of breath—both of surprise and pain. She had to try twice to swallow. Her fingernails bit into her palm.

"It's clear." His whisper seemed as loud as any roar to her mind, and she flinched.

They traded weapons, then, and Saoirse grasped onto Edred's belt like a lifeline as he steered her through the dark, dispatching trowes as they came upon them. One pounced upon her back, screaming a shrill war cry. She staggered backward from its weight and slammed into the wall. Her heart hammered in her ears. The trowe's grip slackened just a fraction, even as it let out a sharp, pained rasp.

She flung herself against the rock once more, hard. A wet crack filled the air and the trowe lost its hold upon her shoulders. She whipped around as it slid to the floor, bone shard swinging, and connected with the side of its face.

She heaved for air, her limbs quaking with the rush of fear.

"Are you hurt?" Edred asked, hastening to her side.

"I'll bide," she said shakily. "Some scratches, but nothing serious."

"We're nearly to the tunnel. Look for yourself."

Edred's calloused hand found hers, and he pressed the stone into it.

Amid the strange, chalked lines of the world, a yawning black tunnel gaped just ahead, like a hole punched through vellum. They stood under a crude arch marked with talismans and sharp etchings. The faintest breeze wafted from the depths of the tunnel, carrying with it the metallic tang of damp earth.

"Ready?" he asked.

Not in the least. The majority of the trowes left alive had speedily disappeared through this tunnel or another unknown to them. "What do you suppose we'll find in there?"

"More trowes, I imagine. Sers," he said, stepping very close indeed. Her heart thudded against her ribs. "No matter what happens, don't let go of me. If we have any chance of getting out alive, it's together."

She couldn't help her small smile. "Like before, when we were children."

"Yes. Like that. Like always."

"We were a good team once," she said, her smile faltering as her heart sagged with an altogether different emotion. Nostalgia? No, not quite. Regret? She frowned. Why had she said such a thing?

"We still are," he said softly.

No doubt, all the terror had addled her brain. She licked dry lips and patted her pocket, ensuring she still possessed the cold iron Edred had given her. "Edred . . . I'm sorry about your hand. I never meant—"

"I know," he interrupted. "I'm sorry about Dafydd and . . . and about my mother. She insisted that I—"

The distant and impossible spatter of rain sounded from the tunnel, growing louder. She strained her ears. Not rain, but the scuttle and scrape of claws on stone.

Edred stiffened beside her, turning his back to her. "Eyes," he said, his large hand clamping down over her wrist. "A lot of them. Saoirse, run!"

CHAPTER TWENTY-FIVE

BROOD NEST

R UNNING IN THE DARK could prove fatal, but they had little choice. The faint glow of the fires, too distant to guide their steps, left them stumbling. Blind, she relied on Edred's modified sight through the hag stone.

They lurched along in stops and starts. She grasped Edred's belt as he led her over rubble, to the far edge of the tunnel. Scree from fallen stalactites littered the ground there, offering a hiding place from the incoming trowes. Edred helped her over a rather large boulder just as the hair-raising sounds of the creature's guttural tongue reached her ears.

Close. Far too close. She held her breath, afraid they would hear every exhalation. Edred pressed the stone into her hand, and she lifted it, her heart hammering.

The strange, skeletal forms of the trowes took shape through the stone. At least a dozen of them exited the wide mouth of the tunnel, some wearing armor, others draped in the same leather strips that hung like rags from their sharp shoulders.

They croaked softly to one another, many sniffing, flat noses raised in the air. Her free hand pressed the Singer's talisman to her skin under her bodice. The cool touch of the crystal told her the magic it held had depleted. No wonder that trowe had attacked her from behind.

Could they smell them? *See* them, despite the dark.

One of the trowes quested the air, its sharp inhale audible even over the pounding of Saoirse's heart. It caught a whiff of something—perhaps the fellow Edred had killed, for it loped off in that direction. Two others followed, chittering in their strange language.

Others stayed, their obsidian eyes gleaming faintly through the hag stone. One turned its head in their direction, peering through the darkness, the sharp planes of its face tilting unnervingly close to their hiding spot.

She ducked behind the stone, her breath catching and pressed the hag stone back into Edred's hand. She kept her grip firm, her fingers tightening around his wrist. *Don't use it. Not now.*

Footsteps grew louder, the crunch of loose stone underfoot unbearably close. She shifted her weight, readying herself to strike if needed. Her knuckles ached with how hard she gripped the bone shard. She slipped her free hand in her skirts, retrieving the iron ore.

Edred prepared himself beside her, the brush of his arm skimming her as he silently readjusted himself as well. Using his left hand might prove awkward, but she knew his strength—trusted him. Together. They'd fight and die together. She swallowed hard, her mouth a desert.

A second trowe joined the first, its guttural voice low and questioning. Saoirse's heart galloped, her muscles coiling.

Suddenly, something swiped the air just above her head. The swift motion stirred the hair atop her head. A clawed hand? A weapon? Clearly, they sensed them, but they could not see them. One of them had apparently taken a literal stab in the dark and come up short.

A distant pebble skittered across the stone, shattering the brittle silence. The sharp clatter drew the looming trowes' attention. Their strange voices drifted away, claws ticking across the stone as they receded into the dark.

Saoirse let out a careful breath, then collapsed against the stone, her chest aching where her heart pounded. Were they really alone? The susurration of Edred's movements told her he intended to find out. She waited, her stomach in knots, for him to dare to expose himself from behind the debris and look through the hag stone.

After anxious seconds, he collapsed beside her. "Something distracted them. We need to move before they realize it wasn't us."

The tension in her shoulders eased slightly. "Lead the way," she said, forcing herself to her feet. Edred rose slowly. His sharp inhale told her his injuries pained him. She couldn't examine his wounds here—couldn't know how much blood he'd lost. His bleeding must have stopped, or the trowes could have simply followed the trail.

They crept from their hiding spot, keeping low and silent. The tunnel stretched before them, narrowing and sloping upward.

As they moved deeper into the cave, Saoirse couldn't shake the feeling of eyes following their every move, and her skin pebbled to life even though the trowes' voices faded behind them. She was growing to despise the dark.

The air turned cooler and heavier as they ascended while the ground beneath them changed from a smooth path to uneven ground. They climbed stairs slick with algae. Treacherous, loose stones spanned the trail. They paused every few steps, straining to hear beyond the echo of their movements and ensure their feet found solid ground.

Some way into the dark, Edred stiffened. She tightened her grip on his belt, her breathing shallow. What? What was it?

A faint clicking noise—more claws?—came from deeper within. Edred leaned close, his lips grazing her ear. "I can't see anything," he whispered, barely audible. "Do you hear that?"

She nodded, afraid to speak, trusting that he understood through his close proximity.

They inched forward, rounding a bend. A faint green glow illuminated the tunnel. The aid of the light allowed them to see that the tunnel split just ahead. One, sloping upward, showed only darkness, the other pulsed with the strange light.

She'd prayed for brightness, but now that it had materialized, her stomach tightened. The unnatural green did not conjure images of leafy treetops or even algae. She'd take a great, scum-skimmed pond any day over this. *This* light smacked of danger and . . . abnormality.

Edred squeezed her hand, offering comfort. It helped, if only a little.

They dared to continue, their footsteps careful, avoiding jagged rocks and uneven terrain. The clicking grew louder. She gulped air.

As they approached, she realized there weren't diverging paths, but an overlook—a natural hole cut into stone, where they looked down upon a cavernous room. The ceiling disappeared into shadow above. Along the far wall, the source of the sickly green glow became clear.

She squinted, taking in the clusters of large, oblong shapes glistening with a viscous sheen. They reminded her of her bees—or of the ant hills that Dafydd loved to destroy—of insect eggs ordered neatly into rows. Something moved under the leathery shell.

Dozens of trowes moved between the rows, their lithe forms silhouetted against the eerie glow. Suddenly, one of the eggs split with a wet squelch, spewing viscous, green goo. The fluid oozed from the shell and spilled over the lip of its little brood cell while nearby trowes hastened over, some of which carried spears and wickedly curved, scythe-like blades.

One pulled the squirming larve from the shell, clicking and chittering, then carried it away, out of sight. The static hum that filled the air wasn't claws, as she'd first suspected, but larva. How many infant trowes were housed in this absurd nursery?

Saoirse pressed herself against the wall, her mind reeling. They far outnumbered the coblyns, who reproduced like humans. She stood on her toes and breathed into Edred's ear. "It's a brood colony. A bleeding nest full of their young."

"I've seen enough. Ready?"

They hastened across the path, past the window into the breeding grounds, and deeper into the dark tunnel. Onward they travelled, until they, unfortunately, came upon the entrance to the room they'd just observed from above. They crouched down, just out of sight.

The green glow illuminated Edred's pallid face. He shook his head, his mouth pulled tight. "I don't remember this," he whispered, his breath on her skin making her shiver. "We can't stay here. We'll have to find another way out."

Disappointment surged through her. They'd have to go back out the way they came and search for another tunnel. Edred, injured and clearly in pain, had started to flag, moving with unusual slowness and hunching over his wounded side.

She eyed her bandage across his middle quickly, taking advantage of the light. Blood spotted the white wrapping, turned black in the green glow. His right hand fared worse. He needed medicine and proper dressing.

"Do you need to rest?" she asked, knowing they could do no such thing. Still, she offered it. She could find a dark space, away from this room for him, and—what? Wait to be discovered? Clearly the trowes searched for them.

Edred didn't speak for a long moment. "I'll be better when I'm out of this hell hole. It looks like there might be another tunnel leading out of there—see it between those two walls full of eggs?"

Saoirse followed his line of sight. She hadn't seen it, distracted by everything else in the cavern, but there, just past two weapon-wielding sentinels and a dozen egg tenders, a dark rift in the rock glared.

Getting across this room unscathed would certainly prove impossible. Only one stone bench, low to the ground at that, offered any cover, and the distance to the fissure in the wall spanned at least twenty feet.

She counted the armed guards in view. Two walked sedately down the center of the room a fair distance away from where she and Edred hid in shadow.

"We could go back the way we came . . . search for another tunnel," she whispered. Going back into the large chamber with the questing trowes they'd only just narrowly escaped filled her with dread, however.

And how long would it take for her and Edred to search for and find the elusive tunnel he'd come through? Did finding it even matter? Any number of pathways could lead them higher, where the coblyns might find them. Even the narrow tunnel across the room could lead to freedom.

One of the guards stopped to inspect a brood cell. As the trowe turned, the glint of light off steel caught her eye. She tensed, her hand wrapping around her friend's forearm. "Edred," she breathed. "Your hammer." How often had she watched him use it? She'd recognize it anywhere.

Anger flashed in his eyes; his lip curled even as his body coiled as if to burst into the room. *He wants it back.*

The corded muscle along his hammer arm twitched under her hand. "Don't," she whispered. "Be smart."

Another squelch sounded and the trowes visible to them gathered around the newest hatchling. Now was as good a time as any. She squeezed his arm, her gaze finding his. "I'll go," she mouthed. "I'm smaller," she added, pantomiming her height to ensure he understood.

An agony of conflicted thoughts played across his face, but she was already sidling against the wall, the cool stone seeping through the thin fabric of her bodice. She dared to peek her head around the edge of the threshold only to dart back immediately.

No less than six trowes stood in close proximity, thankfully each absorbed with the wriggling, clicking hatchling.

Now or never. She sucked in a breath and gathered her courage. She sprinted to the bench and crouched beside it, checking that she hadn't been seen. The wee pew didn't do much to conceal her, and her blood pounded through her veins at a fever pitch.

One of the tenders pulled the greenish, slime-covered larvae from its leathery sac, the armed guards observing with benign interest. Any longer, and they'd resume their pacing. She raced forward, her eyes locked on the black break in the ancient stone. Too tight for her shoulders, she turned sideways as she dove inside and pressed herself against the shadowed wall, her breath thready.

The space widened inside, allowing more freedom of movement. She lifted her bone shard, ready to sink it into anything that materialized, but, against all odds, no guards appeared. No sounds of alarm filled the air.

Her feet hit something solid as she pushed in deeper. Stairs. They led sharply upward; the narrow, well-worn treads fell into obscurity as the green light faded.

Her eyes found Edred—or the vague outline of him. She couldn't see his face clearly, but she reasoned she knew his thoughts. He calculated his odds—plotted how he might retrieve his father's gifted hammer.

Don't. Let them have it.

The guards resumed their pacing. Edred fell further back into the tunnel and she followed suit, sitting uncomfortably, her weapon slipping in her clammy hands. Her muscles ached from constant tension.

Come on, she begged. *Áine, another favor, if you please.*

Edred's chance came after what felt like a very long time. More sounds emanated from the cavernous room of another trowe's birth. Edred inched forward, the lines of his body glaringly, dangerously, visible. He crouched as he ran, not bothering to stop at the bench as she had, and squeezed into the constricted space. He swayed and leaned heavily against the wall, gulping air.

She refrained from shushing him, though the desire to quieten him burned on her tongue. His rasping breaths seemed to announce their location with every exhale. Pale and listing, he stumbled closer and caught his forehead on the low overhang. He sucked in a sharp breath, his teeth clenched against the pain.

Voices from the cavern—footsteps approached.

Saoirse squeezed past Edred, ducking low, and pushed him onto the stairs. She shoved him up with all her might, climbing with him. The ambient light dimmed as one of the guards appeared in the threshold, sniffing.

The world slowed as the trowe's black eyes bored into them upon the stairs. It stepped in, positioning its spear to strike, opening its lipless mouth to rouse its fellows. Without thought, Saoirse reached forward and yanked the shaft of the spear toward herself, pulling the hated creature further into the stairway. Smaller and with the disadvantage of the stair's height, the trowe stumbled forward, grunting with surprise as it fell face-first.

She loosed the spear and, gripping her bone shard in both hands, she plunged it downward in an unstoppable arc, straight into the beast's back. The violent scrape of bone on bone juddered through her hands and reverberated into her arms.

The trowe's blood curdling scream pierced her eardrums.

No way that went unnoticed.

Time resumed its usual pace. Edred's hand fell upon her shoulder, pulling her back. She landed on the stairs with an "oof," as he propelled himself forward, knife in hand. He jerked the iron blade across the still-writhing trowe's throat. Blood poured onto the stone, its cries ending in a wet gurgle.

No doubt slick with blood, Edred fumbled with the knife in his nondominant hand. If fell with a soft clatter onto the stone steps but he did not even pause to pick it up. Instead, he reached for his stolen hammer, pulling it from the dead trowe's body.

He shoved his coveted tool, coated in green-black blood, into his belt.

Suddenly, another guard materialized before them, then a second. A third.

In seconds, dozens of angry, feral faces glared up at them. They couldn't possibly fight them all. Edred leaned down and grasped the fallen spear in his left hand. He whipped the spearpoint around to aim at the throat of the first trowe, which sneered in response.

"Go," Edred growled. "Grab the knife and run, Sers."

No way she was leaving him. Their only advantage lay in the constricted opening, which prevented the trowes from storming all at once. Perhaps, with luck, they could still escape. She crouched, balancing against the wall, and retrieved the knife at Edred's toes, slippery with blood.

Several trowes disappeared through the opposite doorway, shrieking, raising the alarm.

Fear spiked through her. All their screams would bring every trowe down on their heads.

She glanced behind into the dark, but nothing appeared. Yet.

They couldn't stay here. Áine only knew where the stairwell would lead. They could be trapped by incoming monsters descending the stairs at any second.

She tugged on Edred's tunic. "Up, Edred. We'll go together. We can't stay here."

His grip on the spear shaft tightened, his knuckles burning white in the dim. With an explosion of movement, he jammed the spear into the mouth of the closest creature to an outburst of complaint from the shoving, teeming trowes.

The narrow opening kept the horde from attacking them all at once, though some climbed the walls, hissing and clacking their fearsome jaws together. Edred backed up the steps, sticking trowes with the spear. They fell upon the stairs, atop the shoving trowes, writhing and screaming.

Saoirse, knife in hand, reached into the pitch as she climbed; the other fisted around Edred's shirt. She took the stairs as fast as she dared, pulling Edred along. Twice her toes caught the tip of the uneven treads, but the narrow, curved walls of the stairwell kept her from falling. Her shoulder plowed into the rock with a jolt and scrape, but with a frothing flock of monsters at their feet, she barely felt it.

A small rushlight illuminated the cramped space above her head, guiding her feet. Seconds passed; her lungs burned.

As they gained elevation, the top of the curving stairs ended. She slowed, her gaze searching, but no wicked talons nor glittering eyes caught her eye. Her heart lifted in hope.

"We're almost—"

Edred fell. His tunic slipped from her grip as he tumbled down to a volley of squeals and war cries. Edred hit the wall and stopped his plunge, but without the constant use of the spear, the trowes surged, pouncing. He didn't even have time to lift his weapon.

"No!" she screamed, her voice cracking with terror. "Edred!" His broad shoulders and tousled hair disappeared beneath the writhing creatures. Their claws raked at him, tearing fabric and flesh. She barely heard his muffled cry of pain amid the snarls.

She raced down the steps, thrusting her hand into her pocket to fist the cold iron. The uneven stones threatened her balance. Her heartbeat roared in her ears. With a wild, desperate scream to rival the monsters, she plunged her blade into the first creature she reached. It shrieked and crumpled. Another lunged at her, its claws aimed for her throat. She ducked and drove her iron blade upward. A hot spray of blood fanned across her bodice.

"Get off him!" she roared. Slashing and stabbing, her vision blurred with tears and fury. She cleaved through muscle and sinew. A clawed hand grazed her cheek, and she retaliated with a savage thrust, the blade sinking deep.

Blood splattered her face, warm and sickening, but she didn't stop. She moved on instinct, her breath coming in frantic bursts.

A trowe lunged and gripped her arm, its claws scraping her skin as she jerked away. She roared, a wordless scream fueled by anger and panic, slashing at it wildly. She missed, but as the beast lunged for her again, mouth gaping wide in a hair-raising shriek, she chucked the iron straight down its mucous-covered throat. It gaged, taloned fingers scrabbling at its tongue and cheeks.

She kicked it hard in the belly, sending it tumbling, still choking and gasping for air.

Breathing hard, she lifted the knife for the next pouncing monster, but none came. They'd all frozen in place, fear in their black eyes.

The horde atop Edred shifted and shied away. They leaped back down the stairs, whooping and hollering. Their shrieking echoed painfully in her ears.

"Edred, get up!" she sobbed, her voice raw. She grabbed a dead trowe that lay across him by the scruff and hurled it away. She patted Edred's pale face, streaked with blood and dirt. His eyes flickered open and her heart surged with relief.

"You're alive," she gasped, pulling him close. "I thought—"

Edred tensed in her arms. "Saoirse!" he croaked.

She turned her head, following his terrified gaze up the stairs. Two great yellow eyes stared down at them.

A low, rumbling snarl echoed through the stairwell, vibrating the very stone beneath them—too deep, too ancient to belong to anything mortal. Saffron eyes pierced the shadows above, reflecting the faint light like molten gold.

Saoirse froze, every muscle in her body locking tight. Her fingers curled around the useless, insubstantial blade still slick with the blood of trowes. Her lungs burned, and her legs trembled from the battle's toll, but none of it seemed to matter now.

They would die here.

The thought came quietly, like the final note of a dirge. It should have terrified her—should have ripped through her like the claws of the creatures she'd just fought—but instead, a strange calm settled over her. She'd fought for her life and for Edred's, spent every ounce of her strength. And still, this was where it ended.

She almost welcomed it—the exhaustion too great, the constant fear too suffocating. To stop, to rest—even in death—would be a release. She had made it farther than she'd dared hope.

She glanced at Edred, his body limp in her arms. She recognized the acceptance in his eyes, for they mirrored her own thoughts.

Chapter Twenty-Six

Deliverance

C LATTERBY'S VOW SURFACED IN her mind, clear and
unshakable. He'd promised to take Dafydd to Áine.
Promised to return him home to Papa thereafter. Those words
had been her anchor, and now, in the face of inevitability, they
became her solace.

A small price to pay, her death. It would mean her brother
survived, wouldn't it? She'd known this all along—had felt it,
deep in her bones, every step of the way. This quest would take
her life.

Whatever new terror waited above, it shifted, claws scraping
against the floor with the sound of mill stones grinding together.
The snarl deepened, a sound that vibrated through her chest and
into limbs. Her hand trembled on the blade's hilt. Somewhere,
deep in her heart, a spark of defiance flared. Perhaps she had some
fight left in her after all.

"Lady Traveler, are you hurt?" came urgent words from above. A sparkle ignited in the dark. Carreg's face, lined with worry, came into focus as he lifted his burning fingers and set the flame atop the wee candle in his cap.

Relief loosened the tense line of her body. A sound much like a sob escaped her. She trembled uncontrollably. "It's alright," she whispered into Edred's hair, a smile curving her lips. "Friends. They're friends."

With the help of Carreg and the Singer, Edred made it to the top of the stairs. Too battered and exhausted to recoil from meeting a giant, red dragon face to face, he merely stared, wide eyed. They set him against the wall a good distance away where he warily watched their rescue party, his face tight with pain.

Saoirse quickly explained what had transpired since they parted, her voice low and urgent. "They're just below, in a room full of eggs. Or were—they might have scarpered off and abandoned them all now you're here, Eryriaddur." She paused to wrap her arms around herself, shivering. Her teeth chattered. "Just beyond is the great cavern I lowered myself into. I can't—I can't begin to guess how many there are."

Eryriaddur's gleaming eyes burned with fury. The air grew thick with heat and smoke, even though the dragon hadn't yet loosed her fire.

Saoirse's chest tightened as the dragon's growl echoed through the narrow passage.

"I can smell them," snarled the dragon. Her lip curled, exposing more razor-sharp teeth. "I'll grind their bones to dust and burn them to ash."

"The opening is too narrow for you to get in and kill them all," the Singer warned. "Perhaps if we trap them—collapse the tunnels—"

"We can't just let them go," Eryriaddur snapped. "They'll regroup, breed again. This isn't the end unless we make it so."

Saoirse glanced at Edred, slumped against the wall, his face pale and his tunic damp with blood. He clutched at his side, but his eyes met hers, steady despite the pain.

Her heart ached anew at the sight. He'd endured such terrible fright and pain, all on Dafydd's behalf. And her own. If it hadn't been for his concern for her wellbeing, he'd currently be working the forge. He'd have all his fingers. He might take Gwenllian on stroll in the orchard before supper.

A dull ache spread in her chest, savoring of loss and grief, but she didn't understand from where it came.

She moved to his side and the debate around them fell away.

"I'd ask how you're faring, but you look about as good as I feel, and I'm about as good as one of Buttercup's manure piles."

He chuckled weakly then grimaced, his lips going pale. "Don't make me laugh. It hurts."

She shot him an apologetic look as she knelt down beside him. Her hand trembled as she brushed sodden curls from his forehead, smoothing them back with gentle fingers. Cool and clammy—but far too early for fever sickness anyway. She prayed that it stayed that way. She was no healer, but she tended to Dafydd and Papa enough to know the signs.

She bit her lip in concentration, the stubble of his beard raspy against her palm as she cradled his cheek. His eyes appeared glassy but focused. He stared back at her, his hazel eyes nearly black in the dim light.

"I thought I was going to die," he confessed. The whispered words caressed her cheeks. "Those—those *things* were ready to kill me—eat me," he added, disgust pulling his features.

He swallowed, his gaze going slightly unfocused, as if replaying a memory. "After they set me upon that pyre, I thought of you . . . worrying about how you and Dafydd would ever get out. I hoped at the same time . . . hoped that perhaps they'd be satisfied with just me. I'm big, you know," he said absurdly.

Saoirse squeezed his hand, her heart pinching for the terror he must have felt.

"And then I *saw* you," he said, staring at her as if he couldn't account for her. "You were suddenly there, staring down at me from above. Your face . . . it just appeared in the dark out of nowhere. At first, I thought that I was seeing things—that I just *wanted* to see you. A last gift to me . . . before I died."

Saoirse's mouth had gone suddenly dry. Something in her heart stirred, as if waking. It stretched and yawned, but she couldn't account for the sensation. It warmed her all the same.

He continued: "But then you appeared again, amid the huts. You fought like—" he swallowed, searching for words. "Like you were fearless—or mad. Probably a bit of both." He laughed faintly and then winced, a sharp intake of breath cutting him short.

She shook her head. "Not fearless. Inside I—" But she could not find the words for how terror had hollowed her out, had clawed at her with every swing of her blade. Every part of her ached. Tiredness weighted her bones to the stone floor, and suddenly, their circumstances overwhelmed her.

"I want to go home," she confessed, her voice tight. "If only I hadn't fallen asleep that night, or maybe if I had gone to bed with Dafydd, we wouldn't be here now. You wouldn't have followed me into the Wild Wood. You'd still have a working hand and—" Emotion choked her.

"Don't be stupid," chided Edred, though without any real venom. He turned his head, which rested against the stone wall, in her direction. His matted hair clung to his forehead and the pallor of his skin had weakened further, but his eyes shone bright and intense as he met her gaze.

"The witch wove powerful magic against you—against all of us. If she had chosen any other child that night, she would still be free to terrorize people. No one else had guessed to check the faerie hill or would dare pass through such darkness."

She sniffed and looked away. "You did."

"Even I doubted you, and I'm sorry for that. I didn't *want* it to be true. I'm a coward." He lifted his left hand and hooked his finger under her chin, pulling her to face him. "When she chose Dafydd, the witch couldn't have known it would be her undoing; she never could have accounted for your courage—or the fire that burns in you, far brighter than any spell she could weave."

The world swam out of focus as tears gathered in her eyes. The urge to be comforted, to press his hand against her cheek, nearly overwhelmed her. "Look what following me has done to you. Your hand—all your cuts."

"You fought through a swarm of nightmares to get to me," he said, his gaze unwavering. "I owe you my life, Sers. I was a dead man." His voice cracked on the last word, and he cleared his throat, blinking. He paused, the knot in his throat working as he swallowed. "I don't regret following you. Besides, this will all pass, one way or another. We'll go home together, all three of us."

At his soft smile, her heart flipped. His uninjured hand settled over hers, tentative and warm, rough from work.

She dropped her gaze to where he touched her. Why did her pulse leap and her blood race?

"I had to come for you in the trowe den," she answered, her voice tremulous. "I would never leave you to such a cruel fate, but you would have done the same for me, Edred."

"Yes." The word fell between them like a promise. "Yes, I would have."

She smiled and turned her hand under his so that their palms kissed. The friendly gesture morphed into something newly intimate, as if they shared a secret. Whatever confidence whispered between them, however, she could not decipher it.

She could not hold his gaze any longer. The weight of it seemed to pluck at a tightly tangled thread in her breast. She pulled her hand away, busying herself in gingerly lifting the edges of his torn tunic. "I need to tend to your injuries soon. We can't stay here."

As if the red dragon had heard Saoirse, it drew in a long, rattling breath, the dark maroon of her throat glowing bright as a furnace through her scales. The coblynau retreated, coming to stand with Saoirse and Edred.

"She's agreed to collapse the tunnels," Carreg informed them, his expression bright with anticipation. "Containment is paramount. We can figure out a more permanent solution later."

"She intends to kill as many eggs as possible, and I will sing the tunnel closed. Take them back to the burrow, Carreg. Eryriaddur and I have much work to do."

Carreg agreed but seemed reluctant to go. Saoirse, too, stared fixedly at Eryriaddur, unmoving. She would witness this.

Tendrils of sulfuric smoke trailed from Eryriaddur's nostrils, filling the cavity with the scent of brimstone as she positioned herself before the narrow stairway much like a pouncing cat. The scales along her neck brightened further, radiating white-hot. Heat rolled over Saoirse, instantly pulling moisture from her nose and eyes.

Eryriaddur opened her maw, roaring, as molten fire spewed from her mouth into the rock fissure. Liquid fire coated the walls and oozed down the stairs. Saoirse clapped her hands to her ears.

The ancient stone surrounding the opening absorbed the onslaught, changing from dull gray to brilliant orange. The rock beneath Saoirse's feet shivered and she realized that the singer had begun her song. So loud and absorbing was Eryriaddur's vengeance, she hadn't noticed the little coblyn near her, arms held aloft, her mouth working in a song. She couldn't hear her over the tumult.

Carreg tugged on Saoirse's sleeve. Yes, it was time to go. Who knew if the ceiling would hold.

Saoirse helped Edred to his feet. He swayed but steadied himself after a moment's hesitation. Saoirse took his good arm and pulled it around her shoulders. Her stomach erupted into a mass of butterflies at his nearness.

Carreg motioned them toward the darkened edge of the room into the next tunnel, the little candle atop his cap lighting their way.

THE WAY BACK TO the coblyn burrow did not take as long as she'd feared. Carreg led them through a twisting labyrinth of corridors and tunnels until he came upon a system of quarry pullies with great vats attached to them.

"I recognized this abandoned Fire Quartz stope before we found you," explained Carreg as they loaded into three of the quarry buckets—one for each. "The trowes discovered us, and we had to leave it lest they capture us all. Lost a lot of good coblyns here."

Thankfully, the trowes hadn't destroyed the conveyance. Carreg used his magic to lift them up, up, up, a long chimney until they came to horizontal shaft cut through the stone. Saoirse nearly wept with gratitude as a set of parallel tracks came into focus—atop which sat a wheeled cart– not only grateful that they hadn't had to walk the entire way, but Saoirse couldn't wait to see Dafydd again.

They'd helped a rather green Edred into the cart and squeezed in around him. With a bit more magic, Carreg sent them rocketing through the mountain, the rumble loud. "This sound is what frightened us so badly when we first came through the doorway," she shouted to Edred over the noise. He merely nodded, his mouth pressed closed as if he fought the urge to be sick.

They rushed past clear mineral lakes, through countless dim corridors, and over hair-raising crevasses. Coblyns, pickaxes and shovels in hand, stopped to watch as they zoomed by.

At last, the trolley slowed to a stop in a vast, domed chamber that seemed to breathe with the heartbeat of the mountain. Tracks converged from every direction, crisscrossing the cavern floor like veins of silver, their ends meeting at a massive, circular turntable crafted from gleaming steel and stone. The air shimmered faintly, humming with latent magic, as if the mountain itself watched over its industrious inhabitants.

Towering piles of ore and raw gemstones glittered in the flickering light of forge fires that dotted the edges of the chamber. Coblyns bustled about, their movements swift and purposeful, their voices a low murmur of work songs and shouted orders.

In the center of the turntable, an ancient, intricately carved pillar of granite rose, its surface adorned with runes that glowed faintly blue, pulsing in time with the vibrations of the cavern. A series of chutes and ramps radiated outward from the turntable, carrying mined materials deeper into the labyrinthine depths or up toward the burrow.

High above, bridges of rope and stone spanned the chamber, allowing coblyns to move between elevated platforms stacked with tools, supplies, and crates. Glimmering veins of quartz ran through the walls, their light refracting and scattering a rainbow of hues across the bustling scene below.

Carreg hopped out, followed by a less nimble Saoirse, who stumbled and tripped on her skirts. She helped Edred out last, who swayed slightly as he took in the controlled chaos.

Saoirse hesitated, her gaze drawn to the glowing pillar and the steady rhythm it seemed to emit. The coblyns barely acknowledged their arrival, too engrossed in their labors to spare a moment for curiosity.

"Runs on Star Fire Quartz magic," Carreg said, raising his voice to be heard over the noise.

"I can understand your need to mine it," Saoirse said, "but what will you do once you've exhausted its resources?"

Carreg ran a finger under his rather long nose. "It does replenish itself with time, but we must be careful. King Clatterby must have permission to mine any new veins the Singer finds from the summer goddess herself." He drew himself up importantly. "Which is why I'm so often at Herself's court. This way," he said, directing them across several sets of crossing tracks. "This path will take us directly into Clatterby's counting room, where we first met."

Another swift and stomach-dropping ride, and they found themselves rolling through the heart of the burrow. The towering walls with their countless homes carved into the stone seemed to stare down at them.

Coblynau cheered as they entered, chasing after them as the cart drew closer to Clatterby's counting room. Saoirse searched the crowd for Dafydd, who would be heads taller than any of the faeries, but he remained glaringly absent.

"He'll be with his minder, Basalina," said Carreg, no doubt reading the worry in Saoirse's eyes. "I'll send for him as soon as we're out."

She nodded, some of her worry abating. It wouldn't be gone for good, however, until she saw him with her own eyes.

She explained as quickly as she could to Edred about her having to leave Dafydd behind, but in no time at all, they moved through the crowd of excited coblynau and into Clatterby's presence. She recognized Kraglin there, his eyes bright with interest.

Clatterby looked up from where he inspected a gem through the strange glass, one eye magnified so that it filled the lens with his black, glittering pupil.

"You!" he bellowed, his voice echoing off the stone walls. "What have you done? Do you even begin to grasp the chaos you've unleashed?"

Edred shifted beside Saoirse in the cart, his shoulders squaring despite his obvious fatigue.

"We did what we had to do—what should have been done long ago."

Clatterby's hand shot out, pointing a trembling, clawed finger at them. "Had to? *Had to?* You woke the red dragon! The scourge of the mountain! Do you think it will just help you and leave us in peace? Do you think it will show mercy?"

Saoirse slid from the cart, brushing her hands down her skirt to steady herself. "We didn't have a choice," she said, trying to keep her tone calm, though her voice wavered under the weight of his glare. "The trowes had Edred, and we—"

Clatterby cut her off with a sharp laugh, the sound bitter and full of disbelief. "You traded one catastrophe for another! We kept that beast asleep for a purpose! Do you know the cost?"

Kraglin stepped forward, his pickaxe slung over his shoulder, his expression worried.

"Did you have a hand in this, Carreg?" demanded the king.

Carreg hopped from the cart, nimble as a bird. He bowed in apparent humility and stayed there as he spoke, staring at the floor. "Yes, the dragon—Eryriaddur—is awake now. The Singer roused her from sleep."

"I expected reckless stupidity from humans, but you, Carreg? They've doomed us! Dragons do not share. Dragons burn and horde and eat creatures like us!"

Saoirse raised her chin, her temper flaring despite her exhaustion. "Eryriaddur saved us. And the dragon wants to destroy the trowes—she's collapsing their tunnels as we speak with the help of your Singer."

Clatterby's glare didn't waver, but he fell silent for a moment, his jaw working as if chewing over her words.

"If it hadn't been for the dragon," she continued, "we'd be dead—and the trowes would still be free to prey on your people. Eryriaddur is not compassionless. I believe you can come to a peaceable accord."

Clatterby shook his head derisively, still unconvinced. "All you've accomplished is to bring a storm down upon us, girl. If this dragon turns its wrath on us, we'll have no one to blame but you."

Edred stepped forward, his hand brushing against Saoirse's arm as if to steady her—or himself. "You've more than enough treasure here. Barter with her. Riches for protection."

A thick, tense silence pressed in on them, broken only by the distant clang of pickaxes and the rumble of the mountain's heart. Clatterby's scowl deepened, but something in his posture softened, just a fraction.

"Protection? And who will defend us against her? I ought to toss you both into the deepest shaft and be done with it."

"But you won't," Saoirse said. "Because you know as well as I do that Eryriaddur has every right to this mountain and all that you've stolen from her."

Clatterby's lips pressed into a thin line, his dark eyes narrowing as he looked between them.

"Your Majesty," she said softening her tone. "Eryriaddur grieves the loss of her sister, Ishara, and all their offspring. The trowes destroyed their eggs. She may well be the last of her kind. If anyone is in a position for bargaining, it is her. Once her wrath is made complete against the trowes, she will listen."

Clatterby narrowed his eyes at her. "Let's hope you're right, girl. Get back to work!" he barked. Instantly every eavesdropping faerie sprang back to work. Carreg raised stiffly from his bow.

Clatterby whirled around but, thinking better of it, met their gazes once more. "I want you gone. Now. Leave your cream and honey for us at the borderland gate or you *will* feel our wrath.

Saoirse's mouth fell open. "I will do no such thing. The bargain I made stated that if I lived, I would owe you nothing."

Clatterby's face mottled crimson. "Cunning human. Sly girl. You couldn't have survived on your own, so you woke Eryriaddur! You tricked me! You dare to make a fool of me?"

Edred took one step forward, his jaw clenched tight, but a room rang with the pull of knives from all the coblyns and he stopped short.

Carreg and Kraglin alone stood stupidly, their gazes darting between their king and the humans.

"No," said Saoirse to Edred. "Don't." Then to Clatterby: "We'll leave you, but know that your wise Singer also saw the benefit of waking Eryriaddur. You will too, in time. Come, Edred. Let's retrieve Dafydd and go."

Edred nodded stiffly.

"You'll report this to the goddess," Clatterby demanded of Carreg.

The faerie bowed. "As you command. This way," said Carreg softly, his shoulders hunched like a frightened dog. "Quickly now."

As they exited, Saoirse's knees wobbled in a threatening manner. She glanced at Edred, pale yet resolute. "Well," she murmured, "that went about as well as I expected."

Instead of bringing them straight to Dafydd, Carreg directed them down a winding path deep within the coblyn warren, the lantern light flickering off damp stone walls.

The air grew cooler, and a faint earthy aroma filled the corridor as they approached a low doorway framed by woven vines.

Inside, warm golden light illuminated clusters of glowing fungi that clung to the walls and ceiling. Shelves carved directly into the rock held jars of powders, dried herbs, and vials of liquid in every imaginable shade. A male coblyn with a long, braided beard and spectacles perched on his wide nose turned from a stone counter where he crushed something into a paste with a mortar and pestle.

"Carreg," the healer greeted without looking up, his voice gravelly but kind. "I see you've brought trouble."

"Always," Carreg replied, gesturing to Edred. "This one's got wounds that need tending."

The healer finally looked up, his keen eyes scanning Edred. "Sit," he ordered, pointing to a flat stone bench cushioned with moss.

Edred lowered himself onto the bench, his movements stiff and pained. Saoirse hovered beside him, biting her lip as he peeled away the bloodied dressing from his middle. The wound along his ribs cut deep, the edges red and angry, though mercifully not weeping pus.

"Lie back," the healer instructed. "You'll want to keep still for this."

Edred hesitated, his hand bracing his side. "I can manage."

"Lie back," Saoirse said firmly, placing a hand on his shoulder. "You've done enough managing."

With a grimace, he obeyed, wincing as his back met the cool stone.

The healer leaned in, inspecting the wound with a practiced eye. He muttered something under his breath in the coblyn tongue, then turned to his shelves, plucking jars and vials seemingly at random. Saoirse watched as he mixed a thick, greenish salve in a small bowl, the pungent smell of crushed herbs filling the room.

"This will sting," the healer warned, dipping a smooth, narrow stone into the paste and spreading it over Edred's side.

Edred hissed through gritted teeth, his knuckles white as he gripped the edge of the bench. "You weren't lying."

The coblyn didn't reply, instead murmuring a low, melodic chant as his hands worked over the wound. The hairs on Saoirse's arms stood on end as a faint shimmer of light pulsed from the healer's hands. The green paste seemed to sink into Edred's skin, the redness fading slightly before her eyes.

"What is that?" she asked, her voice hushed.

"Old magic," Carreg replied, his tone reverent. "The mountain's gift to us."

The healer moved to Edred's right hand, his brow furrowing as he examined the stubs where two fingers were missing. "I can't restore these," he said bluntly, "but I can ease the pain and help the hand mend properly."

Edred nodded, his face tight. "Do what you can."

The healer prepared another mixture, this one a golden ointment, and applied it to the wounded hand with the same chanting rhythm. Edred's tense expression softened slightly, the lines of pain around his eyes easing.

Finally, the healer stepped back, wiping his hands on a cloth. "Drink this," he said, handing Edred a steaming mug of tea.

"What's in it?" Edred asked warily.

"Things better not to question," the healer replied with a wry smile. "It will dull the pain and help you rest. Mushrooms," he added as Edred hesitated. "Drink, human."

Edred took a cautious sip, grimacing at the taste but he gulped it down. Saoirse sat beside him, her hand lightly brushing his arm. "How do you feel?"

"Tired," he admitted, his voice softer now. "But the pain has eased . . . it's not as sharp."

The healer nodded, satisfied. "You'll heal faster with the salve. Rest as much as you can. And don't move more than necessary."

Edred gave a faint, dry laugh. "I'll try."

"You next," said the healer, offering her a cup of steaming liquid. She gulped it down and warmth spread throughout her body, radiating from where the potion sat in her stomach.

Saoirse met the healer's gaze. "Thank you," she said earnestly.

The coblyn waved her off. "Thank me by refraining from anything foolish. It's not my job to fix stupidity."

Carreg chuckled as the healer shuffled back to his workbench. "Best take the salve. Can you put this in a vessel for us?"

Saoirse smiled faintly, her relief tempered by the knowledge that their journey was far from over.

CHAPTER TWENTY-SEVEN

REUNION

"Sit. Eat," commanded Basalina, Dafydd's tender. "You look about as dim as a dying torch. You too," she added, assessing Saoirse with a keen eye.

Saoirse reluctantly released Dafydd from her embrace and settled him on the stone bench carved into the wall. She sat beside him, her body protesting every movement. Exhaustion weighed her down but with the immediate danger miles behind them, relief softened the ache in her heart. A weight lifted from her shoulders, lightening her mood.

With the bench so close to the ground to accommodate the coblyn's smaller stature, Saoirse's knees rose nearly to her ears. She repressed the inane urge to laugh at her position and pushed her feet out into the center of the room.

Edred groaned as he lowered himself to the ground against the wall opposite. He settled like a battered shield propped against a battlement, stiff and full of holes. Their feet nearly touched, taking up the greater portion of the room.

"Did you have a nice time while I was away?" Saoirse asked Dafydd.

He blinked at her.

Not further harmed, in any case. Saoirse pulled his hand into her lap and sighed.

"He's been no trouble," Basalina said as she offered Edred a bowl of food. "Easy as a falling stone."

Saoirse's stomach growled at the prospect of something hot and watched with interest as Edred lifted the tiny spoon in his awkward left hand.

"What do you Coblyn's eat anyway?" she asked, curious.

"Oh, the usual. Mushrooms, fish, bats, frogs . . . grub worms. Whatever our halls provide us."

Saoirse swallowed convulsively and tried her best not to let her disgust show. Her stomach churned. Perhaps she'd forego food . . . wait until she could catch something in the woods outside of the mine. She couldn't wait to get going. It felt like a month since she'd seen the sun.

Edred sniffed the white and green mush on the end of his utensil and took a tentative bite.

And Edred called *her* brave.

He must have approved, for he eagerly took another heaping mouthful—well, at least as much as he could fit on coblyn table-ware.

Basalina handed Saoirse a bowl of the unknown mush. Nothing writhed inside. No way Edred would eat worms, any-way—no matter how hungry.

The scent wafting up—like lake trout and water weeds—made her mouth water despite her worries. She pinched the too-small spoon between her fingers and dove in. "Better to venture than to rue idle hands," Papa always said.

Not trout, certainly, but fish all the same. She repressed a groan as the food's warmth soothed the hollow ache in her belly. She shoveled more in, too hungry to savor the sensation.

"Slow down or you'll toss it back up," advised Basalina.

Edred, who similarly and rudely shoveled his meal, apolo-gized around a bite. "-orry." Food sprayed from his mouth. He clapped his mouth shut, ears burning red, and wiped his forearm across his whiskered chin.

Saoirse couldn't contain her laughter causing flecks of mush to spatter across her lap.

Dafydd blinked. Edred laughed then winced.

Basalina let out a chuckle herself. "Did you lot knock your heads together?" she asked, amused. "You're half senseless."

Saoirse repressed giggles. "N-no," she sputtered.

Edred sobered first. "No, Fadam, though if I'd hit my head, I might not be in such a sorry state."

"Because he's got a hard head," said Dafydd, deadpan.

DESPITE HAVING A STONE floor for a bed, Saoirse slept hard. Warm and safe, her body had relaxed into slumber as swiftly as a feather settling on still water. Sometime in the night, a sound awoke her, and she blinked open blurry eyes. "I'm here, Little Prince," she muttered as she sat up.

Only she hadn't awoken in her cottage and Dafydd hadn't asked to come sleep with her. She remained—as Edred and Dafydd did—in the wee coblyn house, deep in Monmouth Mine.

Edred snored softly nearby under his cloak, retrieved from the pack he'd lost when the trowe had taken him. Basalina had kept it safe, and a good thing, too. Nothing the coblynau made was large enough cover him. Dafydd's small body no longer lay beside her, offering warmth. She shivered despite the borrowed blankets. He stood in a dark corner, his shirt glowing faintly.

A hum of whispered words floated through the room, too unintelligible to decipher.

"Dafydd, what are you doing up? Who are you talking to?"

He glanced her way then whispered fervently into the shadows. "Saoirse and Papa will. You'll see."

Who did he speak to?

Brow furrowed with concern, Saoirse pushed her to feet and padded closer.

He stood alone.

"You're dreaming, Little Prince," she whispered. "Come lay down by me and get warm again."

Dafydd hesitated but ultimately obeyed. He slid under the covers and stared at the corner.

Saoirse ensured the blankets covered them both and then she settled against him, worry niggling in the back of her mind. Had the witch done something worse somehow? Addled his brains along with stealing his soul?

It doesn't matter what's been done to him. Áine will heal him.

Why, then, did uneasiness persist?

"Tomorrow we will see the sun again," she whispered, determined. "And trees. That should help us both feel more like ourselves, don't you think?"

When Dafydd said nothing, she turned to face him, her gaze tracing his profile, searching for a sign that any part of him lingered.

Dafydd drew in a slow breath. His eyes fluttered closed. "Will Papa be there?" he asked.

Relief and sorrow warred within her. "No, Little Prince, but I'll bring you to him. First, we must follow the trail through the wood to Áine's keep."

"Papa needs help."

Alarm rang through her. She stiffened. "What do you mean, Dafydd?"

"The valley is flooding, and Buttercup is stuck in the mire. We need to help Papa."

Saoirse's mind spun. The fear she'd barely held at bay, rushed into her heart. Lips numb, she asked, "How can you know about the valley, Dafydd?"

He yawned wide and his words slurred together sleepily. "—e told me."

"Who, Dafydd?" she asked, nudging his shoulder. "Who told you?"

But he did not rouse; his chest rose and fell, calm and unworried.

A terrible thought darkened her mind. The witch controlled the afanc. Did she also—somehow—control Dafydd? Is that who he spoke to? Did the spell she'd used on him *connect* them somehow? Had the witch broken free of her bonds? Did she wreak havoc on her village?

Sleep did not come for many hours. Terrible visions of a bellowing, frightened Buttercup and a hobbling Papa falling in the pasture as he endeavored to help their milch cow played in her dreams.

Chapter Twenty-Eight

Summer's Forest

They rose early, but despite Saoirse's poor sleep, she easily shook off her tiredness. Dafydd's restoration spurred her on.

Basalina pressed a mushroom tea upon them and an odd, bitter moss cake Saoirse dared to nibble. Only after one bite, she pocketed it quickly, trying to hide her grimace.

She thanked the coblyn and set some carrots upon the table. While a poor exchange for seeing to their comfort and watching over Dafydd, Saoirse had little else to give. "You eat these," she explained, just in case the faerie didn't know what to do with them.

Basalina lifted one, sniffing. "What a wonderful color," she said. "I'll, uh, stew them with . . . snails?"

Saoirse couldn't wait to get home. Snails, indeed. "Yes, you could do that. I'm sorry I couldn't give you more."

Despite surviving and slipping free of Clatterby's contract, Saoirse vowed to herself to leave honey and cream at the bottom of the long stair for those who'd aided them. Carreg would ensure that Basalina got her share, surely.

Carreg came soon after, accompanied by a wilting Stone Singer, her feet dragging.

"I canna come along," she explained. "There's much to do and King Clatterby is as angry as a trapped bat."

"And what of Eryriaddur?" asked Saoirse, slipping her pack over her shoulder.

"She's agreed to discuss matters with the king," said Carreg, his face tight with worry.

The Singer chuckled. "Dinna tell Clatterby that. He thinks *he* deigned to meet with the dragon." Her tired grin widened. "I'm just glad she decided to clean her teeth beforehand."

Saoirse's stomach turned. "Trowes?"

"Trowes," confirmed the Singer, inclining her head. "Gobbled them up as they fled the collapsing tunnels. She won't need to eat for a month at least, though she asked for a sheep to rid her mouth of their foul taste."

"What's a sheep?" asked Basalina, looking between the Singer and Saoirse for answer.

"Wooly bit of food that walks around on four legs," Edred said at the Singer's shrug. "Tasty, too. Delicious when paired with carrots." He lowered his voice conspiratorially. "If Clatterby is wise, he'll strike a bargain that benefits all parties, and you'll have a more varied fare, easily provided by a dragon."

With the farewells said, they made their way down the winding ramp. As ever, the squeak of ropes in pullies and of wooden carts filled the cavern. Life had a way of continuing, even when desperate circumstances mounted. The wee folk's existence had changed dramatically overnight, yet still the great wheel of life turned on.

Carreg slipped them past Clatterby's counting room, where his angry shouts could be heard over the tumble of stone, and down a winding tunnel. This corridor eventually led to a stone wall with an etched arch upon it—much like the cave entrance. Thankfully, this exit did not require a sacrifice, much to Saoirse's relief.

Two coblynau guards stood at attention as they neared, bedecked in leathery mushroom armor, spears in hand. With a word from Carreg, they opened the gate to a grating of gears and the high-pitched squeak of pulleys.

Instead of melting away, as Áine's gateway had, this stone door rolled aside, exposing dazzling light in increments.

Each of the party squinted, hands held to block the brilliant rays, save for Dafydd, who simply closed his eyes tight, wincing into Saoirse's side. They followed Carreg into the blazing hole of sunshine. Warm air, perfumed with honeysuckle, wafted against her skin.

Simply exiting the dark, close quarters of the mine eased the weight in her chest. She drew in a deep breath, savoring the fresh air.

Her eyes adjusted slowly, but soon, the glittering world of Summer took shape. The spark that had ignited within her upon feeling the warmth of the sun on her face spread to her extremities. Her heart lifted despite the worry that had trailed her since Eva's disappearance.

"One step closer," she told Dafydd, squeezing his hand.

They stood on a narrow mountain path, high above a sea of treetops that rolled like green waves to the horizon. Shafts of sunlight pierced the dense canopy, reflecting in flashes of gold and silver where streams twisted and danced along the forest floor.

In the middle distance, white spires reached for the sky, their facades shimmering opalescent. An intricate, filigree crown topped each pinnacle, winking as if spun from sunlight itself.

"It's as beautiful as I imagined," she said, hungrily taking it all in.

"Spoken like a true Brightlander," Carreg said. "The sun gives us headaches and we dinna care for all the open space . . . the birds—" He sized her up. "Maybe because you're big, this world isn't so dangerous for you as it is for coblynau."

Saoirse bent and placed a comforting hand on the coblyn's bony shoulder. "You're very brave, Carreg. No wonder Clatterby chose you to be an envoy."

His spindly fingers patted her fingers. He shrugged as one sluffing off a deserved compliment. "Well, I do try."

She shared a private grin with Edred, who looked equally relived to be out of the caves. Even Dafydd, face turned to the sky, seemed to relax.

"Who are they?" Edred asked, shielding his eyes. He pointed into the distance. "There, by the water."

Saoirse followed his finger to a silver river winding its way through the foliage. Glimpses of the gleaming surface winked at them from between dark leaves. In a bend of the waterway, she spotted tiny figures, almost too small to see. They moved along the bank, like ants.

"Those'll be the *bendith y mamau*. Nay so beautiful faeries, aye, and mischievous. Dinna take anything they offer. What you perceive as a gift, they take as trade . . . and if you dinna give in return, their playfulness turns to ruthlessness." He gave a lingering look at Dafydd. "Mind ye keep a close watch on him."

"Why?" she asked, warm relief eroding. Of course, she would watch over her brother, but Carreg's warning frightened her.

"Steal children, they do. Swap human children out with a Fetch."

"You mean like a changeling?" Saoirse asked. *Of course* child-stealing faeries roamed the woods.

"Aye, fashioned from mud and sticks along the river." He glanced at Saoirse's expression and added, "Eh, I wouldna worry o'er much. We can avoid them easily enough. Just follow me . . . no wandering off."

She sighed. Could nothing ever be simple?

"I presume we're headed to the castle," said Edred, clearly ready to start moving.

"Aye, that's right. Come on. We'll never get there if we keep standing here, gawping. Should reach there tomorrow, midday, if we dinna dally."

B Y THE TIME THEY made it down the side of the mountain and delved under the towering, reaching limbs of the
ancient forest, the sun had passed its zenith. They stopped to
eat near a bubbling stream, where shafts of golden light bathed
the rocks and the water glittered like so many of Clatterby's
gemstones.

Her tiredness had increased as the day progressed, and she
wanted nothing more than to sit in the shade of the towering
trees. Her back ached and her feet protested every movement,
but poor Dafydd fared even worse. He whimpered with each
step and his confused eyes swam with tears.

"Sit here, Little Prince," she said, settling him upon a fallen
log. "The shade will keep you cool. I'll get you some food."

Just as she made to pull off her bag, a dragonfly as large as
Edred's hand zipped in front of her nose. Eyes crossed, she stared
at its sparkling green wings, shimmering like emerald glass in the
sunlight. It hovered with an uncanny precision, and just as she
reached out to swat it away, the insect stopped mid-air.

"Excuse you," it said, in a voice high-pitched and tinkling, like wind chimes in a storm. Saoirse blinked, startled. Not an insect, then.

The tiny creature's humanoid shape, its body no larger than her thumb, was clad in what appeared to be shimmering blades of grass and dew. It furrowed its sharp, impish face, framed by wild tufts of golden hair. Its large, luminous eyes glinted angrily.

"Oh!" Saoirse pulled her hand back. "I—sorry. I thought you were a—"

"A bug? A *bug?*" the creature squeaked, wings buzzing furiously. It flitted backward, its tiny hands on its hips. "A fine compliment for a noble Ellyllon! Do I *look* like a bug to you?"

Saoirse swallowed her ungracious reply in deference to the furious expression on the creature's face. "My apologies, noble Ellyllon." She curtseyed, casting a glance at Carreg. "I mean no slight, but you *did* fly right into my face."

"I did no such thing!" The creature spluttered, shaking a tiny fist. "*I* came to see what great, lumbering fool had the audacity to sit on my house!" It jabbed a finger toward Dafydd, who didn't seem at all alarmed that a faerie scolded his sister.

"How would *you* like it if a giant sat on *your* house?"

"Enough," said Carreg, waving a dismissive hand. "Clearly an accident. Don't get your wings in a twist."

The wee faerie creature turned on Carreg then and stuck out her tongue.

"Come, Dafydd," said Saoirse. "Let's move you over to that rock." She pulled on a sluggish Dafydd, his face pale, and maneuvered him to safety.

The tiny creature buzzed off in a sharp arc, still muttering to itself about disrespectful ogres, before vanishing into a cluster of wildflowers nearby.

"Always a bit too grand for their wingspans, Ellyllon," muttered Carreg. "Right, we best get some food in you. Especially this lad. Looks a bit wrung out."

Edred inspected the log, apparently unafraid of the wee creature's wrath. "Why, there's a little door cut into the end, here," he said, amazement coloring his tone. "And a window!"

"Here, drink this," said Carreg, plucking an oversized flower from a trumpet vine that clung to a tree. He cradled it in his hands, carrying it as one does a full bowl of soup.

"I see a table inside!" Edred announced. "And a chair!"

"Best move away from there before she comes back," Carreg advised.

Saoirse took the coblyn's offered gift, peering inside the orange petals. Three pollen-coated stamen poked out the end, bobbing and swaying as she pulled it close.

"Nectar," he explained, "and as sweet as honey."

Saoirse stifled a budding sneeze from the pollen dusted stems and helped Dafydd to drink from the open blossom. After one taste, he took it eagerly from her and tipped the flower higher, downing the liquid.

She laughed as he swiped a finger into the would-be cup, scraping out as much as he could before licking it off.

"I take it he likes it," she said.

Carreg handed out more of the summer punch, some for each, then offered a second dose to Dafydd with a wink. "We've got a few miles to go before we'll bed down for the night. This will help."

She had to hold the nodding stamen to the side so they didn't poke up her nose and took a tentative sip. The nectar clung to her tongue, sweet and light, and filled her with a giddy lightness that lifted her flagging spirits.

"Wow," said Edred. "This is far better than Basalina's tea."

"Aye, but take care not to take too much," Carreg warned. "Four or five of these and you'll be as drunk as a tunneling mole in a mushroom patch."

After eating, on they marched, avoiding areas that Carreg proclaimed unsafe due to whatever creatures inhabited it, skirting the river and the trickster fae. No one complained at the wandering path. No way she'd risk Dafydd's second disappearance.

Hours later, the nectar's powers worn thin, Carreg brought them to a clearing, carpeted with moss. "We'll sleep here tonight," he announced. "I'll start a fire for Master Friend's medicine."

She smiled to herself at the faerie's name for Edred, but withholding true names was a precaution she would not forego, even with Carreg.

Saoirse settled Dafydd against a wide beech tree as the sun dipped low, painting the summer kingdom forest in hues of molten gold and rich amber.

Edred insisted on finding limbs to burn for Carreg's tea, grumbling about needing more nectar to sweeten the medicine.

"Eat," she commanded her brother, pushing a limp carrot and a stale piece of bread into his hands. The meal, while not great, proved far better than tough mushrooms and wriggling grubs that Carreg pulled from his pack. The cheese she'd brought had developed a stiff rind and the bread could compete with a stone for density, but still her mouth watered.

"I wonder what Papa is eating tonight," she said, hoping to draw Dafydd out of his stupor. "Beef stew with turnips and fresh brown bread, I'll bet." Her smile faded. Likely he ate just as sparingly as they had. No doubt worried sick over them, Papa likely didn't eat much at all.

She forced her solemn thoughts aside. Hope lived, strong and free. They'd escaped the twisting tunnels of Monmouth, hadn't they? She'd doubted she'd live to ever see the sun again, yet here they sat, amid shafts of light that pierced the thick canopy, highlighting floating motes of pollen that shimmered like mica in a streambed.

Nothing feels so ominous under a blue sky.

Saoirse set aside some food for herself and Edred, wishing she'd brought more, when Carreg wandered off a short distance. He stood before a soaring elm, speaking right to its furrowed bark.

"... well-intentioned humans, if not ill-prepared." And then, inexplicitly, he bowed, his stockinged cap nearly scraping the trunk, and returned to the circle of stones he'd gathered for the fire.

She stared at him as he unloaded his pack, his brow wrinkled.

"All right, Carreg?" she asked.

"Aye." He set a clay pot on the ground with a soft clatter and promptly dropped a satchel of tea leaves and ground mushrooms inside. "Just giving the trees a message for Herself is all. She's been waiting for an answer as to who breached her gate."

A message to Áine? She sat straighter. "Through . . . *trees*?"

"Certainly," Carreg replied, giving her a curious look, as if *she* was the odd one to ask such a question. "Don't tell me trees on yon side of the borderlands don't speak."

Saoirse raised a skeptical brow. "If they do, I've never heard them."

Carreg sputtered. "What—Next, you'll tell me that rivers don't sing and stones don't eavesdrop."

Her mouth fell open. "Be serious, Carreg. Rivers may babble, but they don't *sing*. And stones? They're not even alive."

"Ah, Lady Traveler," he quipped lifting a finger, "perhaps it's not the trees, rivers, or the stones that have ceased speaking—perhaps it's *you* who's never stopped to listen."

She couldn't help her bemusement. "Rocks that eavesdrop?"

"You're telling me that nature in the human world is silent?" Carreg pressed.

"Not exactly," she answered, considering. "The trees rustle in the wind, but that's hardly language."

Carreg lifted a brow. "What of your beasts? You do have them, I suppose?"

She nodded. "Yes, we keep cattle and—" she trailed off. Buttercup told her quite plainly when she wasn't in the mood to be taken from the warmth of the barn or when she needed milking. And she spoke to her bees, didn't she? And they to her, in their way.

Perhaps Carreg spoke truth after all, and she just hadn't paid attention.

As if on cue, the elm Carreg had spoken to swayed, its branches creaking, leaves whispering. The next tree followed suit.

"Ah," he said, his eyes twinkling. He tapped his long nose. "So, I'm right. Are all humans so dismissive of nature?"

"Well . . . yes, I rather think we are." She eyed the nearest moss-covered boulder with interest. Why would it be interested in anything she had to say? Then again, it didn't have anything else to do. Why not listen in?

"Pity." He frowned at her for a long moment before announcing, "Let your time here be a lesson to you, then. Tea coming shortly."

With a snap of his fingers, a flame erupted to life on the end of his thumb. He touched it to the twigs and dead leaves that Edred had collected for them, scattered in the circle of stones.

Edred—slow but determined—still picked through fallen limbs a good twenty paces away.

He fared much better after the coblyn healer saw to his injuries, but despite his new bandages and the hot, medicinal tea they poured into him, he could not hide his pain from her. He held his injured hand close to his middle and winced whenever he brushed it against something.

His hammer hung uselessly from his belt, glinting in the setting sun. The ache in her heart sharpened at the sight. Despite apologizing for what role she'd played in his current trou-

bles—and his subsequent denial that she held any responsibili-
ty—guilt still weighed her down.

The desire to insist he rest pricked at her, but she knew him
well enough. He *wanted* to work—to prove his usefulness, either
to himself or to her. *Stupid man*, she thought with fond exasperation. She watched him work as she pulled more food from her
bag, a hidden corner in her heart swelling with affection for her
friend.

She ensured Dafydd still nibbled on the fare and moved toward Edred. He struggled to lift a rather large tree limb; his face
red, he swore under his breath.

"Good thing your mother didn't hear that," she teased.

He barked a laugh, chasing away some of her melancholy
thoughts. "Where do you think I learned to swear in the first
place?"

She grinned. "And then you taught them to me. I've always
been able to count on you for such things." She picked up the
opposite end of the limb.

Edred's answering smirk faded. "Saoirse, I can get it."

"I'm sure you can, but you're still recovering. Next, I suppose
you'll claim you're ready to take on a dragon bare-handed."

"That depends—how big is the dragon?"

She rolled her eyes. "Bigger than you, I'd wager." Her middle
fluttered nonsensically. That nectar must have muddled with her
system. "I've nothing else to do and I like to feel useful, too, you
know."

"That obvious, am I?"

She shrugged, her gaze lingering on the strong line of his brow and the slope of his nose. His hazel eyes looked more green than brown in this light. When had he grown so handsome? She forced her gaze elsewhere. "Well, I've known you a long time," she said. Her cheeks warmed uncomfortably, and she pressed a hand to her face, feeling the heat in her skin. What was wrong with her?

"Yes," he answered, his tone as soft as his gaze. "That's true."

Something in his look made her blood race. "Don't forget, I've seen you lose at knucklebones—badly." There, the teasing dampened the sensation of unexplained exposure, for she suddenly felt as a hare under a hawk's shadow. What she wanted to hide, she could not say. "Even young Dafydd handles losing better than you, and you're a grown man."

He mocked an affronted look. "How dare you. I let him win."

Saoirse tugged on the branch they shared, ready to be serious. "Look, I know that this—" she said, gesturing with her chin to his bandaged hand "—worries you, and for good reason, but it won't stop you."

Something flashed across his face—a mixture of vulnerability and resolve—but it died quickly, and silence stretched between them, the only sound that of their feet shuffling upon the grass. Finally, he said, "I'm not so sure it matters any longer."

"What do you mean?"

"Sers, what did you give up? At Áine's door."

She frowned in thought. Somewhere in the back of her mind, a shadow stirred—a memory veiled in fog, faint and elusive.

"Funny, I—I can't seem to recall. How strange. Do you remember your sacrifice?"

His gaze bored into her, expectant. "Yes," he said quietly. "I remember."

"Then why can't I?"

"I don't know," he said, "but you seem different. You've changed."

She raised her brow. "I should think we're both altered after what we endured in that mine."

He shook his head. "No. With *me*, I mean. You . . . touch me more. Tease me." His ears tinged a slight shade of pink. "You stopped doing that . . . before."

She blinked at him in confusion. Had she? Her mind raced back, sifting through moments shared and lost, trying to pinpoint when that might have been true, but came up short. "I don't remember." That troubled her. Was her mind going, like Dafydd's? Would she be talking to the wall in the dead of night soon, too?

"I'm sure it's fine, Saoirse. Forget I said anything."

She wasn't so sure. "What did you give up, Edred?"

"Tea's ready!" chimed Carreg. "Drink it up, healer's orders. We can't have you falling ill." He barked out a creaky laugh, looking Edred up and down. "Can you imagine trying to carry that behemoth into Summer Court?"

Edred heaved a sigh. "I'll tell you later. Come on."

As dusk deepened, the forest around them shifted. The ancient trees seemed to lean in closer, their branches heavy with soft whispers, their leaves drooping as if they, too, had grown weary.

Carreg found the stoniest bit of ground in close vicinity and settled himself upon it, his cloak draped over his body. "Sleep well," he said with a yawn. He turned over, his back to the dying fire, and lay his head atop a mossy rock. Within moments, his soft snores filled the silence.

She steered Dafydd closer to the fire and sat with him upon a fallen log. He stared, unblinking at the fire. She put her arm around him and kissed his curls. "We'll set you to rights in no time, Little Prince."

Edred, sitting adjacent on a rock, rummaged, then with a huff of impatience, upended it. A myriad of objects tumbled out. Some rolled close to the fire, and she lunged to gather them.

Edred held out a brown bundle that she recognized as his cloak. "You and Dafydd can use this," he said, gruff. "It's bigger than yours and can cover you both."

She took it, her gaze lingering on the tight lines of his face. She wanted to fix his hurt, wished she could take his place. Perhaps Áine would restore him as well as Dafydd. The thought lent her hope.

"That's awfully kind of you, Edred. Here, take mine," she said, fishing through her own bag. "It'll likely be too short but it's better than nothing. And, if we . . . if we sleep close, you won't get cold." A sudden shyness rose up in her, heat inching up her neck. She found she couldn't look at him. Why should sleeping close in the summer kingdom's forest embarrass her?

"Let's hope the summer kingdom lives up to its name and we won't get chilled." He took her cloak all the same, muttering his thanks.

"I set out some food for us to share," she murmured so as not to disturb Carreg. "Just there, on that log."

"I've brought some food from home, too." He lifted the small, lumpy sack he'd dropped when the trowe had snatched him and set it in his lap. The drawstring proved too difficult to undo one handed. His impatience and frustration grew, a palpable reaction that knotted her belly.

She plucked the offending bag from his lap and ignored his sour attitude. "I hope it's your mother's fruit bread," she said airily.

She found heavily bruised pears and a few small summer apples nestled amid crumbling oatcakes and dried venison. Underneath, a package caught her eye, wrapped neatly in one of her beeswax-coated cloths.

She paused, the sight unexpectedly striking her. She'd gifted him that cloth two years ago, made in a rare, quiet moment at home. She'd used the last dregs of her beeswax to coat it, carefully drawing her initials and a little bee in one corner with charcoal before sealing the design under the wax.

"I use it every day," he said, his gaze steady on her face. "I keep it away from the heat of the forge . . . Da is jealous," he added with a half shrug. "He wants one to keep his bread from going stale at the shop, too, but is too polite to ask."

She unfolded the parcel, exposing dark, crusty bread and traced her finger over the smudged lines of her drawing, marveling at how time and use had softened but not erased her mark. Something stirred within her—soft and insistent, not unlike the hum of a bee. The strange twinge tightened in her chest, unfamiliar and unwelcome. What was happening to her?

She glanced up at him, her hand stilling on the cloth. His unguarded expression, warm with a kind of quiet gratitude, made her heart skip. "You teased me about drawing bees on everything."

Dafydd reached into her lap and chose a bruised golden-green pear for himself. His huge bite sent dribbles of juice down his chin. At least he still had an appetite. The sight warmed her so thoroughly that she clutched him to her. Tears sprang to her eyes, and she blinked them away.

Exhaustion made her weepy, that was all. She simply needed this ordeal to be done, then she would be back to her usual self.

Edred took a pear as well. "A man after my own heart," he said, lifting it as in salute, and took his own bite.

That night, Saoirse stared at the heavens long after everyone else had fallen asleep. Though the sky was beautiful and awash with silver stars, she missed her own constellations back in Cymru.

"Soon, Papa," she whispered into the dark. "We'll come home soon."

Chapter Twenty-Nine

Land of Light

THE NEXT MORNING CARREG led them from the forest. They waded through vast fields of swaying grass. Horses lifted their heads, their curious, intelligent eyes watching them as they passed. The sun beat down upon them, and sweat beaded upon Saoirse's brow while Carreg grimaced continually about the brightness of the world, but before long, they arrived.

Áine's castle, white and resplendent with diamond-paned windows and cluttered with climbing roses of every color, sat in the middle of a sprawling meadow. The turf was cropped short here, softer than the finest rug and cushioned their every step. Languid bees bobbed by, the deep buzz of their wings welcoming. A tree—Saoirse did a double take—*strolled* from a glittering, domed building on the right side of the castle. At one point, the trunk had split into legs, complete with knees that bent. Two limbs served as arms, but the rest of the branches speared skyward, leaves swaying.

"A Greenman," Carreg explained at Saoirse's open-mouthed stare. "Servants of Áine. See, he comes this way to greet us."

The Greenman lifted a thick arm in acknowledgement, its leafy fingers splayed. "We've been waiting for you, Carreg," it called out, its voice deep and as comforting as a drowsy summer day.

"Can all trees walk and talk like this Greenman?" she asked, her voice lowered so it didn't carry, lest she offend the creature.

"Nah, nah," said Carreg, waving back. "Greenmen are guardians o' the forests. Keep and tend trees, don't they? Hush now; let me do the talking."

The tree stopped before them and pressed its lush hands together in some semblance of a bow. "Master Coblyn, Herself received your message and requests an audience in her hall."

"Thank you, Brakenholt." Caregg gestured around the group. "This is Lady Traveler, Brother, and Friend."

The Greenman's strange, green-gold eyes lingered upon them, its oakish face unreadable. "Welcome to Summer Court, Land of Light. The Fair One wishes to meet you. Follow me into the atrium."

Saoirse stared at the building, a marvel of construction—not of stone or timber, but of glass. It shimmered like a captured sunrise, the light shifting and refracting in dazzling colors. Wide sandstone stairs led up to the entrance, radiating warmth, as if endlessly kissed by the sun. Towering, carved pillars framed arched doorways along the curved surface, each draped in gauzy white curtains that billowed languidly in the golden light.

Inside, trees sprouted from the floor, their roots twining seamlessly with the stone—nature and architecture sculpted as one. Their branches stretched skyward toward the crystal ceiling, heavy with fruit that gleamed like polished gems—unknown plump red fruit, golden pears, and dusky figs. Petals drifted lazily through the air, their perfume thick and heady, mingling with the warm, honeyed scent of the breeze.

Somewhere, water flowed, mingling with the chirps of birdsong. A winding path of smooth, river stone led through the vast chamber. Fireflies danced in slow, somnolent patterns at the base of trees and in the ferns, their glow adding to the golden haze of eternal summer. At the heart of it all, where the path ended, a throne appeared upon a dais, woven from vines and gilded leaves. Red and orange poppies bloomed in brilliant color all around the occupant: the summer goddess herself, Áine.

As Saoirse neared the goddess, she couldn't help staring. Áine had imperious blue eyes, bright as the sky, and her bronzed skin shown as if the sun radiated from within her. Wild, wheat-toned hair cascaded around her shoulders, crowned with a spray of golden gorse heather. Her rich green gown flowed around her body like delicate mist. While radiantly beautiful and commanding, the summer goddess's expression did not evoke warmth.

Saoirse swallowed hard as Carreg led them on, stopping a few feet from the bottom step of the throne's platform. Stupid with amazement, Saoirse caught sight of Edred's open-mouthed expression and promptly closed her own. She probably looked like one of the trout Papa brought home from the river.

Áine stared down at them, her gaze lingering on Saoirse for a long moment. She squirmed under the goddess's full attention, and only when her interest moved to Edred did Saoirse's breathing come easier. Edred bowed at the waist with only a slight twinge–his ribs, while much repaired, apparently still pained him. Dafydd, of course, showed the goddess no such deference. He blinked with benign detachment as he had ever since the witch had stolen a part of him away.

The goddess narrowed her eyes on her brother. *Surely the goddess could see his ailment and not find fault with him.*

Saoirse's hands grew clammy as she glanced at Dafydd, silently urging him to, just this once, acknowledge those around him. But before long, Aine's gaze drifted away to land squarely on the emissary.

"At last," the goddess said, her voice as rich and full as summer wine. "You've kept me in much suspense, Master Coblyn. How is it you've gained four souls under your care? Rise and speak."

Saoirse's mind stuttered and caught. *Four souls?*

Carreg for his part, looked just as confused. "Three, Fair One.

Áine waved an errant hand, a small smile playing about her lips. "Oh, that's right. Pay me no mind."

Carreg squared his shoulders and drew in a long breath, his chest expanding importantly. "Much 'as happened, Fair One. We beg yer pardon; we came as soon as we might."

"Of course," Áine said patiently. She folded her elegant hands in her lap and raised expectant brows. "It's not like you to neglect your responsibilities. Please, go on."

The coblyn's gaze darted to Saoirse and back. "Er . . . bit of a funny story, really. I'm sure you'll recall Eryriaddur. Great, hulking dragon that . . . that lived under the mountain. *Lives*, rather," he corrected.

The goddess's other brow lifted in apparent surprise. But wouldn't she know of everything that occurred in her kingdom? "What's this? Brackenholt has said nothing of Eryiaddur's waking."

A rustling from just behind Saoirse startled her. With all the splendor around her, Saoirse had quite forgotten about the servant, Brackenholt, and no wonder. He blended thoroughly in with all the other vegetation.

"The trees have sent no such message, My Lady," said the Greenman.

"Eryiaddur hasna left the mountain, Fair One," Carreg supplied. He fiddled with his hat, not meeting Aine's eye.

"That would explain the tree's ignorance, but what of the stones? Why do they keep silent?"

Saoirse's mouth dropped open, despite Carreg's earlier instruction on the way of the forests in the summer kingdom. Trees and rocks communicated—sent messages to Aine. *Amazing.*

"Perhaps they, too, wished to see a wrong made right," Carreg offered. "Her vengeance is just, after all."

"Mmm," mused the goddess. "But who convinced Clatterby to awaken the dragon? I never thought such a day would come."

Saoirse's cheeks warmed uncomfortably, even as her mind whirred. If the goddess agreed that the trowes had sinned against the dragons, why hadn't she done anything to stop them in the first place?

"Er, weel . . . the Stone Singer did the heavy lifting there, o' course," Carreg said non-committedly, pulling Saoirse from her thoughts. "I told her not to. I said, 'Singer, what would the Fair One say? What would Clatterby say?'"

Summer laughed, clapping her hands together in apparent delight. "You mean to say that King Clatterby didn't even know? Oh, I'll bet he's in a *rage!*"

Saoirse smiled tentatively, catching Edred's relieved expression. Áine wouldn't fault them for waking the dragon, but even with one less worry nagging her, Saoirse's uneasiness did not abate. What of Dafydd? What of the witch wreaking havoc on Summer's very doorstep?

As Carreg explained about Ishara's unfortunate death, of Eryriaddur's hunt for trowes in the depths of the mountain, Saoirse's rescue of Edred, and the Singer's help in collapsing the tunnels to entrap their shared adversary, the weight of the goddess's stare bore down on her. With the radiance of Summer focused so completely upon Saoirse, she wanted to wither and shrink like a flower scorched beneath an unrelenting sun.

"You came through my doorway to awaken the fire drakaina. Why?" she asked.

Saoirse licked her parched lips. "Well, not exactly. Awakening the dragon came about after the trowes stole Edred. He came in after me, you see. He didn't want me to go alone," she added hastily, as if this might lend Edred some grace should Aine disapprove of them entering Faerie in the first place.

"Yes, I'm aware. The stones told me as much."

Saoirse's eyes widened. "Oh . . . well, yes, you mentioned they–they speak to you."

"Communicate," Aine corrected. "They do not speak as you and I do, but let's stick to the point. Why did you come through the mine gate?"

Right. "My brother has been harmed by dark magic." Saoirse gripped Dafydd's cool hand and urged him closer. "You might have noticed he's not quite usual for a boy. He's—he's had a bit of himself stolen away by a witch. I knew the village healer could do nothing for him, and even the witch goaded me that nothing save you or . . . or someone named Agatha could save him."

Áine sat up straighter in her chair, a dark glint in her eye. "Where is this witch now?"

"We left her tied up in the afanc's cave," Saoirse explained.

Áine's expression hardened. "And just what, exactly, has been done to my door's guardian? I wondered how you'd gotten past him. He isn't to let humans near my gate."

Saoirse fumbled for words. "I don't know how to explain it. Sh-she spoke to the creature—the afanc—and it obeyed."

Aine exchanged a dark look with her Greenman servant, Brackenholt. "She's bound, you say?" the goddess confirmed.

"Yes. She was when we left her," Edred said, his voice raspy. He cleared his throat. "I tied her up and left her weeping there, with the sleeping afanc guarding the cave's exit . . . and a little girl. She'd died some days ago. Maybe even a week or more."

"This is troubling news, indeed," whispered Áine, her mind working behind her eyes. Silence filled the room, save for the odd twitter of a bird or the soft susurration of leaves. "This explains your presence, of course," said the goddess, staring at a spot to the right of Saoirse.

She followed Áine's gaze, but the space stood empty.

"Speak, child. I would hear your side of things," the goddess commanded. "Who are you, and why do you linger where you don't belong?"

Saoirse's confusion grew by the second. What could the goddess be listening to? For she *was* listening. The intensity on her face told Saoirse as much. Time stretched slowly as all of Saoirse's concerns replayed in her mind. What of Papa? Had anyone helped him feed and milk cows? Had the witch escaped? She might have. Dafydd had said something about Papa and the beasts being burdened with rain, not that she could understand how he might know such a thing.

"This is vexing news," the goddess said, finally. She stood and paced along the top of her dais, her green gown whispering over the stones. "Why have you not passed through the black gates of Annwn?"

Saoirse froze. Aine spoke of the Underworld. Was she communicating somehow, with Dafydd's bit of soul now nestled in her bag? Did the goddess wish to send Dafydd *on*?

She followed the goddess's line of sight, to where it rested not on her brother, but just beside him. Dafydd, as if following Saoirse's thoughts, turned his head to stare at an invisible spot just to his right. "What is it?" she whispered hoarsely, her voice cracking. "What do you see?"

No answer came from Dafydd, only the quiet rise and fall of his breath.

With a sigh, Áine sat primly on her throne. Her cerulean eyes softened with a flicker of something Saoirse could only describe as pity. When the goddess spoke again, her words rippled with finality. "How very foolish, but you are not to blame, child. Do not fear. I know just the thing. Brackenholt," Áine called, her voice cracking like a whip.

The Greenman emerged from the shadows of a towering tree, his wizened frame creaking. "Fair One?"

She gave him a meaningful look. "Send a message to Annwn. I've located one of Arawn's missing subjects."

The Greenman inclined his head. "Of course, Fair One."

Saoirse didn't bother tracking the servant's exit. Her stomach knotted as she dropped Dafydd's hand and sloughed off her bag. She fished out the clay jar and clutched it to her middle. Warmth radiated from it, pulsing heat into her hands. "But—Dafydd . . . he lives still. If you would only restore him, he'd have no need to go to Annwn."

Áine's piercing gaze landed on her. "Hush, now. Do not assume you can command here as you did in Monmouth Mine. I am no simple king."

Saoirse bit back her words, her throat tight. The urge to argue, to demand answers, to weep, bubbled up inside her, but the weight of Áine's authority pinned her in place. She could take Dafydd and leave. As the witch said, even half a soul was better than none, but what sort of life could Dafydd have?

"Soon all will be righted. Let us discuss other matters while we await Death's response."

As Carreg explained about the dragon and the trowes, desperation filled Saoirse. She did not wish to speak of anything but Dafydd. She barely registered Carreg's patter, detailing the plans for his king to meet with Eryriaddur and his desire for each to come to a satisfactory agreement.

She reached a toe out to nudged Edred's boot with hers. "What should I do?" she whispered. Dafydd couldn't go to Annwn. Not after all they'd suffered and sacrificed to save him.

Edred's uncertain gaze flitted over her face, his eyes searching. The pity in his eyes told her he had no answer.

Desperate, Saoirse gathered her courage and stepped forward. Her boots touched the bottommost step of the goddess's dais.

"We need your help," blurted Saoirse, interrupting Carreg. She dared to step closer, her legs trembling beneath the weight of hope and panic. "Not only has this witch harmed my brother, but the trowes—under the mountain, they took two of Edred's fingers and injured his side. Help us, I beg of you. *Please*. Do not send Dafydd away." She offered the jar to the goddess, lifting it high.

Take it. Fix him.

Aine's sharp gaze pinned Saoirse to the spot. "Gods do not insert themselves in the lives of their subjects so wantonly. Doing so would go against life's very purpose. We give aid where we can, and do our best to influence, but we never *choose* a course of action for *any* creature. In the case of this man," she said, gesturing to Edred, "he *chose* to enter Faerie and, as a consequence, came upon a bloodthirsty creature. I cannot rightfully restore him."

As Saoirse's heartbeat thudded powerfully in her ears, Dafydd sidled closer to her, either unable to remain far from his bit of soul, or for comradery's sake. Edred, too, stood resolute and pale on her left side, and her heart swelled with affection for him. He refused to abandon her, even at his own peril. He always had.

"And what of you?" Áine asked Edred, her voice quiet. "A man of courage and folly, equal in measure. What do you *demand* from your goddess?"

Edred's shoulders lifted, and his chest expanded as he drew in a breath. "I make no demands, but I request, as does Saoirse, for Dafydd's healing. That is why I entered the mine."

Saoirse lowered her arms, too tired to hold the jar aloft any longer. Carreg had been right about Áine. He'd warned her, but she'd held out hope that the goddess would continue to bless her. "I—I thought that you cared. Even the dragon said you favored me, but clearly, I was wrong."

The goddess raised an imperious brow. "You prayed for a way to help your family, and I sent you bees. You asked for help in finding your brother and I used the same blessing to guide you through the Wild Wood. You asked me to help you in the Trowe's pit—pleaded for Edred to safely cross the trowe hatching grounds—and here you, all three, stand." Her look turned thunderous. "And now you question my providence? You dare to stand before me and claim I failed to show you the proper amount of *concern*?"

Saoirse's knees wobbled beneath the weight of the goddess's gaze. Heat flushed her cheeks, shame rising swift and sharp. "Forgive me," she whispered, bowing her head. "I'm so grateful for your blessings. All of them. I didn't mean insolence, it's only that . . . I've traveled so far and endured much." She fell to her knees, desperation coloring her voice. "I have little aside from the breath in my lungs, but I give it willingly in payment. I cannot let Dafydd die. T-take my soul in exchange for his."

CHAPTER THIRTY

SOUL SCARS

"Saoirse, no," hissed Edred, his voice low and fierce. His hand gripped her elbow. The warmth of him rolled across her skin as he leaned into her. "Don't do this."

Áine lifted an interested brow. "A noble offer, to be sure, but perhaps you haven't thought through the consequences of such an action. Your brother would live his days with the weight of your death, knowing you sacrificed yourself for him—a heavy burden for one so young."

Fear and uncertainty knotted in Saoirse's throat and wetted her eyes. She searched for words. Either way Dafydd lost. Which course would prove less painful for him? "Not if—not if you helped him to forget me." Even as she spoke, her heart squeezed, but she could not regret her choice. Not if it saved her brother from guilt or loss.

The goddess raised her brow. "And what of him?" she asked, gesturing languidly in Edred's direction. "Would you have him forget you as well?"

Saoirse turned to look at Edred's tight face. He shook his head, urging her to say no. She faltered. Something stirred in her heart as their gazes met—an unfurling of such keen-edged yearning that she lost her breath. Suddenly, she knew herself—as if the sun had finally risen, exposing the landscape of her heart. Every tender feeling she held for her friend swept through her in a rush. She *loved* Edred. How had she never realized it before?

She lost all the air in her lungs even as her heart lurched. *I love Edred.*

Saoirse could not meet his gaze any longer. Wresting it away, she reminded herself of her plea for Dafydd. She could not think of herself now. "H—he is a man grown," she said, her voice thick, "and will soon have a wife and . . . and children. In time he will forget me." The sharp blade of truth cut through the fragile twine holding her heart together. It unraveled, pieces of herself sagging, slipping away.

She found she didn't want Edred to forget her either. *But Dafydd is your brother and Edred does not love you as you love him.*

"You believe his heart so fickle, that he would forget a favored friend?" Áine asked. "What if you're wrong and your memory endures in his mind?"

Saoirse blinked rapidly, forcing the watery world back into focus. She swallowed heavily. "Then he can—can tell Dafydd of his sister, who loved him fiercely."

The goddess assessed Saoirse, her blue eyes penetrating her. "I see now how you persuaded the Stone Singer to wake the dragon. Almost you persuade me, but rest easy, human. I've no intention of sending your brother off to Annwn."

"You don't?" Relief loosened her joints even as her confusion mounted.

"No, I refer to this persistent spirit," she said, gesturing a graceful hand to Saoirse's left, "who tells me she dogged your steps once you interrupted her mother's spell." A pause, as if listening to unheard words, then, "Yes, I quite agree," Áine said.

Saoirse gaped at the empty air. *Spirit.* Suddenly, Dafydd's knowledge of the encroaching trowes within the tunnels and his whispered conversation with the wall in Basalina's wee cave made sense.

"That's how you knew about Papa needing help," she all but whispered. "Ursa's child told you."

"Her name is Elenwin," supplied Áine. "And she's rather impressed by your selflessness. Has she always been this way?" This last, directed at Edred.

"Yes," answered Edred. "And stubborn as a nanny goat." The soft look in his eye belied his words.

"I see," said Áine. "It's no wonder that you've sacrificed your birthright for her."

Saoirse whipped her head back in his direction. *Sacrificed his birthright?* Surely not. Not for *her.* "What can she mean, Edred?"

Edred's face flamed.

"Explain. There must be some mistake."

Áine sighed, a soft smile pulling at her pink lips. "He gave up his inheritance to enter my doorway—and to ensure freedom from wedding the butcher's daughter. One sacrifice with two benefits, much like your own, it would seem."

Saoirse's gaze bounced between them, her disbelief and desperate hope battling within her. Could it be true?

"Foolish   humans,"   the   goddess   muttered. "He's-in-love-with-you," Áine said, enunciating every syllable.

The painful grimace on Edred's face confused Saoirse all the more.

He's in love with you.

But he courted Gwenllian. Saoirse had seen them kiss in the public street.

Saoirse fumbled as she sank to the dais steps, her legs no longer able to support her. She set the little jar holding Dafydd's soul upon the stairs, afraid she might drop it in her stupor.

"Is this true?" she asked him. Every part of her had come undone—she couldn't even stitch a complete thought together.

He dropped beside her. "Don't worry. You don't . . . you don't have to love me back."

Áine's laughter broke through the tension. "Oh, you mortals," the goddess said with a shake of her head. "Such a delicious mess you make of your hearts. You'd think that, with such short lives, you'd be bolder in declarations of love."

"You don't love Gwenllian?" asked Saoirse.

Edred shook his head. "No."

"But . . . why court her?"

"Mother."

With just one word, everything made sense. Well, almost everything.

"Oh ho, a meddling mother, too! How predictable."

Saoirse ignored the goddess, her thoughts trapped in the tangle of memory and doubt. She swallowed hard, forcing the words past the tightness in her throat. "I saw you. I saw you kiss her in the lane."

Edred shook his head, his expression stricken. "No," he said quickly, his voice raw. "What you saw—I . . . I told her I didn't wish to court any longer. She kissed *me* goodbye."

The tight fist clenched around Saoirse's heart released its hold, and she took what felt like her first unfettered breath in a very long time. "You love . . . me?"

His nod was almost imperceptible at first, but then it became resolute. "Yes, for quite some time, but you didn't seem to share—"

"Let me help you along, shall I, since you both seem to misunderstand subtlety?" Aine leaned forward in her seat to stare at them in turn. "It's true. He's in love with you, just as you are in love with him. Though she will not remember it," she said conciliatorily to Edred, "as she sacrificed any reminiscence of her feelings for you at the mine gate."

Edred's gaze burned into her.

But Saoirse did remember. Maybe not her past feelings, which in light of recent events, she greatly regretted giving up, but she remembered the shape of memories just beyond her purview. She had never forgotten his kindness, his industry, his selflessness—those quiet, steady traits she admired most in him.

Even now, the magic of her sacrifice could not sever her feelings for him. Not totally. Love, it seemed, had bloomed twice in the same heart.

She met Edred's gaze, full of joy and conviction. Warmth spread through her chest. She reached out her hand, and he took it, his rough palm sliding against hers. "I think I've always loved you," Saoirse whispered.

"Hear me," said Áine. "What remains between your souls is yours to untangle. The day grows late, and much needs to be done. Edred, I cannot return the sacrifice you willingly gave at my gate, nor can I repair the consequence of your actions thereafter. Your hand will remain as it is."

She turned her gaze upon Saoirse. "Your brother's ailment is another matter. The witch's dark magic removed his agency. Because of this, it is within my power to aid him."

Saoirse's fingers tightened upon Edred's, sorry he would not regain full use of his hand, but relieved for Dafydd. Missing fingers, they could deal with.

Brackenholt reentered then, accompanied by a tall woman in leather armor that squeaked when she walked. Her onyx hair fell in a ribbon down her back, her pupilless eyes equally dark. Saoirse stared at her long legs, exposed in *trousers*.

"Arawn's servant, Fair One," announced Brackenholt.

Hearing that the god of death's servant had arrived, Edred tugged Saoirse to her feet. She reached out and grasped Dafydd with her free hand. Flanked by two men she loved so dearly, the intense rush of love and relief left her breathless.

"Ah, yes. Good of Arawn to reply so quickly. Thank you for coming, Lady Selkie."

A selkie? Saoirse gaped. She'd only ever heard tales of the creatures—drowned sailors and maidens turned to seals. If legend rang true, they could don their selkie skins and transform into the sea-loving animals, then slough them off again and take upon them once more their human form.

Death's servant bowed. "Captain Selanna, Fair One. At your service. Arawn sends his regards and regrets that he cannot come himself; other duties have waylaid him."

A smile grew upon Áine's radiant face. "I'm not quite sure spending time with his wife counts as duty."

The servant said nothing to this remark, only stared, expectant. If only Saoirse could learn such poise under Áine's gaze.

"This child is in need of some assistance," said Áine, motioning once more to a spot of empty air. "The poor girl avoided the pull of Annwn to linger overlong with her mother but has since separated."

The selkie turned her black eyes upon the same spot, the formidable planes of her stoic face softening. "We've been waiting for you, Elenwin, daughter of Ursa."

A sensation—like static in the air—prickled Saoirse's skin. If only she might hear what Elenwin said–or see her.

"You needn't fear," Captain Selanna coaxed. She lifted her pointed finger and drew a wide circle in the air, the track of it burning silver. In the center, where the fabric of reality had shone vibrant and immediate, faded and dulled, then fell away completely. A tear in the very essence of the world gaped open, exposing a second scene—outside of the summer court.

Edred's sharp intake of breath told Saoirse his amazement matched her own. *Annwn. The realm of the dead.*

Saoirse stared through the doorway, blinking against the brilliant light that spilled through. "Do you feel it, Elenwin?" asked the selkie captain. "Your family calls to you."

If Elenwin did not, Saoirse certainly felt them. An outpouring of warmth and love washed over her, lifting her heart. With every trouble suddenly forgotten, Saoirse longed to enter the hole the selkie had created herself, but didn't, largely because, at that very moment, Elenwin appeared.

As the girl stepped into the corona of brilliant light, she coalesced into being. Pearlescent and half-formed, as if made of light itself, the young girl looked back at Dafydd, uncertainty in her eyes. "Won't you come along, Dafydd?" The ghostly voice echoed strangely, both immediate and far away—a whisper in the marrow, a question that pressed against the edges of her mind.

Dafydd stirred under her hand, as if he wished to obey and accompany the ghostly Elenwin.

The prospect of Dafydd choosing the afterlife despite Summer's promise brought Saoirse to her senses. She tightened her grip on her brother's hand.

The selkie eyed Dafydd with interest. "Who has sinned against you—against nature?"

"My mother," said Elenwin, her eyes downcast and ashamed. "It's my fault," she said, forlorn. "I disobeyed her—opened her witching pantry and . . . and the viper bit me. Mother—she only wished to fix me."

"You needn't concern yourself with your mother just now, Elenwin," the selkie soothed, smiling softly. "She is beyond our help just now. Can you wait here for me?" She waited for Elenwin's nod of agreement before stalking toward Dafydd, her eyes narrowed in interest.

Saoirse stiffened, bracing to yank Dafydd away from the creature should she need.

The selkie seemed to read Dafydd as one does a book, her eyes roving over him. "He's forgotten himself," she said, her voice soft. "He is but form without substance. Are you weary, child?" she asked him.

Dafydd nodded, his large, soulful eyes seeming to plead with the selkie, though he likely did not even know for what he appealed.

The selkie's gaze settled upon Saoirse. "He cannot rest as he is, nor truly live." The selkie frowned in thought. "I am but a ferryman, shunting souls. I am no god. If Áine does not knit him together, he will diminish, for his will to live—to remain—wanes as time goes on."

The selkie looked upon the goddess with no small measure of expectation.

"I have agreed to mend his soul, though it is no small thing."

"No," agreed the selkie. "Any injury to the soul is slow to heal, but it can be done, if you are patient with him." She eyed Saoirse and the same sensation overcame her as when Áine regarded her, as if they sifted through the dregs of her mind.

"I will do all I can to aid him," Saoirse promised.

"That is good," said the selkie. "Come, sweet Elenwin. There are many people waiting to see you. They've gathered in Arawn's hall to greet you."

The ghost took the selkie's offered hand. "Will I see Dafydd again?"

"Oh, yes. When it's time," she answered cryptically.

Apparently satisfied, Elenwin lifted a hand in farewell, then she stepped into the radiance that waited beyond the rift.

Once they moved through, the rent in the world closed behind them, leaving summer's kingdom dim and lacking in comparison.

"Bring Dafydd closer," commanded Áine.

Saoirse exhaled shakily, her hands trembling as she led Dafydd up the stairs. He came willingly but craned his neck as if to search for Elenwin.

Saoirse lifted the vessel from the step and placed it into Áine's waiting palm. Her fingers brushed the goddess's skin, warm as sunlight. Her heart pounded as Áine examined the vessel.

The goddess uncorked the jar and peered inside, her expression unreadable. She gently swirled the contents as though appraising the facets of a rich gemstone. "A good sort of boy for a human," Áine mused. "Industrious, curious—playful, too. A little stubborn, I see, but aren't you all? Ah, yes, there it is . . . his sense of self and kindness were also stolen away from him. You will feel much more like yourself very soon, Dafydd."

She tipped the bowl gently, letting a faint shimmer of light seep from the opening. Dafydd's soul reminded Saoirse of the night sky, swimming with silver stars.

Áine tilted her head, her gaze still fixed on his bit of soul as if listening to something only she could hear. "One cannot simply pour a soul back into a body, as if tipping a jug of water," she informed. "Fractures run deep, especially when torn asunder by dark hands."

Saoirse swallowed, her fists curling. That witch had much to answer for.

The goddess's mouth pressed thin. "You're not wrong there," she said, as if sensing her thoughts. "I could not stop her–nor any free-thinking creature–from doing harm, but nor can those that do wrong escape their consequences."

Was that why she hadn't interfered when the trowes plotted against the dragons? Why, too, so many humans were allowed to wound others?

"I can mend what was taken, but some scars will linger. Even I cannot erase all hurt—nor would I wish to. He will be changed, just as you have by this experience, as all things in life." Áine settled the clay vessel upon her lap and lifted her hand into the air. With a neat wave of her fingers, a finely pointed needle and small, ornate sewing shears appeared upon her outstretched palm, both glinting silver.

The needle rose an inch above Áine's right hand while, with a pointed left finger, she circled the rim of the bowl containing a portion of Dafydd. A glistening wisp of spirit twined into thread, as thin as gossamer and just as ethereal, and soared into the air. Áine curled her fingers, coaxing the delicate strand of soul to the eye of the needle, where it threaded itself.

"Hold him steady," Áine said to no one in particular, though the shimmering strand seemed to quiver and pause as if it waited for her command. Edred moved to stand behind Dafydd, his big hands resting on his shoulders.

With delicate precision, the summer goddess pinched the tiny silver implement and began to weave the fibers of soul into an invisible form, the needle flashing as it pierced the air. Saoirse gasped as a faint outline of Dafydd appeared—a ghostly reflection of an identical boy.

Áine worked with the casual expertise of a tailor, yet each motion radiated power. "The missing piece knows where it belongs," she explained, her tone almost offhand. "But the rest of his soul must accept it, and that will take time. Souls are stubborn things." She flicked her wrist, and the last stitch sealed itself with a soft hum.

Áine rose to her feet. "This will hurt, I'm afraid." Without further warning, she lifted the silver needle between thumb and forefinger, and pierced Dafydd's chest, right over his heart.

Dafydd gasped, shrinking away from the pain, but Edred held him in place. The goddess instructed Edred to turn Dafydd around. There, glowing a faint silver-blue, the sharp tip of the needle poked free from Dafydd's back.

Pinching it, Áine drew out the needle, shining filament of soul still attached, and tugged the spectral image of Dafydd closer. It wavered as it faded into his skin—as his body absorbed the portion of his sundered soul. Áine tied a knot and, with a neat *snick*, she severed the thread, which fell against Dafydd and disappeared just as quickly as his likeness.

Saoirse watched Dafydd's face intently, breath held, and caught a spark of *something* ignite in his eyes. She pulled him into her arms with a cry, then kissed his face.

Áine returned the vessel to Edred, now empty. "It's done. He will heal with the proper care."

Relief washed over Saoirse, tears stinging her eyes. "Thank you," she whispered, still clutching Dafydd, who squirmed against her, wishing to get away. She'd never been happier to have him resist her embrace.

"Ugh, ger-off. I can't breathe, Sers," he complained.

When she let him go, he wiped the kisses from his cheeks. His face flared with embarrassment, a sullen look on his face. "Do you have to kiss me in front of everyone?"

Saoirse laughed, her heart lighter than it had been in a week. She didn't think she'd ever stop smiling.

"Now, in exchange for reuniting your brother's pieces of soul, let us discuss your payment," said Áine.

Saoirse's stomach dropped and her smile faltered.

"Oh, don't look so forlorn, child. Everything comes at a price." Summer settled upon her throne once again, the poppy blossoms opening as if to smile in welcome. "There is a witch in need of capture. She's meddled with lives enough—*and with my afanc*. Now, let's discuss the particulars."

Chapter Thirty-One

The Descent

CARREG BROUGHT THEM SAFELY through the mine once more, guiding their small party over rickety tracks and through shadowed tunnels that seemed to stretch endlessly. The steady clink of coblynau tools echoed around them as they passed the industrious fae still hard at work. Saoirse's heart ached with an odd mixture of relief and reluctance. Soon, they would step back into the human world, leaving this strange, other-worldly journey behind.

Life would go on for the coblynau, as it must for her and Dafydd. And Edred. A bubble of nervous anticipation grew within her. After the goddess revealed the truth about their shared feelings for one another, they'd stolen countless glances at each other, but little else. What could she say?

How were they to begin? How could they settle back into ordinary society after the strange beauty of the faerie realm, even with its dangers? She stole another glance at Edred, seated across from her in the cart, his profile cast in soft shadow. He loved her, as she did him. Her heart thudded in an unsettled, uncertain way.

"Nearly there," Carreg announced. Darkness enclosed them as the rumble of the cart slowed to a stop. Saoirse drew a deep breath, her resolve hardening. Whatever lay ahead for them, surely they could face it head-on.

They'd bested the trowes and faced a formidable goddess. Capturing a human witch who'd plagued the town and controlled a magical beast would be nothing. Right? And as far as her and Edred's relationship . . . well, first things first, she supposed.

Carreg stopped the cart and they exited. The faerie lit his wee candle and led the way through the close, twining tunnels to the familiar gateway. When they'd left, the witch's candlelight had glowed softly through the rock into the mountain. Now, the afanc's lair loomed dark through transparent stone.

"Do you think she's still alive in there?" Saoirse asked Edred, her voice small so as not to alarm Dafydd. As much as she hoped the witch had simply given up and died of sorrow or whatever else, that would leave the afanc under its own control. How could they possibly defeat it?

"She must be alive—and free," Edred replied, his voice equally low. "Otherwise, why would Áine charge us with capturing her and dealing with her 'in the human way'?"

She sighed. "Yes, I was afraid of that."

"No sacrifice is needed to return," Carreg supplied, pushing past them to stand at the gate. "The magic will sense your humanness and allow you back home."

"So simple?"

The faithful little faerie shrugged. "To us fae, simple is best."

"Simple sounds perfect," Edred said. His warm, rough hand slid into Saoirse's; her heart jolted happily. Edred smiled softly at her, his skin winking pink through his stubbled beard where he blushed.

"I don't know how to thank you, Carreg," she said, her voice softer than she intended. Her throat tightened uncomfortably. "You and the Singer—and Kraglin."

The coblyn tipped his head, bowing in his courtly, endearing way. "Just remember ol' Carreg when you're dashing the cream in the churn, Lady Traveler," he replied, his tone light and teasing.

Her laugh wobbled at the edges. "I will," she promised, her affection for the little coblyn warming her. "Perhaps—yes, perhaps we will see one another again."

A flicker of polite confusion passed over his face, but he covered it quickly, his expression growing solemn. "Aye, there's always a chance, I suppose."

Before she could second-guess herself, Saoirse leaned forward and kissed his cheek, her lips brushing the cool, stony texture of his skin. Carreg froze, his small frame stiff with surprise. She lingered, an idea forming in her mind. Before she could think better of it, she whispered a promise.

The dislikable sensation of farewell abated as she pulled away and she met Carreg's wide eyes. "Farewell, Carreg."

The coblyn cleared his throat and straightened, rubbing the back of his neck. "Aye," he murmured, his gruff voice quieter now. "Go on, now. Dinna linger here."

Saoirse turned to Edred, her pulse quickening, and grasped Dafydd's hand. Together, they would step forward, into the uncertain future, leaving behind the faerie realm. "Remember what we discussed," she whispered to Dafydd. "Stay at the back of the cave until we say it's safe to come out."

Dafydd's skin grew sweaty under her own. His pale face shone with pure terror, making her heart ache and her worry increase. "Remember," she said, steel in her voice, and imparted the last words her father had said to her. "Courage, Dafydd."

He nodded, his little face resolving into a visage of determination.

Edred's hand slid into her own once more, and they stepped as one through the gate with the sensation of walking through a spider's web. The etched archway that formed the door glowed softly upon their exit, lending them light. The stench of Elenwin's moldering body made bile surge to her throat. She gagged. Dafydd began to cry.

She shushed him, a finger held to her mouth as her stomach churned. They didn't know what else might lurk in the cave.

She pulled her tunic up, over her mouth and nose and helped Dafydd do the same. "It's all right, Dafydd," she whispered, so close to his ear her lips grazed the shell. "Elenwin is not here. She's moved on, remember?"

He nodded, unspeaking.

Edred held up a hand in a "wait" gesture and crept forward, peering into the dark. He picked up a candle and tucked it in his elbow, then grabbed another.

"Here, light these," he said. "I think we're alone but I don't want to step in . . . anything."

She understood his meaning. She didn't want to walk on poor Elenwin either.

Edred pulled his hammer from its loop, hefting its weight awkwardly in his good hand, as if to acquaint himself with the strange, new sensation.

Saoirse got to work, pulling a flint from her bag. Sparks flew, dazzling her eyes. One wick caught, and she lit the other candle from the first. She replaced her flint and stood, slinging her bag over her shoulders.

"Here, Dafydd. You carry this one," she said, pressing the narrower candle into his hand. "Wait here. I'll be right back."

She edged through the opening that separated the proper chamber from the doorway, lifting the candle high to broaden the halo of light. No afanc guarded the door. No witch lingered in the cluttered space.

She retreated, nodding at Edred. "We're alone." Then to Dafydd, "Don't look too closely, if you can help it. Just watch your feet."

"Ready?" asked Edred. Dafydd nodded, but his eyes showed his fear.

"Stay close," Saoirse instructed. "We don't know where she or the afanc might be."

They crept through the cave. Saoirse stepped over top-pled candles, baskets, vegetables, and crocks of milk—most likely stolen from the temple—and avoided looking at the body-shaped mass along the left wall.

They walked through the narrow throat of the cave that led to the waterfall. Sheets of pelting rain washed the world away, shrouding the trees and rocks as thoroughly as any curtain of fog. Their candles instantly sputtered out, not that they would do much good under the watery sun.

Dafydd tugged on Saoirse's dress. He had to shout over the noise of the falls and the deluge. "Elenwin said the rain came so fast, it flooded the river and spilled into the village streets."

Saoirse's shared a worried glance with Edred. How much worse would the town fare now, so many days since Elenwin's warning? Did their homes still stand, or had the raging river pulled them from their foundations?

"Best we move along then," Edred said. "Keep a keen eye out for the witch and that monster."

She didn't need the reminder. Already, Saoirse craned her neck, squinting through the downpour for the smallest glimpse of potential danger, but the relentless rain blurred the world into a shifting haze of color, as if reality itself dissolved before her eyes.

In a matter of moments, their clothes grew heavy with rain, clinging and uncomfortable. Saoirse's skirts tangled about her legs, and she worried constantly that she might miss a step, tum-ble down the rocky slope, and fall into the bone-littered pond.

She'd never learned to swim. None of them could. She gripped Dafydd's hand all the harder.

By some miracle, they descended the precarious tumble of stones along the falls, across the meadow, and into the relative shelter of the pine forest where the push and pull of the angry wind could not reach them so easily. An ache settled deep in her neck from the constant strain of glancing over her shoulder, searching for the lurking afanc or the fleeting shadow of the witch creeping closer.

So, too, Saoirse sought out her bees at every turn, but they'd likely holed away in some hidden crevice to escape the rain. Still, she hoped that they'd spotted her and would follow her home.

They teetered across the fallen tree that spanned the ravine and hurried past the open saddle in which she'd found Dafydd's lost shoe and onto the topmost stair that overlooked the eastern face of the mountain.

Dafydd's sharp gasp echoed in her heart. "It's like the edge of the world."

Saoirse squinted against the gray sky, unable to tell what time of day it might be. The weak sun hid behind angry, bruised clouds. She could not make out the valley far below. Indeed, the visible path extended a mere ten feet, then dissolved into thrashing sheets of water. She crouched, meeting Dafydd's eye at his level. "Stay between us. Go slow."

"Tie up your skirts, Sers," Edred called over the torrent's roar. He pulled off his pack and rifled through it, producing a line of rope. "Bind this around my waist, would you? Then to Dafydd and yourself. I don't want anyone being swept away."

Saoirse shoved sodden hair from her eyes and forehead and nodded.

Thankfully, the long stair had no chance of eroding. Each carved step, while slick and puddled, held true. Still, she placed her boots carefully, following behind Dafydd. Even the slightest misstep upon the slick stone could prove devastating. Whenever Dafydd looked over his shoulder as they descended, she shot him reassuring smiles.

When they came to the second narrow switchback in the trail, Saoirse held tight to a branch to ease around the corner, just as a brilliant finger of lightning struck, instantly followed by a crack of thunder that rebounded in her bones.

Dafydd squealed and scrambled up the steps to clutch tightly to her waist. Her heart leaped into her throat as his movements jerked the rope and pulled Edred off balance. Edred fell with an *oof*; the steep angle of the mountain pulled him down several steps, bumping him along, but Saoirse grasped the length of rope connecting Edred to Dafydd and held on tight. Thankfully, the tree limb Saoirse fisted kept her and Dafydd from tumbling over the edge, but she swayed from the force of the rope's pull.

"Are you all right?" she shouted.

Edred gingerly got to his feet. When he turned, the drawn look upon his face slackened as he saw the depth of Dafydd's fright. "It's all right, Dafydd! Be calm. You mustn't jerk us about, lad. It's a long way down."

"I'm s—sorry," Dafydd wailed. His whole body shook.

They slowed even further, and by some miracle, they made it down the teetering mountain face without injury. She shivered with nerves and cold, but her determination flared. So close. So very close.

Grime clung to her boots as they squelched through the meadow; her skirt weighed her down, saturated and mud-stained. She gripped Dafydd's hand, pulling him along, her mind lingering on Papa.

Thunder rolled overhead. She barely heard Dafydd's squeak of fear over the gale. Rain battered their exposed skin like tiny, cold arrows.

"There's the temple," Edred shouted, pointing to a faint blocky structure in the distance. The rain plastered his dark hair smooth against his skull, flattening his curls. His shirt clung to him, exposing the hills and valleys of his strong shoulders and chest.

Edred caught her stare, and her face heated mightily. Quaking, she changed trajectory. "Come on. Let's cut through the woods to the house."

They marched through the leveled grass, her limbs trembling and her tired muscles complaining. As they pushed through the elms and beeches along the slope, the village came into view. The river that ran through the town roared as it tumbled, roiling and churning debris. A submerged tree popped up and turned end over end, catching on an unseen obstruction.

The sheer power of the waterway stunned Saoirse. If the bridge should go out, a goodly portion of the village would be cut off from the other. Indeed, even from so far away, the swollen river visibly lapped against buildings along the water's edge. Edred's family forge, which sat across the lane from the riverbank, couldn't be seen, but she doubted it had been spared the flooding.

"The bridge won't hold much longer," she warned. "Best you go and see to your family. We'll check on Papa!"

"Is our house washed away?" asked Dafydd.

Their farm sat uphill from the river. She wiped her face, peering through the rain, but a line of trees blocked her view. The well, downhill from their parcel of land, hadn't been overcome as yet. She pointed it out to him, "See there, Dafydd. The house should be spared."

But what of Papa?

The river raged, its waters clawing at the bridge's stones, threatening to pull the village into its tossing depths. Every moment mattered. They needed to move—now.

"You go," she shouted over the roar of the storm. "We'll be all right."

Edred's jaw tightened. His good hand curled into a fist, rain dripping from his soaked tunic. "I'm not leaving you."

She reached for him, gripping his forearm, desperate for him to listen. "We'll be all right! Check your family! Bring them to us—to higher ground—if need be."

He didn't move. Instead, he caught her wrist, his grip sure and warm despite the cold rain pouring upon them. His eyes searched hers, stormy and unsure, his gaze lingering on her mouth. Then, without another word, he pulled her close, his bandaged hand pressed lightly against the small of her back. Their wet bodies connected; she lost her breath. She stared up at him, startled.

With a soft growl, he bent his head and pressed his mouth to hers once more, his left hand coming up to cradle her cheek;

his fingers tangled in her hair. Urgently, fiercely, his lips claimed her. Saoirse gasped against his mouth, her fingers curling into the fabric of his tunic. The world narrowed to nothing but the press of him, to the slow heat that radiated into her.

As she returned his embrace and kissed him, his fervor gave way to tenderness. She'd never kissed anyone before—had never wanted to if she couldn't kiss Edred. It was just as she'd imagined. Wild and breathless and perfect.

Saoirse's breath faltered, the fragile balance inside her splintering like glass. Warmth flooded her.

"Ugh!" Dafydd made a gagging noise. "Gross!"

Edred pulled away, his thumb wiping rain from her cold cheek. "I've wanted to do that for a very long time."

She smiled stupidly at him and threw her arms around his neck, laughing.

"Come on, Saoirse!" Dafydd yelled. "You can kiss him later. Let's go check on Papa!"

Edred squeezed her tight and let her go, a wobbly smile on his face that undoubtedly matched her own.

No matter how dire their current circumstances, she'd always make time for kissing Edred.

Renewed, her heart full to bursting with love for Edred, she grasped Dafydd's hand and ran through the pasture toward home. As they reached the trees separating them from the cottage, she spied Edred racing past the well at the bottom of the slope.

Chapter Thirty-Two

Homecoming

S AOIRSE THREW THE DOOR open. "Papa?"

No answer.

No candles burned in the shuttered house. No fire crackled in the hearth; no dinner simmered in the pot.

All the elation racing through her veins after Edred's kiss slowed, stalled into disquiet.

"Papa!" Dafydd shouted.

Half-filled buckets of rainwater sat under thatch leaks. Dafydd raced into Papa's bedroom, but he came out instantly. "Maybe he's in the barn," Dafydd offered, and then he tore past Saoirse and flew out the door. Saoirse followed, her feet sliding in the six-inch deep mud.

Dafydd pushed at the heavy barn door, using all his body weight to roll it aside.

"Papa!"

But he wasn't in the barn either. Buttercup lowed, covered in mud up past her belly. The bull Griff, chewed his cud in his stall, equally dirty.

"At least he saved the beasts from the mire," said Dafydd. "He's got to be around here somewhere."

True, but it wasn't like Papa to leave the beasts so filthy.

"He'll be in the village, helping, I'll bet. Injured or no, he wouldn't sit idle when there's trouble. Maybe he's helping someone else with their animals."

Madoc must have come to help—perhaps Papa had returned the favor? Could he bail out water from the forge in his condition? He'd likely try.

"Let's go," Dafydd urged, yanking on her hand. She paused long enough to close the door, and then they hurried down the lane, their boots heavy with mud, their clothes plastered to their bodies.

The river had swollen around the bridge, forcing them to walk through two feet of water as it circumnavigated the stony obstacle. When she set her feet upon the ramp, the rough vibration of the surging water echoed in her bones. Despite its sturdy construction, with much more of this weather, the mortar would fail and the weighty stones would be washed away.

"Hold on," she cried to the bridge, recalling Carreg's words. If the rocks did hear her, maybe a little encouragement might help.

The river had overcome the street, flowing through the thoroughfares into the heart of the village. They waded into it, the water rising to her knees. Dafydd's hand fumbled for hers and she caught hold of it.

Not far from the bridge, water lapped against the forge's office door. The open-air portion, where Edred and Madoc worked, a conflagration of floating odds and ends had gathered, bumping and swaying against the far wall.

An empty barrel floated past her and Dafydd as they drew nearer. Down the lane, Emrys, the wool merchant, loaded their goods into a fishing boat, helped by his family. They stood in a line, passing down bundles of spun wool from out of a window to their father.

She pulled Dafydd through the rising water toward the family. "Excuse me, Syr Emrys, have you seen my father?"

The merchant spared her a glance as he took a lumpy bag from his son, then looked again sharply. "Well bless my soul," he said with a gasp. "You're alive!"

She didn't wish to get into the particulars of her misadventure just then, so she simply said, "Yes. Have you seen my father?"

"He'll be in the square, won't he? With the rest of the town. How they'll burn a witch in this weather, I'll never know! Best to save such things to fairer weather, I say, and save our stock!"

Her heart lurched. Had she heard him wrong? "Wait—what?"

"I say, we should spend our energy now saving our stores!" He took another bag, tossing it amongst the others in the bottom of the boat.

"No," she blurted, "what did you say about the witch?"

"Oh! Well, it was your father that done it! You should have seen him, mistress ferch Rhys. He's the one that brought the idea o' the faeries to our minds, you see . . . said as how you went up the Wild Wood stair tae fetch Dafydd back from them—and by certs you *did*!" He beamed at her, then Dafydd.

"How did he catch her?" asked Dafydd, an edge of fear in his voice.

Emrys nodded importantly. "Used cold iron tae subdue her. Knifed her, right as he caught her carting off little Llew from his home. She hollered and the lad cried something awful—and good too. The stramash broke us from our stupors." He looked thoughtful then. "Funny thing, she somehow made us all rare tired, so we all slept while she carted away the wee ones."

Saoirse didn't want to hear any more. Urgency gnawed at her. She would ask Papa what happened later. "Is the lad all right—and Da?"

"Oh, yes! Llew's parents swept him away. Full o' fight your ol' da. Only the iron didnae kill the witch, only cut her some. They've got her just down the lane."

She didn't wait to hear what he said next. She tugged Dafydd along, the water pulling at her dress as Emrys shouted after her. "Glad you both made it home!"

"Sers!"

She whipped her head around as Edred emerged onto the lane from between the forge shop and the milliner. He drove through the water with much more power than she and Dafydd had. In a short time, he met them, his face white to the lips. "Sers, your father . . . he's caught the witch! He's got her—"

"Yes, Emrys has just told me!"

"Come on!" He grasped Dafydd's hand so that she could pull her skirts up enough to move her feet with some efficiency.

Walking came easier the farther they traveled away from the river, and by the time they reached the next lane, which led into the square, their feet only splashed through puddles. In the center of the town, just in front of the alehouse and the carpenter's shop, a sodden crowd had gathered.

The villagers—or her father—had tied Ursa to a horse post, her wrists bound with iron chains. Her soaked cloak clung to her wiry frame, her shoulders shaking from cold or fear. They had her. Finally, they had her.

As they neared, the witch's maniacal laugh could be heard over the villager's angry shouts. Not fear, then, but crazed delight.

"Hurry," Edred urged needlessly.

Dafydd gripped his side, no doubt holding a stitch but they could not slow.

They pushed through the throng, jostling and maneuvering to the center. Across from the open space that held the apprehended witch, stood Papa. He leaned heavily on his crutch under the eave of the alehouse, a grim expression on his face.

"You!" Urse shrieked, her excited gaze settling upon Saoirse and a repaired Dafydd.

"Papa!" shouted Dafydd. He broke free from Edred and raced across the small clearing, skirting around the witch, no doubt terrified to get too close.

Papa's grim expression lifted into one of pure relief and joy. Dafydd wrapped his arms around Papa's middle and sobbed openly into his cloak. Her father stroked Dafydd's wet head, speaking words Saoirse could not hear over the murmurs of the onlookers, his gaze scanning the gathered faces. Only when it landed upon Saoirse, did it soften fully into relief. He waved at her to come to him as Dafydd had and she wanted nothing more than to fall into his arms, but she first needed to speak about what she'd witnessed.

The villagers, now taking notice that Dafydd and Saoirse had returned from proverbial death, quieted. She stepped closer to the witch, but out of her reach, so that all could see and hear her.

"What happened?" someone asked.

"Praise be! They're alive!" another cried.

Ursa straightened against the post her dark eyes wide with fear. "What did you tell the goddess?" Spittle flew from her mouth. "What has she done with my Elenwin? She's taken her against her will, I know it. My daughter would not abandon me."

More questions spilled from people's mouths, confused and impossible to decipher. Saoirse signaled for quiet. "Her name is Ursa," said Saoirse, her voice ringing clear over the rain-dampened hush. "She weaves powerful spells to catch children in her web."

"And us!" the butcher's wife cried. "We all slept while she stole our children!"

Saoirse nodded. "Yes. She killed Eva and Carys—attempted to kill Dafydd, too, but Edred and I—we interrupted her dark magic deep within the Wild Wood." She turned her gaze over the gathered crowd, her heart pounding. Fadam Fortwin, her face pale, had found Edred. She inspected her son's wounds, her mouth moving soundlessly as she no doubt pestered him with questions.

Edred, though, only had eyes for Saoirse. He met her gaze and her heart skipped a beat. "She took children to harvest their souls," she finished.

Gasps. Shouts of outrage. Fists shook in the air. Someone threw a clog at the witch. It hit Ursa's shoulder then fell to the ground with a wet splat.

Saoirse held up her hand, waiting for quiet once more. "To repair the injury done to my brother, we, all three, entered through Áine's gate. The goddess has charged us with justice, for Ursa has also sinned against Summer herself."

"Justice!" someone shouted.

"Burn her!"

Saoirse glanced at the witch. She'd slid into a crouch, her head thrown back so that it rested against the slick post. Her mouth moved restlessly, as if speaking, and her eyes—her eyes had rolled back into her head, glaringly white.

What had happened? Was she casting a spell even now? Before Saoirse could react to the woman's trance, before she could move to stop her, a tremor rippled through the earth, reverberating through her boots.

Somewhere in the distance, a great tree cracked and fell with a splintering crash. Water surged in a wave from around the buildings, spilling over the cobblestones and into the square.

A mighty roar pierced the air, rumbling through Saoirse's chest, nearly stopping her heart in fear.

The afanc had come.

CHAPTER THIRTY-THREE

SAOIRSE'S SPELL

THE AFANC SURGED FROM the water in the same manner as it had in her childhood nightmares, its terrible body glistening with riverweed and brackish foam. It moved with unnatural grace, dragging itself onto the flooded village square. Its long, toothy maw gaped, lined with rows of jagged teeth, and its eyes—deep, black, and filled with a sickening intelligence—locked onto the terrified villagers.

The witch's cackle raised Saoirse's flesh. The afanc shuddered, its spiny mane undulating as if it responded to Ursa's silent summons.

"She's controlling it," Edred shouted.

"Get Papa and Dafydd out of here!" she commanded of him. "Everyone, go! Run!"

Saoirse lunged for the witch and shook her, but the woman only laughed harder. "Stop it! Release the creature!"

Desperate, Saoirse slapped the woman's face, hard. Her fingers stung from the impact and the laughing ceased abruptly.

People scrambled in all directions. Screams pierced the air. They shoved past Saoirse, past others. Some slipped and fell in their haste. Doors slammed shut. Someone prayed volubly.

Edred's mother suddenly appeared at her side. She grabbed Saoirse's wrist, her fingers digging in. "Sing," she urged. "Sing, Saoirse!"

"What? What can singing possibly—"

"I know the old stories, Saoirse!" she shouted as more people rushed by.

King Clatterby's words came back to her in a powerful rush. What had he said? *You could charm even the most sinister of beasts to slumber.*

Sleep. I need to sing it to sleep!

Fadam Fortwin was still speaking. "Do it, quickly! Now!"

The afanc's tail thrashed, sending a wall of water crashing into a cottage, splintering the door from its hinges. The witch let out a breathless whisper, her lips barely moving, her grip on the beast clearly still intact. It lunged forward.

No more time.

Saoirse opened her mouth and sang.

Her voice, raw and trembling at first, rose above the storm. A melody from a mother to a babe. Alys had sung it to Dafydd.

"Sleep my darling, on my bosom, Harm will never come to you; Mother's arms enfold you safely, Mother's heart is ever true. As you sleep there's

naught to scare you, Naught to wake you from
your rest; Close those eyelids, little angel, Sleep
upon your mother's breast."

"It's working!" shouted Fadam Fortwin. Saoirse closed her
eyes and sang louder.

Sleep, my darling, night is falling. Rest in slumber
sound and deep; I would know why you are smiling, Smiling sweetly as you sleep! Do you see the
gods smiling? As they see your rosy rest, So that
you must smile an answer, As you slumber on my
breast?

The afanc let out a low, uncertain growl.

Saoirse kept on, her throat dry.

Did the rain began to slow? The wind had certainly softened,
no longer howling through the trees. Saoirse opened her eyes
as the afanc's great body swayed. Its snarl lessened, its claws
loosened their grip in the mud. The beast, once poised to tear
the village apart, now blinked slowly as if waking from a deep
dream.

The witch let out a guttural scream.

"Obey me!" she shrieked, her voice cracking with fury. She
stood, straining against the chains that bound her. "I command
you! Kill them!"

The afanc blinked once. Twice.

Then, its black eyes locked onto her.

A moment stretched, a single, breathless instant where the witch realized her mistake. She had lost control. Fadam Fortwin yanked Saoirse away, nearly pulling her off her feet. They stumbled under the eaves of the alehouse just as the afanc lunged. Saoirse's heart pounded in her chest as the guttural roar from the beast filled the air.

The witch's desperate cry cut through the rain, but it was drowned out by the sickening sound of snapping jaws. The massive form of the afanc, its scales glistening with sullied water, shot forward like a serpent lunging at its prey.

The witch barely had time to scream before the beast's jaws clamped down around her, yanking her from her chains as effortlessly as a fox catching a hare. The ground beneath Saoirse's feet quivered with the power of the monster's movements.

A scream tore from any scrambling villagers. The afanc reared back, its head twisting unnaturally as it swallowed the sorceress whole. Its mighty throat worked as Ursa's feet disappeared from view.

The rain stopped—like a spell had been broken. The air hung heavy with an unnatural stillness. The thunderous roar of the river, the screeching winds, all ceased. The last droplets fell, pattering softly against the drenched earth as if the world itself exhaled in relief.

The afanc, no longer bound to its cruel mistress, turned toward the river, its massive body rippling with muscle. With slow, deliberate movements, it slithered around the apothecary shop, disappearing from view. Saoirse pulled free of Fadam Fortwin and stumbled out from under the relative safety of the alehouse eave, staggering over slime-slick cobblestones. Fadam Fortwin followed at her side.

Together, they watched as the afanc slunk between Emrys's and the butcher's shop. Poor Emrys and his sons stared from their bobbing boat, their faces ashen. But the great creature paid them no heed and slipped into the black depths. It disappeared under rippling water. For a moment, it seemed as though the beast had never existed at all.

Saoirse let out a long breath, her legs trembling as though they might give way at any moment. She pressed a hand to her chest, feeling the rapid thrum of her heartbeat beneath her fingers.

Fadam Fortwin, her grip tight on Saoirse's arm, swallowed visibly, her eyes wide with fear, her face pale. The older woman's other hand shook slightly as she adjusted her hold around Saoirse's shoulders. When had Edred's mother embraced her?

"You did well, Lass," she said, her voice barely above a whisper, a tremor beneath her words.

Saoirse nodded numbly, eyes flicking back to the spot where the witch had stood moments before. Her heart twisted with a strange mix of relief and unease. She had done it. A restored Dafydd now huddled somewhere safe with Papa. Edred had made it out, too, albeit injured. So, too, Áine's justice had come to fruition. The witch had died.

But now what? Would it simply creep back to its pond in the Wild Wood? She certainly hoped so.

The silence in the street hung thick as Fadam Fortwin helped her keep steady. Her hands—strong and firm, anchored Saoirse, even as the world seemed to tilt beneath her feet. How strange, for Edred's mother to attend to her. Why had she stayed? Why did she help?

"Come on," Fadam Fortwin said quietly, pulling Saoirse gently but firmly away from the scene. "Let's . . . let's get you seen to."

Saoirse could only nod, too exhausted to resist. She glanced at Fadam Fortwin as they walked. Something had shifted between them here, the unspoken tension that had plagued them for so long loosened. "Edred needs help," Saoirse said, her voice cracking despite her best efforts. "Trowes—"

Fadam's face darkened at the mention of the terrible faerie creatures' name, a flash of something raw and fierce crossing her features. "How bad is it?" she demanded, a catch in her voice. "He wouldn't let me see."

Saoirse's mind flashed to the gruesome sight of Edred's hand—stumps where fingers should have been. The memory made her throat tighten. Her heart ached for him. "I'm afraid he won't be able to wield a hammer."

Fadam Fortwin did not react as she expected. She did not wail in despair or berate Saoirse for what part she'd played in the whole business. Instead, she merely sniffed and tightened her arm around Saoirse's shoulders. "Well," the woman said, voice firm, "we'll just have to see about that, won't we?"

They continued on, splashing up the lane. The crowd that had dispersed from the square trickled back. Shutters opened, heads appearing from windows. People edged out of their homes and called out to them, endless questions shouted their way.

"Go back inside," Fadam Fortwin called to them, her voice carrying a quiet authority. "The lassie broke the witch's spell. Stay indoors until we're certain the beast has gone for good."

Gratitude swelled within Saoirse. The townsfolk's eyes followed them, but the woman led her with such quiet confidence that Saoirse's chest tightened with unexpected appreciation.

"You stayed," Saoirse murmured, her voice soft with surprise. Only now did she realize that Fadam Fortwin—Gwenda—had not steered them toward Saoirse's home, but directly toward her own house.

Gwenda spared her a glance, her mouth pressed tight. "Well, if Edred risks his life for you, it's the least I can do make sure it wasn't all in vain."

Saoirse stopped walking, forcing Gwenda to do the same. "Why?" she asked, her eyes searching the older woman's gaze. "Why did you drive a wedge between us? Between you and me, and then Edred?"

Gwenda exhaled sharply through her nose. "It was, perhaps, selfish of me," she said. "I knew he cared for you—loved you as a friend—but you—" She seemed to weigh her words carefully. "I didn't want to lose him. He'd do anything for you, even if it cost him his life." She sighed, her shoulders slumping. "Clearly, nothing has changed."

Saoirse, numb from recent events, could not find her voice.

Shame flickered behind Gwenda's eyes. "I knew he cared for you, but I thought that . . . I hoped that if he wedded Gwenllian, he'd let you go. He, and my future grandchildren, would stay safely rooted here. But once he rushed after you into the Wild

Wood, I knew well enough I couldn't stop him. He's made it very plain that he is his own man. Whatever you might think of me, Saoirse, I do love my son."

Anger coiled within her belly like a striking snake. "You think I would endanger a child?" She thrust a finger in the general direction of the Wild Wood. "I climbed the long stair to rescue Dafydd, and entered hell itself to drag Edred from the trowes."

"I know your bravery. I've seen it before, remember? But can you appreciate the fear of a mother?"

Some part of Saoirse wanted to further scold the woman, but she could only conjure enough energy to walk away. Edred waited for her with her family. She would hug Papa and Dafydd. She would kiss Edred soundly, and then she would lumber home to bed and sleep for a week entire.

"Can you forgive me?" asked Gwenda, hurrying to catch up to Saoirse.

"I've loved him since I was a wee thing," she confessed, stopping at the Fortwin's stoop. Water lapped against the stone foundation, the bottom three steps leading to the door lay submerged. "And I loved you like a mother—once."

Gwenda's anguished expression softened Saoirse's heart. "I hope it's not too late for us. I failed you then, Saoirse, but I would make amends if you allow it. I never stopped loving you, too."

After everything she'd experienced at the hand of the witch and under the faerie hill, Saoirse supposed that *never* was a word best left unspoken. "Yes," said Saoirse. "Hope lives still."

Gwenda reached out an uncertain hand and lifted sodden hair from Saoirse's cheek. She brushed it behind her ear. "I'm glad he chose you, Saoirse, for no one could love him so well. He told me in the square—said that you saved him." She laid a warm hand against Saoirse's cheek. "Thank you for bringing my boy home. Forgive me. Please."

Saoirse, not one for holding a grudge, nodded. She allowed Gwenda's embrace, and for the first time in many years, sank into something like warm affection from a mother. Perhaps, with time, the wounds between them would heal. What had Áine said about healing soul scars? They required patience and understanding to mend. Time, they had.

The door flew open and an anxious Edred emerged, looking ready to battle the afanc himself. He stopped short as he took them in. He glanced up the lane, toward the square "You're all right."

Saoirse pulled away from Gwenda. "Yes, it's gone. It—I think it's going back to its cave." She spared a quick thought for poor little Elenwin. Did they dare return to bury her? Probably best if they didn't. Witnessing her soul entering the afterlife somehow made her burial unimportant.

Edred stuck his head back in the door and spoke to those still inside. "They're here. They're well," he called, then turned back to them. He splashed down the stairs, shin-deep in muddy water. "Da helped me with your father and Dafydd—we settled them here and I was just coming back to help you. "How did you defeat the afanc? What happened?""

Gwenda eyed Edred's bandaged hand. "Oh, I've told you the story of the milkmaid and the afanc, surely."

Edred took Saoirse's hand in his good one, declaring to his mother his choice. "I don't recall this story."

Gwenda pursed her lips. "Yes, well, it's been some time, but I must have . . . the milkmaid and the blacksmith worked together to drown the creature. Surely you recall that tale?"

Saoirse blinked, searching for and finding a vague memory of a hearthside story told by a younger Gwenda.

Edred squeezed Saoirse's hand; she met his soft gaze. "Come inside and tell us?"

The Fortwin's house was illuminated with dozens of candles. "I'm tired of the dark," he explained. Yes, light sounded perfect.

Rosamund sat at the table, openly staring at Dafydd as he gobbled down cold ham between gulps of milk. Madoc industriously sliced bread while Papa spread the pieces with butter. When they entered, Papa left his work and stood with effort, using the table for support. "There's my brave girl."

Saoirse strode forward and fell into his arms, awash with relief and love. Finally, she was home.

CHAPTER THIRTY-FOUR

ARAWN'S JUDGEMENT

URSA ENTERED DEATH'S GREAT hall, a glittering, high-ceilinged affair that dazzled her eyes. Her escort, a rather surly selkie, nodded for her to join the gathered crowd of milling, assorted spirits at one end of the room.

Excitement lanced through her. Could Elenwin be here? Ursa did not hesitate to enter the crowd. She jostled other spirits out of the way as she plunged into the assemblage. Some jabbed her with an elbow or shot her a sour look, but many shrank away from her.

"Ele, Mummy's here, Dearest. Where are you?" When her daughter did not immediately answer, she tried again, raising her voice. "Speak, Daughter. Do not hide from me any longer." But even as the words left her, the bubble of hope within her breast deflated. Elenwin had left her some days ago. Would she linger here, in a hall full of spirits?

A dozen unfamiliar eyes stared back at her. Fear grew in her heart. Would she ever see her daughter again?

Just then the door opened, and Death stalked in, his billowing, smoldering cloak murmuring against the wooden planks. She stared in wonderment and no small amount of trepidation for the god who would soon judge her.

He stopped next to a great, white throne, assembled out of dry bones, but he did not sit. How could he? For atop the seat rested a deer skull mask, its proud antlers stretching toward the ceiling.

"Welcome to Annwn," he said, his rich baritone rolling through the room.

His gold eyes seemed to pierce through her, to *see* to the very heart of her.

He knows all.

She shrank further into the crowd, hiding herself. Her initial concern for finding her daughter fell away and a different kind of terror gripped her. Even hidden from his view, his gaze still touched her, unwavering. Aware.

"Your judgement awaits you," Death said to the room at large. Ursa flinched and worried her hands, her mind racing.

How does one escape the god of the underworld? They cannot, for he sends his selkies and his hell hounds to round them up. The thought stopped her short. Had Elenwin been dragged away by one such? Her stomach soured and a fuming rage bittered her tongue.

He had no right to take her. Elenwin belonged to *her*. She was her mother, after all. No one could love her so well.

Death called out a name and bade that soul come forth for judgement. Ursa only half-listened to their cries of regret, of their acceptance of their given fate. They were to make restitution for a wrong made long ago, to go to a place in Annwn, and there meet their long-departed enemy, and make peace.

Peace? What solace could Ursa find in a world without her daughter? Death stole Elenwin away from her and no doubt made plans to punish her for her mother's zeal. But what had Ursa done that any mother with power and knowledge would not?

Another name was called and another judgment made. Ursa's hatred for the god grew. Where had he stowed her daughter's soul? Did Elenwin cry for her even now?

Were gods immune to hexes or curses? She did not know. Perhaps he would bargain with her, should she threaten him with some ailment—some injury, but Ursa's frantic mind could not settle on what she might do.

Another two souls called forth found judgement, both of these with smiles and rejoicing. Ursa ground her teeth, glaring at their jubilation. How unfeeling—how self-righteous of them to boast of their blessing within the other souls' hearing.

The double doors opened and in walked a raven-haired beauty. Selkie servants and other attendants bowed in deference to the woman. Her pale skin shone with an inner light, as the morning sun on the blush of a rose petal. Her lush green robes trailed behind her as she approached Death's throne.

He removed his mask, revealing a most beatific smile, transforming his solemn expression into the handsome face of a man

in love. And then she saw her chance, for as he stood to greet
the visitor and bent to brush a kiss upon her brow, Death's hand
settled upon the bloom of the woman's pregnant belly.

A child. *His* child, if she had to guess. Either way, he cared
for it. If Ursa could not curse a god, she could at least affect the
growing babe. Perhaps Death would be more amenable to Ursa's
plight if he fully understood the desperate circumstances she'd
undergone. Yes, what parent wouldn't bend the laws of nature
to keep what belonged to them? She had.

As Ursa racked her brain for any spell she might use,
the woman conjured a throne made from flowering May tree
saplings for herself adjacent to the bone seat.

She'd read of the Withering Womb hex, which sapped the
vitality from the mother or child, causing complications in pregnancy or birth.

Its effects might manifest as physical weakness, an unnatural
pallor, or even a chilling sensation in the womb itself, leaving
the victim feeling drained and fearful, but she understood that
spell to happen over a long period of time. She needed something
more instantaneous. Besides, she could not recall the words.

The Cradle Curse also took too long and was best used at the
moment of birth.

Once the woman settled, Death turned to replace his mask.
A flash of silver caught her eye, there in his belt. What was more
immediate than a blade?

Ursa's hands itched to hold it. She wetted her ghostly lips,
her eyes fixed upon the hilt of the weapon. It jutted from his hip

where he sat. She could retrieve it easily, should she employ all her arts.

The woman's moss-bright gaze lingered on the souls in the room, her hands moving to the roundness of her middle.

Two more souls met their judgement before Ursa's name rang through the room. She approached, bowing her head in a show of humility, while her mind spun a web to catch hold of the woman. Her abilities might prove useless against Death, but what of his mistress?

How much better, if she could persuade the woman to pull the blade herself—to hold it over her own child. It needn't be harmed, if Death complied.

She cast out her mind, searching for the woman's consciousness and found it easily. Irritatingly bright, the woman's aura radiated outward, as if reaching for her.

Ursa came to a stop a few feet from Death's feet, her eyes downcast, fighting a smile. "My Lord Death."

"Ursa, daughter of Morganthe, witch of the Black Fen."

The words echoed in the vast chamber, each syllable a stone sinking into the abyss of eternity. Death's voice was neither cruel nor kind, but it carried a weight that bent the very air around her.

Ursa flinched despite herself, though she willed her spine straight and her breath steady. She would not cower before him. Not truly.

She bowed low, a smooth, practiced movement—submission crafted with care. Let him see humility. Let him think her tame.

"You forget my most favored title, Lord," she murmured, voice like honey laced with thorns. "That of Mother. Pray, have you had the chance to meet my sweetest Elenwin?"

A silence stretched between them, deeper than any mortal pause.

The woman seated beside Death shifted, her gaze heavy and unsettling. A thing of radiance and unnatural grace, she watched Ursa not as a woman regarded another, but as a wolf studied prey caught in its teeth.

Ursa could not help but shudder beneath the weight of that attention. So much light. She had lived in shadow too long to bear such scrutiny.

"I have seen her," said the woman. "She came to us in need of comfort."

Ursa's breath hitched.

To us.

Who was this woman? What claim did she have over Elenwin?

Carefully, subtly, Ursa reached her mind outward, brushing against the woman's consciousness with the barest whisper of sorcery—soft as a gossamer thread.

Pain lanced through Ursa's brain, hot and bright.

She would not be able to persuade the woman after all, it seemed. She eyed the hilt of Death's dagger, her mind spinning. A single lunge, and she could have her way.

"You have many deeds to answer for," said Death. "Even now you scheme against innocents."

A flicker of annoyance passed through her like the tail of a striking serpent. *She* was innocent! Everything she'd done had been borne of selflessness—everything for Elenwin. She lifted her chin, her voice a shade colder. "I did only what was necessary. And I, god-blessed with power, used it accordingly."

She could not discern Death's thoughts, hidden as he was behind the mask, but his words had fallen between them cold and unfeeling. She looked to the woman, instead, but only found revulsion there.

"You murdered children," said the woman, cradling her burgeoning stomach.

"They felt nothing," insisted Ursa. "Like falling asleep. I retained the balance of Annwn. I sought to retrieve a soul, and I gave you one in turn."

Death stood suddenly. "Do not presume to tell me what a soul feels when it is torn asunder. You have no authority to peddle souls." His booted feet thundered on the planks as he approached. She could not meet his gaze. She withered, wrapping her arms about her middle. His presence pressed upon her, suffocating and torturous.

"You have bartered lives and stolen what was not yours to take," Death said, his voice neither cruel nor kind—only inevitable. "But before judgment is passed, you will know what suffering you've brought upon others."

"*I* have suffered!" she wailed.

"You took lives to avoid your own pain."

He reached out a long-fingered hand and touched her temple. A cold wind, unnatural and piercing, swept through her mind. It slipped into the cracks of her fractured soul, forcing them open, revealing wounds she had long ignored.

The fearful desperation of countless animals forced against their will to do her bidding. The heart-stopping wail of mothers who searched for children who would never return. The hollowed faces of fathers who had buried their daughters, grief striking their hearts as painfully as any whip. Last, the confused despair that had taken hold of Elenwin, as she watched her mother's slow turn into madness.

Their pain became her own. The crushing weight of stolen futures, the severed bonds of love and life, unraveled within her like a festering wound laid bare to the sky.

She wrenched away and clutched her head, gasping, desperate to shut out the cries that echoed in the hollow spaces of her newly awakened mind. "Make it s—stop. Please," she begged, gasping.

Something like tears tracked down her face as the weight of her choices settled within her mind and upon her heart. Every sorrow she had borne since Elenwin's passing magnified, doubling and redoubling as she tasted the agony of others.

"I cannot stop it, Ursa, nor would I wish to. You alone have set this trap for yourself," Death continued, his voice heavy with finality. "Now you feel the sting of its teeth."

Anger at his callous indifference to her plight wheedled through the relentless pain, giving her strength. It might threaten to drag her under, to root itself within her bones, but she would not let it. She steeled herself against the ache, forcing it into the farthest corners of her mind.

It is not mine to carry. With a sharp breath, she willed it away, sealing her heart against the tide.

"Even now you will not welcome change," said Death his tone sharp. "You used others cruelly to soothe your own hurts. Even now, before this judgement seat, you plot to harm my queen and unborn child. You, Ursa of the Black Fen, stole and butchered, murdered the hopes of children and parents, and cruelly manipulated nature. Worse yet, you shun even the smallest seed of remorse within you."

He could read her thoughts? Fear slithered through her ribs, coiling tight. She should have realized. She'd sensed his awareness as he arrived, but in her desperation, she'd ignored his power.

"I have regrets," she said, a surge of bitterness lacing her tone. "I should never have left Ele alone that day." Emotion made her words tangle in her throat so that they came out thick and halting. "If I had stayed home, the viper would have never struck."

"Then you would have had no need to steal away other parents' children and sever their souls," answered Death. "Is that right?"

"Yes," said Ursa, lifting her gaze to the two blank sockets of the deer skull mask he wore. But there was no pity there to be found. "Don't you see? A life for life—the balance of nature must be preserved. Annwn . . . this realm should have been appeased."

Foreboding silence pressed in on her.

Death removed the headdress so that his golden eyes bored into her, pinning her to the spot. Anger stirred in his eyes, steely and as cold as a winter gale. "Annwn is *not* appeased."

The woman's cold glare and Death's anger filled her with dread. She sank onto her knees, her mind reeling. Where had it all gone wrong? Should she have pounced upon Death's knife as soon as she'd seen it? Clearly, her hesitancy had cost her.

"Your child's death affected you greatly. I see this, but meddling in darkness and stealing life—that I cannot excuse." Death stared down upon Ursa so that she felt like one of her many gathered sacrifices, forced into a jar, awaiting her demise. "You, who have murdered without thought or contrition, who has mastered the dark arts of manipulation and control, will now be stripped of your own. You will not see your daughter, Elenwin—"

A sob erupted from her. "No!" she wailed. "Have mercy, Lord Death."

"Like the mercy you bestowed upon those poor children?" asked the woman.

Ursa hissed, lunging, scrambling toward the woman. She'd tear her apart with her bare hands if she needed to.

Ursa's body flew backward. She landed with a smack against the hard planks. Though dead, and with no breath in her lungs, still the echo of losing her wind gripped her chest. She gulped uselessly as Death loomed over her.

"*You dare to touch my wife?*" he growled. "Hear me well, Ursa of the Black Fen. You will be henceforth bound to The Deep, to dwell amongst others of your same persuasion. You will find no rest. You will find no solace. You will search endlessly for that which you can never have."

Fear pierced her heart. "Not The Deep!" she wailed.

"I cannot send you back to make amends," Death said. "Not as you are. You have no wish to change, and I cannot allow you to inflict any more of your pain and suffering upon others a second time. This is my judgement. Let it be so."

Ursa sobbed into her hands. "At least tell me . . . what has become of my Ele."

Silence stretched out for a long moment. Finally, he said, "I will tell you this: your daughter condemned your actions as she was judged, and she now rests with family peaceably. Let that be your only comfort."

Ursa had no power here. She could not persuade or command. Utterly stripped of her capabilities, there was nothing she could do but accept her fate.

Someone helped her to move against the wall, away from the judgement seat. She didn't fight them. She could not escape. A selkie guard stood over her as Death passed judgement upon other souls. Ursa paid them no heed, too absorbed in her own misery.

A feast was laid soon after, but Ursa did not join the others. She could conjure no will to move. She'd lost everything. Not just her magic, but her Elenwin. Her daughter had denounced her—discarded her own mother after everything she'd done to save her. A well of bitterness filled her breast.

The sentencing came next. Selkie servants and even a banshee spirited away judged souls, taking them to their respective resting places. Death's footfalls fell hard upon the planks as he approached her where she'd slumped against the wall.

"Are you ready, Ursa?" he asked.

What a stupid question. She did not spit curses or voice her unkind thoughts. She merely stared at a knot in the wooden planks. She would not go willingly. He would have to force her.

Knowing her thoughts, he lifted her by the arm. A strange current of energy raced through her at the contact, compelling her. "Rise and walk, Ursa."

She did so—obliged—and followed him from the hall, down resplendent corridors, and out of the keep. They crossed a stone bridge, flanked by banshee, and moved through a black gate guarded by headless riders upon black steeds.

All too soon, they came to a black sea, the high moon reflected perfectly below. The Deep.

"This is your new home, Ursa," said Death. "It will suit you well."

She sniffed and eyed the expanse with a sideways glare. "You think it will hold me?"

"It's held others just like you for eons of time."

Surely none so talented as herself. Curious, Ursa drew closer to the lapping water, where the lacey edge of foam surged toward her toes.

Where the rushing waves touched her, coldness gripped her. A finger of shadow surged from the water, a living tide that hungrily grasped her. She staggered, splashing into The Deep up past her ankles. The bitter cold spread to her knees.

"I will not be made captive!" she shrieked. She glared at Death. "It will not hold me for long!"

A half-dozen ghostly hands seized her feet and her knees, pulling her further into the water. "Unhand me!"

Water swelled to her thighs. She thrashed, nails clawing at empty air, but there was nothing to hold onto—nothing to stop the inevitable pull.

"No—please, wait—"

Shadows curled around her wrists, pulling her to her knees. Water spilled into her mouth and stung her nose. "Please," she begged. "I will do better. I—I'll give up my craft. I will never enter another's mind!"

"Yes, that's right," he said, a note of pity in his voice. "In The Deep, you will have no such ability. I will visit you again, Ursa, and determine then if your heart has changed. A hundred years of this, then we will see."

The last of the moonlight fled as the ghastly faces in the water and their mauling hands pulled her under. Darkness closed over her head as she fell down, down, down, into the abyss.

The last sound that of her own, echoing scream, swallowed whole by the endless void.

The End.

Epilogue

Reunion

O<small>NE YEAR LATER</small>

The brilliant sun kept the shadow of the mountain to heel, forcing it to pool its gloom amongst rills and to slip between trees instead of stretch along the meadowgrass. Saoirse squinted into the sun, shielding her eyes as she tried to make out the trail of stairs cut into stone. Drooping firs obscured the path, however, and she let her hand drop.

Edred took the crock of honey nestled in the crook of Saoirse's arm with a wink and placed it in the moving ox cart beside them.

"Where, exactly, are we to leave all this?" panted Fadam Fortwin from the opposite side of the cart. She eyed the overhanging tree boughs ahead with trepidation. Perspiration formed on her upper lip and brow, her sharp eyes wary.

"Won't you sit in the cart, Gwenda? It's right hot out." Madoc asked his wife, but she flapped a hand at him.

Even now, the Wild Wood elicited the same unease in Saoirse, and she'd been up and back down the long stair twice as many times as her mother-in-law.

Dafydd stumbled as he walked alongside the ox, glancing over his shoulder. "Not to the top," said Dafydd worriedly.

Saoirse nodded to him, reassuring. "We needn't climb the mountain. Carreg will find our gift easily enough at the bottom. He knows to come looking at the solstice."

"Six jugs of cream," muttered Papa from atop the cart, reins tight in his hands. "Easy, there, wee Griff," he soothed. The ox—Griff—no doubt sensed the same ominous outpouring the Faerie Hill exuded. It rolled its eyes and blew nervously, but did not bolt. Yet. "Just a bit further."

"And three jars of honey," Rosamund chimed in from where she sat on the back of the conveyance. Her legs dangled amongst the long tassels that brushed the underside of the wagon.

"A small price to pay," said Edred, giving Saoirse's elbow a squeeze.

"Right indeed," said Gwenda with a firm nod.

Madoc grinned at Saoirse. "One you needn't pay at all, from what I heard. Clever lass."

Saoirse shot him a warm smile. "I only wish to offer a token of thanks. They did help me rescue my men, after all."

Dafydd slowed his steps as they drew near the base of the mountain, coming even with Saoirse. She slung her arm around his shoulders and whispered into his hair. "You needn't fear, Little Prince."

"Will we see them?" asked Rosamund. "The wee folk?"

Gwenda looked equally interested in the answer as her daughter, but Saoirse could not say.

Papa could only coax Griff so far. The beast blew and lowed in a pitiful fashion before refusing to take another step, and stopped a fair distance from the base of the mountain.

"Well have to carry it the rest of the way, I'm afraid," Papa informed them. He climbed down and stroked Griff's flank. "That's a good lad."

"I'll take the honey," said Rosamund. "Here, you take this one." She offered a jar to Dafydd, who accepted it with a reluctant grunt.

Madoc and Edred pulled out the jugs of cream and handed them out. Despite Edred's missing fingers, he got on very well. Madoc's insistence that he work the forge with tong and hammer despite missing his first two fingers had forced Edred to cope—and cope he had.

His left hand equaled the former strength of his right, and the special gloves Papa had stitched for him—reinforced with metal loops that gripped tools—enabled him to maneuver the tongs with dexterity.

Saoirse sung as they blazed a trail through the grass, hoping to ease some of the tension presently bearing down on Dafydd.

They placed their gifts on the first stair. Gwenda peered upward into the boughs as if she expected the trees suddenly wake and pelt them with pinecones.

Saoirse grasped Edred's hand and searched the shadows for any sign of the coblyn but came up short. He might not wish to expose himself to more humans. "If you're here, thank you."

Papa removed his hat, his cheeks pink. "Erm . . . I'd like to offer my gratitude as well." His gaze roved from rock to branch. "I couldn't do without my children. Thank you for helping Saoirse in the mine and . . . and for escorting Dafydd to Áine." He replaced his hat and cleared his throat, stepping back as to give someone else a turn.

A sudden rustle of leaves. A branch swayed overhead.

Carreg's stocking capped head popped out over a boulder, followed quickly by Kraglin.

"Very generous of you, Lady Traveler, Brother," said Carreg, climbing atop the boulder they'd hidden behind.

"Fie!" Rosamund breathed, her eyes wide.

"We can lighten the load between us, I'd wager," said Kraglin, rubbing his two knobby hands together, his eyes bright with anticipation. "I could polish off three jugs o' that cream myself."

They hopped down the craggy hillside as easily as any goat, pushing through brush, to stand upon the steps, squinting into the sun.

Gwenda curtsied but eyed the coblyns with an untrusting eye, as if worried they might spring from the steps and take a bite out of *her*.

"They dinna call this the Brightlands for nothing!" said Kraglin. He removed his cap and used it as a handkerchief.

"You got your bees back, I see," said Carreg, lifting a jar of honey, big enough that he had to employ both hands. He sniffed at the wax seal.

"Yes," said Saoirse. "They came back home . . . swarmed under the eaves of the barn."

Kraglin took the jar from Carreg and peeled back the wax seal with long, dexterous fingers. He lifted the edge of the container to his mouth and let the thick, amber liquid slide in. He slurped happily, smacked his lips in satisfaction.

Saoirse laughed. He'd already eaten half the jar. "Just be sure to save some for the others—Basalina, the Singer, and Clatterby. He's not still upset, I hope."

"Dinna you worry about him," Carreg said. "He's just as rich as he ever was and growing fatter by the day. Us too," he said, patting his belly. "Eryriaddur keeps us all well fed in exchange for gold."

"Or she did," said Kraglin, licking his sticky fingers.

As if on cue, a shadow fell over them, eclipsing the sun. Far above the trees, soaring, the great shape of a dragon stretched across the pale blue sky.

A deep, powerful roar made the ground tremble.

Madoc swore under his breath, his awed expression matching his wife's.

"I never thought to see a dragon!" said Rosamund, excitement coloring her voice.

"That's Eryriaddur," Dafydd explained. "She breaths fire."

"Where is she going?" asked Papa, no doubt thinking of his cattle not far away.

"Why, she's off tae search the caves and corries of the north, o' course," explained Carreg. "She's in want of a mate."

Kraglin, honey pot abandoned, had started on the cream. He paused drinking long enough to add, "What we'll do with a great, brooding dragon, I don't know." The smear of milk across his upper lip softened his disgruntled words.

"A good omen," said Carreg pointedly. "A sign of things to come."

Saoirse's heart lifted as she watched the dragon disappear into the distance, a magnificent, fiery streak across the sky. "I hope she finds what she's seeking."

"Did she rid the caves of all the trowes?" asked Edred.

"Oh, aye. It took a bit of doing, but the Singer opened a path large enough for the dragon to enter their den."

"We've been right busy mining all the new veins of ore we've found."

"Oh! That reminds me," said Carreg. He dug in his pocket and pulled out a handful of winking gems. "The Singer asked me to give this to you."

Saoirse held out her hands and Carreg let the colorful stones fall against her palms. She stared, awed, at the gift. "But why?"

"You helped to remedy a great wrong, Lady Traveler. Yes, Clatterby wasna too chuffed about waking a hulking dragon, but the right decisions are often uncomfortable."

Too true.

Silence settled over them. The time for goodbye had come.

"We're only a flight of stairs away," said Kraglin.

"Oh, no," said Papa. "There's far more than a stairway separating us, and a good thing too. I don't want any of them going back up there."

Saoirse had to agree. She'd had enough excitement to last two lifetimes. All she wanted now was to live simply with Edred at her side.

"Goodbye for now, Saoirse," Carreg said, his voice gentle. "I'll see you next solstice?"

Kraglin perked up at the promise of more honey and cream. She laughed. "Maybe."

They waved goodbye and walked back to the cart. Saoirse, heart full, turned back for one last glimpse, but Carreg and Kraglin had gone along with all the food.

"What will you do with the gems?" asked Rosamund.

"Your forge doesn't need expanding, Rosamund," said Madoc. "It's doing well enough."

"I might buy half of it back from you," said Saoirse. "For Edred."

"He already has half," Rosamund said. "I don't mind sharing."

"What about your bees, Saoirse," Gwenda asked. "You could expand your business."

Saoirse pocketed the Singer's boon and took Edred's hand.

"We can't stay in the little room at the forge for much longer," Edred said.

"I told you you're welcome to stay at our cottage until we can build you your own place."

"Or ours," said Gwenda.

Saoirse smiled and squeezed Edred hand. She'd told him only two days ago what she'd suspected. Come mid-winter, their twosome would become three. Walking back and forth between the cottage and the forge to tend to her bees wasn't a burden, but a child changed things.

"Eryriaddur isn't the only one anticipating a child," Saoirse announced.

Papa's mouth fell open.

"Áine blessed!" cried Gwenda, clasping her hands in front of her. Her eyes sparkled with tears.

"Yes, quite right," Saoirse agreed. "Blessed."

AFTERWORD

<u>Betws-y-Coed</u> is a real place in Wales, boasting The Faerie Glen, or Ffos Anoddun in Welsh (beats me how you pronounce that!). This secluded and beautiful alpine village inspired the location of this faerie tale. You can learn more about the village and the mythology associated with fairy gorge that inspired this story by visiting the following sites:

https://www.youtube.com/watch?v=YBgKUEPKFWY

https://folklorethursday.com/legends/the-magic-of-the-fair y-glen-merlins-hiding-place/

The song Saoirse sings to put the afanc to sleep is a real Welsh lullaby called *Suo Gân*, written by the composer Morfydd Llwyn Owen. The first recorded in print around 1800. I highly recommend listening to it in its native tongue. You can find it easily by searching the tile on YouTube. While this song is not from the time period of this novel, I liked the lyrics and felt they worked well for the plot. I only changed one word, swapping out "angels" for "gods," since I thought it fit better with this pagan-worshipping people.

Welsh Mythology:

I came across a variety of interesting mythological creatures and the lore associated with each. I thought it prudent to list those that I included in the story and their true origins (for those interested).

Afanc: What better guardian for Áine's doorway than a lake monster? In the same vein as the cockatrice or the basilisk, this half-beaver-half-crocodile creature conjures an interesting image. I tried to make it sound as dangerous and hideous as possible, which would be terrifying to come across as is, but I found its actions far more sinister. There are various accounts, but all describe the beast as able to wreak havoc on humans (eat us, drown us, flood our towns, and even bring the plague). You can learn more about it here:

https://www.historic-uk.com/HistoryUK/HistoryofWales/ The-Legend-of-the-River-Conwy-Afanc/

The Beithir is a dragon-esque creature in Gaelic folklore that is often described as serpent like. According to legend, the beithir, a cave-dwelling creature, could bring bad weather and could kill with its venomous bite.

Bendith y Mamau: is a figure from Welsh folklore, often translated as "Blessing of the Mothers." The name refers to a group of fairies or supernatural beings believed to inhabit the Welsh landscape. Despite the name sounding benevolent, the Bendith y Mamau were often considered mischievous or even malevolent, depending on how humans treated them. They are known for abducting human children and replacing them with changelings, often frail and troublesome faerie children. It's said that this race of faerie can be placated with offerings of food, milk, or honey, which were left outside homes to avoid their mischief. They are said to sometimes bless homes and lands if treated kindly, but their curses could be devastating if offended. So, careful how you treat bendith y mamau. You can learn more about them here, if you wish:

https://pursiful.com/2014/07/18/bendith-y-mamau-ugly -welsh-faeries/

Branwen ferch Llŷr: This story features Bendigeid-fran—meaning Blessed Bran in Welsh—who is so large that no house can contain him. His story—and his sister's—like any Welsh tale, is very tragic. Bendigeidfran arranges the marriage of his sister, Branwen to Matholwch, king of Ireland, to strengthen ties between the two countries.

Things aren't so great for Branwen, though. Her husband mistreats her and forces her into servitude. Branwen, with little recourse, raises a starling and sends it to her brother, Bendigeif-dran, with a message of her suffering. Enraged, Bendigeidran gathers an army and crosses the Irish Sea to rescue her. His sheer size allows him to simply wade across and carry his warriors upon his back.

The Irish plead peace (wouldn't you!?) and build a massive house for the giant, but they hide warriors inside to ambush him. After a bit more trouble I won't get into here, Bendigei-dfran is mortally wounded and, knowing his death is imminent, instructs his men to sever his head and take it back to Britain. Magically, his head retains its ability to speak (of course) and keeps his companions company for many years, but is eventually buried at the White Tower of London to protect Britain from invasion.

The Cockatrice of Castle Gwys: This Welsh legend involves the mythical two-legged dragon (or wyvern) with a rooster's head. This monster is reputed to kill people by simply looking at them or—sometimes—breathing on them (can you say morning breath?) or touching them. The legend of Castle Gwys and the infamous cockatrice goes something like this:

A notable family in the Welsh region now known as Wiston, declared that the estate would belong to anyone who could gaze upon the monster without it seeing them (A risky venture considering the stakes, but we humans often minimize the hazards when prosperity is offered.).

To up the ante, Castle Gwys' beast was blessed with hundreds of eyes. One man managed to win the offered lands by hiding in a barrel, which rolled past the monster. He, apparently, looked through the bunghole and announced to the uninterested monster that he'd successfully beguiled it. Success! I couldn't find any sources that explained what happened next, unfortunately. Did the beast just shrug and walk off? If anyone knows, please share!

Coblyn: In Welsh folklore, Coblyns—or coblynau—are traditionally small, subterranean creatures akin to dwarves of goblins, known for inhabiting mines and caves. While there is no mention of king that I could find in Welsh mythology or folklore, I liked the idea of one—a king to serve as guardian of hidden treasures and a protector of miners. Coblynau are commonly referred to as "Tommy Knockers" in more modern times, said to help human miners find the best veins.

Dragon Sentinels: The story of the feuding red and white dragons is based upon a legend of Dinas Emrys. Apparently King

Vortigern attempted to build a fort there, but it kept collapsing. Merlin—yes, that Merlin—revealed that two dragons (one red, one white, battled underground, causing the instability.

I pulled the name of the mine from Geoffrey of Monmouth's Historia Regum Britanniae, who wrote that the red dragon, symbolizing the Britons, fought the white dragon, which symbolized the invading Saxons. Monmouth reiterates that the red dragon's ultimate victory foretold the triumph of the Britons (hence the white dragon being slain in this tale).

Ellyllon: (plural of *Ellyll*, pronounced "el-lith" or "el-luh-th" in Welsh) are creatures from Welsh folklore. They are often described as small, light-hearted, and mischievous faeries or spirits, similar to pixies or brownies in other traditions.

Greenman: This creature is depicted as a face surrounded by foliage, often with leaves or vines sprouting from the mouth. This, supposedly, symbolizes rebirth and the cycle of nature. Images of the Greenman are commonly found in carvings on ancient Welsh churches and are considered a symbol of pagan fertility deities. It should be noted that "green man" is widely used across British folklore and is not inherently Welsh. What better subject in Summer Court than a walking, talking tree?

Trowes: Sometimes called trows (also trowe or dtrow) depending on where you live, these malignant fairies come from the Orkney and Shetland islands. Folklore describes them as monstrous giants or, in the case of this story, short-statured troll-like elves that dwell in the deep, dark places of the world. While there is little to no evidence of trowes in Welsh folklore, I needed something sinister that lived in the mines and liked the idea of a goblinish troll that preyed on humans and faeries alike.

Acknowledgements

Summer's Reaping came together in fits and starts. I knew I wanted to build off of Winter's Handmaiden by creating books for each of the Celtic seasonal goddesses, but I wasn't quite sure how I could fit my favorite fairy tales in with each (There're more books to come!).

A huge thank you to my friend and incredibly talented editor, Ellie Whitney, who sat with me for hours to "talk shop" in a little Starbucks. Thank you to my critique partners, Paige Edwards, Cindy Hale, and Ellie. Thank you to the talented Kelly Horn, who reads whatever I put in front of her with such optimism that she alone feeds my little author's soul and chases away imposter syndrome. Kelly has such an intuitive sense of stories that I trust her judgement without fail.

I must also thank my best friend, Kristal Winsor, who always answers my calls, even after so many years, and helps me fill plot holes. She plods along with me to events, sells my books like a champ, and is all around my greatest cheerleader. I love you.

Many others helped to make this book what it is, name-ly my lovely beta team: Tresha Beard, Michelle House, Laura Carver, David Calhoun, Christina Reams, and Debbie Calderwood. Thank you for your feedback, your pointed questions, your praise (because we all need that from time to time), and for your willingness to wade through the unpolished version of Summer's Reaping.

Thank you to my ARC team. A book launch is no simple thing and I'm so grateful for your willingness to read and leave an honest review. Special thanks to Author Emily Barlow for her special attention to the manuscript. She found several mistakes that my brain failed to see after so many read-throughs. You are worth your weight in gold!

Last, but certainly not least, thank you to my husband for your reassurance, for your belief in me, and for holding space for me when I'm overwhelmed. I love you. I'm one lucky girl.

ALSO BY

reuniting with the only family left to her, Edyth is tormented as a keeper of a dangerous secret—one that she is only just beginning to unravel. As King Edward I of England dismantles loyalties and spills innocent blood, Edyth traverses the deadly landscape with little hope of success. On all sides bitter conflict looms yet help comes from an unlikely source. But can Edyth trust Ewan, the heroic, young Scots knight with her secret -or with her heart?

A Conjuring of Valor: Book Two
1296 Scotland:

In the village of Perthshire, Edyth Ruthven finds that life as the new mistress of the household is not as comfortable as she'd hoped. Rejected by her husband's people as an outsider with a dangerous reputation, Edyth struggles to make a place for herself amid the rampant rumors of her past.

What's more, Edyth struggles to make sense of her nightmares, forewarning of a deadly event fast approaching. When her only friend and good sister Caitriona is forced into an arranged marriage, the full weight of a divided and prejudiced people falls upon her shoulders.

Ewan, meanwhile, walks along the edge of a twin blade, forced to choose between loyalty to his own people or to embrace the English King. When a nefarious sheriff is appointed to their lands, the life the Ruthvens had hoped for unravels before their very eyes, leaving them in a tangle of wicked machinations set forth by the wicked sheriff.

A Storm Summoned: Book Three

From twice nominated Whitney Award finalist, J.C. Wade, the thrilling true history of Scotland's first fight for independence comes to life in this, the final installment of The White Witch's Daughter trilogy.

1297

Scotland

A Storm is coming.

While England's king conscripts Scotland's sons for a war not of their making and his sheriffs tax and repress a burdened people, the seer Edyth Ruthven foretells of an uneasy future. Even as King Edward's fist tightens around Scotland's nobles, a whisper of rebellion spreads.

The world holds its breath as the very fabric of a divided kingdom is held together by conspiring men. Men who know well at what cost freedom is won. For Ewan and Edyth, life has taken a difficult and uncertain turn. But political machinations would be nothing if Edyth was not also navigating a difficult pregnancy.

Iain, meanwhile, is thrust into the midst of a treasonous act all while traversing a new and unwanted relationship. As Iain and his betrothed, Alice Stewart, work toward mutual compromise, their burgeoning relationship is put to the test.

Last, Cait, who has always craved action, learns that getting what you wish for is not always so sweet. With the escaped fugitive, Andrew Moray, in her new home, Cait no longer must listen at doors, but is she ready for what is surely to come?

With new alliances comes unfamiliar territory, thrusting the Ruthvens into treacherous waters. Can Ewan navigate his scattered family through the clashing swords and scheming hearts that pervade the political landscape? Can Edyth's efforts keep her men alive and free?

<u>Celtic Goddesses Series:</u>
<u>High Fantasy</u>

Winter's Handmaiden

Winter's Handmaiden is a heart-stopping Hades/Persephone retelling, told through the lens of Celtic Mythology.

Plunged into a world of gods, fairies, and monsters, modern-day archaeologist, Maryn Ferguson, must find the missing spring goddess if she has any hope of returning home (and saving the world from an endless winter.).

Gods, fairies and monsters? What could go wrong?

When circumstances force her and her grumpy sidekick into the underworld, Maryn's determination to return to her safe life wanes in the wake of Arawn, god of death.

Will she ever get to the bottom of the missing goddess and save the world from a bitter end? Can her heart withstand the alluring yet broken god of death who befriends her?

Arawn's Remaking
A companion novella to Winter's Handmaiden

Arawn's life as a merciless sword hand brought him riches and infamy.

Only one followed him in death.

At his life's review, Death offers him two choices: submit to eternity in The Deep, an ocean of endless torment, or return to life and endeavor to repair the darkness he'd sowed in his heart.

Remaking himself, however, isn't as easy as he anticipated. Will he ever school his selfish impulses and modify himself? Will he ever learn to forgive himself for his murderous past?

If you'd like updates on current works, sneak peeks, and free books, you can join J.C. Wade's monthly newsletter by visiting her website (www.jcwade.com).

About the author

J.C. Wade is her hometown's resident weirdo. She gets excited about archeological finds, loves folklore, and would spend all her time holed away reading books and petting cats if her family didn't need her. She currently resides in Northern Virginia with her husband, three sons, and (only) two cats. She wishes she had more feline friends, but her husband might divorce her if she dared.

Married to a military man, she has had the great opportunity to move often and fall in love with people of all walks of life. Her works merge multiple genres, featuring elements of historical fiction, romance, fantasy, and adventure, all deemed "clean." She has been a public educator—specifically a teacher of the Deaf and Hard of Hearing—for most of her career but has dabbled in creative writing her entire life. You are likely to find her out and about on book tours along the eastern coast of the U.S. Check out her website (www.jcwade.com) for all upcoming events.